STAR TREK®

CAST NO SHADOW

JAMES SWALLOW

Based on *Star Trek*
created by Gene Roddenberry

POCKET BOOKS
New York London Toronto Sydney

Pocket Books
A Division of Simon & Schuster, Inc.
1230 Avenue of the Americas
New York, NY 10020

This book is a work of fiction. Names, characters, places, and incidents either are products of the author's imagination or are used fictitiously. Any resemblance to actual events or locales or persons, living or dead, is entirely coincidental.

First Pocket Books paperback edition August 2011

POCKET and colophon are registered trademarks of Simon & Schuster, Inc.

For information about special discounts for bulk purchases, please contact Simon & Schuster Special Sales at 1-866-506-1949 or business@simonandschuster.com.

The Simon & Schuster Speakers Bureau can bring authors to your live event. For more information or to book an event contact the Simon & Schuster Speakers Bureau at 866-248-3049 or visit our website at www.simonspeakers.com.

Designed by Leydiana Rodríguez-Ovalles
Cover art and design by Alan Dingman

Manufactured in the United States of America

10 9 8 7 6 5 4 3 2 1

ISBN 978-1-4516-0717-8
ISBN 978-1-4516-0721-5 (ebook)

For *Endeavor,* and all who sailed in her.

1

even years.

Gedda felt every day of them like a weight upon his back. Seven years since the ink soaked into the paper of the Khitomer Accords, seven years since the revelations and the handshakes, the recriminations and the reconciliations.

Almost a decade of his life dedicated to this, and only now had the wheels truly started to turn. He felt a curious mixture of elation and sorrow as he walked the rough metal corridors of the space station. On one hand, he was uplifted and energized by the thought that at last he could make a difference; but on the other, he was troubled by the time that had been wasted just to get to this point.

There had been moments when he felt as if he were banging his head against a brick wall. The Klingons, even when they were trying to be open, were obstructive and cantankerous—and what drove Gedda to distraction was the fact they were spiting themselves to do it. He understood that they had pride, that their martial code made it difficult for them to accept charity from others—worse still if it came from a former enemy like the United Federation of Planets.

But surely there had to come a point where that bellicose behavior became self-destructive? He'd lost count of the number of times he had been shouted down or outright ignored when he dared to state the obvious—the slight, wiry human snapping at the hulking warrior and getting nothing back but sneers and dismissal. The Klingons did not like Gedda, but they didn't dislike him enough to consider him worthy of their true enmity. General Igdar, the military chief of staff in the sector, had once compared him to a *glob* fly—something that would have to rise to reach the level of an irritant.

And then there had been days when he had wanted to quit. Gedda recalled those quite clearly. How many transfer requests or resignation letters had he written? Hours spent putting down his disappointments on a padd and then hesitating at the last moment to press the TRANSMIT key.

Gedda had never done it, because he would never have been able to look himself in the mirror again. To go home, back to New Bangalore, would be to admit defeat.

He had been on Qo'noS when Praxis ripped itself apart, he had seen the horror and the terror on the faces of the most fearless people in the galaxy. It seemed like a lifetime ago; he was an adjutant with the Federation diplomatic envoy in the First City, little more than a functionary if he was honest with himself. When the moon exploded, when the spatial shock wave tore into the Klingon homeworld, Gedda had gone with the others, out into the streets to render what aid they could.

He looked down at his palms, remembering the red earth that clogged his pores and his nails. The scars on his fingers from ripping up the rubble with his bare hands. The hours of backbreaking work in the aftermath of the disaster. But most of all, he remembered the living and the dead he had uncovered.

When the Accords were signed, when the articles of the treaty enacted and the lines of support opened, Gedda had volunteered to join the Federation relief effort. He wanted to keep helping.

But for all the honorable words and honest intent of Chancellor Azetbur, the Klingon people found it hard to take the outstretched hand. Like her father, Gorkon, before her, Azetbur's bold initiatives and offerings of concord were not to the taste of many of her kind. Stubborn Klingon pride dragged like an anchor on every overture the Federation made, and never let up. In the end, it took the atmospheric contamination, the steady rise in infant mortality due to radiation exposure—the corruption of the very soil of the homeworld—to convince the Klingons to allow the Federation to take what General Igdar dismissively referred to as "a minor support role."

In seven years, despite all that had happened, all the setbacks and the politicking among the fragile peace, there *had* been little victories. This platform was one of them, along with the ships drifting out beyond it in orbit over the Da'Kel III colony. Finally, the Klingon Defense Force had turned over a facility to serve as the sole staging area for the ongoing relief efforts. Now that the station was up and running, it would be the core of all resource distribution to Qo'noS and the other worlds brushed by the death throes of Praxis. Ships from Federation space could cross the border and off-load here, the cargoes of supplies then taken up by Defense Force ships and indentured transports.

It would have been far simpler to send the vessels straight to the reconstruction sites, but even Azetbur could not muster the backing for a vote to allow a steady train of alien starships passage to the heart of the Empire. Da'Kel would have to be enough.

After years of slow going, hardheadedness, and hindrances born of political pressures and old prejudice, they had passed a milestone. Gedda wanted to make a difference; he wondered if he could allow himself to believe that now he *had*.

A gruff voice called his name as he entered the operations dome, and he looked up to see Supervisor Kol approaching. He straightened in her presence; it was a reflex action he couldn't break.

"Look at this," she said, without preamble. The Klingon woman beckoned him over to one of the large viewports.

Gedda followed with a nod. Kol was a good head taller than him, and her skin was a shade darker than his tawny

complexion. She had one of those ridge-crests that lay flat and
complex across her forehead, unlike the massive wrinkles of
bone and skull visible on many of the Klingons he encountered. Kol was the closest thing to Gedda's opposite number
here, but still she had the ability to make him feel like he was
her inferior. He didn't correct that assumption: Gedda learned
early on that Klingons were much easier to deal with if they
were allowed to think that they were in charge of everything.

Kol pointed. The curved triangle of the window also dou-
bled as a control panel, holographic panes projecting directly
onto the surface. She was indicating a shipping manifest, and
several items were blinking in red. "The Tellarites have displayed their inability to follow simple commands once again,"
she told him. "The cargo pods containing these medical supplies are not on board their ship."

Gedda peered out into the darkness and found the spade-
shaped Tellarite freighter that had earned Kol's chilly ire.
"There must be a good reason," he offered. "They're usually
very conscientious about this sort of thing."

Kol shot him a look. "I understand that is true of some
outworlders. But I have yet to be convinced they fall into the
same category."

He wondered if that had been some kind of backhanded
compliment, and then pushed the thought away. "It might
have been moved to one of the other ships in the flotilla," he
suggested. "Let me look into it. I'll sort it out."

"Vessel dropping out of warp," reported one of the operations crew. Gedda looked and saw a display screen showing
a nondescript *Monarch*-class merchantman. The manta-like
ship transmitted a series of pass-codes that identified it as part
of the Tellarite convoy.

"There," he said. "A straggler. I imagine they'll have the
missing supplies on board."

Kol looked down at a padd in her hand. "The Tellarite
Shipping Commission only authorized four ships for passage
into the Empire. That one will be the fifth."

"Oh." Gedda blinked. "I suppose . . . we should contact

them?" Kol snapped out a command in Klingon, stalking away from him. "It's probably just a clerical error," he added.

Kol gave him the look again, and he wilted a little, sighing. Sometimes it could be extremely trying how the Klingons treated every problem, no matter how large or how small, as if it were a matter of utmost martial import.

"They're hailing us," said Leru, crouched forward over the main console.

Zennol didn't look away from the merchantman's forward screen. "That was quick." Framed on the display, the angular, copper-green shape of the orbital platform floated in space, catching the glow of the distant red Da'Kel star. He smiled without warmth, the skin around his narrow eyes wrinkling, tightening the pattern of pigment-spots that passed down the sides of his face to disappear into his collar.

Leru stared at him across the empty bridge of the freighter. "Do we answer?" He ran a nervous hand through his lank, pale hair. The younger man's pigment-patterns were stark against his fairer skin. "If we open a channel, I'll need to activate the visual mask," he went on. "If they don't see us as Tellarites, the ridge-heads will—"

"We'll answer them," Zennol said, silencing him as he climbed to his feet. "There *will* be an answer," he repeated. The older man left the helm chair and went to the makeshift panel wired into the merchantman's engineering station.

"Now?" He heard the gasp in Leru's voice. Zennol frowned slightly. He had always believed that the youth would be hesitant when the moment came, but he had hoped that Leru might, at the end, show a little more strength of character.

"Now," Zennol replied. "We're close enough." He activated a control and sent a signal to the device sitting alone down in the ship's main cargo bay. He imagined it there, power moving through the activation grid as it awoke from dormancy. Finally he turned back to his comrade. "It's time. Send the message."

"We . . . we're really doing this . . ." Leru said aloud, as if he had to give voice to the words before his actions could become real. He reached out and tapped a keypad; the merchantman's subspace radio began to broadcast a prerecorded string of words. "Done," he added.

Zennol walked up to the main screen, counting the number of ships orbiting in orderly rows alongside the transfer platform. He saw more than he expected, and nodded at their good fortune. He made out the shape of a Starfleet tug, civilian barges of Vulcan, Tellarite, and Caitian design, but what drew his smile wide were the Klingon ships beyond them. Bulk cruisers and tankers suckling at the station, their crews ignorant of what was about to happen, and in a slightly higher orbit, the shapes of D-7M battle cruisers billeted here on missions of escort and security.

The latter they had failed to perform, thanks to information passed on to Zennol from the rest of his group. He didn't wonder where the pass-codes and the transit route details had come from; all Zennol cared about was that they had gotten him to this place, at this moment. He would fulfill his purpose here and now. His life had been building to this one moment.

Zennol's hand went to his pocket and he pulled out a flattened holograph and unfolded it. The plastic panel gave a soft chime and he was suddenly looking into the eyes of his wife. She was frozen in that moment, as beautiful as she had ever been, full of life. This was how he wanted to remember her, instead of how she was when he found her: charred and dying from the kiss of a Klingon disruptor.

Leru's eyes were closed and he was muttering something under his breath, some litany or invocation. Zennol nodded to himself. Whatever helped the youth to get the work done . . . He himself had never believed in Higher Powers. He needed no other motivation than the face of the woman in the holograph.

He watched the ships and listened to the words of the message . . . and waited.

• • •

Sent on all channels, wide-banded to every subspace receiver in the star system, the message was clear and concise. In flawless, unaccented Klingon, the words were picked up by every vessel. Many of those who heard them did not understand the import of the phrase; those who did—those who knew the truth of what was said—were granted enough time to become angry at the insult they bore.

"*Maghwl' chuH ghobe' QIb,*" said the voice.

The merchantman vanished in a sudden liberation of uncaged energy.

The detonation was not a conventional blast, not nuclear or electrochemical in nature. Instead, it was initiated by a forcible shattering of key physical laws; inside an envelope of projected power, fundamental rules of the universe were twisted and bent to the breaking point, and beyond. It was a bastardization of the principles and technologies that allowed starships to break the light-speed barrier and transmit messages across vast interstellar distances.

A mailed fist of corrupted energy punched down through the layers of reality, briefly opening up a tear in the fabric of space-time. Nature would not stand to let such a brutality exist for more than a few microseconds, but even that was enough to release vast quantities of extradimensional energy from the realms of subspace.

At the heart of the expanding shock-front, the merchantman was already gone, the atoms of its structure and everything aboard it instantly reduced to their component particles. A cloud of crackling, shimmering power, blue-white and wild like auroral lightning, unwound and whipped at the space around it. The discharge destroyed dozens of vessels outright, and others it tore open as it passed, venting them to vacuum; but the core power of the energy flared along the axis of its spin, mirroring the motion of a singularity. The rippling wave engulfed the orbital platform and sheared through its low-level deflectors.

For brief moments the blast cut at the station, stripping it layer by layer from the outermost hull plating, down through the superstructure and into the internal pressure spaces; compartments popped and disintegrated, the life within them snuffed out. Then, mercifully, the over-wash of subspace energy caused the station's fusion core to implode, and the platform died in a final flash of light.

Less than a minute had elapsed from the moment the voice had begun to speak to the subspace surge released by the merchantman. As the wake dissipated, unguided wreckage began to tumble into Da'Kel's gravity well. Those few ships that still had survivors aboard them could only watch them fall, and hope that they would live beyond the next few hours.

Starfleet Penal Stockade
Jaros II
United Federation of Planets

"I need you to be open," said the Betazoid. "If you hold back, our progress will be slow."

The patient didn't look up, but she raised one arched eyebrow by the smallest of increments. "Is the speed of our . . . progress . . . a mitigating factor, Doctor Tancreda?" The question was flat and devoid of weight, or so it seemed.

The Betazoid gave a little frown and reached up to brush her shoulder-length brown hair back from her face. She was pale—too pale for the warm, steady sun of Jaros II—and even though she sat in the shade across the eastern side of the meeting room, she appeared uncomfortable. After a moment, Tancreda leaned forward, her slender fingers coming together in a steeple, her dark eyes returning once again to her subject. "This is supposed to be a guided meditation. I can't guide you if you won't follow me." When an answer didn't come at once, she went on. "I understand this may seem simplistic to you, at first—"

"At first?" she echoed.

Tancreda continued past the implied slight. "I'm aware

that Vulcan telepathic therapy techniques are quite complex compared to Betazoid ones. But I think we can find some common ground."

"For what purpose, Doctor?" This time she looked up, and met the other woman's gaze. Her expression remained cool and unconcerned. Sitting opposite the Betazoid in her hide of shade, the Vulcan was in the full glare of the yellow-white rays of the sun overhead. If she allowed herself to believe it, the warmth was almost like that of home. *Almost.* "Will you tell me what kind of progress you hope we can make? I would like to know."

Tancreda sighed, and she felt a slight pressure at the edges of her psionic senses. The woman was trying to take an empathic read of her mood. "Your rehabilitation is the reason you are here," she said. "But you continue to obstruct the process, and frankly, I'm having difficulty understanding the reason why." Tancreda frowned. "We've been meeting for these sessions for over three months now—"

"Three months, two weeks, four days." The correction came automatically, "Federation standard calendar."

"—and in all that time, you've given me little to work with. You keep yourself closed, and I understand that Vulcan reserve is hard to drop, I really do. I respect that. But the fact is, I have a lot of information about who you are and what you have done. Your . . . past actions mean that things you have held private have come to light." Tancreda tapped a padd at her side. "I've read your personnel files, your logs, seen your psychotricorder scans . . . I know a lot about you. It's my job to keep that trust and, in the keeping of it, help you. But if you don't let me in, then all I can do is make my best guess at the drives that motivate you, and report that to my superiors. Is that what you want?"

An admission of failure on her part. It was a tiny victory in the game that had unfolded between the two of them over the past few weeks and, for the Vulcan, the only real diversion aside from playing chess with the penal colony's computer or the slow march of reading every book in the stockade's digital library. But now, like the pointless physical labor they made her and her fellow convicts perform, it was becoming tedious.

For a moment she looked away, eyes falling to the black oval at her waist where a belt's buckle would be positioned. The device blinked silently, sensors inside the module constantly broadcasting every aspect of her physiological status and, more importantly, her precise location to the prison's mainframe. Every resident of the Jaros II stockade wore one; they were legacy technology from the old perscan medical modules used by Starfleet in the 2270s. There were no bars on the windows or fences surrounding the prison, no guards patrolling the corridors in great number; every barrier and shackle here hid in plain sight.

"What I want . . ." She almost answered honestly, and stopped herself. She gave Tancreda a long look. "What I want is for this to be over." The Vulcan's elfin eyes narrowed slightly. "I am Valeris, the traitor and the killer. I am the assassin's cohort. The shame of Vulcan and Starfleet. As all those things, convicted by a jury of my peers as guilty of treason and murder, do you truly believe that for one single moment what I want has any meaning whatsoever?"

"Do you want to go home?" Tancreda watched her carefully, fishing for a reaction. Valeris almost gave it to her, but she was careful.

Instead she went on the offensive. "Perhaps we should consider a different question, Doctor. Perhaps you should tell me what you want to hear."

"I want to hear the truth."

"Do you?" Valeris cocked her head. "Or would it be more expedient for you to hear the *right* truth? So you may complete your work and move on to another subject. I imagine it would reflect well on your future career to be known as the woman who reformed a traitor." An edge of something that might have been irritation crept into her tone. "I regret the choices I made," Valeris continued. "I was misled. I was naïve and foolish. I allowed my own innate arrogance—which I have now totally overcome, thanks to your stewardship—to blind me to reality. I am sorry for what I have done and beg forgiveness." She halted for a moment. "Is that enough? Or would you like me to attempt to portray some sort of emotional display? Tears of remorse, perhaps?"

Tancreda's lips thinned. "Some people say Vulcans aren't capable of feelings, but you get sarcasm pretty well, don't you? Don't insult me, Valeris. It's beneath you."

"Doctor, I consider this entire endeavor to be beneath me."

The Betazoid shook her head. "No, that's not going to work. The high-handed manner, that's the easy play. You can do better than that." She shifted in her chair. "Come on. Have the courage to show me something real."

Valeris looked away. The irritation was real enough, grinding at her like a stone in her shoe. On some level she was disappointed in herself for letting it take root; but then, she had been here for a long time, and her skills had naturally atrophied in the prolonged company of so many emotional beings. "What can I show you that you do not already know?"

Tancreda picked up the padd and tabbed through the pages. "In 2293 you played an instrumental role in the assassination of Chancellor Gorkon of the Klingon High Council." She read out the words as if to an unseen audience. "You were a coconspirator under the guidance of the then-admiral Lance Cartwright. Following his direct orders, you—"

"I know what I did." She spoke over her. "We both know."

"Are you squeamish about it?" Tancreda asked, seizing on the moment. "You don't want to hear me say it out loud?"

"There is no point reiterating facts that we are both already aware of."

"Very well." The Betazoid paged on through the padd's memory, throwing a sideways glance up to the discreet shape of a monitor bead at the corner of the ceiling. "Let's not speak about the assassination. Let's talk about what happened after Gorkon was murdered, after you framed James Kirk for the deed. After you killed two men in cold blood at point-blank **range**." Tancreda's tone turned cool and judgmental: *Almost*

Vulcan, Valeris thought. "When they caught you, how did you feel?"

"Disappointed." The answer slipped out before she could stop herself. It was the most honest thing Valeris had said since she entered the room.

"Who disappointed you, Valeris?" Tancreda asked. "Not Kirk. He was a Terran, a human. An emotional being. You couldn't expect his behavior to measure up to your standards. But your mentor, Captain Spock . . . That must have been difficult for you. When he let you down."

She didn't answer. Inwardly, she reached back to the techniques she had learned as a young girl, the patterns and mental structures that built walls between her thoughts and the silent turmoil of emotion. She let her hands lie flat on the arms at the sides of her chair, the carved wood warm beneath her fingertips.

Valeris saw the moment again in her thoughts, there on the bridge of the *Enterprise*. The moment she had relived a hundred times over. Kirk's angry demands and her refusal to answer them. Spock's challenge . . . and the assurance she had felt in that instant, as if her arrogance were shield enough against them both. The memory came back with brutal clarity, and she allowed herself to hate it, just for a fraction of a second.

"A lie?" Spock had asked.

"A choice," she replied. But she had been mistaken to think it would end there.

Valeris remembered the flash of surprise when Spock came to her, and the sudden, sickening knowledge of what he would do next.

She tried to fight him. Another mistake. His skills were so much greater than hers, and the barriers she put up were like paper compared to the steady, fluid pressure of his thoughts. Kirk ordered Spock to reach into her psyche through a mind-meld to draw out the names of her fellow conspirators, and to her shock and embarrassment he had done so without question.

She fought as best she could, against reason, against logic. Some primitive animal part of her mind refused to give in, but on his captain's orders, Spock opened her and took the truth from where she hid it. And the horror of it was, she was powerless to stop him. There was nothing Valeris could have done to end the invasion of her self, nothing except capitulate—and the thought of surrender never once entered her mind.

While races with a comparatively crude telepathic nature like the Betazoids could only mind-speak and cruise atop the surface of another's thoughts, the Vulcan mind-meld was something of much greater magnitude. It was not just communication but *communion*. More than the touch of thought on thought, it was a temporary merging of two psyches. In the right instance, a transcendent bond of minds sharing a brief, perfect union.

Valeris's feelings toward Spock had always been complicated, and if she were truthful, neither he nor she had correctly navigated them; but she hoped that one day they might have been able to share each other's thoughts as equals. Not like this. Not under such dark impetus, driven by lies and distrust.

The worst thing of all, worse than the disgrace and the violation of it, came in the sharing of them. Valeris showed Spock her disappointment in him—at his weakness, his illogic, his failure to live up to the expectations she had for him; and in return, Spock showed her a fathomless well of regret and sorrow, the blame he took upon himself for her actions.

When it was over, both of them had been ashamed—not just by what had been done, but by what had been left unsaid and unfulfilled between them.

The silence of the meeting room was suddenly broken by a percussive snap, and Valeris looked down at her right hand to see that she had grasped the arm of her chair with such force that the wood had splintered. She let it go and found Tancreda watching her steadily.

Another unwelcome jag of fleeting annoyance passed through her: Valeris had let her control slip and given the psychoanalyst exactly what she wanted—a reaction, an *emotional* reaction. Now that Tancreda had pushed her into it, would the doctor gloat? Would she take this moment as *her* tiny victory?

"I think we'll end this session here," said the Betazoid. If anything, the other woman's expression was more sympathetic than critical—and, in its own way, that was more insulting. "I can see we're not going to make any more progress today."

Valeris gathered herself and crossed the room to the door, which opened at a command from Tancreda's padd. She paused on the threshold. "I would suggest, Doctor, that if you wish to proceed with these meetings, you make an effort to engage me with something of import in future sessions. I dislike having my time wasted." Before the other woman could answer, she strode away into the corridor.

Malla Tancreda watched the Vulcan woman go, and once she was alone, she blew out a breath. The doctor knew going in that Valeris would be a difficult subject—years of working in telepsychotherapy had exposed her to dozens of different species and the Vulcans were always the toughest nuts to crack—but she had rarely met someone with the same degree of emotional scarring that afflicted the disgraced former officer.

When she accepted the assignment to work with the inmates on Jaros II, there were those among her colleagues at Starfleet Medical who questioned her willingness to engage with Valeris's case. In seven years of confinement, the woman had never shown any kind of contrition or any desire to atone for her part in the Gorkon conspiracy. Valeris seemed, for all intents and purposes, to be in this for the long run. With a life sentence imposed for her crimes, that would be a long time indeed. Given the life span of an average member of her species, Valeris might conceivably live to see the twenty-fifth century from the window of her cell in the western wing of the prison complex.

There was some truth to what Valeris had said before. Tancreda's work with the last surviving member of Cartwright's conspiracy of hawks might mean a paper in the *Federation Journal of Psychology*. It might mean academic kudos both here and back home on Betazed. But that wasn't the only reason Tancreda was interested in Valeris, and the longer she knew her, the more the doctor wanted to understand her. The scars the woman carried were very deep, and not just from the incident with the meld. As much as the Vulcan wanted to believe that she was governed by cool logic, something darker and deeper churned below, and Tancreda was only just starting to see the edges of it. She glanced at the broken chair arm and wondered if Valeris would ever be able to make her peace with the choices she had made aboard the *Enterprise*, and elsewhere.

She paused, taking a moment to clear her thoughts and center herself. The doctor's innate psionic abilities favored her with a strong empathic sense, and one side effect of her work was the ghost of emotion she felt from her subjects, sometimes long after they had ended a session. It was one of the reasons she preferred to work with Vulcans: they kept themselves in check as a matter of course, instead of wearing their emotive nature broadly like Andorians or Deltans. Valeris's aura still hung in the air like a coil of smoke.

Gathering up her padd, she walked to the door. Even as it slid open, she had the sudden sense of another being present out in the corridor, the faint mental impression of someone watching and waiting.

He stood silently examining a glass sculpture out in the hallway. The door closed behind Tancreda and she took a step toward him. He wasn't a detainee or a member of staff. He wore a simple grey tunic with squared-off shoulders and matching trousers. She saw the side of a lined face, the rise of an upswept eyebrow, and those characteristic Vulcan ears.

"Spock." She said the name aloud before she was aware of it. To do such a thing, to address someone not known to you, was considered coarse behavior in Vulcan society, and Tancreda instantly regretted it. But the man said nothing, turning away from the sculpture to give her his full attention.

It was him. Some residual flicker of Valeris's emotions toward the man remained in Tancreda's mind. She felt a faint stir of need and of anger.

He approached her, his expression unchanged but the light in that steady gaze alert and penetrating. "Doctor Tancreda. I would take a moment of your time." His voice was metered and resonant.

She looked around, nonplussed. Even out here on Jaros II, they had heard the barrack-room discussion about the famous Captain Spock and his resignation from the service. The fleet had wanted to handle it with pomp and ceremony, some said, but others noted rightly that Spock's years of duty to the Federation had earned him the right to select a quieter form of departure from the rigors of the uniform. The rumors said that he had traded in his insignia for a role in the Federation Diplomatic Corps, following in the footsteps of his father.

And now here he was, apparently a civilian, appearing from out of nowhere. Tancreda glanced at the padd in her hand containing the files on Valeris. This could not be a coincidence.

"My office—" She began to gesture down the corridor, but he gave a slight shake of the head.

"I will be brief. I do not wish to delay you on your rounds."

They were near a monitoring room, where observers could look in on meetings and therapy sessions from any part of the complex. A suspicion came to Tancreda and she played it. "You were watching."

Spock nodded. "Your sessions have a . . . uniquely proactive nature, Doctor. I am reminded of the somewhat forward bedside manner of one of my former crewmates."

Tancreda's skin prickled with warmth. She could feel the

echo of Valeris's buried emotions still resonating at the back of her thoughts. They were coloring her own, like ink pouring into water. "These sessions are confidential." Her reply was terse. "I certainly do not recall giving permission for anyone to observe them."

He raised an eyebrow. "My security clearance affords me certain liberties."

"Nothing we discussed in that room had any bearing on issues of galactic security. I think you're well aware of that."

The Vulcan looked away. Was that a flash of guilt she sensed? "Indeed," he allowed. "If you will permit me to confide in you, Doctor Tancreda, I am here for personal, rather than professional, reasons. I admit, I have used my reputation to facilitate that."

"Valeris."

He nodded again, and this time there was regret in his tone. "Yes. I am preparing to set out on a journey of some extended duration. Before that begins, I have been . . . making some rounds of my own."

Tancreda folded her arms, anticipating the unspoken question. "She is as well as can be expected, given the circumstances."

"I see."

The doctor gave him a level look. "You're not going to talk to her." She made it a statement, not a question.

Spock shot her a challenging look, but then he gave a slow nod of agreement. "No. At the moment, that would not be in her best interests. I would find it difficult to speak with Valeris. I only wished to ensure that she was . . . comfortable." He inclined his head in a gesture of farewell and began to walk away.

Tancreda called out after him. "Why did you do it?" she demanded.

He halted but did not turn back to face her.

She went on. "The meld. You could have found out the information you needed another way."

"There was no time," he said quietly. "She gave me no choice."

"What you did could be construed as torture, sir!" Tancreda's voice rose. She wondered where her ire was coming from: Was it hers, or was it the ghost of Valeris's fury speaking through her? "A crime!"

"Yes."

The data accompanying Valeris's case files covered much of what had happened on the *Enterprise* during the days surrounding Gorkon's murder, including copies of the fleet review board conducted after the dust had settled. Spock's actions had been ruled lawful in a crisis of the most extreme nature. What he had done allowed Kirk to break open a conspiracy to reignite the enmity between the Federation and the Klingons. But at what price?

"Have no doubt, Doctor," Spock went on, "I understand, fully and completely, the consequences of what took place on that day. I failed in my duty, as an officer and a teacher, to see Valeris's intentions before she carried them out. I will carry that regret with me for the rest of my life."

Tancreda studied him, extending her preternatural senses toward the Vulcan as he spoke. He seemed to know, and momentarily allowed her a glimpse beneath the surface of his thoughts. She caught the faint shimmer of a guilt that ran deep and long.

Spock walked on, and disappeared around the curve of the corridor.

2

Palais de la Concorde
Paris, Earth
United Federation of Planets

The walk from the secure transporter room in the basement sublevels passed almost without Darius Miller's notice. His thoughts were elsewhere, and he felt the familiar pre-mission tingle of excitement at the tips of his fingers. The activation order was barely two hours old, and he'd grasped it with both hands. Miller's mind was sifting through the briefing he had been given, deconstructing it and weighing every part for nuance and meaning.

His commanding officers in Starfleet Intelligence knew him well: a couple of weeks of downtime after his last mission in Orion space and he was getting the first echoes of boredom. Another few days and he would have been at their door, looking for something to occupy him. Miller couldn't help it; he liked the work, liked the challenge of it. Working in field ops was the career that never stopped being interesting, and Darius liked to be interested. Nothing else he'd ever done for Starfleet could quite match the pace of the cloak-and-dagger stuff. The fact that on more than one occasion it had almost killed him didn't cross his mind.

Even though his body-clock told him it was two in the morning—he was still operating on San Francisco time—here in Paris, it was a rainy weekday and the Palais was busy. He scanned the faces of the staffers who passed him in the corridor; the majority of them were serious and intent, focused on a myriad of tasks. Miller was good at reading the mood of a place, but it didn't test him to figure out what was hanging over everyone here.

A report on the incident at Da'Kel had been cycling on the Federation News Service feed as he donned his uniform before setting off to headquarters, so the word was out to the public at large. Over a thousand deaths and a dozen starships destroyed, several hundred of the victims UFP citizens, and many of the ships under the flags of Federation member worlds. One Starfleet vessel was on the list of the dead—the *U.S.S. Bode*, a *Ptolemy*-class tug lost with all hands. That data hadn't been released to the media yet, but it was only a matter of time before it broke. Right now, the news feeds were suggesting the incident was the result of some kind of accident; that, too, would soon be revealed as incorrect.

Although it wasn't his first time in the Palais, this was Miller's first visit to the Cézanne Room; a midsize conference space, it was dominated by a long oval table and a single window that looked out on the grey Parisian day. The walls at either side each sported one of the paintings of Mont Sainte-Victoire, and the ceiling was dominated by a crystal chandelier that also concealed a holographic projection rig. A mix of civilians and Fleet types filed in ahead of him, filling up the seats.

Miller fell into step behind a statuesque Andorian woman and hesitated a moment in the corridor, pausing to catch a glimpse of himself reflected in the glass frontage of a cabinet. He pulled at the hem of his claret-toned tunic to straighten it and brushed a speck of lint from his shoulder. A calm, steady face stared back at him, square-jawed and dark like carved teak, closely cut black hair tight against his skull. Satisfied that he presented a good example of Starfleet's finest, he walked in and searched for a seat in the rows away from the table proper.

A number of other officers were already there and he gave them a respectful nod. Miller immediately recognized Admiral Sinclair-Alexander; the woman was on the fast track to becoming the new chief of staff, so he'd heard. At her side, a tall man with Nordic features and a shock of blond hair caught his eye. He came over.

"Commodore Hallstrom."

"Darius," said the flag officer, with a warm smile. They shook hands. "I heard you were back on Earth. It's good to see you." His accent had the strong Scandinavian tones characteristic of those born on the Fenris Alpha colony.

Miller nodded. "Thank you, sir. Are you well?"

Hallstrom's easy smile faded. "Not since I woke this morning, no." He paused. "I have to admit, if someone saw fit to put you in this room, then I hate to imagine what might really have gone on out at Da'Kel."

"You haven't been fully briefed yet?"

The commodore shook his head. "There wasn't time. This has all been pulled together very quickly." He sighed. "I'd ask you what you know, but—"

"I think everyone here is going to find out in pretty short order, sir." He nodded toward the entrance as a group of three figures in heavy, steel-colored armor walked in, surrounding a fourth.

Kasiel was rail-thin for a Klingon, but he made up for it with a manner that mirrored his wiry, athletic build. The ambassador was the polar opposite of his predecessor Kamarag, slight where the other man had been broad, taciturn where the other had been bellicose. He took a seat at the far side of the table and his cohort of bodyguards formed a wall behind him, impassive and silent. Seven years on from the Gorkon assassination, and the Klingons still insisted on a full military escort for their representative. It was their way of reminding Starfleet of their failures.

Miller knew a little about Kasiel; Starfleet Intelligence's files on him were sketchy, but they had learned that he served with General Chang in the years leading up to the conspiracy to murder Gorkon. As the commander understood it, Kasiel had been cleared of any involvement in the plot, but his proximity to Chang—the architect of much of the Gorkon assassination's plans—had meant he was forced into a temporary form of exile. In this case, that meant the duty of being the Empire's ambassador to the Federation. Miller had no doubt Kasiel resented every day he was forced to spend on Earth, but the Klingon hid it well enough.

A Grazerite adjutant entered from another door on the far side of the room and addressed them all. "Gentlebeings, the President of the United Federation of Planets."

Everyone rose to their feet as the Efrosian walked in, his expression tense. President Ra-ghoratreii moved quickly to the head of the table and sat, gesturing with a nod for the assembly to do the same. He looked worn and his heavy brow was furrowed. This was to be his last year in the office, his term limit reached, and doubtless the politician wanted to end his tenure on a high note. An incident like this could destroy any hope of that.

"Here we go," said Hallstrom quietly, returning to his seat as Miller found a place where he could observe the proceedings as they unfolded.

"Thank you all for coming," began the president, absently stroking at his thin white beard. He glanced up as the room was sealed. "I think it is best if we go directly to the heart of this." At a nod from him, the adjutant activated the holoprojector in the chandelier and ghostly display panes formed over the middle of the table. Miller saw a tactical display of the Da'Kel System there, centered on the third planet and the orbiting utility platform. "I believe everyone is aware of the reports circulating about what took place at the Da'Kel transfer facility approximately twenty hours ago, Earthtime. A subspace discharge destroyed the station and several vessels in close orbit." The display showed a sphere picked out in white grid-lines, expanding to envelop the image. "I've asked our Klingon colleagues here to provide a more full and frank explanation. Ambassador?"

Kasiel stood and gave a shallow bow. "Mister President." His voice was firm and steady, but Miller immediately got the impression of a man who was working from a prepared script.

"The current public data suggests that a warp drive system failure aboard a Tellarite transport vessel caused a cascade subspace event. That is incorrect. In fact, it was the deliberate and premeditated use of a weaponized subspace device, with the sole intent of taking as many innocent lives as possible, and in a most honorless manner."

Admiral Sinclair-Alexander leaned forward. "Are you suggesting this was the use of an isolytic weapon, sir?"

"I am not suggesting it at all, Admiral," Kasiel countered. "I am *confirming* it. A weapons system prohibited under the addenda to the Khitomer Accords by all main galactic powers, deployed against Klingon citizens in their own space."

"Klingon and Federation citizens," said another voice. Miller saw a Vulcan woman sitting a few seats down from Raghoratreii. T'Latrek had been one of the president's staff for many years and now served as a key advisor.

"Indeed," Kasiel allowed. "As I speak," he went on, "operatives of the Klingon Defense Force and our law enforcement agencies are on site at Da'Kel, conducting an investigation into the cause of this attack. The full weight of the Empire's power is being brought to bear on this circumstance, and you may rest assured that those responsible will feel the blade of justice at their throats in short order." Kasiel paused and gave T'Latrek a look. "In addition, repatriation of remains of all Federation citizens will commence as soon as the investigation is completed. Chancellor Azetbur has personally requested that I extend her most profound sympathies to the families of those who lost their lives in this cowardly attack."

Then Kasiel sat down again, and folded his arms. Hallstrom caught Miller's eye with a look that asked: *Is that it?*

"The chancellor's words are well-taken," said Raghoratreii, "but with all due respect, I think a more detailed explanation is in order."

"Mister President—" Kasiel began to speak, but the Efrosian nodded toward his adjutant.

"Play the recording, please?"

The Grazerite nodded. "Moments before the destruction of the *U.S.S. Bode,* this data was transmitted back to Starbase 24 in an emergency data transfer . . ."

Miller knew that was a lie; an old design of ship like the *Bode* didn't have the subspace capabilities to send that kind of narrowband emergency data packet, the so-called panic signal. But Starfleet still had covert listening posts all along the Klingon border, monitoring every bit of communications traffic they could read, and the explanation was a small piece of disinformation to keep that secret hidden.

"This message was broadcast in the clear a few moments before the detonation," said the adjutant.

The holograph changed to a waveform display as the words were spoken across the room. *"MaghwI' chuH ghobe' QIb."*

Miller recognized the vernacular: an older dialect of Klingon, almost a "classical" form of the language, still used by some Imperial academics. The translation escaped him, though.

Ra-ghoratreii studied Kasiel carefully. "Could you please tell us what those words mean, Ambassador?" The way he asked the question made it clear he already knew the answer.

After a moment Kasiel gave a nod, as if he were conceding something. "It is a proverb, from the era of Kahless the Unforgettable. The literal translation is 'Traitors cast no shadow.' In the past, when a betrayer was put to death for his crimes, those words would be spoken before his execution."

"Who would consider a relief-and-recovery effort to be a betrayal?" said the admiral. "Enough to perpetrate an act like this?"

Miller watched the president. He never once took his eyes off the Klingon. Kasiel's lips thinned. "At this early stage, the investigation is following up many leads. I will inform you in due course what we have learned."

Ra-ghoratreii leaned back in his chair. "I'm afraid that won't do, Ambassador. Once we are done here, I will leave this room and give a press conference that will be broadcast to hundreds of worlds, some of which lost sons and daughters to this atrocity. I will not stand behind that podium and speak in half-truths. Please be clear."

Kasiel's face colored, but he kept his tone neutral. "As you wish. It is the belief of the High Council that this deed was committed by a cadre of renegades from within the Empire. A militia of hard-line isolationists who believe that any peace with the Federation weakens us. They decry any alliance with outsiders as the path to ruin for all Klingons, and advocate that we maintain an adversarial state toward all alien powers."

"Even in the aftermath of the Praxis disaster?" asked the Andorian diplomat.

"They believe that any Klingon who cannot stand alone against what fate throws at him is only fit to perish." Kasiel glanced back at the president, gesturing at the waveform. "That archaic phrase on the recording was their maxim. We believe they have returned to plague the Empire after many years of inaction."

Ra-ghoratreii nodded slowly. "We appreciate your candor, Ambassador. Naturally, the Federation will place its assets at your disposal in this matter. By executive order, I will be dispatching our best people to assist the Empire in its prosecution of these criminals."

Miller blinked in surprise as Kasiel's jaw set firmly; neither of them had expected to hear those words.

"That will not be required," said the Klingon stiffly. "This is an internal matter, directly under the aegis of the High Council and Imperial Intelligence."

"I remind you that more than two hundred victims of this attack were officers and enlisted serving in Starfleet," insisted the president. "I am authorizing Starfleet Command to conduct a full investigation into what happened to them, in accordance with military regulations. Ambassador, as a valued partner in a unity toward galactic peace, I expect the Klingon Empire to extend its fullest cooperation."

Kasiel's silent ire finally burst its banks and he shot to his feet. "Sir, you are questioning matters of Klingon sovereignty and territorial law! You have no authority to make these demands!"

"No?" Suddenly, all the fatigue on Ra-ghoratreii's face was gone, replaced by a steely determination. Miller's respect for the man jumped a few notches. "Tell me, is it not true that while within the borders of your space, the crew of the *Bode* and the other Federation ships at Da'Kel were under the sworn protection of the Klingon Empire?"

"Yes." Kasiel bit out the word.

"And if the circumstances were reversed, would you not at this very moment have a flotilla of warships ready to cross the border into our territory, the treaty be damned?"

"I imagine so."

"Then we understand one another." Ra-ghoratreii glanced at the admiral, who gave him a curt nod in return. "We will send a single vessel, Ambassador. The captain and his crew will respect all conventions of the Khitomer Accords and the letter of Klingon law."

"They may observe only!" Kasiel snapped. "Your vessel will be escorted at all times! Any Starfleet personnel who interfere with the investigations of Imperial Intelligence will be considered obstructions to the inquiry, and dealt with accordingly!"

"That's acceptable," said the admiral.

"Good," said the president. "Let us work together to find the people responsible for this and see that they answer for their actions." He got to his feet, and the room rose with him.

Kasiel and his party were the first out the door after Ra-ghoratreii departed, the ambassador's face stormy. Miller watched him go, and things began to click into place for him. Years of extensive field operations in and around Klingon space, a working knowledge of exotic weapons systems . . . His file had to have been top of the pile when Starfleet Intelligence got wind of the president's intentions.

Ra-ghoratreii had played Kasiel carefully; the man had

been ready to give this order before he entered the room, but now that he had done it out in the open, there was little the Klingons could do to prevent it happening. Any attempt to stop Starfleet going to Da'Kel would look dishonorable—or, worse, that the Empire had something to hide.

He waited for the rest of the people to file out of the room, taking a moment to study one of the Mont Sainte-Victoire paintings, the soft aura of the protective stasis field around the artwork humming at the edge of his hearing.

Miller lost himself in the brushstrokes for a moment, thinking hard. He'd expected to be here in his role as an intelligence officer, to supply a viewpoint from SI if the president decided to call on him; but now he understood he had been sent along to watch as Ra-ghoratreii cut his orders right in front of him.

"Commander Miller?" He turned to find Admiral Sinclair-Alexander standing behind him.

"Sir." He stood to attention.

"At ease." She gave him an appraising look. "Hallstrom tells me you're a talented officer."

"He's very generous, Admiral."

"The hell he is," she countered. "He doesn't suffer fools gladly."

"That's true. I try not to be a fool, if I can help it."

Sinclair-Alexander nodded. "Good advice at any time." She nodded toward the door. "I spoke to Vice Admiral Bur'Gun before I came up here. It seems you're in the frame for this mission, Commander."

Bur'Gun was current chief of operations at SI; Miller's direct superior was a gruff Tellarite with a permanently sour outlook that was perfectly suited to spook work. Miller liked him, but the feeling didn't seem to be mutual. "Sir . . . the president said a single ship . . . Do we know who's been assigned?"

The admiral pursed her lips. "We need someone the Klingons will respect. Someone who has shot at them once or twice. I have an idea. But for now, that's not your concern. Report to Starbase One immediately and await further orders."

"Aye aye, Admiral."

"Stay on your toes, Miller. Give the Klingons half a reason, they'll slam the door on us and we'll never know what happened to our people out there."

Starfleet Intelligence Command
San Francisco, Earth
United Federation of Planets

Outside, the predawn light was turning the sky a shade of pale orange, but in the eternal artificial day of the evaluation center's bullpen, there was nothing to mark the passage of time. Lieutenant Junior Grade Elias Vaughn made his way back to his desk with two cups of *raktajino* and settled into his chair. The virtual workspace in front of him was cluttered with a dozen padds and displays, even a few scraps of actual replicated paper lined with notes. He reached for the comm earpiece slaved to his console, turning it over in his fingers. A few hours of listening to the raw feed from Starfleet's Firewatch monitor stations had turned up nothing but some low-priority chatter from smugglers in the Hromi Cluster; he'd tagged the data and forwarded it to the appropriate analyst, but aside from that, Vaughn had not had a productive night.

"Is one of those for me?" He looked up to see Lieutenant Tracey Dale in the middle of shrugging off her coat. She didn't look happy to be called in so early.

Vaughn shook his head. "Actually they're both mine. I didn't want to make two trips to the replicator."

Dale made a face, her olive skin wrinkling, and took her desk across from his. "You got in early, then?"

He shook his head. "Never went home."

She tutted. "You should try having a life outside Starfleet, Elias. Y'know? A social life? You've heard of those?"

"I'm familiar with the concept," he deadpanned. For a

moment he considered the small, sparse apartment where he stored his personal effects. He thought of it that way because it wasn't really a home for him, just a place where he stowed things he couldn't carry on him, and occasionally parked his body. He'd been there a couple of years now and most of his stuff was still in the shipping crates that had followed him from Berengaria VII. Somehow, he'd never had the impetus to unpack it all. There were always other things to be done, other work.

Dale paged through the alerts at the top of her data queue, talking as she read. "Everyone got a wake-up call," said the lieutenant. "Commander Egan is bringing in the whole team because of this Da'Kel thing."

She nodded toward Per Egan's glass-walled office, at the far end of the room. The stocky, grey-haired officer was working, grim-faced, at his desk monitor. For all Vaughn's dedication to the job, it seemed as if Egan really *did* live every day of his life inside the evaluation center, tirelessly stalking between the desks of his staff. Dale had once, half-jokingly, suggested that Egan was actually some kind of android and not a human being at all; nothing Vaughn had seen from the commander since he had been assigned to this division had convinced him otherwise. The man was humorless and acerbic, and seemed to consider the operation of any other division but his own to be an impediment. He'd taken a dislike to Vaughn early on, and their relationship showed no signs of thawing.

"You saw the President's press conference?" she went on.

"Yeah." Vaughn had watched Ra-ghoratreii's live broadcast from the Palais on the main screen, and the politician had barely finished speaking before Egan was handing out new assignments. "Do you know who they've picked for the investigation team?"

"It's not a team, it's one man. Miller, from field ops. He's one of their top guns, apparently."

"You think he needs someone to carry his bags?"

Dale smirked. "What, you don't like it here?"

The team that Vaughn was part of was just one of several

units working in the Office of Intelligence Evaluation, each dedicated to sifting through the gigaquads of data that flooded into Starfleet Intelligence every day, looking for nuggets of information about threats to the Federation or the galaxy at large. Even with suites of dedicated artificial intelligences working in tandem with them, it was a monumental task— and it never stopped. The agents in field operations had a nickname for the OIE division: they called it the "jigsaw department," for two reasons. First, because the staff who worked there spent all their time evaluating and assembling fragments of a colossal picture that could never be fully completed; and second, because to want to do that kind of job meant you had to have a few pieces missing yourself.

Vaughn had taken a posting to OIE because he believed his analytical skills would be of use there, and also that it would stand him in good stead for eventual advancement to a field deployment. It hadn't quite worked out that way, though, and the steady, grinding pace of the assignment was wearing him down little by little with each passing day.

He sighed and ran a hand through his brown hair. "What do you think about this, Lieutenant?" He indicated his screen, where notes on the Klingon investigation at Da'Kel were displayed. "Isolationist hard-liners, coming out of the woodwork after nearly a decade of silence? I don't buy it."

Dale glanced at him. "Aren't you supposed to be scanning the Firewatch feeds?"

Vaughn didn't answer that. "I took a look at the files we have. The people Ambassador Kasiel was talking about, they were connected to a fallen noble clan out of Ty'Gokor, the House of Q'unat. Very old-school Klingons—strict tradition-alists. That catchphrase of theirs? Comes from a myth from Klingon prehistory," he noted. "There's this story that tells of how their great leader Kahless knew there was a turncoat in his camp, so he made them all stand with their backs to a huge fire. When the light from the fire fell on them, one warrior, who was a spy for Kahless's brother Molor, had no shadow. Kahless declared that because the man was a traitor, his shadow itself had fled because he was such a disgrace. Then he executed him." Vaughn made a throat-cutting gesture.

"While the lesson in Klingon mythology is fascinating, what does that have to do with the bombing at Da'Kel?" Dale asked.

He pointed at his screen. "We've got unconfirmed reports here from a few years back saying the Q'unat clan were wiped out by some internal feud. And then there's the methodology. Isolytic weapons hidden on a Tellarite transport? That's not how they did things. They were open about their opposition: they didn't hide their faces. They *wanted* people to see them coming."

"You said it yourself, ten years have passed," Dale pointed out. "Things change."

He shook his head and shot her a look. "Am I the only one who doesn't think this smells right?"

"Maybe yes, maybe no," she told him. "But the fact is, that's not your assignment, Elias. Egan wants you going through comm traffic, that's what you have to do."

For a long moment Vaughn was silent; then his hand strayed to the old scar that ran along his neck as a thought occurred to him. "You're right, Lieutenant. Comm traffic. That's *exactly* what I should be looking at."

He drained the first cup of *raktajino* to the dregs and then started on the next, bringing up a cascade of new data panes across his screen.

The second cup turned cold and sour as the hours passed by; Vaughn forgot it as he lost himself in a maze of new discoveries.

Commander Egan looked up from his screen as he heard a tap on the glass of his door. He frowned to see Lieutenant Vaughn waiting outside, holding a padd in his hand. Egan beckoned him into his office without breaking the stride of his conversation.

"I appreciate your concern, Commander Gravenor," he told the woman on the monitor, "but you have to understand that we're not miracle workers. I can't simply pull the data you need from thin air. This is an ongoing process."

He directed Vaughn to stand and wait, and the younger officer glanced down, catching sight of the petite woman on the screen.

"We're moving very swiftly on this," said Gravenor. *"Expedience would be appreciated. Frankly, we have no idea how long the Klingons are going to tolerate our presence at the site. The local military commander has already filed a formal complaint with the High Council. If we can show them we have something to offer in this investigation—"*

"I understand," he sniffed. "I promise your people will be the first to get any viable intelligence we have. Egan out." He tapped the console and cut the channel. "What is it?" he asked without sparing Vaughn a look.

"Sir, I think I have something you should see." Vaughn launched into a quick replay of his discussion with Dale out in the bullpen, barely pausing for breath. He explained the disconnect between the House of Q'unat and the line of attack used against Da'Kel, along with the fragmentary report stating that the clan was no longer active.

Egan took the padd he offered and gave it a cursory once-over. "This is what you interrupted me for? A couple of suspicions and a six-year-old piece of intelligence from an unreliable, unconfirmed source?"

"Commander, I think it's more than that."

Egan gave him a level look. "Lieutenant Vaughn, do you think I am unaware of the transfer applications you have made to the field operations division? Do you believe I haven't noticed that you consider the work we do here in OIE to be . . . I think 'deskbound' is the word you used?" He sniffed. "You believe you're capable of undertaking field missions?"

"I have before, sir."

Egan almost rolled his eyes. "Escorting some alien relic is a far cry from SI's standard remit." The previous year Vaughn had been given an atypical off-world assignment to ensure the recovery of a stolen Linellian fluid effigy, and since his return, he had become . . . unsettled. "You were sent on that mission because no experienced agents were available. Don't make too much of it. It doesn't mean you're better than the rest of us."

Vaughn stiffened. "I have the utmost respect for my colleagues and this department, sir."

Egan's face grew a thin line of scorn. "I don't think you do. I think you're so eager to get into the field that you're ignoring your assignments to bring me things like this." He waved the padd in the air. "There are people working on all nuances of the Da'Kel incident as we speak. Let them do their jobs, and you do yours."

"Again, with respect," Vaughn replied, "no one seems to have made the Q'unat connection yet. And as Commander Gravenor just noted, time is of the essence."

Mentioning Egan's opposite number in field ops was the wrong thing to do, and Vaughn knew it the moment the words had left his lips; but it was too late to take it back.

Egan leaned in. "I need team players in this division, Vaughn. Analysts who can think and compose data, not officers who entertain fantasies of undercover missions on exotic worlds."

Vaughn's eyes narrowed. "Sir, may I have permission to speak freely?"

"Absolutely not," Egan replied. "Now, unless you have something of import to say to me—"

"I do," he insisted. Before Egan could stop him, he launched into another explanation. "First, the merchantman that carried the isolytic weapon, I recognized the design. That type of vessel is not Tellarite, even though it was registered to a Tellarite shipping concern. They rarely use alien hardware if they can help it. Second, based on the ship's entry vector into the Da'Kel System, I did some quick-and-dirty calculations and extrapolated a likely course. It looks like it came from inside the Klingon Empire."

"Which lends credence to the isolationists as the culprits."

"Possibly," Vaughn admitted, "but it also means the

merchantman passed through sectors of space being monitored by our covert Firewatch monitors. So, using the subspace fingerprint from the warning message, I set the filters on the communications tracking subroutines to look for something similar." He paused to take a breath. "I got some hits."

Egan looked at the data. It showed evidence of several short-duration signals, each one plucked from the raging noise of the stellar medium by Starfleet's patient, careful scanners. "This is vague at best. A lot of this data is corrupted."

"Actually, sir, I think it might be encrypted."

"How can you be sure it's from the same ship?"

Vaughn pointed at something on the padd. "*This*, sir. Each transmission is prefixed with a single word, broadcast in the clear."

Egan read it aloud. "*Kallisti.* Another Klingon phrase . . ."

The lieutenant was almost eager. "I thought so at first. But it's something else, Commander. A code word."

The officer tapped a control and entered the term into his console. Immediately, it returned a sealed file notation. Only a series of tags were present, the actual file itself apparently redacted out of existence. What was there gave Egan a moment's pause. "This . . . this is data connected to the Gorkon assassination in '93."

"That's right. And it references one of the conspirators. The Vulcan woman, Valeris," said Vaughn, a hard edge of antipathy in his voice. "But there's nothing else there."

Egan stared at the screen for a long moment, silently considering what he saw. Then he looked up and met the lieutenant's gaze. "You're correct, there *is* nothing there."

"Sir?"

The commander shook his head. "The forest for the trees, Lieutenant. You're confusing the presence of vague data with the presence of what you're looking for." He pushed the padd back across his desk. "This is nothing more than a collection of random elements that hang together to resemble a pattern, when in fact it is nothing of the sort. This is exactly the reason that the Office of Intelligence Evaluation exists! To evaluate, consider, and, if needed, *discard* information." Egan's lips thinned. "I suggest you return to your assignment and carry on, instead of stitching together haphazard pieces of data."

"Commander, I honestly believe there could be something to this." Vaughn stood his ground. "I have a . . ."

"A *what*?" Egan demanded. "Were you actually going to tell me you had a *gut feeling*, Mister Vaughn?" He glared at the junior officer. "We do not operate on instincts and raw intuition in my department. We operate on proven facts." The commander folded his arms. "I will pass on what you have here, get another set of eyes to evaluate it. But frankly, this looks like little more than static to me."

"Which means it'll get buried under a pile of other low-priority intel," Vaughn retorted. "Let me ask you this, *sir*. If it was any other officer that presented this to you, would you have heard them out?"

The temperature in the room seemed to fall ten degrees when Egan spoke again. "I *did* hear you out, mister. And I resent the implication that I would dismiss any viable source of intelligence because of personal bias." He pointed at the door. "Now, get out of my office before I write you up for insubordination."

"Aye, sir," replied the lieutenant, and after a long moment, turned on his heel.

Starfleet Penal Stockade
Jaros II
United Federation of Planets

The veranda looked out over the open quad, which was empty except for a pair of mutterbirds jostling with each other for an insect at the edge of the grasses. The sunlight was hard, casting sharp-edged shadows around the rim of the fabric portico. Tancreda removed her polarized glasses as she stepped into the shade.

Valeris sat cross-legged on the ground, staring out at the ring of foothills that marked the perimeter of the facility grounds. "I chose not to return for another session," she said without looking up. "I assume I will be penalized for that transgression. A loss of privileges."

Tancreda found a chair and sat. "We don't have to talk in the meeting room."

"I would prefer it if we did not talk at all."

The Betazoid thought about the conversation with Spock the day before in the corridor. How would Valeris react if she told her he had been here? Would it shock her into opening up? Or would it close her down even tighter than before? Tancreda decided not to mention it for the moment. "You and I have to do this, Valeris. The interviews are a part of the psychoanalytical regimen that forms a key element of your prison sentence. If you ever hope to have the parole evaluation board—"

"Grant me release?" She let out a faint sigh. "We both know that will never happen. I am a convict. I have shown no remorse for the crimes I committed. I will remain in this prison until my life ends."

"It doesn't have to be like that."

"You advocate an alternative where none exists. Nothing I say or do will convince anyone that I should be given my freedom. You labor under the mistaken assumption that I am somehow morally 'broken' and therefore can be 'repaired' by your diligent efforts." At last, Valeris spared her a look. "I reject the implication that I am an experiment, or some puzzle for you to solve."

"I have never suggested that!" Tancreda replied. "I'm just trying to . . . understand you. I don't know why you did what you did, but there had to be reasons that you believed in. You're a logical being. You must have thought you had a logical reason."

Valeris looked away again, out at the sun-bleached rocks. "One would think so," she said quietly.

Tancreda saw an opening and took it. "Until the *Enterprise* made its rendezvous with *Kronos One*, your role in the conspiracy had been relatively minor . . . What changed? Did you regret what you did? Did you feel . . . remorse?"

"Remorse is an emotional reaction." The reply was rote.

"Something Vulcans feel just like any other being, they're just better at hiding it."

When she spoke again, Valeris's tone was cool and conversational, and it lent her words a chilling air. "You would like me to tell you how I felt as I killed two men. Their names were Harlan Burke and Thomas Samno. Both noncommissioned officers, placed aboard the *U.S.S. Enterprise* by Admiral Cartwright. We knew each other. We knew we had roles to play. But, unfortunately for them, circumstances did not follow the expected pattern."

According to the data on the Gorkon assassination, hidden inside EVA suits, Burke and Samno had beamed aboard the chancellor's personal cruiser and killed several members of the crew after a cloaked Klingon bird-of-prey had fired on the vessel and disabled it. The two of them had fired the phaser shots that were ultimately responsible for Gorkon's death, and in the aftermath those actions pushed *Enterprise* and *Kronos One* into a battle stance. It was only the refusal of Captain James T. Kirk to let the situation devolve into open conflict that prevented the ignition of a shooting war then and there.

But for Burke and Samno, their continued presence became a liability, one big enough to threaten the delicate structure of the conspiracy surrounding the murder of Gorkon.

"Captain Kirk was supposed to engage *Kronos One* in battle; had we survived that, the *Enterprise* would have retreated to a nearby Starbase where Burke and Samno would have quietly been reassigned," explained Valeris. "But things changed."

"You were ordered to silence them."

The Vulcan nodded. "Yes. To preserve not only the conspiracy, but also myself. Either man could have revealed my involvement under interrogation. I had no choice."

"There's always a choice, Valeris."

"Spare me the homily, Doctor. Unless you have been in that circumstance, I doubt you could understand."

Tancreda shook her head. "I understand you despised what you had to do."

"You would like that to be true." Valeris slowly got to her feet. "But that would have been an emotional reaction. As you suggested, I killed those men because logic dictated that I do so. I felt nothing."

The Betazoid took a breath, trying to sense the surface thoughts of the other woman; but all she could detect were shifting walls of denial. "I don't accept that. I think you want to believe you feel no remorse, but you're conflicted. You're afraid to acknowledge it, and you're burying it deeper and deeper." She gestured around. "You're imprisoning your emotions the same way you've been imprisoned here."

"What you do or do not accept is of no concern of mine, Doctor," said Valeris as she walked away.

3

Miller stood at the window of the empty embarkation lounge and let his gaze range around the inside of the spacedock bay, the vast walls like sheets of city skyline spun into an inverted cone. A handful of vessels ranging in size from small scoutships to heavy cruisers drifted at station or docked to mooring arms. The majority of them resembled the familiar design philosophy of warp-streamlined discs and elongated nacelles; only a single terra-cotta-colored courier of Vulcan manufacture stood out among the Starfleet-clean lines of the other craft.

Darius Miller had never had a command of his own, and given his career trajectory it was unlikely that he ever would. Intelligence officers didn't usually end up on the road to captaincy. Those who made it to senior rank generally found themselves training or supervising the next generation of their kind, working from the sidelines to keep the Federation safe.

Still, looking out at these ships, for a moment the commander recalled a time when he had dreamed about exploration. Like every other cadet at Starfleet Academy, he had been enraptured by the promise of pushing back the boundaries of the vast night. He found himself wondering what had happened to the men and women in his graduating class; none of them worked for SI as far as he knew. None of them had shown the same aptitude for spook work that had seen Miller plucked from his first posting and sent to serve in the shadows.

Do I regret it? The question crossed his thoughts. Perhaps he did, in a small way. But after all he had seen as an intelligence operative, he knew he would never be able to go back to the life of a line officer. For all the threats and the challenges that faced the captains of the ships out there, a hundred more invisible dangers lurked in the clandestine realms where Miller and his kind worked. A handful of people knew, and that was how it was supposed to be. He would never be able to wear his medals or have a world named after him, but if SI did their job right, the galaxy would spin on in peaceful ignorance and never know they had been there.

Absently tapping his hand against his thigh, he turned away from the window as a spry Asian man sporting captain's insignia on his tunic entered from the corridor. "Commander Miller, I presume?" His voice had a rich timbre.

"Aye, sir." He blinked: it was the first time he'd ever met a man who had a street named after him in San Francisco.

The captain extended a hand. "Hikaru Sulu."

Miller suppressed a smile. "It's an honor, Captain. When the admiral informed me that the *Excelsior* was going to Da'Kel, it was a weight off my shoulders."

Sulu smiled slightly. "Well, let's just say as far as the Klingons are concerned, my reputation precedes me and leave it at that."

"Some of them may consider your assignment to this mission to be . . . provocative."

He shrugged. "I don't doubt it. But as an associate of mine once said, 'We'll burn that bridge when we come to it.' "

"An associate?"

"Curzon Dax, an ambassador. Do you know him?" Miller shook his head and Sulu went on, almost to himself, "Pity he's not here now. We could use him on this."

"I'm sorry you had to have your current mission disrupted."

The captain crossed to the airlock hatch near the observation window and typed in a summons code on the console there. His smile faded. "I won't lie to you, Commander, my crew were not pleased to have a change in orders dropped on them at the eleventh hour. We were ready to ship out from Mars for a three-month mission mapping locations of Debrune archaeological sites . . . But the Fleet asks of us and we follow."

"That we do, sir."

Sulu gave Miller a measuring look. "Commander . . ." he began, eyes narrowing, "let's save ourselves a little time here. I'm not unfamiliar with covert operations and the needs for compartmentalization, information security, and the like. But I want to make it clear to you that I will in no way accept any Starfleet Intelligence operation that will place my ship or crew in harm's way without my full knowledge and consent. Is that understood?"

"That would never be my intent, Captain," Miller replied without hesitation. "You have been fully briefed?"

Sulu nodded. "Indeed, Command felt they needed me to speak face-to-face with them rather than transmit over a secure channel. I appreciate what the effects of the Da'Kel bombing will be if we don't contain the problem immediately."

Miller reflected the other man's nod. "We've worked hard to make the Khitomer Accords happen. It can't be derailed because of this."

The captain's face clouded for a moment. "I agree. I was there when that treaty was made, and I'll be damned if I'll let it collapse because some old soldiers want to reignite a pointless war." He sighed. "I've been told you're very good at what you do, Commander. I confess that I've never come across your name before, though."

"That's precisely because I *am* very good at what I do, sir."

Sulu smiled again. "I think you and I will get along just fine."

A motion at the corner of his eye drew Miller's attention and he turned his head to see the egg-like shape of an automated travel pod rise into view. It settled into the airlock collar with a dull thud and the aft hatch opened.

Sulu beckoned him toward it. "I'll pilot," said the captain. "These days I don't get the opportunity that much, so I like to take any I can get—"

Behind them, the door to the corridor hissed open and Miller turned to see a junior officer clutching a padd in his hand. The young man was flushed and out of breath, and the commander immediately noted dots of discoloration on his uniform tunic: raindrops. He had to have transported up from the surface, and clearly in a great hurry.

"Commander Miller?" he asked. He went to attention. "Captain Sulu, sir. Sirs."

Sulu shot the new arrival a look. "Is there a problem, Lieutenant . . . ?"

"Vaughn, sir. Lieutenant J.G. Elias Vaughn. Starfleet Intelligence Command."

"Oh?" Sulu glanced at Miller. "One of yours, Commander?"

Miller searched his memory for the name, and a vague scrap of recall snapped into place. "You're part of Commander Egan's jigsaw team, yes? Did he send you?"

Vaughn gathered himself. "Uh, not exactly, sir, no. I'm . . . I'm kind of operating under my own initiative at the moment." He held up the padd. "I have some data here I think you should see."

Miller glanced at Sulu and saw what might have been a flicker of amusement in the other officer's eyes, but the captain said nothing. Instead, he hesitated on the threshold of the travel pod.

"Does Commander Egan know you're up here?" Miller asked.

Vaughn took a moment to frame his reply. "I don't believe he's aware at the moment, sir." Before Miller could answer, he pressed on. "Sirs, if I may? I've found what I think may be a critical piece of intelligence connected to the Da'Kel bombing."

"I'm sure if that's so, your department head would pass it on," offered Sulu.

"Yes sir," said Vaughn. "I mean, no sir. I mean, Commander Egan considered the data to be noncritical. And I didn't agree."

"Is that so?" Miller's voice grew cold and he took a step

toward the lieutenant. He knew Per Egan by reputation, and he'd had his issues with the man in the past, but that had no bearing on the fact that this officer was apparently circumventing the chain of command. Miller told him so, fixing the young man with a hard glare.

To his credit, Vaughn didn't buckle. "I understand that, sir. But I feel very strongly that you should be made aware of this information before you set off for Klingon space."

"You can't just ignore the orders of a commanding officer when it suits you," Miller went on. "Isn't that correct, Captain?"

"Oh, undoubtedly," Sulu said innocently.

In retrospect, perhaps the captain of the *Excelsior* wasn't the best choice to bolster Miller's argument, he reflected. Sulu had bucked command more than once in his career, and before that served under a captain who had made an art of it.

"I'm willing to accept any punishment I may incur," Vaughn replied, still stiffly at attention, "*after* you look at this." He held out the padd.

"You feel that strongly about the matter, Lieutenant?" Sulu asked.

"Yes sir, I do, sir."

At length, Miller took the padd and glanced at it. "All right," he said. The commander had to admit, his interest was piqued.

"I have a suggestion," offered the captain, nodding toward the travel pod. "It'll take us a couple of minutes to cross the spacedock to *Excelsior*. Why don't we give Lieutenant Vaughn here that long to convince us both not to have him reprimanded?"

Miller gave a curt nod. "Two minutes, aye." He looked back at the officer. "Clock's running, Vaughn. Start talking."

The pod left the docking collar so smoothly that Elias was only aware of it through the motion of lights outside the panoramic viewing canopy. Captain Sulu stood at the thruster controls, working them deftly and by touch alone.

Miller frowned at the padd containing the data from the comm traffic that Vaughn had hastily uploaded.

This wasn't the smartest thing Elias Vaughn had ever done, and sure as hell wasn't the safest play for a young Starfleet officer with hopes of promotion. But standing there in Egan's office as the man tore him down, and dismissed his work out of what could only be petty departmental politics and personal dislike . . . He couldn't let that stand. A lot of good people had died at Da'Kel, and he owed it to their memories to make sure the truth about what happened to them came out. If Vaughn relied on Egan to funnel the raw intel to the people who needed it, it would come too late. So when he heard that Miller was on Starbase One, he knew he had an opportunity to make things right.

But now, as he explained his discoveries about the tactics of the House of Q'unat, the rumors of their destruction, and the code word used by the fake Tellarite transport, he felt an icy wave of worry fill him, as if he were an empty vessel. What if Miller and Sulu didn't see the connections that he had made? What if they took Egan's side—or, worse, what if Egan had been correct all along?

Have I just blown my entire career on one impulsive act?

"Kallisti." Miller rolled the word around, trying it on for size.

"The only reference to that term in the OIE database links directly to sealed files about the assassination of Chancellor Gorkon," he said, speaking quickly as if he were afraid he would not have time to get it all out.

Sulu looked back at him, his expression deadly serious. "You're certain?"

"Positive, Captain."

Miller paged through the padd. "After Captain Sulu, Captain Kirk, and Captain Spock brought the plans of General Chang and his coconspirators to light, SI moved in to annex and seal all the data we could find. But unfortunately, those involved on our side had prepared for that eventuality."

"Cartwright . . ." Sulu said the man's name, grim-faced.

The captain had been the one who caught the renegade admiral as he attempted to flee the scene of his crime.

Miller nodded. "And his supporters. Drake and the others. We caught them all eventually, but after the revelations at Khitomer, they purged the databanks of almost everything. We managed to rescue some scraps, but little else. The Kallisti reference was part of that."

"The Da'Kel attack," insisted Vaughn. "It has to be the first strike in a campaign engineered to break the Accords! And this proves that someone involved with it was part of the plot to murder Gorkon seven years ago!"

"No, Lieutenant," said Miller. "It doesn't *prove* anything. Egan was right when he told you this was thin."

Vaughn's gut tightened. "Sir . . ." *Here it comes. Miller's going to kick me straight into the brig.* He had rolled the dice and now they were about to come up snake-eyes.

"But it's also *something*." The commander weighed the padd in his hand. "I'm just not sure what yet."

Vaughn swallowed, his throat suddenly arid. He wasn't certain, but it sounded like Miller was agreeing with him.

"May I?" Sulu took the padd and scrutinized it, effortlessly steering the travel pod at the same time. After a moment he spoke again. "The code word is associated here with another of the conspirators. Valeris."

"After Cartwright died in prison in '98, she's the only surviving member of the plot," said Vaughn. "She's serving a life term at the Jaros II stockade."

"Jaros II . . ." repeated the captain. "It's on our way."

"It is?"

"It can be. I'll arrange for the *Excelsior* to take a short detour en route to Da'Kel. I can send a message to an old crewmate of mine who may be able to get us access to Valeris."

A grin threatened to break out on Vaughn's face, but he kept it back. He almost sagged against the wall of the pod in relief. He'd done the right thing; Miller's trust in his discovery invalidated all the doubts Elias had felt, and proved to him that his instincts were valuable after all.

He looked up, out of the forward canopy, and before them lay a curved steel-white expanse of tritanium, lined in cobalt and dotted with running lights. Dark letters picked out the name and registration across the starship's primary hull: *U.S.S. Excelsior* NCC-2000.

Beyond the center of the disc, where the platform of the command deck and the impulse manifolds rose high, Vaughn caught sight of a pair of long, sleek warp nacelles. They glowed an electric blue, the chained power of the interstellar engines dormant but ready to be released at a single word of command. The cruiser seemed as if it were already racing, even though it lay at rest.

"She's something else, isn't she?" said Sulu quietly, noticing Vaughn's attention.

"Aye, Captain," he replied—then the lieutenant shook off the moment and looked away. "I want to thank you both for hearing me out, sirs. I'm sorry I was so, uh, unconventional in my approach. But I felt it was warranted."

The travel pod dropped toward a docking ring at the rear of the starship's command deck, turning as it fell to orient for capture. Vaughn felt Miller's steady gaze on him.

"That's it?" said the commander. "You're done?"

Vaughn blinked. This wasn't the response he had expected. "Uh. Yes?"

"Wrong answer," Miller replied. He held up the padd. "You think you can just drop this in my lap and then go back to OIE without another word?"

"I don't follow you, sir," Vaughn replied. But he had an idea.

"I think you will," said the other man. "If you were so all-fired certain of your interpretation of this data that you would risk censure and reprimand from not one but three senior officers . . . then I would expect you to have the conviction to follow your instincts wherever they take you."

"I don't think . . ." Vaughn ran out of words, unsure of how to proceed.

"I could use an extra set of eyes, Lieutenant. Someone with good analytical skills; someone who can see the unseen, which you clearly have done." He glanced at Sulu. "With your permission, Captain?"

"I think Lieutenant Vaughn might wish to be off-planet when Commander Egan learns what took place here," he agreed. The travel pod settled into the airlock slot and the doors gently eased open.

Those hard eyes bored into Vaughn's, the challenge open and ready. "Are you up for it, Mister Vaughn? Or would you like to take the pod back to dock control for us instead?"

The question hung in the air, and he hesitated. Part of him wanted to accept the offer immediately, while another shied away. Was he really ready for something like this? He thought about Egan's comments; was he just entertaining the fantasy of being a field agent?

There was only one way to be sure.

Vaughn went to attention once more and looked toward Captain Sulu. "Permission to come aboard, sir?" he asked.

Sulu gave a half smile. "Granted."

Xand Depot
Deep Space
Klingon Border Zone

Once, when ships had to struggle to make it past warp factor two, when the space lanes were longer and journeys extended into months instead of days, commercial way stations like Xand Depot were a fact of life. It was little more than a generator spindle surrounded by a cluster of fusion-welded cargo modules refitted for purpose, and bits of decommissioned warp one transports that were not worth the cost of scrapping. Even at the height of its popularity, it had been a raggedy place, a patchwork port adrift along the contested outer edges of Klingon territory. But then there had been accidents and losses of life, piracy and a dozen other smaller problems. In the end, Xand Depot was abandoned and left to decay.

Power failed, ice rimed the corridors and compartments. It drifted, forgotten by crews who no longer needed to stop to rest their engines or seek some shore leave. But nothing is truly lost in the vacuum. For decades, Xand Depot remained derelict—until those who had need of a hidden place that had fallen from the star maps came looking.

The station lived again, if you could call it that. Much of the facility was irreparable, open to the void and too badly damaged to patch. But there were still decks where life support could function, and with some gentle coaxing the generator had been reawakened. Now it served as one of a number of hidden places where Rein's people could move freely without attracting unwanted scrutiny.

He leaned in toward the monitor screen before him, pulling the heavy miner's overjacket tight across his shoulders. It was always chilly on this deck, the bite of the cold like a winter's day along the coast where he had grown up, and Rein's thin frame didn't deal well with it. It made him irritable. He folded back the hood from his head, running a hand through the unkempt peak of his hair and down the line of pigment spots that ran to his neckline. He sighed and drew himself up as the encryption key locked in, and the hyperchannel finally connected.

Seryl's face filled the screen. The other man was older than Rein, and in some ways he had once been a mentor to him. But that was a long time ago, and Seryl's place at the vanguard had long since been taken by his student. "It was done."

The older man nodded. "It was done. But not as we had hoped."

Rein frowned. "Explain."

Seryl looked away from the sensor pickup at his end of the communication, as if glancing at someone out of sight. It was difficult to get a read on where the other man was; the heavily coded signal was thick with static and the images were washed-out and grainy, making the background a wall of shadows. "The weapon did detonate. But not where we had planned. And not with the force we expected."

He nodded. Rein's younger brother Colen was in charge of

monitoring the news feeds and comm traffic throughout the sector, and everything they had seen on the public channels showed that the isolytic device had fallen short of its intended target yield. But there was no way the Klingons could know that. The destruction Rein and his people had wrought was terrible enough. *At least for now.*

"*I have concerns,*" Seryl told him. On the screen, the old man absently traced the line of his own faded pigmentation. It was a gesture many of their kind exhibited in times of stress. "*I think something went wrong with the device. The displacement was asymmetrical. Unbalanced. It was weakened.*"

Rein paused, evaluating this information. "Do you think that, at the end, Zennol was trying to . . . stop it?"

Seryl reacted as if he had been slapped. "*Of course not! Zennol understood exactly what was at stake. He placed his life in service to the First Monarch as . . . as we all have. He was paid in kind with guarantees for his family. He would not have faltered at the last moment!*"

"Leru, then? He was young. He might have had second thoughts."

The other man shook his head. "*Zennol was there to make sure that did not happen. No, Rein. There was another reason. I think the weapons . . . may not be all that they were promised.*"

"No?" Rein smiled thinly. "How many ships destroyed or scuttled? The orbital station obliterated? How many dead among the tyrants and their allies?"

"*It could have been more.*"

His smile grew as chill as the room. "It soon will be. Thanks to you."

Seryl looked away again, static crackling over his voice. "*If we proceed.*"

"If?" Rein snarled the word back at him. "Ah, so it is *you* that has the doubts, then?"

"*Don't put words into my mouth!*" Seryl snapped back at him. "*If we were misled about the weapons, then what if there is a malfunction? If there is a failure and we are captured?"*

"You must ensure that never happens," Rein insisted. "The scheme turns on keeping the Klingons floundering in the dark, putting them off balance. We have to make sure they are looking in the wrong place, so when we strike, they chase their tail like a maddened animal!" He blew out a breath. "Yes, Zennol knew the stakes, and so do you, Seryl. If any one of us is dragged into the light, it will mean the end of our world! They will come and take their reprisals: one thousand dead for every Klingon corpse! We must be ghosts, or we will never find our vengeance!"

"My life is given in the name of freedom, not revenge."

"They are one and the same," Rein retorted, barely catching himself before he chastised the older man. Instead he moved closer to the screen. "Seryl. My trusted friend. You know what you must do. Zennol and Leru, their sacrifice was brave, but it was only the landing of the first blow. What you do next will show our enemies the absolute strength of our resolve. We all must stay the course."

"I have never believed otherwise," came the reply. *"You are right, as always. Whatever happens, they won't see our faces."*

"Not until it is too late," Rein told him. "And when that day comes, the tyrants will be on their knees, drowning in the ashes of their fallen empire." He gave a sad smile. "You will take us there."

When Seryl spoke again, it was as if he had the weight of ages upon him. *"Remember us, Rein. Promise me that."*

He nodded, reaching for the disconnect key. "Promise made, old friend. I'll carve your name on the walls of Akadar's temple myself." Before Seryl could speak again, he cut the signal.

For long moments Rein sat there in the dark and the cold of the comms room, weighing the choices he had made. When he heard footfalls on the rusted deck plates, he wiped his eyes and stood up.

Colen appeared at the open doorway. "It's almost time," said his brother, stifling a wet cough. "The new delivery will be here any moment."

"Of course." Rein stood up and trailed after his sibling.

"You spoke with Seryl?" he asked as they walked up the inclined ramp toward the cargo tier above. "What did he want?"

"What any of us want. Reassurance. A voice to tell us that we are doing the right thing."

"We are," Colen replied without hesitation. "The tyrants pushed us to this with their thuggery and their lies. What choice do we have if not slavery and dissolution?" He snorted. "No one else will help us. The rest of the galaxy is blind to our struggle."

"Most of it, at least," Rein noted as they walked into the open storage space. "A righteous cause can still have some supporters, so it seems."

The cargo tier had once been home to transient shipping modules, back when Xand Depot was in full operation; but now it was a wide, empty chamber. Gattin, Rein's second, was there with Tulo and a few of the others, waiting with tricorders and sensor wands at the ready.

Rein looked up. In the curved ceiling over their heads there was an arc of transparent metal looking out into the blackness beyond. He looked hard, wondering if he might see some visual artifact of the cloaked ship out there with his naked eye; but there was nothing. He wasn't surprised by that: their patrons were exceptionally good at keeping their identities a secret. And for now that served his cause as well as theirs.

At his side, Colen was looking up at the same blank patch of space. "How do we even know they are here?" he asked.

"They could have been out there for days," muttered Tulo. "Watching us."

"Keep your nerve," Gattin said, her tone acid.

Rein was about to add something, but then a glitter of emerald light formed out of nothing in the middle of the empty cargo bay. He heard the humming of energy and displaced air molecules. In seconds, a rectangular capsule materialized, a slab-sided thing bereft of any markings or detail that might suggest its origin.

The similarity between the container and a burial casket was not lost on Rein, and he gave a grim nod. "Check it."

Colen took one of the tricorders and made a slow orbit of the box, scanning the seams. Rein looked up again as he worked; he still saw nothing.

"Trace amounts of subspace radiation and omicron particles. It's the same as before."

"Good." He glanced at Gattin. "Bring the anti-grav up from the ship. I want to get it on board as soon as possible."

"Rein?" Colen looked surprised. "We're moving it? We're not going to assemble the third one here?"

"No. We've stayed here too long as it is." He beckoned his brother closer. "I want you to make sure there are no tracking devices embedded in the container or the parts before we leave this place."

Colen folded his arms. "It's safer to do the assembly work first."

Rein shook his head and jutted his chin toward the window overhead. "They've come to the depot twice now. That's enough. We can't afford to fall into a predictable pattern." His voice went low. "One mistake. We only need to make one mistake and we are done."

"We can't trust anyone," added Gattin.

In the dimness of the cargo bay, Colen seemed pale, his pigment spots dark against his neck and temples. "It's only that—" Suddenly he broke off and gave a hacking, bone-deep cough that bent him over with its force. He wiped his lips with a kerchief, and before Rein could lay a hand on him, he pushed his brother away. "I'm all right. It's just the cold."

Rein watched him for a moment and then nodded. "Have the medic take a look at you after we get under way."

"I don't need any special treatment because I'm your brother," he replied.

"And you won't get any," Rein snapped back, his temper fraying. "Now, do what I told you. Transfer the components and take everything we need from here. We're not coming back to this place." He stalked away, his hands knitting together.

Colen watched him disappear out of sight with Gattin at his side and then hastily discarded the kerchief, the cloth marked with flecks of red.

Starfleet Penal Stockade
Jaros II
United Federation of Planets

At night, the temperature outside dropped sharply and the majority of the inmates retreated back to their cells or the day room. Valeris tested the limits of the prison's regulations by remaining in the courtyard. The Vulcan was careful to remain well within the sensor perimeter atop the light towers, and she knew that somewhere on the roof of the building, a security hover drone sat with its wings folded like a patient raptor, ready to burst into motion and come after her if she ditched her perscan unit and tried to bolt for the boundary line.

There was a rock she favored, a long oblate thing with a surface that was flat and slightly angled. Valeris sat upon it, her eyes closed, filling her senses with nothing but the feel of the stone and the cold brush of the air on her face.

It had been a few days now since her last conversation with Doctor Tancreda, no more than a few meters from this very spot. Perhaps the Betazoid had finally gained a measure of understanding from her. Perhaps at last the psychologist had accepted that Valeris wanted to be left alone to go through the motions of her days without Tancreda's constant probing at the walls of her persona. If a day ever came when Valeris wanted to unburden herself, then she would choose to speak. Until that time her thoughts were her own.

It was important for Valeris that her thoughts *remained* her own.

And then, cool like the night breeze, she felt the ghost of a ripple in the psychic space of her meditation. She knew immediately that it was the aura of another Vulcan: the telepathic resonance was unmistakable. But even as she became aware of that, another certainty pushed its way to the front of her thoughts. A familiarity, a sudden, absolute knowing that triggered—what? *An emotional response?*

It was *him*. There could be no doubt.

Footsteps approached, soft leather shoes crunching lightly over the patina of sand cast across the courtyard by the winds. Valeris turned her head toward him, schooling her expression to maintain her neutral aspect, and at last opened her eyes.

Spock emerged from the pools of shadow between the towers and halted a short distance from the rock. His hands were clasped behind his back, and his face betrayed nothing.

How like him. Valeris studied Spock, allowing the moment to extend into silence. She recalled hearing a ship pass overhead before sunset; perhaps it had been the one that brought him here.

He looked old. It was as if she were seeing him with new eyes, or perhaps it was more truthful to say she was seeing him as he really was, not how she had wanted him to be. The last time she had laid eyes on Spock was as he left the tribunal chamber at Starfleet Command, after completing his deposition to the admiralty board. His statement only added weight to the scales stacked against Valeris by her own deeds, fully revealed in the light of Admiral Cartwright's arrest and imprisonment.

A surge of sensation rose up inside her, and belatedly Valeris realized that it was the churn of buried emotions struggling to take voice against her former mentor. For a moment, she wavered on the edge of allowing them to slip their cage—but she knew if that were to occur, she might never find a way back to any kind of stability. With monumental effort, she marshaled her will and silenced the cry inside.

Then she uttered the first words she had said to Spock in seven years. "What do you want?"

"Are you well?" he asked.

Valeris searched his expression for anything, any minute tic that might give her a clue to his state of mind. He wore civilian clothes, in a style that had been popular with her elders when Valeris was a child, and he carried himself stiffly. She wondered what possible reason he could have to appear before her now, after so long. Valeris had heard about his departure from Starfleet. *Is he dying, perhaps, and come to make amends?* She dismissed the thought, dismayed at how much the notion of that perturbed her.

"My well-being is as one might expect in these circumstances," she said. "Have you come here to apologize to me?"

He watched her intently. "What could I say that would count as an act of contrition? What value would that have?" Spock took a shallow breath. "What could *you* say?" He gave a small shake of the head. "I regret what took place between us. You left me no choice, Valeris."

"There is always a choice," she replied, quicker than she intended.

"We have both had time to reflect on what occurred aboard the *Enterprise* that day." Spock's gaze did not waver. "You feel that I disappointed you, that I failed your belief in me, because I did not see what you saw in the Klingons."

Yes, she wanted to say. But she remained silent.

"I *did* fail you, Valeris," he went on. "As your teacher, your senior officer, as a fellow Vulcan and . . . as an associate. I did not see the path you were taking until it was too late. I did not stop you soon enough, and so you were lost to me."

Annoyance struggled at the base of her thoughts. "You have no right to take responsibility for me, Spock. You are not my father, nor my husband or . . . *associate*. I made my own choices. I understood every one of them."

Valeris placed her hands flat on the cool surface of the rock, to stop them from drawing into tight fists. She knew it would be so very simple to hate him. It would be easy to fall into the trap of an emotional response. All these years on Jaros II without the companionship of other Vulcans and only the company of emotive beings had eroded Valeris's control. On some deep, personal level she was appalled at herself for the need that rang in her thoughts; the primitive part of her wanted to hurt him, make him feel what she did now.

And yet, Spock *had* felt what she felt, just as Valeris

had shared with him during their forced mind-meld. The conflicted recall of that moment came back once more and she turned her thoughts from it.

At last Spock looked away. "I have lost too many friends in recent years. And on each occurrence, one cannot help but wonder, even against logic, if there was not some way events could have gone differently."

She took his meaning. "Captain Kirk . . ." Valeris considered the name. "I will confess that I was dismayed to learn of his death aboard the *Enterprise*-B. Of all the humans I have known, I had the greatest respect for him. I . . . admired him."

"And yet you drew him, and the rest of us, into a plan for war."

Valeris's lips thinned. "I regretted his involvement in the move against Gorkon. But he was Cartwright's selection for the mission. The admiral believed he would act against the Klingons in reaction to his own history with them."

When Spock looked back at her, his gaze was stony. "If you thought he would embrace aggression without consideration or forethought, then you did not understand James Kirk at all. He was an exceptional human, able to see beyond himself and the moment. He let go of his rage against the Klingon people for the death of his son. The conspiracy to kill Chancellor Gorkon went against everything he believed in."

"It would appear so," Valeris replied after a long moment. "So, then. I return to my original question. What do you want with me, Spock?"

"A group of terrorists attacked the Da'Kel utility platform in the Mempa Sector several days ago. A weapon of mass destruction was used. There were many deaths."

Valeris's arms drew up and she folded them across her chest. "A tragedy," she said, almost dismissive. "But not uncommon, given the Klingon predilection for solving all problems with massive bloodshed."

"A contingent of Starfleet officers and Federation citizens were also victims of the attack. Two members of the Starfleet crew were in your year at the Academy." He mentioned the names, but Valeris's recollection of their faces was vague and without consequence.

"I am sure tragic events such as that one occur all over the galaxy every day. Why come here to tell me of this single incident?"

Spock told her of the Klingon statements regarding the suspects in the bombing, and also of some new if rather anecdotal evidence that suggested that the truth might not be so clear-cut.

"A code word was found prefixed to encrypted communications messages, apparently sent and received by those who destroyed themselves to perpetrate this attack. That code was also in use seven years ago by those engaged in the assassination of Gorkon." Spock gave her a level look. "You are familiar with Earth's Greek mythology?"

"A . . . a passing familiarity."

"*Kallisti.*" When he said the word, she almost reacted. It took effort to remain silent, and Valeris wondered if she had revealed something before she could stop herself.

Kallisti. She had not heard that uttered since before the assassination, before Gorkon and the *Enterprise.*

"It means 'for the most beautiful.' The folklore claims it was written on the surface of a golden apple, a gift given at the wedding of Peleus and Thetis that was eventually responsible for igniting the Trojan War." Spock came closer, watching her carefully. "A single act that plunged two nations into conflict on the eve of a great union. The so-called apple of discord was created by the Greek goddess of strife."

"Her name was Eris," she said.

4

Commander Miller watched the courtyard through the glass doors of the annex. Out in the cool night, Ambassador Spock spoke to the convict, his movements small and understated. The woman, on the other hand . . . From what he knew of Vulcans, she was practically animated.

For better or for worse, it was up to Spock now. Sulu had been as good as his word; the captain had spent a half hour in a private conversation with the ambassador over subspace, and when he emerged from his cabin, he gave the order to divert the *Excelsior* to the Jaros system.

"Ambassador Spock understands the situation," Sulu noted. "He will make the arrangements." He didn't volunteer any more than that, and Miller didn't ask.

Lieutenant Vaughn had questioned how that might be possible. After all, despite his respected status, Spock was no longer a serving Starfleet officer and technically had no formal influence over the workings of a place like the Jaros II stockade. But then again, when you had rescued as many worlds as the first officer of the *Enterprise* had, people tended to cut you a lot of slack.

Things became clearer when Miller learned that Spock had visited the prison complex earlier, some time before the news from Da'Kel had broken. He wondered what the Vulcan had hoped to gain. Of all the prisoners incarcerated there, Valeris could be the only one of personal interest to Spock, and the former captain's mentor-student relationship with the woman was a matter of record. Miller decided not to dig too deep—for the moment. He was just a commander, and the motivations of a decorated ex-officer like Spock were not his to deliberate upon. *For now.*

Miller and Vaughn beamed down to the coordinates provided, and were told to wait. Now that time was almost over, so it seemed. Out in the courtyard, the conversation had to be reaching its end point. "Moment of truth . . ." Miller said to himself.

At his side, Vaughn's jaw was stiff and his posture rigid. "He's not what I expected," said the junior officer. "Spock, I mean."

"What *did* you expect?"

"I'm not certain," he admitted. "I've never met someone who died and came back before. I thought he'd seem . . . I don't know, *different* somehow."

"He's a Vulcan," said Miller, and that was answer enough.

"So is she." Vaughn's gaze became a glare as he studied Valeris from a distance. "She's not what I expected either. A Vulcan traitor. I didn't think their kind were capable of that."

"They can lie like anyone else," Miller noted. "They just have a whole different way of doing it from the rest of us."

"She committed high treason."

"I'm well aware," said Miller.

The lieutenant was silent for a moment. "Do you think Valeris cares about what she did? Or does she think betraying her oath was logical?"

"You'd have to ask her." Miller heard the antipathy in Vaughn's voice and gave him a look. "It's not our concern. We're not in the business of judging right and wrong, Lieutenant. We're here for information, that's all."

"How can we trust a traitor?"

"I never said we **have** to trust her. **Valeris has** information we need, so we do what we must to get it. That information isn't black-and-white. It's not good or bad, it just exists. It's only what you do with it that makes the difference. If Valeris can help us, we use her, end of story. The moral issues we can consider another day."

"Aye, sir," came the reply, but Miller could tell the other man wasn't convinced.

Outside, Spock threw a glance back at them and the commander opened the doors.

Valeris looked up as they approached. Vaughn felt her gaze rake over his tunic and the Starfleet insignia on his chest. He wondered if she was remembering wearing a similar uniform.

Spock backed away a step to allow them to come closer. Valeris looked across at her former commander and cocked her head. Her voice was as cold as the night when she spoke to him. "The reality of things becomes clear," she said. "You did not come to Jaros II in some consideration of my well-being. You are here because Starfleet ordered you to come. Because you *want* something from me."

Spock didn't address the comment. "This is Commander Miller and Lieutenant Vaughn, from Starfleet Intelligence. They have questions regarding the Kallisti code." He paused. "It would be in the best interests of all involved if you would answer them as fully as possible."

When he said the code word, Vaughn caught the slightest twitch on the woman's face, a fractional microexpression that even her Vulcan resolve wasn't enough to completely hide. He knew then: she knew *exactly* what that code meant.

Valeris drew herself up. "I do not remember."

"Haven't asked you anything yet," said Miller.

"Nevertheless," she replied. "I do not remember."

"Okay, that's a lie," said Vaughn. "Even I got that one."

"You are being offered an opportunity, Valeris," Spock told her.

"An *opportunity*?" Her answer was almost a sneer. "For what? To once again serve a Federation willing to do anything for the pretense of peace? To help the Klingons?" She turned away. "If you believe I will do so, then you are indeed a poor judge of my motivations."

Miller shook his head. "No, I don't think so. I've got a pretty good idea of what will motivate you, Valeris. Lieutenant?"

Vaughn had been carrying a padd with him, and now, at the commander's direction, he offered it to the Vulcan. He kept his expression neutral as she took it from him.

"What is this?" she asked. "A list of my crimes?"

"No," said Miller. "It's a document drawn up by the Office of the President of the United Federation of Planets. It's not quite a pardon, but it's in the same ballpark."

The lieutenant gave the commander a sharp look. He'd had no idea what the padd contained. "Starfleet is offering her . . . a deal?"

Miller nodded. "Something like that."

"You understand the gravity of this offer, Valeris?" Spock asked. "I called upon certain favors to help Commander Miller facilitate this proposal. It will not come again."

Miller spoke as Valeris scrutinized the text on the padd. "If you agree to assist Starfleet Intelligence with our investigation into the Da'Kel bombing, and if that information proves to be of value, your prison term will be reviewed."

"Define 'reviewed,'" Valeris replied.

"That depends on what you have to give. Some names and places—that could mean a couple of decades trimmed off your life sentence."

"I will require more than that," she retorted.

"I don't doubt it," said Miller.

Valeris glared at Spock. "I want my life back. I want to leave this place and return to Vulcan."

"That will never happen," Spock said firmly.

"A colony, maybe," Miller went on. "That we could do. And a new identity. You could . . . start again. *If* you give us everything you know."

"If you really *do* know anything, that is." Vaughn

couldn't remain silent. He was incensed that someone who had betrayed the ideals of Starfleet could be offered the chance to walk away from her punishment. If justice were truly enforced here, then Valeris would have been deported to some barren wasteland world, exiled like the convicts of Earth's eighteenth century. It wasn't right that she could have her crimes erased with the stroke of a politician's pen.

"And if I decline?" she asked. "Will you transport me away in the night, take me to some secret facility, and compel the information you need from me by force?" Valeris ended the words with her eyes on Ambassador Spock.

"No," said the other Vulcan. "If you refuse, you will spend the rest of your life in confinement here on Jaros II. Is that what you wish, Valeris?"

She looked at the ground, and for a long moment the only sound was the low howl of the night winds. Vaughn found part of himself hoping Valeris would reject the offer of amnesty. As much as he wanted to uncover the truth about the attack on Da'Kel, he despised the idea of working with a traitor to do so. It didn't sit well with him that they were here only because of data he had uncovered. But Miller had taken his side, and Sulu with him—and, it seemed, so had Admiral Sinclair-Alexander back on Earth. *Or at least they're giving me enough rope to hang myself.*

"What I wish is to be left alone." Valeris's reply was almost a whisper. Then, with an abrupt motion, she placed her thumb on the padd's reader plate and it chimed. The woman thrust it back into Vaughn's hand. "We have an agreement, then."

"Kallisti," said Spock, wasting no time. "How did the code connect with Gorkon's death?"

Miller nodded. "Was the House of Q'unat part of the conspiracy?"

Vaughn became aware of Valeris watching him. She ignored the others and stared at him. "What do *you* wish to ask me, Lieutenant?"

He said nothing, but a question still pressed at his lips. *Why did you betray your oath?*

When he didn't respond, Valeris looked away. "I have no knowledge of the House of Q'unat. The code word was part of a communications protocol set up with another group. A political activist cadre operating in the Beta Quadrant."

Spock's brows arched. "Klingon?"

She shook her head. "Are you aware of an organization called *SeDveq*?"

"It means 'the Thorn' in common Klingon," said Vaughn.

"That is one translation. It also refers to a form of barbed spearhead used in melee combat," she continued. "The group I refer to are a violent revolutionary sect from the Krios System."

"Krios Prime is a planet on the far side of the Empire," noted Spock. "It is euphemistically designated as a 'protected' world under Klingon aegis."

"In other words, they annexed it and are stripping it for all it is worth?" said Vaughn.

"They gained a foothold there over thirty years ago," Spock went on. "The Krios System is rich in ores such as biltritium and pergium, both valuable to an expansionist galactic power like the Klingons."

"Those elements are used in power systems," noted Miller.

"In short supply after Praxis exploded," Vaughn added. "All the more vital."

Miller folded his arms across his chest and studied the woman. "You need to tell us how to locate and access any files relating to Kallisti that Cartwright left behind."

"There are no files, not any more. Broken remnants at best," Valeris told him. "They were erased the moment the admiral was arrested. All that remains is here." She touched a slender finger to her forehead.

"Fine. Then you give up everything you know about this Thorn group, every detail you can recall."

She arched an eyebrow. "That may take several days."

Vaughn looked across at the senior officer. "We don't have that much time. The *Excelsior* is on a tight clock . . . If we're not at the border when the escort ships from the Klingon Defense Force arrive . . ."

"They will consider it a grave insult," Spock concluded.

Miller frowned. "General Igdar is already looking for any excuse to shut us out of the investigation . . . We can't give him the opportunity."

"Then it appears you have a problem," said Valeris. Vaughn couldn't be sure, but he thought he detected a tinge of amusement in her words.

The commander cut right through her reply. "No, not really." He turned to Spock. "Ambassador, your support in this situation has been vital. Starfleet Command and the Federation thank you for your assistance."

"May I ask how you will proceed now?" said the Vulcan.

Miller drew his communicator from where it was clipped to his belt and flipped it open. "The lieutenant is right: time is against us. We're already pushing it as it is, diverting to Jaros. We can't afford to remain here and conduct an in-depth debrief with a new asset." He glanced at Valeris. "As of this moment, you're now officially transferred to the custody of Starfleet Intelligence. You can brief us on the way to Da'Kel."

"That would seem to be the most expedient solution," Spock offered.

Valeris covered a flash of surprise. "I will not travel into Klingon space."

"Oh, I beg your pardon," Miller replied. "Did you think I was offering you a choice? You signed the paper. You belong to me now." He raised the communicator to his lips.

"Wait." Valeris held up a hand. "Very well. I will accompany you. But I have a condition."

"You are in no position—" Vaughn started to speak, but Miller waved him to silence.

"What condition?" said the commander.

"Doctor Tancreda . . . She has assembled a file on me."

"The doctor is Valeris's psychoanalyst," explained Spock. "Assigned by the Federation Council for purposes of rehabilitation."

"I want her case notes," Valeris insisted. "And I want all other copies deleted."

Vaughn eyed her. "Why?"

She looked back at him. "I wish to keep my own secrets."

Spock gave a nod. "I will see to it."

"Then we're done here." Miller returned the gesture and spoke into his communicator. "*Excelsior*, this is the landing party. Three to beam up. Lock on and energize."

The landing field beyond the penal complex was a small affair, a disc of thermoconcrete wide enough to accommodate the civilian shuttlecraft Spock had been given for his travels. The warp sled remained up in orbit, maintaining a steady position directly overhead, patiently awaiting his return.

There were no crew on board—with his extensive experience on auxiliary craft, Spock did not require them— and the shuttle's sensors detected his approach, waking the ship from its dormant state, the ramp across the rear hatch dropping open. Sulu had made the offer to Spock to accompany the *Excelsior* at least some of the way to the Klingon border, but he declined. While it might have been agreeable to meet with his old *Enterprise* crewmate once again, Spock knew that his presence would have only exacerbated tensions that already existed.

It was important that he keep his distance from Valeris for now—if not indefinitely. His absence would ensure that her mind was not clouded by her attitudes toward him . . . and in turn, he would not be distracted by his own regrets.

At least, that was his hope; he imagined that it would not be so easy to lock away the reactions that had come upon him on seeing Valeris again. Outwardly, Spock remained the stoic, metered example of the Vulcan ideal. Inwardly, the landscape of his thoughts was clouded.

She will never forgive me, he told himself, *nor should she.*

Perhaps one day things might reach an equilibrium between them. But not today.

His thoughts were drawn back to the moment by the sound of racing footsteps across the landing pad and Spock turned to see Doctor Tancreda approaching at a run. The wind was picking up and she wore a *shemagh* held across her face to deflect the blown sand. "Ambassador!" she called, her voice tight with anger.

Spock stood at the hatch and waited for her to reach him. "Doctor."

"What have you done?" demanded Tancreda. "My work . . . You had no right, no authority, to take my files!"

He cocked his head. "Calm yourself, Doctor. That was not done on my order. Your files were seized under the instructions of Starfleet Command. I will remind you that this facility operates under their auspices. It is not a civilian penal complex and therefore does not operate under the same strictures."

"Don't quote rules and regulations to me," she shot back, "and don't insult my intelligence by pretending you're not involved! This would never have happened if you were not here! You pulled strings to get access to Valeris, not once, but twice—and why? Was it to salve your own conscience?" Her eyes flashed with annoyance. "Now months of my work have been deleted from the database and my patient has disappeared!"

"Valeris's presence was required elsewhere."

"Really?" said Tancreda. "And with that vague justification, you spirit her away? Do you understand the progress I have been making with her?"

"Yes. I read the case notes. Your 'progress' appeared negligible, Doctor."

Tancreda scowled. "I was on the verge of a breakthrough! But now you've derailed any chance of psychological healing Valeris might have!"

He raised an eyebrow at her tone. "I disagree. Valeris was my student. I know her well . . ." Spock paused, considering the deeper meaning of his words. "As thoroughly as anyone could. I believe her incarceration in this facility is only hindering her."

"You're not qualified to make that ruling, sir," Tancreda replied. "I'm aware of all your accomplishments, but you're not a criminal psychologist."

"And you, Doctor, are not a Vulcan. Your insights, while well reasoned, will forever come from an alien standpoint." He paused. "As long as Valeris remains a prisoner here on Jaros II, she will never have what she requires to move on in her life."

"And that is?"

"An opportunity to redeem herself. Without it, she remains trapped in that moment."

The Betazoid woman folded her arms and eyed him harshly. "Redemption? That's a rather human conceit, don't you think?"

"Perhaps," he allowed. "Nevertheless, it is applicable in this matter."

"Do you know what *I* think?"

"I am certain you will tell me."

Tancreda met his gaze. "I think your line of reasoning is flawed, on a fundamental level, and that flaw stems from your personal guilt over the mistakes you made in your relationship with Valeris." She took a step closer. "You assume that, if offered the opportunity, Valeris would take a different path from the one she did seven years ago. But what guarantee do you have that she will not betray the ideals of the Federation all over again?"

A memory unfolded in Spock's mind, sudden and clear, as if it had happened only moments ago. His cabin aboard the *Enterprise,* as the ship approached the Neutral Zone to rendezvous with *Kronos One*. Valeris there, speaking in veiled terms of "turning points," with a subtext concealed beneath her words that he failed to properly interpret. His reply to her in that moment returned to him, and he echoed it to Tancreda. "We must have faith."

The doctor's expression grew cold. "That will never be enough," she told him.

Spock watched her vanish back into the shadows surrounding the landing pad.

Tancreda didn't glance up as she heard the shuttle hum past overhead on its impulse thrusters. Instead, she moved with quick purpose to the administration block where her office was located. At this time of night, only one or two rooms were illuminated as some of her colleagues worked long shifts. Unnoticed, she slipped in and secured the door.

Taking a seat at her desk, she drew a small case from beneath her tunic. She kept it concealed in her personal quarters, and after what had taken place today, the doctor's caution had proven prudent. A scan of the case with a tricorder would reveal a few personal votive items of Betazoid religious significance, but the actual contents were much different.

There was a dense isolinear memory drive that contained additional copies of all her case files—Valeris's included—as well as material covertly duplicated from the databases of several of her colleagues; a phaser small enough to conceal in the palm of her hand; and a module that she now removed and slotted into the front of the monitor unit on her desk.

The module made quick work of tapping into the facility's subspace communications gear, erasing any trace of its passage as it went. After a few seconds it asked Tancreda for a code, which she provided, and then opened a link across the interstellar void. With the device in place, there would be no record of the transmission or what it contained.

The screen showed a bald human male seated at a plain desk. He wore a dark tunic that had no insignia, although the cut of it recalled that of a uniform. "Hello, Malla," he began. "I thought we might be hearing from you."

"Hello, Control," she said, frowning. She wasted no time on preamble. "You knew about this? I should have been warned."

He shook his head. *"No. It was better for your reactions to be authentic. What did Miller learn from the subject?"*

"I have no idea," Tancreda told him. "Miller decided to take Valeris with him aboard the *Excelsior*. I believe Ambassador Spock used his influence to smooth the path."

The man on the screen leaned back in his chair. *"Ah. We knew that was a possibility, but . . ."* He considered it for a moment. *"We'll have to adjust. I'll contact our operative on Sulu's ship. They'll pick up the observation from there."*

"Valeris wanted my case files, and Miller gave them up. The data has been purged, but I still have duplicates."

"Good work, Malla. As thorough as ever."

She looked away. "So. What next?"

He leaned in, filling the screen. *"Execute your mission shutdown protocols. Leave the surveillance devices and data-taps in place. Tomorrow morning, you'll have transfer orders, fresh from Starfleet Medical. We'll get you back here, conduct a full debrief in person, and reassign you."*

Tancreda blew out a breath. "That's it? I'm done here?"

He nodded, as if the question was a surprise. *"Of course."*

"What's going to happen to Valeris?"

"For the moment, that's not your concern." The man on the screen reached for the disconnect key. *"But we'll be watching her."*

U.S.S. Excelsior NCC-2000
En Route to the Klingon Neutral Zone
United Federation of Planets

The starship's observation lounge was an elegant affair, a long room that followed the curve of the back of the bridge "island" atop the saucer-shaped primary hull. Through a line of large, circular portals that stretched from the deck to the overhead, Miller could look out down the length of *Excelsior*'s command section and out to the glowing spars of the warp engines. Stars, turned to streaks of light by incredible velocities, fell past him as the ship raced toward the Klingon border. Staring at them, he became aware of the sense of falling, as if the vessel and everything aboard it were plunging down a tunnel toward an unknown fate.

He dismissed the thought with a curl of his lip and turned away just as the door across the room opened to admit Lieutenant Vaughn.

The young officer had done a good job of rising to the challenge Miller had set before him, but it was clear he was also feeling the pressure of it. The commander noted the faint edge of nervous energy about the man; Miller had thrown him in at the deep end, and so far Vaughn had kept his head above water.

He'd meant what he said back at the starbase: someone sharp enough to find the Kallisti link would certainly be an asset to him. If he was honest, at the start he had given Vaughn's suggestion a fifty-fifty chance of panning out, but even those odds were better than what he'd had before. The commander had good instincts, and he'd learned the hard way that ignoring them was usually a bad idea: those instincts had told him that the lieutenant was onto something.

But Miller was under no illusions to the fact that he had kicked over a hornet's nest with Commander Egan and the OIE with his impromptu recruitment of one of their officers. Egan actually had the temerity to demand that Vaughn be placed on a shuttle back to Earth and Miller be put on report for his actions. Commodore Hallstrom had apparently taken those suggestions "under advisement."

Miller argued the point; he'd originally intended to draw someone from Sulu's crew to assist him, but even the best of them didn't fit the bill as well as Vaughn did. He recalled something his mother had once told him about moments of providence: only a fool would stand by and let one pass when the opportunity arose; what happened afterward you could fix later. Darius Miller had always believed that it was easier to seek forgiveness than to ask permission.

Vaughn gestured with a padd. "Updated report from SI's

data trawl," he explained. "They swept the records for any information on Kriosian conflicts and this 'Thorn' group."

"Any hits?"

"Yes and no," said the lieutenant. "We've got some historical background on Krios but not a lot of current material."

Miller nodded. "Start with that." He took a seat at the obs room table and Vaughn followed suit.

"The Krios System is out on the far border of the Klingon Empire, right in the Deep Beta. Humanoid population, got some outward physiological similarities to species like the Trill . . ." Vaughn paused to draw an imaginary line of pigment spots down his face. Miller nodded and he went on. "They've had an ongoing conflict with a nearby system, Valt Minor, for most of their post-colonization history. The Kriosians were originally from the Valt System . . . There was a schism between two ruling bloodlines, and their colony was the offshoot of the group that left Valt behind. They've been trying to kill each other ever since."

Miller took the lieutenant's padd from him and scanned the files. According to Starfleet's xenographic research division, Valt had been the nexus of a small stellar kingdom in the twenty-first century, ruled by a line of monarchs from noble houses—a similar structure to the early Klingon hierarchy or Earth's medieval period. However, at some point, the two brothers who had risen to rule Valt Minor together had fallen out over that most traditional of home wreckers, the love of a woman. The split ended in one brother spiriting the woman away, and thus began the war that tore the kingdom in two. The errant brother was named Krios, and he and his followers made planetfall on a Valtian colony world and called it their own. The battle lines drawn there had lasted for centuries.

"How do the Klingons figure into this?" he asked. "I can't imagine they took kindly to skirmishes on their doorstep, unless they were the ones starting them."

Vaughn shook his head. "No sir. From what we can gather, the Empire annexed Krios sometime in the late twenty-third century, apparently to 'enforce stability in the region.' "

Miller snorted. "But we know what they really wanted."

"More resources. Krios has a lot of mineral wealth. The Klingons suspended the rule of the Kriosian Sovereign Dynasty—for reasons of stability, of course—installed their own governor, and started systematically strip-mining the Krios system for ore."

"Biltritium and pergium," said Miller, recalling Spock's earlier statement. "So let me guess. These Kriosian activists, they're resistance fighters?"

"*SeDveq.*" Vaughn nodded. "They were the literal thorn in the side of the Klingon Empire."

"*Were?*" Miller seized on the word.

"After the destruction of Praxis, all signs of any Thorn activities have ceased. At least until now, with these Kallisti messages."

"How long has Starfleet Intelligence been monitoring the Krios situation?"

"Actively since the 2260s, when the Klingons first started sniffing around there," said Vaughn.

The commander's expression darkened. "So, what are we saying? At some point, Cartwright sets up a back-channel line of communication with the Thorn . . . Why?"

"He could have been cultivating an intelligence source hostile to the Klingons . . ." Vaughn sounded it out. "Maybe even going so far as to encourage and support them in their resistance."

Miller nodded slowly. "All feasible. But those are both covert operations plays, and that wasn't Cartwright's turf. He was in Fleet ops back then." He sighed. "This is all supposition. Pity we can't ask the man himself." The admiral had died in prison, apparently of a respiratory infection, but in his darker moments Miller couldn't help but wonder if Cartwright might not have been helped along the way. There were certainly enough people who had axes to grind with him.

"Cartwright was building his own network of influence," said Vaughn. "The first foundations of his conspiracy?"

The commander shrugged. "Again, feasible." He leaned forward. "What about the rest of the data?"

"That's all there is." Vaughn frowned. "This is a song we've heard before, sir. All intelligence reports we have— or, rather, *had*—were purged from the system by the same hunter-killer virus program that destroyed the data connected to the Gorkon conspiracy. We know Lance Cartwright wasn't alone in what he did. After his arrest, a kill-switch was triggered in an attempt to obliterate anything that could incriminate him."

"It could have been one of his coconspirators that pushed the button," Miller agreed. "God knows, Drake had the means and the opportunity after the fact." Admiral Androvar Drake, a man who had briefly ascended to a role as chief of staff at Starfleet following the Gorkon assassination, had later been revealed to be a silent partner in Cartwright's cabal of pro-conflict agitators. Drake's duplicity was exposed, but at the cost of his own life and the loss of the *Enterprise*-A over the planet Chal.

Miller slowly let out a breath. "So, if we take what we have, and what Valeris told us, what kind of picture can we see?"

Vaughn was quiet for a moment. "Sir, that's assuming that Valeris told us the truth about the Kallisti code word and the link with the Kriosians."

"Do we have a reason to believe she's lying to us?"

The lieutenant matched his gaze. "Do we have a reason to believe she's *not*?"

"Beyond personal dislike?" Miller asked.

"I was thinking more based on her past record."

"I see your point," the commander allowed. "But, for the moment, indulge me."

The other man frowned again. "What we have is the detonation of an illegal weapon, which may or may not have been facilitated by a faction of hard-line isolationists or a radical group of freedom fighters, or maybe both. A connection to a seven-year-old plot to murder the Klingon Empire's first peacemaker in centuries and cause interstellar war. A bunch of deleted files and missing data. Oh, and a prisoner convicted of treason and murder who may well be lying right through her pointed ears—not to mention a command authority who doesn't buy any of that, and may have me cashiered for sticking my neck out . . ."

Despite the lieutenant's dour reply, Miller smiled slightly. "I bet I can guess exactly what you're thinking right now."

"Sir?"

"*Next time, Elias, write a goddamn memo.* Am I close?"

He nodded. "Very perceptive, Commander."

Miller leaned in, his gaze turning steely. "We've got less than thirty hours before we reach Da'Kel. We need something coherent by the time we get there."

The lieutenant nodded again and went back to his padd. "Aye aye, sir."

Valeris opened her eyes. Her attempt to return to a meditative state had failed; it wasn't just the circumstances that she found herself in that arrested any chance of it. No, it was something about being on board a starship, traveling at warp. The faint sensation of motion, coming up through the deck of her cabin and the couch where she had placed herself.

They hadn't given her a room with an external viewport, but still she glanced at the wall and imagined what she might have seen if they had: the warped luminosity of passing stars, the color and motion of faster-than-light travel. On some level, Valeris had never expected to set foot aboard a starship ever again, and now that she was here on *Excelsior,* it was a mild surprise to the Vulcan to realize that she found the sensation curiously agreeable.

She recalled her first experience on the bridge of a starship, as a child in tow with her parents when they visited the command deck of a Vulcan diplomatic courier. It had fascinated her, especially the actions of the helmsman as he took the vessel into warp velocities. Valeris had no doubt that that early, formative moment of her life had led her to train for the same role when she joined Starfleet. There was something compelling about riding with one's hand on the controls of an interstellar vessel. Perhaps it was an echo of that she was experiencing, or perhaps some primitive element of her mind mistakenly associated this voyage from the stockade with freedom.

That was a fallacy. Valeris had left her prison behind, but she was not free, not by any rational measure.

She looked around the cabin once more. It was the same kind of single-occupant quarters given to all junior officers on most starships of cruiser-class tonnage or larger, basic but not without functionality. Valeris had expected to be housed in *Excelsior*'s brig, as befitting her status as a convicted felon, but Miller had ordered her escorted here instead. Still, while the cabin gave the impression of comfort, it was no less a cell than those down in the security section. Outside her door, a pair of noncommissioned crewmen wearing security crimson stood at guard, each armed with a phaser. Valeris had not attempted to open it or operate the intercom, desk computer, or food slot: she imagined all those mechanisms were being monitored for signs of tampering or misuse.

The cabin reminded Valeris of her first billet aboard the *U.S.S. Enterprise,* and once more she was surprised to discover that the thought brought with it the distant echo of an emotion. Was that . . . *regret?* She tried to examine the sensation, but it retreated from her, fading away to nothing.

Valeris considered that for a moment. From a human standpoint, regret would be an understandable reaction, triggered by the visual and sensory stimulus of something so close to her time on *Enterprise.* Her service on that illustrious vessel, first as a cadet and later when she returned as a fully-fledged officer of the line, had without doubt been among the greatest achievements of her life. She had hoped for so much from her posting to Kirk's command—but at the end, it had all turned to ashes.

She cut off the train of thought: it accomplished nothing

to dwell on those past matters. Instead, Valeris returned to her casual but careful scrutiny of the cabin. She understood what would be expected of her, and she understood the offer that Miller had made. And yet, Valeris could not fully trust the face reality presented to her . . .

Her experiences dealing with humans had taught her that they could be by degrees mercurial and challenging. The inconstant nature of emotional beings was what raised Vulcans above their concerns, and as such Valeris knew she would need to remain on her guard.

On the way to the cabin, she had already noted several avenues of approach for potential escape attempts. She estimated a sixty-two-point-two percent chance that she could disable her guards and flee into *Excelsior*'s Jefferies tubes, but the odds against her grew longer beyond that point. For the moment, the situation was too fluid for an accurate prediction. She would watch for an opportunity, even if one would be unlikely to arise.

The fact was, for all her understandable reticence to venture into Klingon territory, Valeris was intrigued by the morsels of data Spock and the intelligence officers had put before her. The logical course of action, she told herself, would be to seek a path to escape as soon as possible. Although she believed that Commander Miller's intention to honor the agreement between them was honest, Valeris had learned firsthand that the actions of the admirals at Starfleet Command were subject to personal whim and political expedience in equal measure.

But the old code had sparked her interest. *Kallisti.* She mouthed the word to herself. Many years had passed since she had spoken it aloud. She could not deny that she wanted to know how it had come to be enmeshed in this new attack on the Klingon Empire.

For the moment, she would remain and do as she had been ordered to. Miller appeared to be refreshingly direct for a human, and that would make dealing with him palatable. But the other one . . . Lieutenant Vaughn struggled to keep his emotions in check beneath a façade of professionalism, but it was clear that the young officer had nothing but antipathy for Valeris. He clearly hated her, doubtless projecting a loathing for all things that did not follow his personal code of conduct onto her persona.

Valeris had seen the same dislike writ large across the faces of other crew members aboard the *Excelsior*, from the officer in the transporter room to the guards who stood sentinel outside her cabin. What did they see when they looked at her? A traitor? A collaborator? A dupe?

She crossed to the table. The handful of personal items from her cell on Jaros II had been beamed up to the ship and deposited here, along with a change of clothes in a commonplace civilian design. Valeris's slender fingers found a memory module among the items and she lingered over it, considering its contents. Finally, she gathered it up and settled into a chair, turning to the computer on the desk.

The memory module dropped into a slot on the side and the screen came to life. A menu scrolled down the length of the display, vid recordings of individual interview sessions arranged by date and time, pages of case notes appended to each one. Valeris chose a file at random, the text unfolding to fill the screen. She immediately recognized Doctor Tancreda's mannerisms from the writing style. The file Valeris had selected was part of a debrief, an "exploration," as the Betazoid had liked to term it, a recollection of key events from the Vulcan woman's past that informed the person she had grown to become. Her eyes narrowed as she read the conclusions Tancreda had made.

Can a Vulcan truly know what hate *is?* asked the psychologist.

5

U.S.S. *Enterprise* NCC-1701-A
The Neutral Zone
Federation-Klingon Border

Valeris entered the botanical gardens to find it empty, as she had intended. The open atrium, spanning the width of the *Enterprise*'s secondary hull from port to starboard, was lush with greenery from a handful of Federation member worlds, although nothing Vulcan grew here: the nutrisoil substrate could not support the hardy desert plants of her home planet. Instead there were dwarf trees, bushes, and flowering vegetation from worlds like Earth, Halkan, and Efros.

She hesitated at the entrance, listening intently to be certain that she was alone. The only sound was the faint murmur of the shallow waterfall at the far end of the compartment, feeding the artificial stream that wound across the space. Satisfied, Valeris strode quickly along the pathway until she reached the rockery where Alyssum and Jaisone flowers provided a spray of color among the green and grey. The lieutenant had memorized the exact positioning of the rocks before the *Enterprise* had left spacedock, knowing full well that she would need to return to them now.

With care, Valeris bent down and turned a pale marble-white stone on its side. There was an indentation the size of a humanoid thumb on the base, and she stroked it with her index finger; then the stone opened like a strange, fossilized blossom, revealing a concealed compartment within.

Inside was a handheld communicator, adapted far beyond

Starfleet standard. The stone closed itself as she moved away and Valeris examined the device. It had a slot for a memory chip, which she dutifully inserted. The Vulcan crossed to a bench beneath the large viewports and sat. In her hand the device came to life, trains of indicators flickering back and forth.

The unit was covertly probing *Enterprise*'s computer network, infiltrating the system and worming its way into the starship's communications grid. Valeris did not need to glance up at the chronometer above the entrance to the gardens to know the time: just before nineteen hundred hours, just seconds from the moment when *Enterprise*'s automated comms array would make contact with the nearest subspace beacon. It was a regular occurrence, scheduled by Starfleet for every ship: *Enterprise* and all the other vessels on deployment would send a stream of crosstalk back and forth across the Federation communications net, transmitting minor updates and ship's logs, getting time-base amendments, mapping corrections for galactic drift and a hundred other minor pieces of data.

The regular transmission also provided the perfect cover to hide a clandestine signal. Done correctly, Valeris could open a channel through the device in her hand, and no one up on the bridge would be any the wiser.

It was almost time; still, she could not stop herself glancing away for a brief moment out through the tall viewports and into the black of space beyond. On the other side of the transparent aluminum windows, the sight was dominated by the elongated, predatory shape of a Klingon starship, moving in steady lockstep with the Starfleet vessel. Valeris's analytical mind processed what she saw; a D-7M *K'tinga*-class battle cruiser, the hull an uncommon stone-grey instead of the usual steel or copper green of the Imperial Defense Force. She noted irregular bulges in the hull, telltale signs that showed this craft sported modifications beyond those of a line warship. *Kronos One* was purported to be a vessel of peace and diplomacy, and yet, Valeris could quite clearly see the maws of photon torpedo bays and the blunt emitter heads of disruptors. Even as it drifted abeam, the ship exuded an air of stately menace. For a moment she wondered if there was a Klingon crew member doing as she was now, staring across the vacuum and weighing up the dimensions of their enemy. She had no doubt there was: the Klingons were almost incapable of anything but a martial, aggressive outlook.

The communicator beeped once and she held it close to her face. "Kallisti," she said, and a faint crackle sounded from the speaker. It recognized her vocal signature, and the channel went active.

"Status?" said a voice. It was laced with distortion and static, but Admiral Cartwright's dour tone was unmistakable.

"Nominal," she replied. "Contact has been made."

"Understood. When will they be coming aboard?"

"Thirty minutes. A formal dinner has been prepared."

Valeris heard something that might have been a chuckle. *"Of course it has. I'm sure that'll be an evening to remember . . ."* The admiral paused. *"Listen carefully. You will proceed to access the ship's munitions database and edit certain files. Details will be loaded onto the data chip. Do it while Kirk and his officers are at the dinner."*

She nodded. "I understand." But she did not—not fully; Cartwright had seen fit only to enlighten her to certain elements of what he called "the operation." Valeris had already placed surveillance taps in certain sections of the ship's computer architecture, notably to monitor key sections of the *Enterprise* such as the bridge, main engineering, even the captain's cabin; but so far she had not been ordered to utilize any of the data she had gathered. This new directive would not be the first time she had made adjustments to conceal activities taking place aboard the ship. Earlier in the voyage, Cartwright had ordered her to ensure that certain items of landing party equipment—notably, a pair of environment suits and two phaser pistols—were logged as in storage, when in fact they had been removed. Not for the first time, she wondered how many operatives working under Cartwright's direct command were stationed aboard the ship. She knew of Burke and

Samno, but were there others? Valeris discarded the thought. It was of no consequence.

"Is that all?" she asked. The Vulcan was mindful of the passing seconds; soon the beacon signal would cease and the communications hidden within it would end as well, or risk detection.

"No," said Cartwright. "*You understand the seriousness of this operation. There are many variables, and it may become necessary . . . to take more proactive measures if the situation demands it. Extreme sanctions may be required. Do I make myself clear?*"

"Yes." There was no question of it: he was asking her to kill. Valeris's hand tensed around the communicator as a moment of doubt echoed in her mind. Of course she was proficient with a weapon, of course she was more than capable of the act. But Valeris had never been faced with the need to take a life in anything other than a combat situation.

"*You'll know what to do,*" he said. "*Don't forget, a single error . . . a single failure of will . . . and all that we've done will come apart. We will all hang together.*"

"I understand," she repeated.

"*I know you do. That's why I gave you this responsibility. One last thing: you may detect an intermittent surge of neutron radiation during the next few hours. Ignore it—*"

Valeris never let him finish. She snapped the communicator shut and buried it beneath her tunic as the footsteps she had heard from the corridor grew louder. Composing herself, she glanced up in time to see a lone figure rounding the corner from the botany lab.

"Captain." She rose to her feet automatically.

Kirk slowed slightly as he approached, his keen gaze searching her face. "Lieutenant. Aren't you supposed to be on the bridge?"

"My duty shift does not commence for another nine-point-two minutes, sir."

"Ah." He nodded and gestured to her. "At ease, Valeris."

"Can I assist you in any way, Captain?"

"No." Kirk gave a slow shake of the head. "I'm surprised to find you down here. Usually at this time of day the gardens are deserted. Sometimes I like to take a walk here . . . clear my head a little."

"It is a tranquil space," she offered, careful to stand so that he would not notice the bulge beneath her jacket. If she were found with the covert communicator on her, it would be difficult to explain away.

However, the captain's attention was clearly on other matters. His gaze drifted to the window and the other ship. "I could use a little tranquillity," he told her. "This is going to be a long day—for all of us."

The right thing to do—the intelligent thing to do—would be for Valeris to excuse herself and allow Kirk the opportunity he wanted to gather his thoughts. And yet, Valeris felt a strong compulsion to stay, to engage him. So far she had found precious little opportunity to speak with the captain directly, and her first overtures to him in his cabin earlier in the day had not gone as she wished.

There were many things Valeris wanted to ask him, and against her better judgment they pressed at her to be said aloud. "Did you ever think that we . . . that *you* would be here, sir?" she said. "After everything that has happened with them?" Valeris gave a slight nod toward the distant *Kronos One*.

Kirk was studying the lines of the Klingon ship just as she had done earlier. Perhaps he was looking for points of weakness or admiring the brutalist design ethic of the alien craft. "Honestly?" He shook his head. "Not in a million years. I always thought that one day it might come to war . . . Or, at best, that Starfleet could stand by and hold the line while the Klingons burned themselves out . . ." Kirk gave a humorless smile. "But peace? A real, honest peace? No."

She had to be careful now. To say too much at this moment could tip the balance. "Do you think we can trust them?" Valeris already knew the answer, but she wanted to hear him say it.

"Trust . . ." he echoed. "I used to have plenty of that. These days I have to dig a lot deeper to find it." At last Kirk turned away from the viewport. "I've shed plenty of their blood over the years. I don't take pride in it. I did what was needed."

"Aye, sir."

"We can't measure them by our standards, Lieutenant. I've known some Klingons who showed courage and honor. They have their code, just as we have ours. But . . ." He halted, frowning. "But they can show you respect in one breath, and then bury a knife in your back the next. You ask me if we can trust them? I don't know that we can. I want to believe it's possible, but I've spent years of my career facing Klingon aggression, and I don't know if they can transcend their nature." He gave the rueful smile again. "I don't know if I can transcend mine."

Valeris took a moment to frame her reply. "I . . . appreciate your candor, sir."

He seemed to shake off the moment of introspection, and suddenly a more vital, more focused aspect was upon him. "It was hardly that, Lieutenant. And ultimately, whatever reservations you and I may have, we still have our orders. And we have a duty to offer the olive branch, even if it's to the devil himself. That's détente."

"A word of French origin. Traditionally, it means to loosen the catch upon a crossbow, but since the early twentieth century it has come to describe a lessening in political tensions."

Kirk nodded. "Gorkon wants us all to take our hands off our guns. That can't be a bad thing, can it?"

"Are you asking my opinion, sir?"

"Always," he replied, an edge of challenge in his tone.

"An easement in Klingon-Federation hostility would be beneficial . . . *if* Chancellor Gorkon does in fact intend to seek it. If this offer of peace is not merely an attempt to take advantage of the Federation and prepare for later acts of belligerence."

Kirk studied her for a moment, and Valeris fell silent. Had

she overstepped her bounds? For a human, the captain of the *Enterprise* was most difficult to read.

Then at length he turned to walk away. "I guess we're going to find out. Hopefully, before the end of the dessert course." Kirk gave her a last nod. "As you were, Lieutenant."

When he was gone, and she was certain she was alone, Valeris removed the isolinear data chip from the port on the side of the communicator and then returned the device to the hiding place inside the artificial stone.

The chronograph read nineteen-fifteen; secreting the chip in her tunic, Valeris made her way toward the turbolift to report early for her bridge duty shift.

As the doors closed, Kirk's words echoed in her thoughts. *I did what was needed.*

I will do the same, she told herself.

6

The briefing room was a blank-walled compartment on the lower decks of the *Excelsior*, little more than a space with a viewscreen and a rectilinear table surrounded by a few chairs. Sulu sat at the far end, in what was traditionally the captain's seat, from which he would normally brief his staff. Today the discussion was going to be led by another. Miller was seated to his right, leaving Vaughn to serve as a functionary and operate the computer mounted on the table.

The lieutenant looked up as the door opened and Valeris entered, a security guard at her back. He glimpsed another, a stocky Caitian, standing at stiff attention out in the corridor, just before the doors closed.

"Reporting as ordered, sir," said the first guard, a human woman with a close-cut cowl of red hair.

"Thank you, Crewman," said Sulu.

Vaughn saw her nod and step back to block the door, one hand resting close to a holstered phaser. Clearly, Sulu's people were on the alert, and the lieutenant took grim comfort in the fact that they had as little trust for the Vulcan as he did.

"Take a seat," Miller told Valeris.

She stood for just long enough to make it an issue and then sat down in the chair at the farthest end of the table. Her hands knit together in front of her and she displayed an air of cool disinterest.

Miller threw Vaughn a sideways nod, and he tapped the activation key on the console. From this point on, every word uttered in the room would be recorded, sifted for meaning, and measured for levels of stress and possible deceit.

Valeris inclined her head toward Sulu by way of a greeting. "Captain," she said. "Thank you for my accommodations. They are preferable to a brig cell."

"Don't mistake it for any kind of generosity on my part," he replied. Sulu's voice was low and wintry. "If it were up to me, you would never have set foot on my ship. But needs must."

"Indeed."

Miller cleared his throat. "Commencing," he announced, for the benefit of the recording scanners. "Interview with asset Valeris, currently in custody of Starfleet Intelligence Command field operations. Present at this time: Commander Darius Miller, Captain Hikaru Sulu, Lieutenant J.G. Elias Vaughn, Crewman Lisle Tiber. This interview is to be considered security level three data."

"I was not aware Captain Sulu would be involved in this discussion," Valeris said, ignoring the implied speak-when-you're-spoken-to protocol. "Given his connection with my . . . conviction, does he not represent a possible bias?"

Sulu's eyes narrowed. "That's a rather obvious ploy, don't you think? Attempting to disrupt the situation before the discussion even begins? Imposing your own rules?" Valeris opened her mouth to reply but he didn't allow it. "This is *my* ship. Nothing goes on aboard her that I don't know about. And I have a perfectly good first officer to see *Excelsior* doesn't get lost on the way to the Klingon Empire while I'm down here. So if my presence in the room makes you somehow uncomfortable, my advice to you is . . . deal with it."

Miller nodded. "Yeah, what he said." The commander picked up a padd before him and checked something. "So. You are going to explain to us the origin and meaning of the code 'Kallisti,' the alleged connection with the Gorkon assassination and this Kriosian activist group."

"The connection is not alleged," she insisted, "it is actual."

"So you said," Miller noted. "But the thing is, there's about a hundred reasons why your so-called information doesn't hold any water. We're going to need a lot more specifics, Valeris. Or else you'll find yourself back on Jaros II so fast, you'll wonder if this was all a dream."

"I doubt that. I am fully capable of establishing the difference between reality and fantasy."

Vaughn's jaw set and his lips thinned. *Hasn't stopped you spinning us a line, though,* he thought to himself. Before the interview the lieutenant had taken the opportunity to review some of the court recordings from the tribunal that convicted Valeris. In all of them, the Vulcan had been withdrawn, sometimes even sullen, in her unwillingness to provide any information beyond the most basic facts. Even when offered the opportunity to reduce her sentence, she had refused to give the full details of what she knew of Admiral Cartwright's schemes, either out of fear of incriminating herself further or through some misplaced loyalty. With his death, perhaps she had reconsidered . . . but even now, she wasn't exactly singing like the proverbial canary.

"Kallisti," Miller repeated. "Gorkon. Krios." He gestured in the air. "Connect the dots for me."

Vaughn saw something so fleeting in the woman's eyes that he couldn't be sure he hadn't imagined it: a shift, a change somewhere deep down. But then it was gone and her aspect was as it had been. Her elfin, almost coy manner was at odds with the words that came from her mouth.

"From what I was made aware of, it appears that a representative of the Thorn contacted Admiral Cartwright directly. He wanted to meet with the admiral to discuss matters of mutual benefit. His name was Seryl."

"A Kriosian freedom fighter looking for a sit-down with an admiral of the fleet?" said Miller. "Why did he go to Cartwright? Why not someone at Starfleet Intelligence?"

"Because of who Cartwright was. You will recall that he was quite open about his feelings toward the Klingon Empire."

Sulu gave a nod. "That's true. While he never overtly contradicted Federation policy, he certainly came close to it. Cartwright wasn't the most politic of commanders. His views were a matter of public record."

"A meeting was facilitated," Valeris went on.

A question crossed Vaughn's mind. "Were you present?"

She shook her head. "Not at the beginning. Later I . . . acted as a proxy."

"Continue," Miller prompted.

"Starfleet was aware of the existence of the Thorn and their opposition to the Klingons, so the admiral agreed to open a line of communication. A covert back channel. This was the first iteration of the Kallisti protocol."

"This man, the Kriosian," said Sulu, "he wanted support for his group against the Klingon occupation force?"

Valeris shook her head. "No. Seryl revealed that he was not acting on the direct behalf of the Thorn. He was, in fact, serving as a go-between."

"For who?" asked Vaughn.

"General Chang."

Miller actually snorted with derision. "Chancellor Gorkon's chief of staff? One of the highest-ranking Klingon officers in the Defense Force hierarchy? And here we have what has to be one of his sworn adversaries working *for* him?" He shook his head. "Come on, Valeris. You can do better than that."

She turned to look at Vaughn. "I know that console contains a psychotricorder module, and I know you already have baseline data on my physiological state. So please tell me, Lieutenant, according to your sensors, has anything I have said so far been a lie?"

Vaughn looked down at the monitor reading: heartbeat, perspiration, pupil dilation—all of it configured to look for even the smallest, most Vulcan glimmer of duplicity or misdirection. "The machine says no," he replied. "But I'll reserve my own opinion."

"As you wish." She inclined her head and turned back to

Sulu and Miller. "What is the human phrase, Commander? 'Keep your friends close, but your enemies closer'? You are of course aware that Chang considered himself a student of Terran culture . . ."

" 'Some rise by sin, and some by virtue fall,' " muttered Sulu, almost to himself.

"Measure for Measure," Valeris noted. "Act two, scene one."

"Let's keep the Shakespeare appreciation to a minimum," Miller interrupted, with a cutting gesture. "Stay on topic. So somehow Chang had a group of radical freedom fighters in his pocket."

Valeris nodded once more. "It was via the auspices of the Kriosians that a line of secret communication was opened between Admiral Cartwright and General Chang. Through it, the framework for the conspiracy to terminate Chancellor Gorkon was created."

"And you were part of that process," Sulu added. "You were Cartwright's agent."

"Among others."

Vaughn held up a hand. "Wait a second. This doesn't marry up. If the Thorn and Chang were working together . . . that would mean that they were talking months before the Praxis incident. *Before* Gorkon publicly sued for peace."

"That is correct. The destruction of Praxis only served to accelerate a process that was already under way. Even before that incident, Gorkon had made it clear to his inner circle that he planned to reach out to the United Federation of Planets with peaceful intent."

Miller paused, musing. "There had been rumors, before Praxis exploded," he noted. "We knew the Klingons were feeling the pressure of decades of unrestricted military spending and social problems. Gorkon was the first moderate chancellor in centuries, certainly the first to suggest ending the cold war between the Empire and the Federation."

"Chang did not wish to see that," said Valeris. "He felt it was a betrayal of his people. He wanted to maintain the status quo, and he was aware that Admiral Cartwright felt similarly. The fallout from Praxis presented an immediate opportunity to remove Gorkon, and the conspirators moved swiftly to take advantage of it."

"An opportunity?" Sulu's words were almost a growl. "I saw that disaster unfold right before my eyes. Do you know how many lives were lost on that day? And how many more have perished since? This ship and my crew were very nearly counted among them."

"I do not have an exact figure," she replied, with apparent unconcern.

Vaughn listened for a trace of anything approaching compassion in her voice, and found nothing. Like her, Elias had grown up in an era where the Klingon Empire was seen as the enemy of right and freedom. Still, he had thought the obliteration of Praxis and its aftermath was enough to stir a moment of regret in anyone. *Clearly not,* he corrected himself.

"I am simply stating the facts, as you requested," Valeris told them. "The code word 'Kallisti' was used as a signifier and pass-phrase for the communications conduit created by the Gorkon conspiracy. That network was abandoned after Admiral Cartwright's arrest and Chang's death."

"Except that it wasn't," Miller retorted. He got up and walked across the room, pacing out his thoughts. "So now we've got more questions than we have answers. More discrepancies."

Sulu shook his head. "This just doesn't add up. The Kriosians have no love for the Klingons, and that's putting it lightly. The Empire annexed their planets, strip-mined them. Why would this man Seryl be willing to become a messenger boy for his bitter enemy?"

"Who knows what Chang had over him?" said Miller. "He may have had no choice."

"War makes strange bedfellows," said the lieutenant, almost to himself.

"I agree," said Valeris, watching him intently.

"Then there's the reason we are all here," continued the

captain. "The attack on the Da'Kel platform . . ." He glanced at Vaughn.

"According to the Klingons, the blame for that is being laid at the door of the House of Q'unat. Radical anti-Federation hard-liners." The lieutenant grimaced. "But honestly, sir, I don't buy that for a second."

Miller turned back to face Valeris. "Clearly there is a lot more going on than the Klingon High Command knows . . . or want *us* to know. The question is: Who is the liar here?"

Valeris raised an eyebrow. "It will become tiresome if you continue to accuse me of repeated falsehoods."

Miller was silent for a moment, turning over something in his thoughts. Finally he addressed Sulu. "Captain, you should know that I've made a number of encrypted subspace communications while I've been on board the *Excelsior*."

"Go on," said Sulu.

Vaughn said nothing, but he had been aware that Miller had secluded himself in his cabin for several hours.

"We're going to be joined by an operative from . . . from another agency, once we reach the border."

Sulu eyed him. "That's all you're giving me?"

"For the moment."

The captain frowned. "All right." But he didn't sound like he meant it.

Miller pointed at Vaughn. "What about the device used at Da'Kel? Does that connect with any of this new information?"

The lieutenant tabbed through the digital files on the padd, coming to the file that showed the long-range sensor readings captured by Starfleet's Firewatch monitor stations along the Neutral Zone. "It's undoubtedly an isolytic weapon. The subspace signature of the detonation is unmistakable."

"Ambassador Kasiel confirmed as much," said Miller. He looked at Valeris. "This Thorn cadre . . . Would a device like that be within their capabilities? Would they be willing to deploy it?"

"With regard to your first question, I do not believe so," she told him. "The civilization on Krios Prime possesses warp drive and related technologies, but I believe the capacity to fabricate the components of an isolytic weapon is beyond them, and certainly beyond a group like the Thorn. But as to your second question, I have no doubt they would use such a weapon without hesitation, if they possessed it. Culturally, the Kriosians are a passionate and highly emotional people, often given to extremes of reaction. They are not adverse to the use of violence as means to an end."

"Perhaps the Thorn and the Q'unat clan are in this together?" Sulu offered.

Vaughn shook his head, putting down the padd. "The House of Q'unat would never ally themselves with aliens. And from what we can determine, they may not even exist anymore. Klingon interclan conflicts don't tend to leave a lot of survivors."

Miller's frown deepened. "Maybe. But Starfleet Intelligence thought the Thorn were dead and gone, too, remember? We still need to figure out who the players are here."

Valeris reached out and took the padd without waiting for permission. She scanned the data on the Da'Kel blast with a quick, steady focus. "These sensor readings of the subspace discharge . . . they are correct?"

"Of course," Vaughn snapped, resenting the implication.

"You have something to add?" said Miller.

She gestured to the main screen on the far wall. "If I may?" Sulu gave her a wary nod, and Valeris manipulated a control on the padd, migrating the display to the bigger screen. She did it effortlessly, deft enough to show that she hadn't forgotten anything about how to operate starship systems.

The screen showed a graphic representation of the moment of peak effect from the isolytic weapon's discharge. Like a series of nested spheres and ovoids, layers of energetic power were shown in grids of color, each one representing a flayed seam of subspace briefly torn open by the blast.

"The pattern of the detonation is asymmetrical," Valeris stated. "Observe." Again, without waiting for consent, she stood up and crossed to the panel to point out certain sections of the display. The security guard never took her gaze off the prisoner. "Here, and here, the phase shift is out of synchrony."

"That's likely just a distortion effect from the sensors that registered the blast," Vaughn countered. "You have to bear in mind that this data is an amalgam of readings from five different listening posts, the closest of which was several light-years from the actual site of the event. Errors are bound to have crept in."

"I understand that," she replied, "but I believe there may be another reason for this discrepancy."

"Which is what?" Miller prompted.

"I am not certain. Perhaps, if I could examine this data in greater detail and build upon Lieutenant Vaughn's work—"

Vaughn raised his hand, interrupting her. "Just a second. Was I not paying attention? When did you go from being the subject of an interrogation to a member of this investigation?" His irritation toward the Vulcan was building by the moment; the woman's arrogance was unbelievable.

Valeris favored him with a look and raised her eyebrow. "However you wish to characterize me, Mister Vaughn, for all intents and purposes I became a part of this investigation the moment you took me from Jaros II."

"You're only here to provide information," he retorted.

"Is that not what I am doing?" she replied. "As I was told, it is in my best interests to provide as much assistance to Commander Miller as possible. My Starfleet officer training and science skill set can be of use in that manner." She nodded at the screen.

"Lieutenant . . ." Miller had a warning in his tone, but Vaughn didn't hear it.

"You are not a Starfleet officer." He bit out every word, his expression twisted in disgust and barely restrained anger. "You gave up the right to call yourself that when you broke your oath to the Federation! You are a disgrace to this uniform and the ideals for which it stands!"

"Vaughn!" snapped the commander. "That's enough."

Valeris studied him for a moment. "Thank you for making your opinion of me clear, Lieutenant. You may be correct . . . but I think you will find that no matter what I may have been convicted of, I am still an active participant in this operation. And I believe I can locate an anomaly in the isolytic effect readings." She held up the padd.

"At this stage, we need all the input we can get," said Sulu.

"Yes, we do," agreed Miller, his gaze boring hard into Vaughn's. "Is that clear?"

Vaughn colored slightly, swallowing his annoyance. "Aye, sir." It left a bitter taste in his mouth.

Miller turned back to Valeris. "You want to help? Go ahead. Read the files. Anything sparks a thought, I want to know about it."

A bosun's whistle sounded from an intercom on the desk, and Sulu tapped the panel. "This is the Captain."

"Bridge here." Commander Rem Aikyn, *Excelsior*'s Rigelian first officer, had a manner that was brisk and businesslike. *"Sir, we're slowing to sublight. Estimate ten minutes to Neutral Zone perimeter."*

"Here we go," Sulu said, glancing at the others. "Rem, anything from the Klingons yet?" he asked.

"Nothing. But we can see them on long-range sensors. A pair of D-18 destroyers, waiting at the rendezvous point."

"All right, you know the drill. Yellow Alert, defensive posture. I'll be up there in a few moments."

"Aye, sir. Aikyn out."

"You're raising the shields?" said Miller. "Won't they see that as combative?"

Sulu eyed him. "Possibly. But anything less would be a sign of weakness, and I find a strong first impression works best with Klingon captains." He glanced at Valeris. "And after what happened to the *Bode* and all those other ships, I'm not willing to cross the border with *Excelsior* in anything even remotely resembling a vulnerable state."

"The Klingons will be insulted," Miller went on.

"A little," Sulu admitted, "but we can weather that. They respect strength. If they don't think we're willing to take the gloves off for this, we won't get within a parsec of Da'Kel."

Gion
Da'Kel System
Mempa Sector, Klingon Empire

Seryl walked across the damp grey earth of the barren little moon, his shoulders hunched forward and the hood of his environment jacket pulled forward over his head. A light, persistent rain had begun as he made his way back from the sluggish creek, and the air was becoming damp and clammy again.

He quickened his pace, the canteens of water thudding against his legs where they hung on the lanyard over his shoulder. The elderly replicator in the cargo shuttle had malfunctioned for the final time two days earlier, forcing Seryl and his cohort Cadik to survive on the sparse ration packs in the storage compartment. They still had a supply of purification tabs, but the sullen heat on the surface of Gion meant they were going through water very quickly. This was his second trip of the day.

Seryl glanced up. Overhead, past the faint green hue of the moon's atmosphere, the surface of its parent world was visible. Da'Kel II was an ocean planet full of turbulent, rust-red iron oxide seas; it had largely been ignored by the Klingons when they colonized the star system: they had instead focused their efforts on the more temperate third planet. The colony of Da'Kel III was visible in the morning sky as a glimmer of light low to the easterly horizon.

He wondered about what was going on there now. The flotilla of first-responder ships drifting around the edges of the blast zone, the Klingons grimacing through their viewports at the sight of all the bloodshed caused by one act of damning reprisal . . . Seryl wished he could see their faces. He wished he could make them know who had done this to them.

But now is not the time, he told himself. *It's too soon.*

That thought drew a mirthless smile from him as he started up the steep incline of the hill. *Too soon.* It was almost a joke: Seryl was one of the few of the group who remembered a time before the tyrants came to their homeworld—not like Cadik or Leru, not like the young ones who had grown up knowing nothing but a life beneath the boot heel of the Klingon Empire. Seryl had once lived free, only to have it all taken away from him. His family had lost everything—status, power, a line of lands ceded to them by the First Monarch himself—and been reduced to poverty, after the invaders had annexed their holdings to take the rich ore buried beneath. Seryl's parents had died destitute, and he had vowed then to oppose the Klingons until the very end.

And now that moment is almost here. He felt a sting of something bittersweet. A distant ring of resentment, deep inside, tempered by a certainty born of age and insight. His time was over; it had been over for a long while now. Perhaps ever since Rein had come to be a part of their group. As a youth, Rein was everything Seryl had once been: a firebrand, a man of charisma and defiant, singular purpose. Rein had been Seryl's greatest apprentice, and he had eclipsed his mentor in almost every way.

"I should be proud," he said to the air, between puffs of wet breath. "I *am* proud." The words still rang a little hollow, though.

He used his hands to pull himself up the last few meters, toward the top of the rise. Up above, the cargo shuttle lay beneath a net of sensor webbing and makeshift camouflage, sitting in the mud where Cadik had landed it after they left Leru and Zennol aboard the merchantman. While their comrades had traveled on to the target, they had put down here and gone silent, unseen by the enemy, waiting for the right moment. They were the second tier of the attack, the greater blow that was to follow. If anything, their mission was more vital than the first, for the effect of it would be all the greater.

As long as nothing goes wrong. Seryl made a negative noise to himself and shook off the idea. Rein had been right, of course. Nothing would be *allowed* to go wrong. They were more than ready. Cadik ventured into the shuttle's sealed freight compartment time and again, checking and rechecking his work, never satisfied with his own perfection. Seryl could not afford the luxury of doubts. They were committed to this, and although he would never live to see it end, he believed in his heart they would succeed.

He called Cadik's name as he crested the ridge, but the only sound was the mutter of the rain. And then he saw the young man lying facedown in the mud, a few steps from the shuttle's open hatch.

Seryl dropped the water bottles and ran the rest of the distance to his comrade, bending to turn him over. Cadik's eyes fluttered and he convulsed with a sudden, fluid cough. There was blood among the mud smeared on his face, and he was ashen.

With effort, Seryl dragged the other man to his feet and together they lurched back under the camouflage net. The night before, Cadik had been pale and sweaty, complaining of stomach cramps. Seryl had written it off as a bad reaction to the rations, but now he wondered if it might have been something else. The younger man was on the edge of unconsciousness.

Seryl managed to get him into the shuttle and he almost collapsed while putting him in the crew compartment behind the cockpit. Cadik raised his hand, trying to point at something, but Seryl ignored the weak gesture. Instead, he loosened Cadik's clothing and the young man's tunic fell open.

He recoiled. Cadik's chest was a mess of fresh lesions that wept thin liquid, grotesque discolorations like burns that were deep in his flesh. Seryl knew radiation exposure when he saw it, and yet he was perfectly well. He cradled the young man's head in his hands, turning his face. "Cadik? Cadik, do you hear me? How did this happen?"

"Nuh," managed the other man. "Nuh-no." He tried to point again.

This time Seryl turned to look, and through the companionway to the cockpit he saw an indicator blinking steadily on one of the control panels. "What is that?"

"Kuh," Cadik sputtered. "*Klingons.* Tried to. Come to warn. Sick . . ."

Seryl frowned; neither of them were carrying communicators, for fear that any signal might be picked up by a patrol ship passing nearby.

Then suddenly, out beyond the sloped canopy of the shuttle where the tree line began, there was a thrashing motion among the branches. Two Klingon warriors in full duty armor stepped into the clearing, each with a disruptor pistol in their grip, grimacing at the sight of a parked ship where no such craft had a right to be.

Seryl scrambled for the hatch. The cargo shuttle's passive sensors must have detected the approach of the Klingons and Cadik had collapsed trying to get to him, to warn him to get back under the sensor web before his life signs were detected.

This is my fault, he realized. *I brought them here.*

They could not be allowed to report in. Seryl exited the shuttle as the first of the Klingons, a stocky female, shouted at him and aimed with her disruptor.

"Identify yourself!" she bellowed. "What are you doing on this world?"

He made himself look weak and pathetic—not difficult to do when his species was by nature a good head shorter than the average Klingon trooper. "Apologies, warrior," he began, closing the distance between them. "Apologies. My ship suffered an engine malfunction and I was forced to put down on this moon for repairs. I mean no harm. If I have transgressed . . ."

"Be silent, *petaQ!*" she snarled. "You are lying! The Da'Kel System is a security-restricted zone: there has been a terrorist attack here!"

Seryl reached for her arm, playing up to the role of a

simpering outworlder. "Apologies, apologies," he went on, head bowed.

"We will search your vessel!" Before he could lay a hand on her, the female trooper grabbed him and yanked Seryl off balance, throwing him to the mud at the feet of the second Klingon, a dark-skinned male who sneered at him and let out a gruff chug of amusement.

Seryl scanned their armor and spotted the status tabs that indicated both of them were *bekk*s, low-level enlisted troopers, doubtless press-ganged into taking on the increased number of patrols of the Da'Kel System following the bombing. He gambled that they would be part of a small crew, perhaps no more than four or five, stretched thin, dealing with too many orders and not enough time. There was probably a picket ship in orbit somewhere overhead.

And then, when the male Klingon's gaze flicked away from him for a moment, Seryl let the shimmerknife fall from the pocket in his sleeve and into his hand. Moving with a speed that belied his age, he pushed off the muddy ground and slammed the blade of the weapon right into the spine of the warrior. The crystalline knife, sheathed in a membrane of energy, found the joint between the leaves of the Klingon's torso armor and pressed through. Seryl knew how to make this attack work from experience: he'd done it more than once, and it almost always worked the same way. The tyrants *always* underestimated them.

With a cry, the male Klingon was already falling, his legs failing him as his spinal column was severed. Seryl drew back the knife and slashed at his throat as he fell, sending a spray of purple blood out across the mud.

The other *bekk*, half in and half out of the shuttle hatch, turned back at the sound of the commotion, but Seryl already had her compatriot's disruptor in his hand. She fired wide in his direction, tried to duck his return shot, and almost succeeded; but the halo of the flame-orange beam tore across her face and neck, throwing her to the ground with the shock of it.

Seryl's chest was heaving as he crossed the distance back to her, and he felt light-headed from the exertion. His hands, the shimmerknife in one, the disruptor in the other, twitched with adrenaline.

He smelled the sweet tang of seared flesh and the odor of burning hair. The woman was a strong one; she was already trying to get back on her feet. Seryl delivered a savage kick to her stomach that put her down again, and then another just to hear her grunt in pain. With a sweep of his boot, he put her gun out of her reach and then took aim with his stolen disruptor.

The Klingon stared up at him, furious and defiant. Her brutal, sneering arrogance once more ignited the fires inside Seryl's heart, the deep hatred that he had nurtured since his childhood—and suddenly he remembered what it was he was here to do, what it *really* meant. The purity of that was exhilarating.

"You have no idea who we are, do you?" he spat. "You don't know who I am, where I am from, what you have done to us." Seryl's voice became a shout. "You don't even know. You underestimate us. You always have!"

There was a flicker of confusion on the *bekk*'s face, and he knew he was right. All she saw was a humanoid, an alien, something beneath the notice of her precious Empire, with all its talk of honor and glory and greatness. In that moment Seryl wanted nothing more than to burn it all down.

"We did it," he told her, through gritted teeth. "Your station, your ships, your brothers and sisters." He jerked his head at the sky. "We did that."

This time his words found meaning for the Klingon, and she tried to leap at him; but Seryl fired a second shot that burned a hole in her chest and made her scream echo through the hiss of the rain.

He kicked her body over the edge of the ridgeline and went back to the shuttle, making Cadik as comfortable as he could on the sleeping pallet before firing up the thrusters and bringing the craft to flight-ready mode. They couldn't stay here now: sooner or later, the ground patrol would be declared overdue and their crewmates would come looking.

Seryl took the shuttle up and hugged the tree line, speeding away over the surface of Gion, watchful for any sign that he had been detected by the picket ship.

He was approaching the moon's night side, the ocean planet beyond rising to fill the canopy, when the computer signaled the arrival of an encrypted communication stream.

"Kallisti," he said aloud. The alien word felt strange on his lips. In return, the message wrote itself across a screen in front of him, the encoded symbols transforming into Valtian script. *Federation cruiser has crossed the border*, it read. *Arrival imminent. Commence attack.*

His old eyes full of renewed purpose, Seryl nodded to himself and turned the shuttle to climb out of Gion's shadow and into open space.

Down on the surface, in a gully half filled with dead leaves and gore-choked rainwater, *Bekk* T'Agga, daughter of Kelmok, turned over and sucked in a breath that cut her insides like razors. Through her one unblinded eye, she saw the ruin of her own torso, and in her nostrils there was the stink of rotting plant matter mingled with the metallic tang of her own blood.

Something bronze glittered in the mud beyond the reach of her arms: her communicator, torn from her belt as she tumbled down the hillside. From here T'Agga couldn't tell if it was still in an operational condition, but the Klingon Empire built things to last. Their machines were as hardy as their warriors.

Some of the people who had perished on Utility Platform *loS pagh loS* had been friends of *Bekk* T'Agga; soldiers she played games of *grinnak* with at the end of a duty shift. If the treacherous, spot-skinned *petaQ* had told the truth about his involvement in the Da'Kel bombing, then she owed it to them to see he did not escape unpunished.

It took all of her effort to move even the smallest increment toward the communicator, and T'Agga could feel things inside her coming apart, breaking, leaking. It would take a while to reach the device, but she would do it, even though the attempt would likely kill her. One word of warning would be all that was needed. One word.

Gritting her bloodstained teeth, she tried again, and split the air with a howl of effort.

U.S.S. Excelsior NCC-2000
Da'Kel System
Mempa Sector, Klingon Empire

"Damn," said Sulu, leaning forward in his command chair. "It looks like a war zone out there."

"Aye, sir," said Commander Aikyn, turning his tattoo-lined face from the science console. "A killing field."

Miller nodded slowly in grim agreement. *Excelsior*'s bridge crew were silent, the view on the main screen moving slowly as it tried to encompass the aftermath of the destruction wrought over Da'Kel III.

A massive shoal of wreckage had settled into the orbital path that had once been occupied by the utility platform. It was a shaggy, ragged-edged cloud of metals and polymers, shards of hull and decking tumbling in slow motion, some of them catching the light from the distant Da'Kel star. Other, larger fragments drifted like icebergs among the morass. Miller saw flickers of energy dancing around the ends of severed power conduits, and slicks of dusty matter that could have been frozen breathing gasses. Now and then he picked out a recognizable shape—a warp nacelle or a support strut—and once or twice he thought he saw what could have been a body. Deep in the debris, something like lightning crackled, sending random discharges out across the span of the remains.

He glanced at the Rigelian. "Plasma discharge," explained Aikyn, his tone bleak. "It seems some of the ships that were wrecked during the detonation are still partly intact and their systems were not shut down."

"It's not just a hazard to navigation out there," said Sulu. "Those derelicts . . . They may still have functioning warp cores."

Miller nodded again. There was a ready danger here: the aftereffect of the subspace blast could easily have disrupted the functions of the warp systems of the ships it didn't immediately destroy. There was no telling what might come of that—anything from an uncontrolled release of antimatter to the spontaneous formation of a spatial anomaly. The work of picking up the pieces at Da'Kel would be laborious, dangerous, and time-consuming.

The commander thought about the crew of the *Bode* and wondered what they had experienced in those fleeting final seconds. *For their sake,* he thought, *I hope it was quick.*

Finally, Sulu sat back. "Mister Lojur, reduce magnification," he told the Halkan officer at the conn. "Take us in, slow and steady."

The screen snapped back to a standard display, and once more Miller saw the shapes of the two D-18 destroyers at the far port and starboard edges of the image. The Klingon ships had flanked them all the way in from the Neutral Zone, never leaving their side as the *Excelsior* crossed Imperial space. The ships reminded Miller of Terran cranes: their secondary hulls were tall, almost like battlements capped by warp nacelles, with slender necks that terminated in slab-sided command pods. Not once in the journey had either ship done anything as obvious as place a weapons lock on the Starfleet vessel, but Miller didn't doubt that their gunnery crews were still ready to fire on them at a moment's notice.

For all the agreements and treaties of the Khitomer Accords, this was still enemy territory, and Miller could never forget that. Despite what his personnel files might state, this wasn't his first time in Klingon space, and he remembered all the others in full and often unpleasant detail.

Sulu turned in his chair, toward the communications officer. "Mister Roose. Alert all decks, all department heads. I want us ready to render any and all support possible for the recovery effort. The sooner this mess is cleared up, the sooner we can get back to the work of the treaty."

Miller eyed him. "You think the Klingons will just go back to the way things were?"

"They have to, Commander," replied the captain. "As horrific as this attack was, it doesn't mean the fallout from Praxis has stopped in the meantime. The Federation made a commitment to stand by the Empire, and we have to keep to that."

"No matter if the Klingons like it or not," Aikyn added, his tone dry.

Roose raised his hand to the earpiece he wore. "Sir. We're being hailed. It's the *I.K.S. No'Tahr.*"

"General Igdar's flagship," said Aikyn. "At last *someone* speaks to us." The escorts had maintained radio silence all through their journey to Da'Kel.

"Show me," ordered Sulu, and the screen shifted to show a D-10 heavy cruiser approaching from a high polar orbit. "*Riskadh*-class," noted the captain, sizing up the alien vessel. "Formidable."

"We're not going to be starting a fight with him, are we, sir?" asked Miller, half joking.

Sulu, was poker-faced as he replied, "The day is young, Commander." He nodded to Roose. "Open a channel."

The bridge's viewscreen became a smoky, red-lit window into the dark, metallic recesses of the *No'Tahr*'s command pod. Unlike Starfleet ships, where the commanding officer sat in the center of the space with his crew arranged around him, a Klingon bridge put its captain at the very fore, metaphorically leading from the front. On a podium, in a chair that was closer to a throne in aspect, General Igdar of the Imperial Defense Force glared out at them with the same expression on his face he might have shown to something he was scraping from his boots.

"I am Captain Hikaru Sulu of the *Starship Excelsior*," said the captain. He indicated the others. "This is Commander Aikyn and Commander Miller."

The Klingon officer was decked in heavy armor of archaic design, the plate crossed with a bronze sash laden with medals and honor-marks. He had a craggy face that seemed cut from granite, and Miller's first thought was of an ex-boxer he'd known as a youth, a man who was all broken nose and dense muscle. Igdar's hair was sparse, but he had a broad, spade-shaped beard that was almost oil-black.

The general made a show of surveying every face on the bridge before ending with Sulu. *"Captain,"* he began. *"We meet again."*

Sulu's eyes narrowed. "Again?" he said. "Forgive me, General, but I do not recall—"

"The K'oyun System," Igdar retorted. *"An engagement in the asteroid belt. I was the first officer of the warship* Barka.*"*

"Indeed?"

Aikyn worked a console, pulling up a log file. "K'oyun is the Klingon designation for the Q-Theta System, sir. There was a border skirmish in 2268 . . . You were serving at the helm of the *Enterprise* at the time."

"Ah. Of course." Sulu nodded smoothly. "I remember it now."

"Your commander, Kirk . . ." Igdar gave an unpleasant smile. *"He was a sorcerer, that one. A rare enemy. He died well, yes?"*

Miller saw Sulu's manner stiffen a little. "He did. Saving lives."

"Oh." Igdar seemed disappointed—then in the next breath he was indifferent. *"I will have my second officer transmit a set of orbital coordinates to your vessel. From there you may hold station and monitor the recovery efforts."*

"With all due respect," Sulu replied, "*Excelsior* stands ready to assist you, General. In addition, we have information that may be of use in your investigations."

"Your assistance is not required," said Igdar. *"You may observe."*

"General, if I may?" Commander Aikyn spoke up. "This vessel has high-acuity sensor grids, numerous transporter stations, fabricator facilities, a fully stocked infirmary, and a crew trained in disaster recovery operations. We can undertake any salvage and rescue tasks available."

"*You may observe,*" Igdar repeated, his manner growing colder. "*And rest assured that the Klingon Empire has everything in hand.*"

"You're willing to dismiss us so quickly?" said Sulu. "There could be lives out there, sir . . . Klingon lives we could help you to save. And we may be able to bring this matter to a conclusion far quicker."

The general's mask of false civility finally cracked and fell away: Miller saw his features shift from showing offhand arrogance to the actual irritation bubbling away beneath. "*Help us? And while you do so, what else will you be doing, human? Looking over our shoulders, interfering, and judging us as we work to find the honorless* taHqeq *who caused this atrocity?*" He snorted with derision. "*I have enough to do without being wet nurse to a Federation starship!*"

The tension on the bridge leapt a dozen notches as Sulu came up from his chair and matched the general's flinty glare. When he spoke, there was steel beneath his manner. "I remind you, *sir*, that many of my people died in this place just as yours did, and, like you, we wish to see swift justice done. I warn you, if you cheapen that loss again, it will not go well between us."

Igdar took pause. "*That has all the color of a threat, Captain Sulu.*"

"Yes," he replied, "it does."

Miller saw an opportunity and stepped forward to take it. "General, perhaps if we were to meet face-to-face, we could better discuss this situation?"

"*Perhaps,*" echoed Igdar. The commander couldn't be sure, but he thought he detected a vague air of new respect in the Klingon's voice. "*We will arrange it.*" He reached for a control on his command throne and cut the signal.

At Miller's side, Sulu relaxed slightly. The commander glanced at him. "I was kidding about starting a fight, Captain."

"Like I said," Sulu told him. "The day is young."

7

ulu chose the observation room behind the starship's bridge to host the meeting with the Klingons, and Vaughn was sure that the captain had picked it for the theater of the place. With the broad, towering windows looking out onto the ruins over Da'Kel III, there was a real and unforgettable reminder to everyone present as to why they were here.

Once more, the captain of the *Excelsior* had delegated the conn to his first officer, and while Aikyn remained on deck, Sulu was joined by Miller, Vaughn, and the ship's towering Capellan chief of security, Lieutenant Commander Akaar. The security officer stood at stiff attention, and across the room a Caitian guard held a sentry post at the door. Both of them bore expressionless aspects, their focus steady and unwavering.

On the other side of the table, their Klingon guests seemed indifferent. General Igdar had two troopers of his own standing at his shoulders, and seated to his right was a lone Klingon female whose clothing did not resemble the standard duty armor of the Imperial Navy. If anything, her gear was formfitting and utilitarian, decked with pockets and pouches—more befitting some sort of technician than a warrior. Still, Igdar and his men seemed to treat her with a wary kind of respect, and the careful way she moved set alarm bells ringing inside the lieutenant's mind.

"Thank you for coming, General," Sulu began. "I promise

you, this discussion will be worth your valuable time." He nodded toward Miller. "The commander here has been dispatched by Starfleet to act as the Federation's on-site investigator into the Da'Kel bombing, and in turn *Excelsior* is facilitating his mission."

"He's a spy," said the woman, the hint of a smile playing around her lips. She brushed heavy braids of dark brown hair back over her ears, revealing a subtly complex crest of bony ridges on her forehead. "Darius Miller, Starfleet Intelligence operative."

Vaughn shot Miller a look and saw the commander smiling right back at her. "As the general didn't see fit to do it, gentlemen, let me introduce Major Kaj of Imperial Intelligence's active operations division."

Sulu gave Miller a sideways glance. "I take it the major is the 'operative from another agency' you mentioned before?"

Miller nodded. "We're . . . acquainted."

Kaj mirrored the gesture. "I tried to kill him once."

"Didn't take," Miller replied. "A good try, though."

Igdar made a rumbling noise in his throat that Vaughn guessed was his equivalent of a chuckle. "Perhaps she'll have the chance again before you leave, eh?"

Miller went on. "Major Kaj and I have an understanding. She's been heading up the investigation here about the attack. I contacted her and suggested we pool our resources."

The general's smile froze on his face and he turned an icy glare on the woman. "Is that so? You have been engaging in communications with the—" He barely stopped himself before he said *"the enemy."* "The Federation?"

Kaj's intense, steady gaze didn't waver. "What Imperial Intelligence does is not your concern, General. It is not a military matter."

Vaughn suddenly found himself in the unusual situation of actually agreeing with the brusque alien general, and he glanced at Miller, who mirrored Kaj's casual demeanor. "Does

Commodore Hallstrom know you were doing this?" he said in a low voice. "Going . . . off book?"

Miller spared him a look and spoke quietly so that only Vaughn could hear him. "Lieutenant, if you really intend to make a career of being a Starfleet spook, you're going to have to learn to modify your definition of what counts as 'off book.' Are you uncertain about my methods?"

"Yes sir," he told him. There seemed little point in hiding the fact.

"Good. Then consider this a lesson in the nature of fieldwork." Miller turned away and back to the Klingons. "So. Why don't we start with what you have so far on the suspects behind the attack?"

Igdar began a brisk and irritable summary of the events leading up to the subspace blast, but even as he spoke, Vaughn found he could not keep his attention from wandering back to Kaj. The major was unlike any Klingon woman he had ever seen before. In another time and place, he might have found her attractive, but here and now she gave off an aura that he could only define as *predatory*. Her manner was cool and detached, and yet it was clear she was taking in everything that was going on around her. Vaughn let his instincts interpret who she was: he got the sense of a professional, someone who functioned like a weapon to be aimed at a target and released.

Kaj noticed his scrutiny and turned slightly toward him, measuring Vaughn for a moment. He got the distinct sense she was figuring out how she'd kill him if the chance ever presented itself. It was hard to determine how old she was: Kaj could be anywhere between five or ten years his senior right up to Miller's age. Imperial Intelligence were known experts in bio-sculpting and surgical alteration, which meant the major could have been serving the Empire as far back as the heyday of the Federation-Klingon conflicts.

First Valeris, and now this? he thought. Once more, a cold spike of fear gripped him, and Vaughn wondered if he was in over his head. *Too late to turn back now, Elias.*

"With the service of Major Kaj and her organization," Igdar was saying, with no little sarcasm, "we have made a preliminary determination as to the identity of the spineless cowards who attacked the utility platform. It sickens me to say that Klingons were behind this craven assault, although with this act they have renounced any kinship with the Empire and its people. Chancellor Azetbur had declared them renegades and they have been discommended in absentia."

"The House of Q'unat," said Sulu.

The general gave a grave nod. "I see you are well-informed, Captain. Yes, the Q'unat clan. Once an honored name in the days of the old dynasty, warriors who fought with courage in defense of our way of life . . . But as time passed, they became hidebound and inflexible. They failed to embrace the future, and grew to be inward-looking and bitter."

Vaughn raised an eyebrow. Considering that a reactionary manner was almost a genetic trait for all Klingons, to hear one of them describe some of their own as overly obstinate was quite unusual.

"The Q'unat . . ." Igdar looked as if he were on the verge of spitting. "They are a disgrace to the Empire. And now this deed has cemented their name in the annals of infamy. When they have been brought to justice, I will see to it that all trace of them is erased from our history."

"What makes you suspect they're behind this?" said Miller.

Igdar glared across the table. "I do not suspect this, Commander. I know it! My own noble house has crossed blades with the Q'unat before, and we know them of old. All evidence uncovered points to them!"

"The declaration broadcast over subspace radio before the attack . . ." said Sulu.

"And more," Igdar insisted. "Once we knew where to look, we found other proof of their activities."

Miller glanced at Kaj. "Have you made any . . . arrests, Major?"

The woman's expression remained neutral, and her reply was without weight. "At this time, no suspects of confirmed linkage to the House of Q'unat are in Imperial custody."

"They hide like *bok-rats*," Igdar snarled. "They will be dragged into the light and put to the sword for their crime, mark me."

Vaughn saw a glimmer of doubt in Kaj's eyes; she didn't seem to share the general's ironclad certainty. "Can I ask what this proof you found was, General?" he ventured.

Igdar sniffed. "A data trail. Movements of illegal funds and bribes." He gestured as if dismissing a nagging insect. "Falsified shipping manifests and the like. The foundations of guile and duplicity. The major will provide you with pages of recovered documentation, if you do not feel my explanation to be thorough enough, *Lieutenant*." The general put hard emphasis on Vaughn's rank.

Sulu came to his defense. "You'll forgive me, sir, but that all sounds somewhat . . . circumstantial."

"Men have been executed for less," Igdar warned. "Unlike the Federation, Klingon law does not mire itself in endless talk and debate!" He pointed a gloved hand at the windows. "There is the crime! We have a culprit. A method, means, and motive! Justice will be done!"

"You're just a little shy on proof," Miller challenged. The general took a breath and was about to retort, but the commander went on. "I fully understand how you must feel, General. This atrocity . . . the Klingon people want retribution, and they want it now. And you seek to be the instrument of that. It's only right, as the Mempa Sector is under your command. Your responsibility."

Igdar's gaze turned flinty, and Vaughn saw the warrior's men stiffen at the barely concealed accusation in Miller's words. Only Major Kaj did not react.

"With that in mind, the Federation would be remiss if we didn't fully disclose to the Klingon Empire certain data that has come to our attention regarding the identity of the Da'Kel attackers."

"Speak!" Igdar growled, his thick-fingered hands tightening into meaty fists.

Miller looked at Kaj. "What if I were to tell you that we suspect the House of Q'unat was not responsible for all this? That the true culprits may be hiding in plain sight?"

"I would call you a fool!" Igdar snarled, his nostrils flaring with anger. "Tell me, Earther! How is it you can know the nature of this act of unspeakable cowardice better than those who were here to witness it? What possible source of information could you have that outstrips mine?"

"I'll introduce you to her," Miller told him, and Vaughn saw the commander nod to the Capellan security chief.

Akaar returned the gesture and spoke into the grille of an intercom on the wall. "Tiber? Bring in our guest."

A moment later the far door to the observation room opened, and the security guard entered with Valeris following two steps behind.

There was a brief, stunned silence. In the next moment Igdar was on his feet, a guttural curse on his lips and a *d'k tahg* flashing in his hand.

Shuttle *Suy'rov*
Da'Kel System
Mempa Sector, Klingon Empire

Seryl put the shuttle through a swift but careful turn, flanking a massive support tender as it crawled slowly along the edges of the damage zone. The big ship resembled a gigantic insect on its back, metallic gantries reaching up like limbs, some bending to gather in large fragments of hull.

Twice the local patrols had challenged him, and each time the false identification beacon had passed muster. The cargo shuttle had been captured from a Klingon military base on the far side of the sector, and in the confusion that reigned after the first bombing, the report of that loss had yet to filter through to the ships in the Da'Kel System. It was a calculated gamble to use such a craft, but so far it had paid off. And they only needed to get close enough. No more than that.

Seryl pulled away from the cover of the tender and applied more speed to the shuttle's impulse engines, pitching it down toward the third planet. He grimaced at the flotilla of first-responder vessels all around him; he had never been so close to so many tyrant ships before, and it reminded him of a story of Great Krios himself. The tale told of how the First of All Monarchs walked through a chamber filled with vicious nighthunters in order to reach the cell where his love Garuth was being held prisoner, picking his way through the sleeping monsters in stealth and silence. Seryl was the stealthy one now, making his way deep into the den of the beasts—but, unlike the heroic king, he would not return with his prize. Seryl's destiny was to end here, in a storm of fire and vengeance.

He glanced over his shoulder, looking back into the crew compartment where Cadik lay. The other man was still breathing, but each inhalation came with a wet, stuttering sound, and Seryl found himself hoping that his comrade might slip away into silence before the moment came. Either way, he would be spared the pain of his radiation burns soon enough.

As long as this works. The rogue, almost traitorous thought made Seryl's face twist, and he shook it away. "It will work," he said to the air. "It will be done."

Ahead, through the canopy, he saw more Klingon ships—battle cruisers from the Mempa starbase—and there, drifting among them, the distinctive white and steel shape of a Federation vessel.

He nodded to himself. It was fitting, he decided. They had allied themselves with the tyrants and turned a blind eye to the crimes of the Klingons. They could perish alongside them, and those deaths would bury the wedge deeper between the two powers.

• • •

U.S.S. Excelsior NCC-2000
Da'Kel System
Mempa Sector, Klingon Empire

The general came at her like a wild animal suddenly set loose from its tethers, his teeth bared and a string of invective spilling from his lips. For one moment all Valeris saw was the shine of the lights on the edge of the blade in his hand, and suddenly she was engulfed by the memory of a similar weapon dancing in the air before her, years earlier.

Then Tiber was shouldering her aside, blocking the Klingon's line of attack. Everyone in the room was on their feet, voices were calling out—

"*That's enough!*" Captain Sulu's bellow was hard and strident. "No one draws blood on my ship!"

But Igdar's eyes were locked on hers. "Valeris," he said, drawing out her name as if it were some arcane curse. "The traitor and assassin!" He stabbed a finger in her direction, still kneading the grip of his knife. "This . . . wretch . . . has a death sentence upon her head, ratified by the Chancellor herself! She is within Klingon space—she is subject to Klingon law! I am within my rights to kill her where she stands!"

"She stands aboard the *Excelsior*," Sulu retorted, "and this vessel is Federation territory. No matter what she has done, Valeris's rights will be protected—by force, if so required. I suggest, General, that unless you wish this room to be the first battleground in a new war between our peoples, you put up that *d'k tahg* and sit down."

Igdar glared at the captain. Valeris's initial evaluation of the general had proved to be correct: he was a typical Klingon, without even the veneer of civility present in most emotional races.

Fury tightened Igdar's face, but at length he sheathed his *d'k tahg* and gestured for his men to holster their drawn disruptors. "In the interests of continued *peace,* then." He spat out the word. "In return, explain to me why you have insulted my Empire by bringing that filth across its border."

The female, the agent Kaj, was the only one who had remained seated, and now she turned a cold gaze on the Vulcan. "I must concur with the general," she said. "Why is this criminal not in shackles or, at the very least, confined to your brig?"

"Valeris remains under armed guard at all times," rumbled Akaar. The Capellan nodded at Tiber and the Caitian. "For her own protection," he added, "as well as that of others."

Kaj addressed Valeris directly. "On our world, you would have been put to death in the public square of the First City, for all the Empire to see."

"I know," Valeris replied. "I understand that your Ambassador Kasiel made several attempts to have me extradited in order to carry out that exact sentence."

"We purged our ranks of all those who sided with Chang and his dishonorable schemes," Igdar went on. "Can you say the same, Sulu?"

The captain couldn't help but glance briefly in Commander Miller's direction. "The Federation believes in justice, not revenge." He took a breath. "No matter how personally objectionable you may find the presence of Valeris, she is here to assist us, and her continued involvement is under my authority. Do you wish to challenge that?"

Igdar's expression remained granite-hard. "Not yet."

"How can this turncoat be of aid to us?" Kaj demanded, eyeing Miller. "I assume she has knowledge of value, if you are so determined to keep her alive."

"Valeris has information about the group we suspect are the true architects of the Da'Kel attack," said the commander. "The Q'unat clan is just a blind, a smokescreen for someone else. *SeDveq.*"

For a moment Igdar was struck speechless; then he roared with harsh, braying chugs of laughter. He brought his fist down on the table with a flat *crack* and the cold amusement on his face vanished like vapor. "Do you think we are fools?" he growled. "You dredge up a name from the past, a pathetic rabble of terrorists hunted down and exterminated years ago?"

"Like the House of Q'unat?" Vaughn broke in. "Weren't they also considered to be destroyed?"

Igdar paid no attention to the interruption. "Those Kriosian agitators were dealt with when they attempted to oust the Klingon peacekeepers sent to their world to maintain stability in the region . . . Nothing of them remains! And if any of them did still exist, they would be no threat to us . . . *SeDveq* can be nothing more than a spent force at best." He shook his head. "No. The renegades of Q'unat are the agitators who caused this atrocity, and to claim otherwise is idiocy! I expected better from Starfleet, Captain Sulu. You have allowed yourself to be taken in by whatever lies this Vulcan witch has spun . . . Their kind are no better than their Romulan cousins! What did she want in return, eh? Her freedom?" The general glared at them all. "Did you promise her that?"

"I have no cause to lie," Valeris insisted.

"Give her to me," Igdar said, studying Valeris with a feral gaze. "I will encourage her to speak the truth." He leaned closer. "They say Vulcans do not feel. That, too, is a falsehood. They merely require a more . . . *forceful* approach to interrogation."

"You're not taking her anywhere." Valeris turned to see Vaughn staring down the Klingon commander. Of all the things that had happened since she entered the room, the lieutenant springing to her defense was perhaps the most unexpected. "Answer me this, General," he went on. "We have evidence that connects to the Kriosians, and not just the word of this prisoner. Why are you so quick to dismiss it?"

"I know the reason why," said Valeris.

"Oh?" Miller turned to look at her. "Care to enlighten us?"

Valeris looked Igdar right in the eye. "Because the general is afraid."

I.K.S. ho'Pung
Da'Kel System
Mempa Sector, Klingon Empire

The *ho'Pung* was barely a starship; having served the Klingon Empire with a completely undistinguished career since before the current crew were born, the elderly K-6 gunboat, while warp-capable, was so unreliable that it had been relegated to service as a patrol ship within the confines of the Da'Kel System. It had been this very quality that had spared the lives of the *ho'Pung*'s crew when the first isolytic device tore through the utility platform and the ships nearby. The gunboat's temperamental engines suffered an overheat and left the vessel drifting out beyond the orbit of the third planet—and so gave the handful of men and women aboard a ringside seat for the destruction that was wrought.

They had been among the first on the scene, along with other ships too far out to be clipped by the blast wave or lucky enough to have survived the detonation. What they saw there hardened their hearts, turning them—like any true Klingons—to thoughts of fierce reciprocity. The crew of the *I.K.S. ho'Pung* took on the mission they were given—to patrol the system as they always had—but now they were watchful for serpents hiding in the darkness. They did so, and hoped they would have the chance to face their new enemy. Just the night before, in the tiny mess room, the crew had discussed in gory detail the revenges they would inflict, if only the opportunity was presented to them.

Then *Bekk* T'Agga had led a landing party down to Da'Kel II's largest moon to follow up on an anomalous sensor reading. Now she was overdue.

Kobor, the officer who was the gunboat's captain, glanced at Junhir, his second. Junhir leaned close to the scanner console that took up most of the *ho'Pung*'s narrow command center; less a bridge, more a roomy cockpit, it still felt cramped and uncomfortable.

"She's missed the check-in," he told Kobor. "T'Agga does not respond to any signals."

"Can you read them down there?" Kobor glanced at his own screen, showing the clouds massing above the surface of the Gion moon.

Junhir made a spitting noise and swore under his breath. "Fek'lhr take this piece of garbage!" He slapped the palm of his hand on the panel. "It's a miracle these sensors can even register the planet! A lens and the light of a flaming torch would work better." He shook his head. Junhir had been poring over the garbled readings for some time—something that resembled the ion trail of a shuttlecraft had appeared there for a brief moment, but he couldn't be certain . . .

An indicator flashed on the communications board and Kobor turned toward it, opening a channel. "This is the *ho'Pung*. What do you want?"

For a moment Kobor thought the communications gear was broadcasting nothing but static; but then he realized that the hissing sound he was hearing was rainfall. Something like a faint animal cry issued out of the speaker grille, and his jaw stiffened.

"T'Agga?" he asked urgently. "T'Agga, is that you? Answer me!" Kobor glared at Junhir. "Sensors!" he barked. "Get me a lock-on, damn you!"

When the *bekk* finally spoke, he could hear how broken she was. Her voice was bubbling with fluid, almost suffocated. "*Shuttle,*" she managed. "*Danger . . .*"

"I knew it!" snapped Junhir. "I knew there was something out there! I saw the trail, heading out to the next orbit . . ."

"*Danger,*" T'Agga repeated, and then she fell silent.

Kobor stared at the console, the grim certainty of what he had just heard settling upon him. The landing party, his crewmen, were dead—and now he had to make sure they had not spent their lives in vain. He stabbed at the panel, opening a new channel. "This is patrol vessel *ho'Pung* to command ship *No'Tahr*. I have a priority alert, repeat, a priority alert . . ."

U.S.S. Excelsior NCC-2000
Da'Kel System
Mempa Sector, Klingon Empire

General Igdar did something entirely unexpected: his craggy, scarred face split in a wide, fanged smile that was utterly without warmth.

"I have killed a room full of men for lesser insults than the words that *petaQ* has just uttered," he told them. "Believe me when I tell you that it is taking every iota of my considerable will *not* to cross this room and rip her bloody throat open with my bare teeth."

"Oh, I believe him," muttered Sulu.

"The captain makes a good point," said Miller. "Our honored guest here doesn't look all that afraid to me."

"It is said that a true Klingon fears only dishonor," Valeris noted, the hint of a sneer creeping unbidden into her voice.

"You dare quote the teachings of Kahless?" Kaj said darkly.

Valeris went on. "Is it not true, General, that the families of the Q'unat and Igdar clans were once staunch allies?"

If the general had been enraged before, now he became livid. "Ancient history, long since turned to dust!" he spat.

"It is true," said Kaj. Her aspect changed: now the Klingon woman was listening, paying attention.

"The House of Q'unat became rivals to the general's family, but a victory over them was never decisively achieved." Valeris gave a sniff, lecturing the room as if she had a lesson to teach them. "The opportunity to redress that balance has come to pass now. The general fears it may slip away from him if he does not pursue it quickly enough."

"You know nothing of my clan or Klingon ways," Igdar retorted.

"I know enough," Valeris told him. "And consider this: If this information is clear to me, then what if it is clear to another?"

"To someone laying a trap that they know the general would chase . . ." said Vaughn.

"No matter where it led . . ." Kaj spoke quietly.

But Igdar was on his feet once more. "I will indulge this parade of insults and absurdity no longer. I am leaving this ship before I commit murder." He stepped away from the chair and nodded to his men, who gathered to him. "You have wasted enough of my valuable time, Sulu. You will take the *Excelsior* to the orbital coordinates provided to you, and you will remain there until such time as I give you the command to leave."

"General—" The captain stood, holding out a hand.

"If you deviate from this directive in any way," Igdar snarled, "I will have your vessel's engines blown out from under you and see this ship towed back to the Neutral Zone by tugs. Do I make myself clear?"

Whatever answer Captain Sulu was about to give, it died in his throat as a lightning-bright flash of energy lit the observation room through the tall windows. Valeris spun to see a streak of coruscating energy lance out from one of the destroyers that had escorted *Excelsior* in from the border. The beam flashed silently through the dark, and the Vulcan had the brief impression of a small craft fleeing the attack, moving at high speed toward the debris zone.

"There—" began Kaj, pointing toward the target.

Then the alert siren began to sound, and Commander Aikyn's voice issued out of the intercom panel. *"Red Alert! Red Alert!"* he called. *"Captain to the bridge!"*

Shuttle *Suy'rov*
Da'Kel System
Mempa Sector, Klingon Empire

The panel above Seryl's head blew out in a cascade of sparks, and acrid smoke swirled around the cargo shuttle's cabin. He blinked furiously, afraid to take his hands off the flight console to wipe his eyes, even for a second. That last disruptor blast had almost consumed the shuttle, and it was more by luck than judgment he had been able to avoid it.

He didn't register the voices shouting at him over the communications channel—not the words, only the tones of the roaring Klingons. They were cursing him, threatening him, warning him of his imminent death, but their demands meant nothing to the old man. He was beyond the point of no return now, and nothing they could say or do would change what was about to happen.

Out past the blunt prow of the shuttle, the great slick of wreckage from the first attack was spread out across space. The first few tiny fragments of debris were already sparking off the navigational deflectors. Ahead of the drift of ruins, Da'Kel III's surface was defined in shadow, the curve of the world deep in its night cycle.

Seryl would bring them a new light down there, a beacon that would illuminate the tyrants and show them the cost of what they had wrought on his species.

Another torrent of energized particles cut the darkness, a near-hit ripping open the cargo shuttle's port-side engine nacelle with a shocking rumble of broken metals. Seryl felt the craft heave to one side and enter a spin, the artificial gravity in the deck plates fading away. He was dimly aware of Cadik's body floating free somewhere behind him, moving as if he were still conscious.

Dazzled by the blast, Seryl felt his hands slip over the console and find the remote activator unit Rein had given him at their last meeting. He had clamped it to the canopy to keep it within easy reach.

The patterns of buttons and switches were committed to his memory, so he did not need to look at them to enter the correct activation code.

His last thought was of Cadik. *I hope the boy did his job correctly.*

• • •

U.S.S. Excelsior NCC-2000
Da'Kel System
Mempa Sector, Klingon Empire

The doors to the bridge hissed open and Sulu led the way, racing to the center seat even as Commander Aikyn got to his feet. At his side, Lieutenant Commander Akaar cut away to the tactical console.

"Status?" Sulu ordered.

"An alert went out across the Klingon general comms channel, sir," said the first officer. "Something about a fugitive shuttle. Then they started shooting."

Igdar, Kaj, and the rest of their party were right behind the captain, and the general made a growling sound. "Another attack?" He looked at Kaj. "Contact the *No'Tahr*—now!"

Valeris watched the moment unfolding, shifting to place herself out of arm's reach of the Klingons, should they suddenly decide to take their frustrations out on her. Miller and Vaughn flanked her, but both of them had their attention firmly set on the main viewscreen.

"I have the target," reported the helmsman. "Klingon F-type cargo shuttle, quad six, moving erratically at high impulse. Two life-signs aboard, one very weak . . ."

"Are we in a position to intercept?" said the captain.

"No!" grunted Igdar. "You are not to interfere with this!" On the screen, flashes of light tore past, cutting the darkness around the fleeing craft. "They must be destroyed before they strike again!"

Sulu ignored him, addressing his officer. "Lojur, can we get a tractor beam on that shuttle, yes or no?"

"We can try," said the Halkan. His hands danced across the console and the *Excelsior* pushed forward, closing the gap.

"What are you doing?" Igdar demanded. "My ships will not hold their fire if you enter the engagement zone! That shuttle is a danger—"

"If that ship is being flown by the same people who

attacked the utility platform, then we want them alive!" Sulu retorted. "Aikyn! Get us a transporter lock on the crew!"

"Sir . . ." Miller's voice held a warning. The commander was craning over the sensor console before him. Valeris turned to see what had caught his gaze and immediately recognized the waveform on the scanner screen: a new bloom of energy was radiating from the shuttle's interior. "Reading a power surge . . ."

Kaj's face turned ashen. "The weapon . . . It's the same weapon!"

"Confirmed," said Aikyn. "Isolytic energy building to critical onset."

"Shields up!" Sulu ordered. "Lojur, veer off!"

"Aye, Captain."

"Destroy them!" Igdar shouted. "Do it now!"

"The subspace field is fogging the targeting sensors," said Akaar with a frown.

The detonation came like a tiny, brief supernova. A flash of punishing white light flared across the darkness and threw stark shadows across the *Excelsior*'s bridge. Valeris flinched, her inner nictitating eyelid flicking down to negate the searing glare.

The pulse of light vanished as quickly as it had come, but in its place there was a seething spiral of unchained energies, spinning and growing. The subspace discharge, the raw power of extradimensional force, propagated outward in an expanding shock-front. Pieces of wreckage left adrift were consumed by it, some liberating new flashes of energy that were sucked into the blast wave.

Off to the starboard, Valeris saw one of the destroyers make a violent kick-turn, the vessel desperately pivoting to escape the edge of the flare. The subspace shock tore through the starship, stripping plates of metal from the hull and exposing the superstructure beneath, a heartbeat before the D-18's warp core imploded and engulfed the ship in antimatter fire.

The wave kept coming, rushing at them, filling the screen.

Sulu shouted into the starship's intercom. "All hands, brace for impact!"

What the first detonation of an isolytic bomb had not been able to accomplish, the second achieved within seconds of reaching criticality.

The blast that spread from the merchantman had been incorrectly placed, and the full force of its potential had not been achieved. It spent what power it had on consuming Utility Platform *loS pagh loS* and the vessels attending it. The detonation triggered by Seryl had no such mass to disturb the full expansion of the subspace effect, and once it reached the point of maximum force, it briefly became self-sustaining. The isolytic shock tore open the barriers between this dimension and those underlying it, allowing uncontrolled torrents of energy to spill out.

Wreckage left by the first blast was consumed by the second, and new deaths were added to the total as ships died in the flash-fire. Unchecked, the storm of unnatural force reached out claws of rippling light and raked them across the outer edges of Da'Kel III's upper atmosphere. The membrane of air cradling the Klingon colony world convulsed and ignited as streaks of fire formed out of nothing. Seen from the surface, lances of flame crisscrossed the skies, bringing hurricanes of heat in their wake.

The methodology of the strike was a classically lethal and callous act of terror: the use of a weapon to take life, followed by a second strike of even greater power, targeted in the same location to murder those who had come to rescue the victims of the first assault. Da'Kel III's sky was wreathed in an inferno, a thousand more lives snuffed out in an instant to join those who had perished only days before.

Once before, when the Praxis moon had been obliterated, the *Excelsior* had felt the force of a subspace shock wave and survived to tell the tale. But the Praxis blast had been light-days away, the majority of its power expended over time and distance. The isolytic blast's proximity rendered it an order of magnitude more lethal.

Valeris barely had time to grab on to the curve of the support rail surrounding the center of the bridge before the discharge connected with the bubble of shield energy protecting the Starfleet vessel. *Excelsior* resonated with a long, tortured moan of stressed metals as the shock engulfed it, and the Vulcan lost her footing, slipping to the deck.

All around her, noise and fire and chaos erupted. Electroplasma conduits across the ceiling of the bridge tore open, vomiting great plumes of heated gas. Consoles, their circuit breakers stressed beyond all tolerances, coughed showers of sparks and went dark. She heard cries of pain and alarm from members of the bridge crew; she felt the sickening lurch as the inertial dampeners struggled to compensate for the crippling torsion placed on the starship's internal structure. Smoke filled the bridge as main lighting died and the hellfire glow of emergency illumination snapped on in its place. A stanchion broke free above her head, and Valeris threw herself aside as a razor-sharp piece of girder impaled the deck.

Through the cloying, hot haze, Valeris staggered to her feet, still gripping the support rail. She glimpsed one of General Igdar's bodyguards slumped against a chair, his head turned at an unnatural angle, eyes staring blank and sightless into nothing.

The deck beneath her was trembling, each iteration of the shock wave growing stronger than the one before. Valeris blinked and tried to peer through the searing smoke. On the main viewscreen, through a veil of static, she saw a dark horizon rising to fill the image. The ship was tumbling out of control, caught in Da'Kel III's steady gravitational pull. From the speed and angle of descent, she estimated they had less than ninety-seven seconds before the *Excelsior* cut into the fiery edge of the planet's atmosphere.

The vibration was growing worse, and the rumble

resonating through the hull made it difficult to be heard over the confusion across the bridge. Valeris guided herself hand over hand back along the support rail. Somewhere in the smoke, she heard Captain Sulu calling out for his crew. He was biting back pain with every word.

Her boot encountered something on the floor and Valeris almost lost her balance. She glanced down and found herself standing over Lojur, his body sprawled in the well of the bridge deck. Blood covered the helmsman's face like a stark mask, leaking from his eyes and nostrils.

Perhaps a human might have paused and stooped down to put a finger to the Halkan's neck to check to see if he was still alive—but to do so would have wasted valuable time, and it would be illogical in placing the potential survival of one crewman over the safety of the *Excelsior* itself. Valeris ignored Lojur and slipped easily into his empty chair at the helm station. Her hands fell into the correct position over the console without conscious thought on her part. She did just as she had been trained to.

"What the hell?" The security guard Tiber reared up out of the smoke with her phaser drawn and aimed. "Don't touch those controls!"

But then another figure stepped out of the haze and put his hand on the weapon. "No," said Vaughn, blood leaking from a gash on his cheek. "Let her do it." He glared at her, challenging Valeris with each word. "You *can* do it?"

She nodded and looked away. The layout of a standard Starfleet helm console had undergone some alterations since she had last been assigned to that post, but the variations were minor and would not hinder her. Valeris quickly took stock of their situation: the starship's shields did not answer the command to raise, and the chorus of alert icons on the display showed that the subspace shock wave had caused widespread shutdowns across most of *Excelsior*'s primary systems. The warp core was off-line, and the impulse engines were trapped in a restart cycle, sporadically firing bursts of thrust that served only to push the starship deeper into the danger zone.

It all came back to her, effortless and quick. For a brief instant it seemed as if the intervening years had never happened, and she was where she was supposed to be: at the helm of a starship, in control of all that power and potential.

Valeris killed the restart sequence and let the impulse drives go dead. Behind her, she could hear raised voices arguing over what she was doing. She ignored them all, submerging herself in the work of flying the ship. The buffeting became horrific as *Excelsior* nosed into the interface zone at the edge of Da'Kel III's atmosphere, but she was ready for it. Careful manipulation of the attitude thrusters kept the ship's angle shallow, paying off the stresses through the length of the hull rather than collecting them all at the bow.

When the moment came, she reinitiated the firing sequence on the impulse engines and the sublight drives fired true. Valeris eased the throttle control to one-quarter velocity and the starship skipped across the interface zone and away, angling back out into orbital space. Like the passing of a thunderstorm, the tremors in the deck ebbed away, leaving the wounded ship to settle into something approaching equilibrium.

The tension of the moment broke, and Valeris looked up to find Sulu standing at her shoulder; she hadn't been aware of him at all. "That's good enough," he told her. "You can stand down."

Valeris got to her feet and stepped away from the helm console. The smoke had all but dissipated under the churning of the emergency ventilators, and now the full scope of the damage across the bridge was visible. Several of Sulu's officers were attending to their crewmates, patching wounds, others pulling modules from damaged consoles. The air was still heavy with the smell of blood and burnt tripolymer.

General Igdar stood at the sensor console, his expression a mixture of barely chained fury and ice-cold shock. "The colony on Da'Kel III . . ." he began, making a wan gesture at the scanner readouts. "It is in flames. Half the recovery fleet does not respond. Another attack . . . another cowardly assault!" He turned a savage glare on Captain Sulu and Commander Miller. "*You* brought this about. This was done because of *you!*"

"You can't know that!" Miller retorted.

"Open your eyes, Earther!" Igdar shouted, letting his anger cut loose. "They waited for you! They waited until the Federation was here, and then they sent another murderer to strike at us! If you had respected our wishes, if you had not come into Klingon space, this would not have happened!" He pointed at Valeris. "You brought this witch here, and now see what has been wrought!" Before Sulu could respond, the general shook his head and stormed away, moving back to where Major Kaj knelt beside the dead bodyguard. "I rescind my former agreement," he went on. "Starfleet is no longer welcome here. You will take your ship back across the Neutral Zone and remain beyond the Empire's borders until this matter is closed."

"No," said Vaughn. "You can't do that! You need us here! You're looking in the wrong place, damn it!"

"We didn't make this happen, General," Sulu insisted. "Chancellor Azetbur—"

"I do not care to hear you any more!" came the reply. "And Azetbur will listen to me when I give her word of what has taken place!" Igdar shook his head. "Take this message to your president, Sulu. Tell him he may demand whatever he wants, but the Empire will deal with this in its own way, and you will have no part in it!"

"And if I refuse to accept that?" said the captain.

Igdar showed his teeth. "Then you will be considered an impediment to Klingon justice, your ship will be seized and your crew imprisoned!" He snatched his communicator from his belt and snarled a command into it.

The glow of a transporter beam shrouded the Klingons and swept them from the bridge. Valeris's last sight was of Major Kaj, an unreadable expression in the woman's dark eyes.

8

Seven Years Earlier

Xand Depot
Deep Space
Klingon Border Zone

The transporter beam's blue-white glow faded into the darkness, and Lieutenant Valeris blinked, her eyes swiftly adjusting to the gloom. The coordinates that had been provided over subspace led them to this derelict, and in turn to the echoing, empty chambers of a decrepit cargo compartment.

She glanced around, allowing her hand to drop to the phaser at her side. With her other hand, Valeris pulled back the hood of her traveling robes and took a deep breath. The air was cold and heavy with the smell of corrosion.

"You don't look like Starfleet," said a voice. She turned toward it as a group of humanoids emerged from the darkness and into the chilly light cast by the few flickering illuminators on the high ceiling above. "You look like a tourist."

Valeris cocked her head. "Then my objective is complete." The robes she wore were ordinary attire, of the kind that any Vulcan traveling off-world might favor. The phaser and communicator band on her wrist were of Orion design, and the transport ship that had brought her to the depot was registered to a nonaligned world in the Triangle. There was nothing about her that could be traced back to the United Federation of Planets, and Valeris knew that if she was captured or killed, Starfleet would disavow all knowledge of her. Admiral Cartwright had been very clear on that point.

There were six of them, the older male who had spoken and then a woman and four younger men. The man walking in lockstep with the elder made an amused noise at Valeris's reply, and she immediately labeled him as the group's second in command.

They came to a loose halt a few meters from her, in a semicircle that was doubtless supposed to be intimidating. Valeris scanned their faces, seeing flesh tones that ran from dusky to pale pink, all of them showing the stipple pattern of pigmentation up along the neck and forehead that was characteristic of Kriosians. Most of them had the humorless, grim aspect of soldiers called to a duty they detested.

"Some of us were not sure you would come," said the older male. "I am Seryl. We are the Thorn."

"Say the word." The woman glared at Valeris, a hard look in her eyes. "Say it, or I'll kill you." To emphasize her point, she drew a heavy laser pistol and let it hang at the end of her grip.

Valeris didn't look in her direction, keeping her eyes on Seryl instead. "Kallisti."

"You'll have to forgive Gattin," said the older man, nodding toward the woman. "Trust doesn't come easily to her."

Despite giving the correct password, Valeris noted that Gattin didn't put the weapon away. "You requested a meeting. I am here. What is it that required a face-to-face encounter?"

Seryl glanced up, toward a window in the roof. The transport ship was visible at the edge of transporter range, a sliver of steel in the darkness. "Tell your admiral that it's safe, Vulcan. Contact your ship and tell Cartwright to come down here."

"You are laboring under a mistaken assumption," she told him. "My . . . commander is not aboard the ship. I was sent in his stead."

The younger man chuckled again, but Seryl's face soured. "I told him to—"

"Your communiqué merely stated that you required a

meeting," Valeris corrected. "It did not stipulate who was to attend it."

"I wanted Cartwright to come here!" Seryl insisted. "This is a matter of conviction!"

Valeris shook her head, even as she sensed the mood in the chamber shifting. "You will never stand in the same room as the admiral," she told him. "None of you. This matter will be dealt with at a distance, for the good of all parties involved. If you believed otherwise, you were mistaken."

Gattin muttered something under her breath, most likely a curse of Kriosian origins. Seryl blinked and his jaw worked: the man had been wrong-footed.

His second stepped forward, and it was immediately clear that he understood the nature of the situation. "You're here because we wanted to look you in the eyes," he said. "Because a voice across a comlink from the other side of the galaxy can't give you the color of a person's soul."

"A fanciful suggestion," Valeris noted. "But I recognize the need of emotional beings to exercise what the Terrans call 'gut feelings.'" She opened her hands. "I will have to suffice."

"Rein," began Seryl, addressing the younger man, but his second shook his head.

Rein came closer, looking Valeris up and down. She noted that he, too, carried a large pistol, but his was a disruptor pistol of a design favored by officers of the Klingon Imperial Defense Force. He saw her looking and nodded. "A spoil of war," he explained.

Valeris sensed a very real aura of aggression simmering beneath Rein's cool smile. He reminded her of a feral *sehlat*, stalking back and forth in front of another predator, daring it to make the first attack. The man was quite capable of killing her at a moment's notice, she realized. If she said or did the wrong thing, Rein would end her. Where Seryl seemed metered and fastidious, the younger man was pulling at his tethers, barely kept in check by his own drives.

And then a moment of understanding came to the Vulcan. It was Admiral Cartwright who had ordered her transferred from her current posting, Cartwright who had secretly briefed her before sending her to Xand Depot. This clandestine mission, she realized, was as much a test of the will of the Thorn as it was a test for Valeris. If she failed the admiral here, she would prove herself unworthy of his patronage. But if she succeeded . . .

"I'm curious," Rein said. "You're a Vulcan. The tyrants say your species is a race of misbegotten pacifists, weaklings who talk away your days instead of living with purpose." He smiled at her, fishing for a reaction. "Is that true?"

"Tyrants?"

"The Klingons," Seryl noted.

"Ah." Valeris shook her head. "The answer to your question is no. The Vulcan people are not pacifists, but neither do we seek conflict. We do not shirk from it if no other method of resolution is available. In our past, my species fought violent wars that led to great bloodshed. However, we rose above the emotions that created that violence and found a unity in the pursuit of logic."

"Logic, yes." Rein was nodding. Valeris noted how Seryl had taken a step back, both figuratively and literally, as the young man continued to speak. She noted the shift in the dynamic of the group and filed it away for later consideration. Clearly, no matter how much Seryl wanted to present himself as the leader of the Thorn, Rein was edging him out of that role with every word he spoke. "I've heard that your kind eschew all emotion. Which makes me wonder . . ." He turned suddenly and glared at her. "How can we trust someone without passion? This is a battle about hate and revenge, Vulcan. And if you can muster neither, then I have to wonder if your Admiral Cartwright is any better."

"He was afraid to come here in person," Gattin sniffed.

"He was cautious," Valeris replied. "Unlike you, he showed restraint and intelligence. Whereas you have shown your hand." Gattin's face grew a sneer, but Valeris kept speaking. "Suppose that we had decided to excise you from this operation? What if there is a Starfleet vessel waiting close by, ready to beam me away and atomize this station an instant later?"

The room grew silent, and Seryl blinked back up at the window. Only Rein's expression remained unchanged.

"You gave us all we needed to find you," Valeris added.

"Kill us and ten more will take our places!" snapped Gattin.

"Perhaps so," said Valeris, "but you will still be dead. And you will never see your world find freedom."

Rein's manner shifted and he laughed, the sound echoing. "Oh, Cartwright is no fool. He's sent us a sharp one!" The younger man nodded again. "I am in this unholy alliance for only one reason, Vulcan," he told her. "Because I hate the Klingons and I want my planet to be free of them. Of all the terrible things I have had to do toward that end, believe me when I tell you that the deeds I . . . that *we* do now sicken me more than every kill. But still I embrace this opportunity." He stepped closer. "I would turn my back on Akadar and the First of All Monarchs if it would see this thing done. Can you comprehend that?"

"I believe so."

"Good." Rein's steady, unblinking gaze searched her face, and Valeris did not turn away. "It is right to say that I do not know the Vulcans. But after meeting you, I think I understand this one." He aimed a slender finger at her.

"Indeed?"

"You *are* like us," Rein said, turning toward Seryl and the others. "She must be. Why else would she come all this way, risk death on an errand like this one?" He turned back, smiling coldly. "Because you want what we want, don't you?"

Valeris took a moment to frame her reply. Was it that she was disturbed to think that the Kriosian, an emotional being, could be so perceptive? The Vulcan knew that a dark vein of antipathy toward the Klingons lay down in the depths of her self, buried like a seam of poison. She saw the mirror of that in Rein's eyes, cut loose and magnified a thousandfold.

She pushed these errant thoughts away, dismissing them.

"You may ascribe whatever motivations you wish to my actions," said Valeris. "My only concern is the transfer of the information Seryl promised to deliver at this meeting."

"Of course." Rein stepped away, smiling as if he had won some kind of contest.

Seryl snapped his fingers at one of the others and a man passed him a data padd of Klingon design. "Here," he said, offering it with a terse gesture. "These materials are from Chang himself."

Valeris took the device and scanned the contents. There were pages of text in brisk, martial Klingon script, files of data on the initial plans by Chancellor Gorkon to make the historic offer of an olive branch to the Federation. The promise behind these words, of disruption for galactic geopolitics, was enormous. Valeris weighed the padd in her hand, considering it. For a moment she imagined herself at the point of a fulcrum around which potential futures were turning. History was replete with such moments, she reflected, and it was sobering to consider that this could be one of them. Had she not been a Vulcan, she might have allowed herself to have doubts.

"This will suffice. You will be contacted if you are required," she told them, and tapped the signal key on her bracelet. The transporter beam enveloped her, and Xand Depot became a memory, replaced by the cramped interior of the transport ship.

The crew of the transport didn't need to hear from her— they knew what to do—and as she stepped into the narrow corridor that ran the length of the craft, Valeris felt the rumble through the deck as the vessel got under way.

She returned to her cubicle-like cabin and worked on the Klingon padd, checking it for tracers, implants, or any kind of malicious software. The work would make the trip back into Federation space pass more quickly and give her something to focus on.

Without it, Valeris was concerned that an emotion would bleed through and affect her performance: *anticipation*.

She had done what the admiral asked of her: performed her mission flawlessly. Now she would reap the reward he had promised her if those conditions were met.

Since joining Starfleet, there had been only one thing that Lieutenant Valeris had wanted, one posting, one opportunity. But despite her best efforts, despite graduating at the top of her class at the Academy and excelling at every challenge, it remained beyond her reach.

But not now, not after this.

When she returned to Earth, under the orders of Admiral Lance Cartwright, Valeris would report for duty at her new station: as chief helmsman of the *Starship Enterprise*.

The flagship of the fleet, she told herself, *where I should have been all along.*

9

Vaughn pressed his head against the port of his cabin and closed his eyes. Even the deflectors and life support systems aboard the starship couldn't stop it from holding some measure of the chill of the void outside. The cold leached the warmth from his skin; it was like a tonic, in a way. It brought him back to the moment, to the harsh reality of where he was and what had happened.

With effort, he turned away and frowned. The faint burnt smell of damaged components still dogged him, even though he had taken the time to get a clean uniform and a brief moment in the sonic shower. It was as if the echo of the bomb blast was still resonating all around him, still sounding through the tritanium bones of the *Excelsior*.

They had all come very close to death out here, and many had not been so lucky. The isolytic device on the shuttle had wreaked terrible damage, and according to Commander Aikyn, it was likely that the effects of the discharge on Da'Kel III would render the colony uninhabitable. There were civilians down there, families. The Klingons were already evacuating them, but not all would make it off the surface before the geological instabilities and atmospheric inversions grew too powerful.

Vaughn thought of Captain Sulu's face as the *Excelsior* limped away on a course back toward the border. He remembered the sorrow and the regret hiding in his eyes.

The captain had to be asking the same question that troubled Vaughn: *Was General Igdar right? If they had not come to Da'Kel, would this attack have happened?*

Part of him knew it was foolish to play a game of what-if. The terrorists had shown they were willing to take life without warning or compunction, and he had no doubt that they would have used their second device even if *Excelsior* had stayed on the Federation side of the border . . . Perhaps not here at Da'Kel, but somewhere. *Of course they would have.*

And yet, he couldn't shake the sense of responsibility that dragged him down like iron chains. He sighed and took a seat on the narrow bunk, staring blankly across the space of the cabin Aikyn had assigned him. He had been ready for this for so long: Elias Vaughn insisted he was ready for field duty, and perhaps his arrogance had blinded him to the fact that, *no, he really wasn't.*

Command training was something that every officer candidate in Starfleet went through, and buried in that curriculum was the lesson that every leader had to learn: *people will die because of choices you will make.*

Intellectually, Vaughn knew that could happen, but somehow he thought it would never happen to him. Placing his own life in danger, that he could handle, but suddenly shouldering the responsibility for the lives of men and women, for Klingons, for civilians, for people he had never met and would never know . . . Suddenly it was all too real.

"Did I make this happen?" he said quietly, to the silent room.

His answer was a chime from the door. Vaughn stood up and pulled his rumpled undershirt straight. "Who's at my hatch?" he demanded.

"Tiber, sir," came a weary voice. He opened the door and found the security guard standing with Valeris at her side. "She wanted to see you, Lieutenant," explained the woman.

Vaughn found himself nodding. "All right. You can wait outside."

"Are you sure?"

He nodded again. "I'm sure." Vaughn walked to the food slot and summoned a cup of *raktajino* as Valeris followed him in, the door sliding shut behind her. "What do you want?"

"I do not require a beverage."

He gave her a hard look. "With me," he went on. "What do you want with me?"

"There are questions I require answers to, and Commander Miller is unavailable."

Vaughn took his cup and sipped at it. "I imagine he's on subspace to Commodore Hallstrom and the admiral of the fleet, trying to convince them that we didn't just incite an act of mass murder."

Valeris glanced at the window. Matching *Excelsior*'s velocity in close formation, a D-7 cruiser hung off the starboard bow. With the damage suffered by the starship still being repaired, the journey was progressing at a comparatively slow warp factor one. "There was no way we could have known what would happen," she said in her usual matter-of-fact tone.

Her manner grated on Vaughn. "Are you sure about that? Because if you—"

She raised an eyebrow. "My telepathic abilities do not extend to reading the minds of the Kriosians, Lieutenant."

"If it was them," he replied. "Igdar swore otherwise."

"Igdar cannot appear to be wrong," said Valeris. "His pride and egotism have blinded him. You heard his words: the moment the second attack concluded, he took the opportunity to place the blame on us. He refused to accept any measure of responsibility." She looked away. "It is a Klingon trait. They cannot accept that any failure may be theirs. It must always be caused by an outsider. That is why the House of Q'unat is the perfect scapegoat."

"Because they are Klingons; but they're renegades, so they're not *true* Klingons." Vaughn's lip curled. "And, of course, the idea that the Federation might be right about the Kriosians . . . If he agreed with that . . ."

"It would weaken him. Therefore, we have returned to

the same state of affairs we were in before you took me from Jaros II. Nothing has changed."

"Except that now more people are dead," he said bitterly. "And we're no closer to tracking down the Thorn."

"What will happen to me?" she asked. "Commander Miller told me that if my information was of value . . ." Valeris trailed off. "If the investigation ends here, then I will not be able to prove my worth. You will return me to the prison."

Vaughn studied the Vulcan for a moment, trying to put aside his prejudices about the woman. "We would all be dead if it wasn't for you. What you did on the bridge . . ."

"It was not altruism on my part, Lieutenant," she told him. "I was saving my own life."

He snorted. "Is that what you want me to put in my report? That you didn't give a damn about the rest of us?"

"I want you to be clear about me," Valeris told him. "I want to ensure there is no misunderstanding between us."

Vaughn eyed her. "Lojur's healing in the sickbay. He said he wouldn't have been able to do what you did. Whatever you say your motivations were, everyone on this ship owes you their life, so if I were you, I'd take that as a win and shut the hell up. Because right now you need all the goodwill you can get."

"No amount of 'goodwill' will be enough to grant me my freedom. But perhaps that was the intention all along. Perhaps I was foolish to believe the Federation would ever be able to forgive me for my transgressions."

The intership sounded: *"Lieutenant Vaughn, Commander Miller. Report to Captain Sulu immediately."*

Vaughn put down the cooling *raktajino* and tapped a control. "Commander Aikyn? Is something wrong?"

"Lieutenant, bring the prisoner with you," said the Rigelian officer. *"There's been a development. The captain will bring you up to speed."*

The cabin was an office-like affair on the bridge deck, essentially a workspace for the ship's commanding officer. The ready room had been a fixture of Starfleet ships in the early pre-Federation era, but the notion had fallen into disuse through the twenty-third century. However, with the refit of ships in the *Excelsior* class and the newer designs rolling out from the construction yards, the concept had come back into fashion.

Sulu's ready room should have been an oasis of calm for the captain, but, like a lot of his vessel, the cabin was a half shambles, panels on the walls hanging askew and sooty marks marring the ceiling where electroplasma conduits had taken damage. Vaughn's nose twitched as he caught the burned scent again.

The *Excelsior*'s captain and first officer were already waiting for them with Miller. The expression on the face of Vaughn's commander was stoic and unreadable; that didn't bode well.

As Vaughn had done in his cabin, Sulu ordered Tiber to remain outside, and as soon as they were alone he gave the lieutenant a steady, level look. "I'm going to ask you this just once, Mister Vaughn, and if I don't get an answer I like, you're going back to your quarters and you'll stay there until we reach Federation space, is that clear?"

"Crystal, sir," he replied. His throat felt arid and he licked his lips.

"Are you certain that the Thorn are the antagonists behind these attacks? Beyond any shadow of a doubt?"

Vaughn hesitated, and his gaze flicked to Valeris, who stood silent beside him. She gave an imperceptible nod. He looked away. "If I didn't think it was them, I would never have come to you on the starbase," he said. "Frankly, sir, I may have destroyed my chances of a future career in Starfleet with the choices I've made, but I know the data." Vaughn looked back at Valeris. "And matters of trust aside, I've come to believe what she has told us is true. The Kriosians killed those people."

"I agree with him," said Miller. "But then, you knew that before I walked in here, right, sir?"

Sulu gave a nod. "Commander Aikyn, show them our surprise gift."

The first officer opened a small equipment case on the ready room's desk. Inside was a bed of grey foam, and on it lay a thick, bronze rod studded with gunmetal keys and glassy insets. "A damage control team found this in the observation room after we left orbit of Da'Kel III."

"The design is clearly of Klingon origin," Valeris offered.

"Correct," said Sulu. "We can only conclude that one of our guests secreted it there when they were aboard."

"So, what is it?" Vaughn peered at the object. "A surveillance device? A weapon?"

Aikyn shook his head. "Quite the opposite, Lieutenant." The officer carefully picked it up. "Aside from a small anti-tamper charge, there's little that's dangerous about it."

Miller tapped a finger on his lips. "It's an encrypted communicator."

Sulu gave him a sharp look. "You've seen this sort of thing before?"

"No," said the commander, "but I know Major Kaj well enough." He held out his hand to the Rigelian. "If I may?"

Aikyn warily handed over the device, and Miller fingered it, finding an activation switch. "Kaj," he said into the air. "I'm here."

The reply was almost immediate. "Good. It took you long enough."

A crystalline node at one end of the rod shimmered and a beam fanned out, sketching a humanoid figure. The holographic image gained substance and the illusion of solidity. The Klingon intelligence operative stood before them in the ready room, her virtual ghost glancing around as if she were really there.

"You left a concealed mechanism on my ship, Major," said Sulu. "What would General Igdar have to say about that? I wonder."

"I needed a means of contact that we could keep between us," she replied smoothly. "The general and I do not agree on all matters of protocol."

A thought occurred to Vaughn. "A holographic transmission

like this one . . . that's a lot of data being transmitted. There's hardly any signal degradation or response delay . . ." He smiled thinly. "She's close."

Valeris glanced at the monitor screen on the far wall, where a tactical plot of the *Excelsior*'s course and the parallel flight of the D-7 was displayed. "Aboard the escort ship?"

Miller watched the image of Kaj carefully. "I don't think so. The captain of that cruiser is one of Igdar's fleet officers."

"*I am nearby,*" Kaj admitted. "*What matters now is what we discuss in the next few moments.*"

"You've gone to a lot of trouble to talk privately with us," said Sulu. "I'm listening."

Kaj folded her arms. "*As Commander Miller will doubtless agree, it is often true that operatives in our line of work are unable to influence the choices made by the policy makers in government, even if they are clearly in error.*"

"Can't argue with that," said the officer.

"*General Igdar has influence with certain members of the Imperial Intelligence hierarchy. Political pressures within the High Council and the power games he and his clan are playing have made his position all but unassailable . . . for now. Even Chancellor Azetbur understands that Igdar's fealty is required to maintain the status quo.*"

"Yes, we've seen firsthand the breadth of his influence," Aikyn noted. "What is your point, Major?"

"*Prior to your arrival, I conducted my own inquiries into certain avenues of study that the general considered a waste of time.*"

"The Thorn," said Aikyn.

Kaj gave a sharp nod. "*The information presented by Lieutenant Vaughn . . .*" She glanced at Valeris. "*And the convict . . . it matches my own suspicions. I believe there is a high probability that the Kriosian terror cell known as the Thorn has been instrumental in the Da'Kel attacks.*"

"Nice to know we're on the same page," said Miller, "but that ship has sailed. Literally, in our case. Or did you forget Igdar's little 'Get the hell out' speech?"

The Klingon woman showed her teeth. *"I do not support the flawed decisions of the general, nor will I stand by and allow this charade to continue in order to protect the vanity of his clan."* Her lip curled in a sneer. *"It is my intention to pursue this 'Kallisti' network and hunt down the Thorn."*

"You will fail," Valeris said, without weight. "The Kriosian freedom fighters have remained beyond the reach of the Klingon Empire for more than twenty years. You have not been able to find them in that time. You will not be able to find them now."

Kaj's hologram flickered, as if in concert with the Klingon's mood. *"That may be so. But you can find them, convict. You know the protocols set up by that traitor Chang and your scheming master, Cartwright. You know where to look."*

"You want us to turn Valeris over to you?" said Sulu. "We've already had that conversation. The answer is still no."

Miller's smile widened. "That's not it, Captain," he said. "I think what the major is looking for here is some cooperation."

"Think of it," said the Klingon, *"as a secondment to another agency."*

"Ah." Sulu paused, taking it in. "I see."

Vaughn blinked as the import of Kaj's words settled in on him. "Uh, sirs? Just so I'm sure I understand this, I'm going to say it out loud." He swallowed hard. "We're actually entertaining the idea of . . . what? Disregarding the authority of a ranking officer in the Klingon Defense Force, a politically connected sector commander no less?"

"Lieutenant Vaughn's point is well made," Aikyn noted. "We're already looking down the barrel of one interstellar incident as it is."

Sulu remained silent, turning the situation over in his thoughts.

Miller drew himself up; his manner became formal. "Captain," he said, "we have no guarantee that the Thorn are done with this terror campaign of theirs. And they have shown a willingness to take Federation lives as easily as Klingon ones. We have an obligation to stop them."

"I'm more than conscious of my obligations as a Starfleet officer, Commander," Sulu replied. "Once we've crossed the Neutral Zone, we can contact Commodore Hallstrom—"

"And do what?" Miller broke in. "Ask permission? You know as well as I do how that's going to go. After Igdar's statement, President Ra-ghoratreii won't risk antagonizing the Klingons any further. We'll be reduced to watching this all unfold from the outside in, and if and when the Thorn destroy another one of our ships, we'll be looking the wrong way."

Sulu's gaze was flinty. "Are you done, mister?"

Miller drew back, realizing he had overstepped his bounds. "Yes sir."

Vaughn watched the captain weigh up his options; he didn't envy the man. After a long moment Sulu spoke again. "A covert operation inside the borders of a nonaligned galactic power, conducted without oversight or support from either side . . . That would not only be illegal but reckless and dangerous. Starfleet could not allow itself to be connected to such activities in any way."

"I've been there before," said Miller.

"I'm willing to take the risk." Vaughn heard himself say the words, almost by reflex.

Valeris folded her arms. "Is there an option here that does not require my presence?"

"There is not," Kaj sniffed.

The Vulcan gave a nod. "Then it appears I have no choice but to make myself available."

Aikyn's brow furrowed. "We're really going to do this?"

"Yes, we are," said Sulu.

The damage the *Excelsior* suffered during the attack was being repaired en route as best the ship's engineering team could manage. However, it was a piecemeal job and there were problems. It did not seem unusual when, two hours after the meeting in the captain's ready room, the starship's warp field suffered a sudden collapse that dropped the vessel out of light speed as it passed near to a rogue planetoid. The escort cruiser's crew reacted quickly and came about, swiftly returning to *Excelsior*'s position, but for several minutes they were out of direct contact. The Klingons found the Starfleet vessel adrift, plasma streams venting from its nacelles. The gaseous discharge caused ghost images on the D-7's sensor grid and made it difficult for them to get a thorough scan of the vessel or the surrounding area, but the point became moot as Sulu's officers brought the ship back up to operational status. After a terse exchange of words, the cruiser's commanding officer warned Captain Sulu to keep a better eye on his ship's systems. Any more unscheduled stops would be considered disruptive and force the ship to take the *Excelsior* in tow.

The captain was contrite, and soon the two ships were under way once more. Had the sensor officer aboard the Klingon cruiser thought to run a comparative scan of *Excelsior* after it returned to warp, he might have noted the absence of three humanoid life-signs from the crew complement.

I.K.S. Chon'm
Mempa Sector, Klingon Empire

"They're moving off, Major," said D'iaq. "No sign of detection. As long as we remain in the shadow of this planetoid, we are invisible." He glanced up at her, his one cybernetic eye glittering in the light of the cramped bridge pod.

Kaj ran a hand through her hair as she stalked across the room toward him. "Power status?"

"Adequate, for the moment," reported Gadan, the ship's whipcord-thin engineer. "I recommend raising our veil as soon as they are out of visual range."

"Noted." Kaj looked at D'iaq. "Our guests are safely aboard?"

"I put them in the cargo bay," he replied.

"Good. Stand by to get us under way as soon as possible."

D'iaq bobbed his head in reply. On any other vessel in the Klingon fleet, answering the order of a superior officer with anything less than a salute would have earned him a punch in the mouth, at the very least—but Kaj's command style was far more relaxed than the usual standards.

The major's interest was less in regulations and salutes and more in competence and loyalty. Indeed, the interior of her ship bore closer resemblance to a privateer than a serving ship flying Imperial colors, but that was reflective of the unorthodox missions the *Chon'm* engaged in. Her ten-person crew was just as eclectic; they wore no uniforms and carried no insignia. Some of them were not even Klingons, and some did not appear to be Klingons, although it would take a detailed genetic scan to determine which was which.

Kaj made her way from the bridge down the long corridor that sloped to the keel deck, dismissing the guard at the heavy iron hatch leading to the cargo bay. She slapped at a control with the heel of her hand and the hatch ground open. Inside, the Starfleet officers and the convict did their best not to appear intimidated.

"Major," said Miller, with a nod. "Permission to come aboard?"

"Granted," she said with an incline of her head. "But then, this isn't the first time you've been aboard one of our ships under . . . irregular conditions, is it, Commander?"

He gave her nothing in return. "I'm sure I don't know what you're referring to."

"It's *my* first time," offered the younger human, Vaughn, "if that counts for anything."

"We are aboard a Klingon combat vessel," said the Vulcan, reverting to type immediately. She made a show of looking around the interior of the bay. "Judging by the drop-hatches in the floor and the dimensions of the internal hull spars, this is a *B'rel*-class K-22 scout, more commonly known as a bird-of-prey."

Kaj glanced at Miller. "You allow the convict to speak out of turn whenever she wishes? The Federation is as lenient as I expected."

"We prefer to consider ourselves as compassionate," said the commander.

"I don't doubt it." Kaj studied them. Like the Vulcan, the two humans were now dressed in civilian attire of a utilitarian cut, similar in design to the major's own functional gear. Both men appeared unarmed, although she doubted that was so. Vaughn carried a daypack over his shoulder and made no attempt to set it down on the deck.

"So you were pacing the *Excelsior* all the way from Da'Kel?" Miller went on. "What would you have done if we'd ignored your little invite?"

Kaj smiled thinly at Valeris. "I would have exercised a different contingency in order to secure the information I required. Suffice to say that it is better for the crew of Captain Sulu's ship that you did not."

"And now you have us right where we want you," said Vaughn.

The lieutenant's idiom was lost on Kaj, and she ignored it. "Commander, I suggest that you and your officer make yourselves . . . comfortable . . . while I discuss our objective with the convict. Once I have the information I require—"

"Discuss?" Miller spoke over her. "By that, can I assume you mean, use a mind-sifter?" He shook his head. "I think we need to lay down some ground rules right now, if this is going to work out."

Kaj stiffened at his tone. "Remember where you are, Miller," she told him. "You are on your own now, beyond Federation intervention, light-years within Klingon space. You draw breath only because I allow it. Do not mistake the . . . the *lenience* I have shown to you so far to be *compassion*."

Miller seemed unfazed. "That's how it is, huh? So, what next, you threaten to turn us over to General Igdar if we don't do as you say? I guess that could work for you. You could tell him you caught us spying, maybe even gift-wrap Valeris here for him to send to public execution . . ."

"Sir," Vaughn broke in, "this is just a suggestion, but could you *not* give her any ideas?"

The dark-skinned human went on. "You could do all that, score some points with the general, maybe even get on his team." The lightness faded abruptly from his tone. "Then, when the Thorn attack again—"

"And they will," said Valeris.

"When they attack again and hundreds more Klingons perish, you can be right there with him laying the blame, once again, in the wrong place."

Miller's flippant tone chafed on Kaj and set her teeth on edge; the Starfleeter had struck a nerve. With effort, she pushed aside all her personal desires for vengeance and forced herself to concentrate on the matter at hand. "I am pleased to see we have a clear understanding of each other, Commander. Very well. We will proceed, for the moment, as you suggest." She glanced at Valeris. "How do we find them, criminal?"

The Vulcan concealed her irritation at the label Kaj had given her. "I am aware of a location that the Thorn used as one of its bases of operations. The coordinates are out on the far side of the Klingon Empire, on your colonial border."

"That's quite a trek from here," Miller added. "How do you propose to get us across Imperial space without raising any alarms? A ship this small . . ."

Kaj allowed herself a smile. "Ever since Kirk took one of our craft, you think you know all our secrets, don't you?" She gestured at the walls. "This is the *Chon'm*, a variant of the bird-of-prey design with some very uncommon properties. These ships are unique, Commander. Their construction makes them well suited as test beds for exotic weapons and experimental tactical systems. I imagine you recall the *Dakronh*?"

"General Chang's flagship," said Vaughn, without hesitation. "A bird-of-prey like this one, capable of firing its weapons while still cloaked."

Kaj nodded. "The *Dakronh* and the *Chon'm* were sister ships, drawn from the same research program. But where Chang's vessel was designed as a first-strike weapon, this ship is more suited to an espionage role."

"What do you mean?" asked Valeris.

In reply, the major drew her communicator and spoke into it. "D'iaq, status?"

"About to move off, Major. Orders?"

"Activate the veil. Pick something . . . innocuous."

D'iaq grunted his acknowledgment. *"A cargo tender, perhaps?"*

She nodded. "I leave the choice to you. Kaj out." She stepped out into the corridor, and the others followed her through the ship.

"A veil?" Miller raised an eyebrow. "What is this, a costume party?" A quiver ran through the deck as the ship's drives came online.

"In a way," Kaj replied. "The *Chon'm* is like your Terran chameleon, Commander. It can take on the appearance of anything I wish it to, to blend in and pass unseen. A matrix of holographic generators embedded in the outer hull project a three-dimensional visual image that allows us to take on the guise of any other craft of similar size and mass."

"Intriguing," offered the Vulcan. "But such a mechanism would work only as camouflage against visual scanning. A standard sensor sweep would reveal the true nature of the vessel immediately."

"Do all Vulcans share her tendency to state the obvious?" Kaj asked. Before anyone could reply, she went on: "The veil system is also capable of generating a focused dispersal field that can mimic the sensor profile of anything in its holographic library."

"Hiding in plain sight. I guess that's Klingon guile . . ." said Vaughn. "Which begs the question: Why be so open about how it works? I'd have thought you would want to keep something like that secret." He paused as a thought occurred to him. "Or are you just going to kill us when we're done here?"

Miller smiled again. "She told us because it's not a secret," he said. "Starfleet Intelligence has been working on holo-ship concepts for years. They stole the technology from us in the first place."

"More accurately," Kaj explained, "*I* stole the technology from you."

Kaj deposited them in the cramped mess hall of the *Chon'm*, with a burly Orion standing guard by the door. He carried a plasma shotgun cradled in the crook of one arm, and if it had not been for the sound of his breathing, Valeris could have mistaken him for an extremely lifelike sculpture. The Orion stood immobile, ignoring any attempt to engage him in conversation, and eventually Lieutenant Vaughn gave up, returning to sit at the far end of the dining table with Miller and the Vulcan.

Valeris used her time as productively as she could, poring over the data files and information they had brought with them from the *Excelsior*. She isolated herself in the data, shutting out the constant bass rumble of the ship's warp engines and the riot of stenches wafting through the ship, which threatened to overwhelm her. Still, as she worked, Valeris kept an ear open to listen to the humans.

"You think Kaj is coming back anytime soon?" asked Vaughn after a while. "We've been in here for hours."

"She said she had to visit the sickbay," said Miller.

"The major seemed well enough to me."

The commander nodded. "It's not that kind of medical attention she's getting," he noted, gesturing at his face. "Don't be surprised if she looks different next time you see her."

Vaughn frowned. "So those stories about II agents are true, then?"

"Let me put it this way: last time I saw Kaj, she didn't appear the same as she does now. Of course, she was shooting at me at the time, so I didn't get that good a look."

The lieutenant leaned closer. "For a woman who tried to kill you, you're pretty well-disposed toward her."

Miller shrugged. "This mission is nothing personal, Elias. It's just the work. Yesterday Kaj was our enemy, today she's our ally."

"It's tomorrow I'm more concerned about," admitted the other man.

"Good instinct," said Miller. "But just keep your focus on the job. You mix emotion into it, and that's what causes problems." He glanced at Valeris. "Isn't that right?"

"Undoubtedly," she replied without looking up. "But the lieutenant does raise an interesting point."

"Which is?"

"Your association with Major Kaj. I suspect it might be based on more than just exchanges of weapons fire."

Valeris had observed that Commander Miller liked to display an outward manner of casual directness, but for a moment she saw a brief flash of the man that lurked beneath that façade: the veteran covert operative and spy. "Call it mutual respect," he said. "You spend that long hunting someone, or being hunted by them, and you get to know their personality. Let's just say that Kaj and I have been playing a long game and leave it at that."

Valeris looked up at last. "Do you trust her?"

Miller's easy manner reasserted itself. "I trust Kaj to be Kaj. Same way I trust you to be you."

For a moment Valeris hesitated on the cusp of voicing her thoughts out loud: *You think you know me. You do not.*

Vaughn indicated the padd in her hand with a jut of the chin. "What is that you're reading?"

She glanced at the lieutenant. "It is your report, Mister Vaughn. Specifically, the collation of the sensor readings from the first detonation at the utility station. With the addition of data from the *Excelsior*'s sensors at the time of the second blast, I have been able to undertake a deeper analysis."

"I thought you were trained for the helm, not sciences," said Miller.

"My talents are numerous," Valeris replied with a sniff. "My minor at Starfleet Academy was in weapons technology. I am more than familiar with the function of offensive subspace munitions."

Vaughn took the padd and studied. "Isolytic weapons. Every major galactic power has banned these things . . . The Klingons and Romulans, the Federation, Tholians and Orions . . . Every time one of them is detonated, it slams the barrier between this dimension and subspace like a hammer. Next thing you know, there's fallout of spatial anomalies, warp field distortions, singularities . . ." He shook his head. "How much hate do you need to have to use something that can break space-time like glass?"

"I have observed that if any emotions have a limit, hatred is not among them." Valeris's words seemed to come from a long way away. She felt unwilling to dwell on the deeper truth of them, for fear she would touch on her own buried feelings.

"Before," said Miller, "on the *Excelsior*, you said you thought the dispersal pattern of the first blast was flawed."

She nodded. "Correct. There is a similar asymmetry to the second discharge, but it is not identical to the first." Valeris indicated the patterns on the padd. "I believe that while each isolytic device produced a powerful destructive effect, neither detonated at their full potential."

"You're saying those bombs were malfunctioning?" asked Vaughn.

Miller stared into space. "No, it's not that. I see where she's going with this. It's all to do with how the weapons were manufactured." He made a spherical shape with his hands. "Constructing an isolytic subspace weapon isn't like brewing up some bathtub chemical explosives. It's difficult work: it requires highly advanced hardware and, most of all, time." He gave a slow nod. "I think Valeris is right. I think the Thorn mishandled the weapons. They botched the construction because they were hasty. They wanted to take advantage of the situation at Da'Kel, and they couldn't wait."

"If those subspace devices had operated at maximum capacity," Valeris told them, "it is my belief that the Da'Kel III colony and everything in orbit around it would have been consumed by a spatial rupture. As it was, the isolytic reaction could not maintain a long enough period of criticality. The decay rate was too short."

They were all silent for a long moment. "A planet-killing bomb, small enough to fit inside a cargo shuttle." Vaughn was grim-faced as he said the words. "How the hell did a group of minor-league freedom fighters get hold of something that dangerous?"

"Someone is backing them," said Miller. "There's no other explanation."

From out of nowhere, a strident Klaxon began to bray, the raw-edged sound slicing through the room. Valeris's eyes snapped up to see the big Orion guard suddenly spring into motion, bringing up his plasma weapon to a ready position.

"What's going on?" called Vaughn, raising his voice to be heard over the sound of the alarm.

Miller was already on his feet. "Combat alert! We've got to get to the bridge!" He pointed toward the corridor, after the Orion. "This way!"

Valeris gathered up the padds and followed.

"I thought we had some kind of disguise for this ship?" said Vaughn. "You know, low profile and that sort of thing?"

A shuddering impact slammed up from the decking beneath their feet, and they stumbled against the wall, the lights along the corridor of the *Chon'm* flickering and buzzing from the force of the hit.

"It would appear otherwise," said Valeris as she picked herself up.

10

Had they considered the ship an honorable foe and one worthy of respect, they might have given the *Chon'm* a warning; but instead the two D-7 cruisers swept in behind the vessel, one taking the wing of the other as it fired a salvo of disruptor fire into the hull of their target.

The shape of the cargo tender—a bulky, blocky craft lacking any grace in its design—flickered and hazed as the bolts passed through it. Backwash from the energy nimbus cracked into space and the holographic veil abruptly collapsed, revealing the true form of the bird-of-prey beneath, wings outstretched in cruise configuration.

At the helm of the *Chon'm*, D'iaq was nimble and turned the agile ship quickly, barely avoiding the next pulses of shimmering green fire. The second D-7 came about and presented its bow to the smaller ship—but instead of firing its cannons, it discharged a throbbing wall of high-energy antiprotons that washed over the bird-of-prey. The pursuers were clearly well aware of their target's capabilities; until it dissipated, the antiproton wave would collapse any attempt to activate warp drive.

Only then, after they had struck the first blows and hobbled their quarry, did the commander of the attack wing deign to address the crew of the *Chon'm*.

• • •

The hatch hissed open as the bird-of-prey lurched again, and Valeris fell against Vaughn, her feet slipping out from under her. He caught her before she could strike her head on the wall of the corridor. Her body was warm through the thin sleeve of her jacket, and the randomness of the realization struck him; Vaughn had somehow expected her to be cold to the touch, as cool as Vulcan logic.

Valeris pulled away from him and followed Miller into the ship's forward pod, and Vaughn fell in behind her.

The red-orange light of the Klingon bridge was a stark contrast to the well-lit brightness of a Starfleet command deck, and with all the crossbars and armored supports it seemed cramped and utilitarian. Vaughn was reminded of the interior of an ancient iron tank he had seen in a museum on Earth, a tight space given over to the functions of movement and battle and nothing else.

On the screen, a Klingon cruiser swept past the bow of the *Chon'm*, seemingly close enough to reach out and touch.

"What now?" said Miller.

A figure at the gunnery console turned and Vaughn had to look twice to be sure who he was seeing there. It was Major Kaj, except that it was not. Her hair was gone, leaving a bald scalp framing her hard features; the color of her flesh was odd, patches of it lightened and others still the dusky shade she had been when he first saw her. But most strange was the dissolution of her cranial ridges: where there had been defined lines of bone, now there were only a few chevrons of cartilage, and her eyes . . . her eyes were now a piercing green. Kaj was no longer Klingon.

"Vaughn!" Miller called to him, and he snapped out of the moment. "Make yourself useful, Lieutenant." The commander was pointing at an empty engineering console, and he went to it.

Valeris went with him. "The warp engine," she said, scanning the Klingon text on the screen.

He nodded. Vaughn's grasp of written Klingon was basic, but he knew enough to interpret the data. The rain of antiproton energy had crippled the functions of the drive system.

"That's a new look for you," Miller was saying as Kaj crossed the bridge, giving up her station to one of her men.

She ignored him. "Gadan! Where did they come from? How could they attack us without warning?"

The stocky crewman at the primary systems console waved at the air as if dismissing a nagging insect. "Don't know, Major. They appeared out of nowhere. Their firepower is vastly superior to ours."

Valeris threw a quizzical glance at the Klingon engineer and then stepped away, finding another panel she could use. Vaughn watched her bring up the sensor logs.

"We are being hailed," said the warrior at the helm console.

Kaj spat out a guttural curse and nodded. "Let me hear it."

A booming, officious voice filled the room. *"Attention, fugitives. You are to stand down and render your vessel inert immediately, under the command of General Igdar of the Fourth Fleet. Any attempt to flee will mean your destruction. Comply now, or we will fire on you."*

"'Fugitives,'" echoed Miller. "Damn it, Kaj . . . You said you didn't see eye to eye with Igdar, but you never mentioned anything about armed ships!" He fixed her with a hard stare. "What are you not telling us?"

"D'iaq," said the major, disregarding Miller's words. "Give no reply." Her expression was stony.

"They will not hesitate," said the helmsman. "We must escape—"

"No can do," said Vaughn. "If I'm reading this right, we've got at least another ten to fifteen minutes before the engines can reinitialize. What about the holographic veil?"

"What good would that do?" said Gadan. "They are upon us. We cannot escape them . . . We never had a chance." He looked back at Kaj. "Major . . . Perhaps—"

"Perhaps *what*?" Kaj's manner shifted in a heartbeat, from controlled to boiling fury. She took a step toward the engineer's station, and Vaughn heard silence fall across the bridge as the rest of the major's crew watched and waited. *"Surrender?"* Kaj said it like a curse.

"Major Kaj, of the House of Tus'tai." The voice across the comm channel returned. *"Consider yourself under arrest. You have acted in a manner unbecoming to a Klingon warrior. You have deliberately ignored the directives of Imperial Intelligence. You will stand down now, or your crew will suffer for your folly. Respond immediately!"*

Kaj glared at the ships on the forward viewscreen. "How did they find us so quickly?" she demanded, scanning the faces in the room. "We left no trace! How did Igdar know?"

Miller faced her. "I'm going to ask you one more time: What are you not telling us, Kaj?"

She wheeled around to glare at the commander, and Vaughn saw her eyes flash. "The charges are correct," she told him. "After the second detonation, Igdar removed me from the investigation team and ordered me to stand down and return to Qo'noS. He claimed I broke protocol for reasons of personal revenge . . . That I was 'not operating in the best interests of the Empire.' As if *he* would understand the meaning of that!" Kaj looked away, searching the bridge once more. She caught Vaughn's eye, then turned past him. "My commanders, the general . . . They refused to follow the leads I found, that you confirmed, for no other reasons than petty prejudice."

Miller watched her carefully. "But it's more than that," he said. "This is *personal* for you, isn't it? It's not just about the Thorn."

Kaj gave a slow, icy nod. "Her name was Kol. Of the House of Tus'tai. My sister, the only living family to share my name. She perished aboard the station in the first attack." The major's glare could have cut through steel. "I will have vengeance for my sibling's death."

"That's why you came to us on the *Excelsior*," said Vaughn. "Because we're the only chance you have."

"I will not be denied," she growled.

"Major," said Gadan. "The crew respects your anger and

your need, but we cannot fight two battle cruisers! Even now, the general will be vectoring more ships to this location—"

"How do you know that?" Valeris's question cut through the air.

Gadan snorted. "The convict dares to interrupt me?"

Kaj turned her iron-hard gaze on the engineer. "Answer her."

He hesitated. "What?"

"How could they have found us, Gadan?" Kaj advanced on him. "We were hidden. There are a hundred ships in the space lanes of this sector. Igdar would have had to chase every single one of them to locate the *Chon'm*. Unless he already knew where to seek us."

Valeris indicated the console before her. "These logs indicate that the ship's sensor dispersal field has been deliberately attenuated. Anyone who knew what to scan for would be able to pinpoint the *Chon'm* from light-years away."

Gadan's face went crimson. "Am I dreaming? Did a Vulcan *petaQ* just accuse me of being a traitor?"

"Are you?" snarled Kaj. "How many times have you been absent from the ship in recent days, Gadan? Where were you?"

"Attending to my duties—"

"With the general?" asked D'iaq, solemn and quiet. "Swear it is not so, Engineer. Say the words."

Gadan's mouth worked, but only exasperated half sounds emerged. Then, with a flurry of motion, he tore at something concealed beneath his console and his hand returned with a heavy disruptor in it. "Curse you all," he spat. "I have a wife and a family! I won't follow one woman on a foolish personal crusade . . . I won't let my clan be disgraced by association with hers!" He aimed the gun at Kaj. "Answer the summons, Major!" Gadan snarled. "Surrender the ship and end your disobedience! You cannot defy a man like General Igdar!"

An alert tone sounded loudly from D'iaq's console. "Weapons lock," he reported. "They're going to fire."

Gadan's eyes flicked away from Kaj for a moment. "No . . . No . . . !"

It was all the time she needed. The major flicked her wrist, and something bright and silver flashed across the chamber from a hidden holster in her cuff. A metallic rod buried itself in the engineer's right eye and he let out a chattering gasp, paralyzed where he stood.

Miller came forward and tore the gun from Gadan's grip as other members of Kaj's crew pulled the traitor away.

"Get that off my bridge," she told them.

"What now?" said the commander.

Kaj dropped into the bird-of-prey's throne-like center seat. "We fight."

A ship like the *Chon'm*, whose martial prowess sprang from guile instead of the brute strength of the D-7s, was not expected to be a formidable opponent. Placed head-to-head with just one of the cruisers and denied its cloaking device, the *B'rel*-class ship would not win an engagement. Against two, destruction was assured.

The commanders of the cruisers waited for the surrender they knew would come. Any other response would be suicide.

And so Kaj surprised them both with her defiance. At her order, maximum power was dumped into the impulse drives and the bird-of-prey shot forward, passing under the command pod of the closest D-7 and along the line of its keel. The major ordered D'iaq to elevate the wingtip cannons as far as they would allow, and as the *Chon'm* shot by, a cascade of blind-fire tore through the other ship's shields at point-blank range, scoring a dozen hits.

Had the captain of the second cruiser followed protocol, he would have waited to engage the bird-of-prey in clear space. But he was one of General Igdar's inner circle: he knew Kaj and he distrusted her. The general had made it very clear to the captain that things would be better if the troublesome intelligence agent met with an unfortunate end; if that included her crew into the bargain, then so much the better. The only thing of value here was Kaj's ship.

The instant his gunner had the first ghost of a targeting solution, he gave the order to fire a photon torpedo. The shot erupted from the prow of the D-7, glowing fire-red like a cinder thrown from a volcanic eruption. The torpedo crossed the distance to the target, and the bird-of-prey saw it coming, veering down and away to avoid the detonation,

Set to a proximity fuse, the photon torpedo exploded clear of the target vessel, but close enough to strike it with the concussion wave, and close enough that the other pursuit ship took a good measure of the blast. The captain cared little for his cohort: it was Kaj he wanted, the major's head as his kill and the general's gratitude at his feet.

The *Chon'm* took the brunt of the explosion and spun away, trailing fumes. The halo of energy protecting it flickered and faded.

"Our shields have failed," called the helmsman, through the thin wisps of smoke that curled in the air. "They were eager with the shot . . ."

"Not enough to save us from it," Kaj replied, peering at a console. "Get those barriers back up—quickly!"

Vaughn tried to obey the order, but the Klingon controls were counterintuitive to him, almost as though they were fighting him with every action he took. "Damn this thing," he muttered under his breath.

Valeris came to his aid. "Use this protocol," she said, working the panel as if she had been born to it. "It will circumvent the initiator lock-outs."

"How do you know so much about Klingon systems?" he asked.

"I am a quick study," she replied. "And I learned early on that it is important to understand the ways of your enemies."

He jerked a thumb at the main viewscreen. "Our enemies are out there!"

"Perhaps," she replied. Valeris turned away and addressed

Kaj: "The shield emitters will not cycle. Manual override is required."

"Engine room," Kaj barked into her communicator. "Status!"

Over the open channel came the sound of beam weapons and the cry of someone mortally wounded. At Kaj's side, Miller's face turned grave. "They must have had a boarding party on the pads, ready to beam over the moment the shields collapsed."

"We can't allow them—"

Miller waved Kaj into silence and gestured with the phaser he had taken from Gadan. "Don't worry, I'll get down there, see what I can do."

Kaj gave him a nod. "Take Urkoj with you," she said, indicating the big Orion. "And be careful. We have no idea how many of them came aboard."

Vaughn looked up as Miller dashed past him. "Commander?"

The other officer threw him a nod. "Hold the fort up here, Lieutenant. We're in this together now." Miller vanished through the hatch, the burly Orion at his side.

"We cannot wait for the commander to secure the engine room," said Valeris. "Every second we are unprotected, we are vulnerable to attack."

"Again she voices the blindingly evident truth as if we are all simple children," Kaj snapped. "If you have a solution, convict, speak! Otherwise, be silent!"

"I have an idea," Vaughn broke in. "Give me main power control at this panel. I think I can divert power from another system and kick-start the shield emitters."

Valeris raised an eyebrow. "Given your lack of familiarity with these systems, I doubt you would be able to achieve that."

"Which is why you're going to parallel me," he told her. "But we need to do this now, Major."

"If the human makes a single error, the whole ship will go dark," said the helmsman, shooting Vaughn a frosty look. "We'll be adrift. Nothing but a floating target."

"Second cruiser is coming back around," shouted one of the other crewmen. "Eight hundred *qell'qampu'* and closing."

Kaj frowned. "Give the lieutenant what he requires," she said. "Just be certain of this, Vaughn. If you fail me, your body will strike the deck a heartbeat after hers." She nodded toward Valeris.

"Right," he replied. "So. No pressure, then."

"Six hundred *qell'qampu'* and closing," came the call.

Vaughn leaned in and stared at the strings of bloodred cuneiform characters teeming on the screen before him. He placed his hands on the panel and went to work.

Despite his size, Urkoj was swift on his big feet, and he charged down the inclined corridor and into the *Chon'm*'s engine chamber at full tilt. He blasted down a Klingon warrior in full Defense Force combat armor and spun around to engage another in close combat, deflecting blows from a *bat'leth* with the long stock of his plasma shotgun.

Miller took in the room in a single glance: Kaj's crew was fighting hand to hand with the boarding party, fists and blades flying back and forth in an angry melee. He fired a shot at a warrior looming over a crewman with a wicked-looking blade, and the Klingon fell. Something blurred at the edge of his vision and he ducked, narrowly escaping the slashing cut of a serrated *yan* sword. The blade was curved, like some monstrous pirate's cutlass, and the hand behind it belonged to a towering Klingon with a face that was a web of scars. The *yan* spun and danced, coming at him again. Miller fired a brace of phaser bolts, but they went wide, and he was too afraid to cut loose with the weapon for fear of a missed shot striking some vital engine component.

The tip of the sword slashed at him and he dodged—but not enough to escape it completely. Miller snarled in pain as the blade made a shallow cut across his bicep, the agony jerking the phaser from his grip. It was lost through a gridded deck plate.

The Starfleet officer threw himself out of the path of the

attack that followed, snagging a heavy hyperspanner where it lay atop a tool chest. He brought up the spanner to block the fall of the sword and they connected, sparks flying.

The *Chon'm* sped away, the thruster grid flaring. Behind it, the damaged D-7 began a sluggish turn to follow, but lucky hits from the disruptor barrage had lit fires on the lower decks, and it was slow to react. The other cruiser had no such concerns, banking as it moved to keep the bird-of-prey centered in the sights of its forward weapons. The *Chon'm*'s cannons threw a brace of shots against their enemy, but they slammed harmlessly into the D-7's forward shields, the lethal energy dissipating in flares of radiation. The only advantage the smaller ship could call upon now was its speed and agility, but they could only run so far, so fast.

Lines of disruptor fire reached out, raking claws of flame across the wings of the raptor-like scoutship.

Valeris felt the energy bolt strike the *Chon'm* as if it were a crash of distant thunder echoing up through the ship. Surge baffles flared in gouts of sooty smoke and fat blue sparks, and she heard Vaughn utter a human curse word under his breath.

"Keep us out of their range," Kaj ordered. "If they land a direct hit on us, we will be lost!"

"Major," called one of the other crewmen, a warning in his tone. "I read an energy surge . . . A second boarding party—"

The Klingon had barely spoken the words before three pillars of red light hazed into being at different points on the bridge. Warriors in combat armor and bearing edged weapons attacked.

One of them, a female with a wild topknot of night-black hair, was closest to Vaughn, and she threw herself at him, bringing down a blade-chain array that glittered in the gloom of the bridge. The lieutenant barely avoided a sweeping cut that would have opened his throat, but the blunt, heavy weight at the opposite end of the black iron chain followed and creased his scalp. Vaughn grunted in pain and stumbled to the deck.

Then the Klingon trooper came at the Vulcan, bloodlust in her eyes. Some higher, more analytical portion of Valeris's mind registered the crudity of the weapons the boarding party carried. Phasers or disruptors would have ended any opposition to them within seconds, a handful of precise shots killing anyone who stood in their way; but instead they fought with weapons that were more suited to boarding actions in an age of sailcloth and galleons. There was some logic to the use of such archaic technology, she had to concede—a missed hit from a blade could never open a hull to space—but Valeris doubted that was why the Klingons were using them. They were a race that liked the taste of blood. They wanted to prolong the moment of the kill, savor it . . .

In the close confines of the *Chon'm*'s bridge, the blade-chain whistled as the warrior woman spun it up into an attack posture. Lacking anything to parry the stroke, Valeris dodged as best she could. The Klingon repeated the pattern she had used on the lieutenant, and the Vulcan kept clear of the blows. As the heavy weight on the end of the weapon hummed past her face, Valeris threw out her hand to catch it.

The barbed orb of black iron smacked into her palm and drew emerald blood. The Klingon tried to yank away the chain, but Valeris pulled back, and for a brief moment the women were in a tug-of-war. Although she was slighter in build than her opponent, Valeris resisted, muscles bunching. Vulcan strength was not to be underestimated.

The warrior spat in fury and brought up her other hand. Valeris saw the glitter of a pronged blade as it rose toward her face. The Klingon had backed her up against a console, and she had nowhere to go.

Then, from nowhere, a patch of stark purple blossomed on her opponent's chest, and Valeris saw the woman stagger. The Klingon choked, and dark, arterial blood trickled from her lips. Her attacker dropped to the deck, revealing the hilt of a slender throwing knife protruding from the small of her back.

Valeris looked up as Kaj stalked across the bridge to recover her weapon. The rest of the boarding party were already dead, the metallic tang of spilled blood harsh in the air.

The major took her weapon and wiped it clean. "Don't look so shocked, convict," she said. "You're on my ship, so I keep you alive."

Valeris eyed her. "You did not do so for any reasons of honor. You did not let me perish because you need me. Do not insult us both by suggesting otherwise."

Kaj hesitated, as if she were considering executing Valeris there and then; but then she turned away and returned to the command throne. "True," she said over her shoulder. "So don't make me regret my decision. Get the human to his feet and raise the shields, or we will *all* die."

Valeris bent to help Vaughn rise shakily from the floor, and they set to work.

Distantly, Miller registered the sound of the bird-of-prey's warp core drawing more power, and the ship shivered slightly, lights dimming. *Deflectors are back up,* he guessed. That meant that, for now, the *Chon'm* was protected from the arrival of any more troopers from the pursuit ships—but it did nothing to assist him with the ongoing melee in the engine room.

The hyperspanner in his hand bore scrapes and gouges of bright metal where the Klingon swordsman had struck it again and again. Miller fought back, making solid hits on the warrior's head and neck, but his opponent seemed unaffected. There was nothing in the Klingon's eyes but violence.

The commander feinted back a step and the Klingon came on, eager to draw blood from him. At the last second Miller shot out his arm and used the massive spanner in a stabbing motion, jamming it hard into the soft tissues of the warrior's throat. Something gave a wet crack and the swordsman let out a strangled howl and clutched at his neck.

"Give it up!" Miller demanded, panting with effort. "Lay down the sword!"

"Die first," said the Klingon, choking out every word.

Miller wasn't sure if that was a promise or a threat, but then the *yan* blade rose high once more, and the question became moot.

Vaughn's head was ringing like a struck bell, the humming pain from the blow echoing thorough the bones of his skull. His hands seemed to move of their own accord across the systems panel, setting the cycle to reactivate the shield emitters, running through the motions with Valeris paralleling him every step of the way. She didn't wait for Kaj's permission: she touched the activator pad and a long second passed in silence. It seemed like an eternity, but then the shields re-formed and the major gave a sharp hiss. Elias decided that had to be some kind of compliment.

His timing was perfect. Light flared as disruptor bolts crackled through the void and the *Chon'm* was at their point of confluence: if the ship had been unprotected a few seconds longer, they would have been vapor and fragments.

Red Alert signals were flashing all around him, and the smoky air of the bridge was split by loud, braying alarms. Or perhaps the noise and the lights were all in his head, an echo of the damage done by the strike to his skull.

He blinked at the power curves displayed before him and heard a voice say, "We can't take much more of this." It took a second for him to register that the words were his.

"I am open to all suggestions," snarled Kaj.

Vaughn shook his head and immediately regretted it. He tried to marshal his thoughts, and his brow knitted. "We . . . need to outthink them. Can't do this as a stand-up fight . . ." He blinked owlishly at the panel, his thoughts clearing. "Wait. The holo-veil . . ."

"Useless," began D'iaq.

"No," Vaughn insisted. "We're not going to use it to hide." He looked toward Kaj. "How much energy can the holo-matrix on the hull put out in one go?"

"It's not a weapon," said the Klingon. "What are you thinking, Lieutenant?"

"My head is killing me," he told her. "We can spread that around a little."

"Your words make no sense." D'iaq scowled.

Vaughn shot the crewman a look. "Let me put it another way," he said. "Do you know what a flash bomb is?"

The damaged bird-of-prey began to drift. The cherry-red glow from the impulse manifolds dimmed, becoming dull yellow as power bled off and the scoutship listed to starboard. The *Chon'm* was no longer accelerating; instead it was directionless, as if there were no one at the helm.

That was how it appeared to the pursuit vessels. The leading D-7 cruiser moved in, with the second vessel now coming up to join in formation. There was hesitation. Neither ship could communicate with the boarding parties they had transported to the target, so they could not know if their men had taken the craft. A steady rattle of jamming kept any signal from reaching the cruisers. The commander of the lead vessel waited, watching as his gunnery officers found firing solutions and trained all their weapons on the bird-of-prey. It was suddenly an easy target, but like a pair of careful predators, the pursuit ships were wary.

General Igdar's orders had been direct. Major Kaj was wanted dead or alive, but preferably dead. Agents of Imperial Intelligence had a tendency to be survivors—they were trained that way—and it was better to see them terminated with extreme prejudice than chance a last-second revival or escape from custody. Such things had happened often.

But the ship . . . The ship was a different matter. One of a handful of experimental prototypes built in a secret manufactory that had since been obliterated, the *Chon'm* would be a valuable prize for any officer who could take her intact. It was that greed that slowed the commander's impulse to order a barrage of photon torpedoes and disruptor blasts, a hesitation that now turned to ruin.

It happened with great speed. In the first few seconds the levels of power across the *Chon'm* dipped, and the ratings working the scanner hoods aboard the D-7s saw what looked like the start of a cascade systems failure. They reported this to their captains.

But the energy was not lost: it was being rerouted, diverted from the impulse drive and life support, the weapons grid, and any other system that could spare it. With the help of Valeris and Kaj, Elias Vaughn assembled a holographic program on the fly, something simple in concept but complex in execution.

And after a few moments it was ready. The cruisers were poised over the scoutship like winged carrion eaters hovering above a dying man. They came closer.

The system of the *Chon'm*'s holo-matrix was designed to simulate the three-dimensional image of another vessel in perfect detail; the plan to use it was crude and risky, but it was inspired.

Every holographic emitter on the ship's hull released a burst of light at the exact same instant, a pulse of white auroral display that blazed like a starburst. The light frequency was harsh, and through Valeris's ministrations it had been carefully tuned to a wave band that matched the sensing apertures of the detector grids mounted on the D-7s.

A flash of brilliant, intense color dazzled the pursuit vessels, momentarily overloading their optical sensors and radiation-ranging gear. Automatic baffles cut down the brightness of the flash as it washed across the bridges of the two cruisers, but the glare was so bright that a handful of crew, unfortunate enough to be looking out of viewports at the wrong moment, found themselves blinded. The searing glare lit the dark for less than a few seconds, but it was enough. The crew of the *Chon'm* had shut off their sensors, blindfolding their ship to survive the pulse. Now they shrugged off the pretense and the bird-of-prey's engines went live with power.

The smaller ship shot away as lances of particle-beam energy extended outward, stabbing sightlessly toward where the *Chon'm* had been. Kaj's vessel wove through the rain of fire and left its enemies reeling behind it.

• • •

"It actually worked," said D'iaq, half disbelieving. "*Kai* the human!"

Vaughn seemed to be capable of only a shallow nod. Valeris noted he seemed pale and sluggish, and she wondered if he was suffering the first effects of a concussion. She had to remind herself that human skulls were not as resilient as those of her species or the Klingons.

"Don't praise him yet," said Kaj, scowling at her console. "That ploy was clever, but it won't last long. We need to make warp speed now, or else they will catch up and run us down once again . . ."

D'iaq worked the helm panel. "Major, there's a field of cometary fragments two points off our current course. If we can swing closer, we can use the backscatter effect there to break up our ion trail."

"That would buy us some valuable time," Valeris noted.

"I'm so glad you agree," Kaj said, sneering slightly. "Do it, D'iaq. Put all power to the engines. I want you to wring every fraction of speed from this ship."

"Understood," said the helmsman, and he bent forward, almost as if he were encouraging the ship along with him.

On the viewscreen, the star field shifted as the *Chon'm* accelerated away from the stalled cruisers. Valeris turned back to the major. "Commander Miller—"

The Klingon waved her away. "Engine room," she called, speaking into the intership. "Report! Is the warp core secure?"

From the speaker grille came the sound of a strangled scream as a throat was cut with a blade.

Miller sensed the ship was in motion, but he couldn't give the thought any more than the most cursory consideration. Over by the main controls beneath the matter-antimatter stack, he saw Klingon fighting Klingon as one of Kaj's men tussled with a tall warrior in armor. A *bat'leth*, rimed in dark blood, cut a brutal upward arc, and the crewman died with a cry as he was opened by a wound that started at his sternum and ended at his jaw.

The Starfleet officer had his own fight to deal with. The snarling Defense Force trooper with the *yan* sword was on him with every step, trying to block his path or force him into the corners of the cramped engine room. The light of a berserker's rage was in the warrior's eyes, and Miller knew that a single mistake would cost him.

He tried a new tactic, dodging toward a support stanchion as the sword danced in the smoky air. Miller grabbed at the sloped support with one hand and leapt to it, scrambling up the steep angle, his boots taking purchase on the massive rivet heads that stuck out of them.

The Klingon swore at him, cursing him for fleeing like a coward, and overextended with the blade in his haste to strike a killing blow. The razor-edged *yan* struck the metal support and the sword bit, a good two centimeters of it cutting into the stanchion before it stopped dead. The warrior tugged at his weapon, but it refused to budge.

Miller took the opportunity and let go of this handhold, dropping back to the deck with the battered hyperspanner in his grip. With all the brute force he could muster, the commander brought the heavy tool down on the flat of the shining blade. The weapon, stressed beyond its tolerances, snapped with a sound like breaking bones. Most of the blade remained stuck in the stanchion, and the rest of it, the hilt and pommel, clattered to the deck.

Miller didn't arrest the momentum; he let the club carry on and used it to swat away his adversary. The Klingon took the broad head of the spanner in the face and dropped hard, a fan of blood sputtering from his nostrils.

At last, Miller tossed the tool away, his hands stinging with the impact of his blow, and he panted, drawing in breaths of hot air. He glanced around, seeing that the invasion had been stalled, that the assault team from the pursuit ships had all been neutralized. The warp core's pulses quickened, casting fiery light through the chamber, and he caught the eye of Kaj's Orion enforcer. "Urkoj," he gasped. "Tell the major we're secure."

The commander began to say something else, but his words fell away as he caught the sound of boots scraping over the gridded deck plates. Miller turned as the warrior he had just put down came hurtling at him, blinded by a mask of blood from the cuts on his face. He tried to block the attack, but the Klingon had the blunt stub of the broken *yan* blade in his hand, and he buried it in Miller's stomach, right down to the guard.

Miller struggled with the rage-blinded Klingon, fighting to stop him from ripping the jagged metal up, cutting him deeper. Pain like he had never felt ran through him, and it was cold, like deep space.

A green shape blurred at the edge of his vision and Urkoj was suddenly there, slamming the Klingon away with the butt of his heavy plasma shotgun. Miller stumbled and fell back against the stanchion as the Orion spun his weapon around and executed the swordsman with a point-blank shot.

His eyes fell to the alien blade protruding from his belly, and the blossom of crimson growing across his tunic. "I . . . can't die here," he managed.

But even as the words left his mouth, he realized that choice had been taken from him.

Vaughn entered the *Chon'm*'s engine room at a run, Valeris a few footsteps behind him. His boots clanged across the metal as he sprinted to where Miller lay slumped against a heavy metal support. The first thing that struck him was the thick, coppery scent of the other man's blood.

Valeris had secured a Klingon medical kit and she produced a tricorder, dispassionately sweeping it back and forth to gain a reading on the commander's condition.

It was hardly worth the effort, though. The man's teak-dark skin had a pallor that horrified the lieutenant, and he was drenched in sweat. Miller's breath was coming in short, tight chugs that pained him with every inhalation.

"This isn't how it's supposed to go," Miller managed. "It's all wrong, Elias."

Vaughn shot a look over his shoulder. Major Kaj had followed them down the corridor, and she stood in grave conversation with the burly Orion. He looked back and fell into a crouch. "Sir, you're badly hurt. We need to get you into a stasis chamber . . ."

"If we move him, he will die," Valeris said flatly.

"That's gonna happen no matter what," Miller retorted. He groaned with pain. "Elias. Listen to me." With difficulty, the commander fished in a pocket and produced a small padd-style device. "The code is 'reindeer flotilla,' right? Say it back to me."

Vaughn did as he was told, and Miller pressed the unit into his hands. "Sir, I don't—"

"Operational command of this mission now falls to you, Lieutenant," he went on. "You're going to see this through, Elias. Through to the end. Remember what I said to you in the travel pod?"

" 'Have the conviction to follow your instincts.' " Vaughn nodded. " 'Wherever they take you.' "

Miller nodded toward the Vulcan, the simple action causing him great pain. "She's your responsibility now. Don't screw it up."

Vaughn looked to Valeris and met her gaze. Without warning, the tricorder in her hand emitted a long, uninterrupted tone.

When he turned back to Miller, the commander's eyes were still open, staring blankly at the throbbing colors of the warp core.

"He died well," Vaughn heard Kaj say. "In battle. With honor."

The lieutenant came to his feet, propelled by a swell of anger. "He's dead because of you," he snapped. "Because you didn't tell us Igdar had death squads looking out for this ship! Because you had a traitor on your bridge crew!"

Urkoj snarled and took a warning step forward, but Kaj stopped him. "Take care, human. Miller earned my respect, and so he had it in return." She nodded toward Valeris. "And I need her. But you? That is a different matter."

"*Respect?*" he spat. "The man is dead! This mission is blown!"

"Incorrect," said the Vulcan. "Commander Miller's demise is regrettable. But we can still proceed without him. He knew that."

Vaughn's hands tightened into fists. *This is turning into a nightmare,* he thought. *Everything is going wrong.*

I'm not ready for this.

At a nod from the major, Urkoj came forward and gathered up Miller's body. "With care!" she demanded. "He was an honorable enemy, and a willing ally. The commander's remains will be treated with the reverence they deserve."

Vaughn cast his gaze down at the patch of blood on the deck and then turned away. He found the Vulcan woman studying him. "Perhaps," she began, "I could—"

"Take charge?" he cut her off. "Don't push your luck, Valeris."

"That was not my intention," she told him. "I wished only to remind you—and Major Kaj—that our mission will require all our skill sets to meet with success. We must work together to find the terrorists that attacked Da'Kel. Without the commander, that is truer than ever."

Kaj grunted. "I find myself in rare agreement with the convict." The agent studied Vaughn with her peculiarly modified, not-quite-Klingon features. "We three cannot afford the luxury of hating one another anymore. Our shared endeavor grows beyond that petty concern."

Vaughn closed his eyes and shut out his doubts. "Agreed."

11

U.S.S. BonHomme Richard, NCC-1776
Sol System
Sector 001, United Federation of Planets

"I once met an Academy cadet who asked me to define the word 'duty.'" The voice carried out across the rec deck, over the sea of wine-dark uniforms and upturned faces, all of them listening intently to the speaker. A hover-drone was relaying an image of him to the screen on the high wall above, but the officers and enlisted men were focused on the man himself. They wanted to see him, to look him in the eyes. They wanted to be able to tell people that they had stood in the same room as James T. Kirk.

The captain gave a crooked smile as he remembered. "I'm not a philosopher," he went on. "And there are a thousand answers to that question. So I went with the one that was the closest to my experience. I told the cadet that for a Starfleet officer, 'duty' means 'challenge.' It can be a myriad of other things, but challenge is at the heart of the duty we perform." Kirk touched the insignia on his chest. "It's at the heart of the oath we've sworn, that gives us permission to wear this."

Ensign Valeris listened intently, hanging on the man's every word. There was a polite mutter of applause from some of the *BonHomme Richard*'s senior officers, and she noticed the young executive officer, Commander Mancuso, nodding and smiling. Perhaps he had been the cadet Kirk spoke of.

The captain's gaze crossed the assembled group. Like Valeris, many of the assembled officers and noncoms were new graduates from Starfleet Academy, fresh from training and ready to take on their first deep-space assignment. The sense of anticipation in the air was palpable. The *BonHomme Richard* had recently completed a series of refits and upgrades at the Utopia Planitia yards, and her new crew marked the beginning of a new lease on life for the starship.

"I remember when I served my tour on this ship as a junior officer. It was almost three decades ago . . ." Kirk grinned. "I'm dating myself. But I stood where you do now, and I heard another visiting captain say something similar. And it is as true now as it was then." Valeris saw her commanding officer, Captain Pollard, return the man's respectful nod.

"You *will* be challenged," he told them. "Have no doubt about it, you and your shipmates will be tested in ways you cannot begin to prepare for. But I have every faith in you, and I have no doubts each and every one of you will rise to meet whatever comes. You've been trained by the best instructors in the galaxy. Your ship is state-of-the-art. All you need do is to have faith in yourselves. Look around you, at the officers and crewmen who stand shoulder to shoulder with you. Trust them. Learn by doing." He gave a nod. "And I know you'll make us proud."

The applause came again, and this time Valeris joined in, as it was expected of her. Captain Kirk's words were simple and direct, exactly what she had anticipated from the man, and yet they clearly stirred the hearts of the men and women who stood with her. She was forced to admit that Kirk's charisma was more than evident; he seemed every bit the legend.

Respect, especially for non-Vulcans, did not come easily to Valeris, but James T. Kirk had impressed her. At first she had doubted that the reality could match the myth that surrounded the captain of the *Enterprise*—but truth was often stranger than fiction. Kirk talked of challenges, and he knew whereof he spoke. This was an officer who had stood toe-to-toe with the Federation's greatest enemies in the Klingon Empire and defeated them on many occasions, who had lost his son, his friends, his ship, in battle with them and yet never faltered. Valeris considered her admiration for him to be fully deserved and not at all rooted in emotion.

Pollard and Mancuso stepped up to speak, shaking Kirk's hand as the formal part of the launch ceremony approached its conclusion. Valeris listened at a distance to their words of encouragement, instead watching Kirk as he took his seat and nodded to the captain's speech.

As she watched him, the ensign could not let go of the disappointment she felt at where she found herself, the lingering dissatisfaction. The *BonHomme Richard* was a fine ship, but it was not the flagship. Not Kirk's *Enterprise*.

It was not what Valeris wanted.

The tone of the gathering changed as Captain Pollard gave the order to stand easy and the assembled crew broke up into smaller groups, grazing at the tables of finger foods or sampling glasses of synthehol wine. Valeris accepted a flute of the sparkling liquid only for reasons of social convention, leading with it as she quickly and carefully navigated across the recreation deck, toward the area near one of the light-cube tables. She could see only the back of Captain Kirk's head. He was already surrounded by a cluster of younger officers, all of whom wanted a moment of his time.

Valeris wanted the same. Listening to Kirk speak was one thing, but she wanted to truly meet the man, to gain some sense of him. She considered what she might say to him as an opening conversational gambit; it should be something he would respond to, something that would impress him—

"Valeris."

She felt the ghost of a familiar aura and turned to find Spock standing nearby, his hands folded behind his back. He seemed to have appeared from out of nowhere. "Captain." She nodded coolly to her teacher. "I was not aware you were a guest at this ceremony."

Spock inclined his head toward Kirk. "I am the captain's . . . plus-one."

"Of course." Valeris deposited her untouched glass of wine on the tray of a passing server and turned all of her attention on the other Vulcan. "It has been some time since we spoke," she went on. A gossamer trace of ill mood gathered in her. In truth, Spock had been distant for some time, his attention lessening toward her as other duties took up the bulk of his time. She understood the reality of the situation—that as a seasoned senior officer his expertise was often in great demand—yet, there remained a small kernel of dissatisfaction within her. Spock had done much to mentor her admission to Starfleet at the start, but recently contact between them had lessened to almost nothing. She went on, the question pressing at her: "You were not present at my graduation ceremony at Starfleet Academy . . ."

"I was detained. A secure conference with the Klingon ambassador," he noted. "A regrettable absence. I was gratified to learn that you passed at the top of your class. Well done, Valeris."

"In no small part, I have your guidance to thank for that," she admitted. "But it appears that I have not done well enough."

Spock raised an eyebrow. "You are the first Vulcan to achieve such a position of academic excellence. That merit in itself is a valuable achievement."

"Some would not agree." Even after hundreds of years, there were still many Vulcans who considered Starfleet to be a human-centric organization of lesser value than the more esoteric, academic pursuits of the Vulcan Science Academy and other, similar institutions. Valeris came from a family that shared such a viewpoint. She continued: "I must also question the validity of my . . . achievement. For all its apparent value, it did not earn me the posting I requested."

"The *Enterprise* . . ." Spock said, sounding out the name of the ship. His gaze drifted to Kirk, who stood telling some story, the captain's hands forming shapes in the air; then he looked back. "You are unsatisfied with your position aboard the *BonHomme Richard,* but your tour aboard this vessel has yet to commence. Do you have an issue with Captain Pollard that I should be aware of?"

She shook her head. "No. Captain Pollard and his crew are all adequate officers. I respect their skills."

"Do you?" Spock asked, without weight.

Valeris went on, ignoring the implication. "Given my graduation performance, I can only assume there is some factor I did not consider that prevented my assignment to the *Enterprise* as a helm officer. Perhaps you have knowledge of why my request was denied?"

She let the question lie between them. It was almost an accusation. Valeris had performed exceptionally well; she had assumed—no, she had *expected*—that she would be rewarded with a posting aboard the flagship. A chance to serve directly with Kirk, with some of the best officers ever to wear the uniform. It seemed right. But instead she was here, on a ship about to embark on a mission to map supernova remnants in a backwater corner of the Beta Quadrant.

"My sponsorship of your application to the Academy is a matter of public record, Valeris. As with Saavik before you, I saw the potential in you to become an exceptional Starfleet officer."

A tiny flash of irritation registered at the mention of the other woman. Valeris dismissed it immediately. She had first met Spock's protégée on Vulcan some five years ago, in the province of Raal. At the time, Valeris had been considering the direction of her life; her parents were steadily propelling her toward a future that followed in their footsteps as part of the Diplomatic Corps. But her frustrations with what she saw as the slow pace and weak manner of the Federation's handling of the affairs of state made that course less and less attractive to her.

It was only after crossing paths with Saavik that Starfleet had seemed like a viable career choice. After all, if a woman rescued as a feral child from the ruins of a desolate prison world could garner a commission in the fleet, then it was clearly well within Valeris's capability.

It seemed obvious that a full-blooded Vulcan would be

able to improve upon the performance of a half-Romulan. It had always been her opinion that, unlike Spock, Saavik had never truly been able to grow beyond her non-Vulcan traits.

"For you to reach your potential, you must do it alone," he concluded.

"I have," she told him. "I will."

Spock nodded. "I have never doubted so. But it is important that your career be free of any suggestion of . . . partiality."

Valeris stiffened. *Was he saying that he turned down her application to the* Enterprise? *Had Spock denied her what she wanted, what she deserved, for the sake of reputation?* "Of course," she replied woodenly. The realization struck her hard. On some level, it felt like a betrayal.

The ensign heard a peal of human laughter and her gaze flicked back to Kirk. He was shaking hands with Pollard and Mancuso, saying his farewells, and as she watched, he stepped away, heading toward the turbolift bank.

When she turned back, Spock was watching her intently. "If I were human," he ventured, "I would say I was proud of your accomplishments, Valeris."

"But you are not," she told him. "And I do not require such platitudes to bolster my sense of self-worth. I believe I am quite capable of measuring that myself." Valeris continued before Spock could respond. "I will be assigned to the *Enterprise* in due course," she said, as if the statement were already undeniable fact. "And from there I will take the first steps to a command of my own."

"An admirable goal," Spock replied, "and a good challenge to any new officer."

"As Captain Kirk said, it is our duty is to be challenged." She matched his gaze, daring him to question her words.

But instead he only nodded. "It was agreeable to see you again. I must depart, as my duties require me once more." Spock paused. "I will leave you with a few words of advice, if I may."

"Go on."

"Do not allow your reach to exceed your grasp. The

captain was correct in his definition of the nature of duty, but he also said that it supports many others—and one of those is *service*. Always remember that the Starfleet oath means we serve the good of others. Our own wants and needs must always be subordinate to that."

"Of course," she replied, but her answer was rote and without conviction.

Spock raised his hand in the Vulcan salute. "Live long and prosper, Valeris."

"I intend to," she told him, returning the gesture.

12

The bright, sodium-white beam cast by the Klingon flashlight threw a pool of stark color over the frost-coated walls of the metal corridor. The air was thin, enough to carry a wisp of vapor from the exhalations of their lungs but not enough to support sustained breathing. Like the rest of the landing party from the *Chon'm,* Valeris wore a breather mask over her face, with a hose that snaked to a weighty support pod on her belt. The mask reeked of old sweat and polymers, but she ignored the smells, focusing her will to expunge them from her thoughts. There were far more serious concerns that required her full attention.

She picked her way across the freezing deck plates, careful to avoid the patches of black ice that could rob her boots of all traction. At a rough estimate, Xand Depot had been occupied sometime within the last ten Standard days. After their departure, those who had been here had left the extant life support mechanisms to cycle down to a dormant state. With only the light of distant stars touching the patched and barely functional solar arrays, the power running through the station was next to nothing.

Valeris held her tricorder out in front of her, the purring of the sensor oddly loud in the creaking metal spaces. A steady train of null data scrolled down the screen of the sensing device—nothing but one empty, abandoned compartment after another, sections left open to the void or cut to the bare bones by salvagers. Xand Depot was empty.

She glanced over her shoulder to where Lieutenant Vaughn and Kaj's Orion thug followed in her footsteps. Urkoj wore a set of low-light goggles and a heavy survival mask; Vaughn had the same gear as Valeris, but the beam from his flashlight made only desultory progress along the ground near his feet.

"Lieutenant?" she said, the mask muffling her words. "Any readings?"

He glared at his tricorder, the light from the display playing on his grim expression. "Nothing. Same as the last time you asked me." Vaughn fixed her with a look. "I don't know what kind of game you're playing here, but this place is abandoned. The Thorn aren't here. We can't be sure they ever *were*."

"I am sure," she told him. It had been some time since Valeris had come to this place, but the memory of the journey—moving through cutouts and blinds, her covert orders from Cartwright erased from all records, her passage to the border zone kept secret—was strong.

Seeing the derelict station from the bridge of the *Chon'm* had immediately brought it back to her; on some level she had been concerned that Xand Depot would not be where she expected it to be, or perhaps destroyed by the Thorn after the collapse of the Gorkon conspiracy, to cover their tracks. There had been a good chance she would be wrong about the location. Finding the old Kriosian hideout was the last card she had to play, and Valeris had no doubt that Major Kaj would cut short what little liberty she had, if this lead proved worthless.

That still might occur, she thought. As soon as the bird-of-prey closed to sensor range, it became clear that nothing lived on Xand Depot. Vaughn suggested that a scanner blind might be in use, but Valeris suspected otherwise; she kept that to herself, however. She did not wish to give Kaj additional cause to exercise her ire.

They transported across in four teams of three, Kaj sending Urkoj to watch Vaughn and Valeris closely, and they began a deck-by-deck survey of the station. The major's second, the helmsman D'iaq, had called in some twenty minutes earlier to report a find: remnants of Klingon fleet-issue ration packs and other detritus, but nothing else.

The *Thorn* *had* been here; she was certain of it. But they were long gone now, and with them any chance for Valeris to prove her worth to Kaj and Vaughn. The Klingon would want to wring her mind for every last piece of information and then discard her, and the Vulcan wondered if Vaughn would do anything to stop that. The lieutenant was morose and sullen over the brutal killing of Commander Miller, and he appeared more concerned with his own circumstances than anyone else's. He was now the ranking Starfleet presence on this mission—such as it was—and Vaughn appeared to be in over his head. Valeris's thoughts turned again to possible escape ploys.

Ahead, the corridor ended in a hatchway that had been left in the open position. Beyond the threshold, Valeris's flashlight passed over dull steel shapes like the limbs of a robotic insect. They were manipulators, designed for carrying and handling hazardous cargo; but it was clear from the bright scars of recent welds they had been modified for different duties.

The tricorder in Valeris's hand ticked and she glanced at it. As Vaughn drew level with her, his scanner emitted the same tone.

Urkoj immediately brought his weapon up, but the lieutenant waved him away. "Take it easy, big man." He looked at Valeris. "You getting that?"

She nodded once. "Exotic particle traces, from inside that chamber."

"Dangerous?"

She gave another nod. "With extended exposure, quite so. I estimate we can remain inside for no more than fifteen-point-six-two minutes at a time." Valeris entered the room, and Vaughn followed gingerly after her. The Orion hesitated at the hatchway, kneading the grip of his plasma gun and frowning.

Inside, the dynamics of the room became clearer. There were locations where force field generators had been emplaced, others where thick barriers of radiation-dampening metals stood around workstations and the tables beneath the manipulator arms. Valeris took it all in; her immediate impression was one of a manufacturing center.

Vaughn saw it too. "What were they building in here?"

The tricorders were humming now, the readings peaking. The deeper they ventured into the chamber, the stronger the particle density became. Valeris took a few steps and held up a hand to halt the lieutenant. "That is far enough. Beyond this point there exists a viable risk of tissue damage."

The human turned in a slow circle, letting the sensors sample the cold air. "I'm reading decay signatures from tetryons and verterons. Those are by-products of subspace effects . . ."

"Agreed." Valeris adjusted the sensing envelope on her tricorder and mapped the dispersal of the emissions.

"Was there some kind of radiation surge in here?"

"No. The particle spread has left traces in the hull and the deck. It is not the remnants of a detonation or a spatial tear . . . It is a slow stream, something that built up over time."

"A leak?" Urkoj volunteered, the low rumble of his voice echoing from the doorway. He still had not followed them in.

"Correct," said Valeris. "Lieutenant, do you recall Commander Miller's hypothesis about the isolytic devices?"

"The detonations were stifled because the Thorn botched their construction." She saw the understanding strike him. "And this is where they did it . . ." He looked around. "It makes sense. A remote location, all the equipment needed for the assembly could fit in here . . . And the particle traces prove it." Vaughn gestured around. "We're standing in the middle of their bomb factory."

"What the traces prove," Valeris replied, "is that whoever worked in this chamber exposed themselves to high levels of subspace radiation over a sustained period. There are very few life-forms that could experience that without suffering major systemic damage."

"Damn . . ." Vaughn muttered. "They poisoned themselves to build the bombs. How many of those things did they make? There could be dozens of isolytic weapons out there."

A guttural chirp sounded from Urkoj's communicator and the Orion snatched it up, grunting an acknowledgment. Major Kaj's voice carried through the cold air. *"All teams, regroup at the main hub. This place is a worthless tomb. We're wasting our time here."*

"She doesn't sound happy," Vaughn noted.

The blunt maw of the plasma shotgun rose to aim at them both. Urkoj jerked the weapon in a beckoning manner, the gesture making it clear he expected no defiance.

Valeris studied the Orion before she began to walk. There was going to come a moment, and soon, when she would need to make a choice. The Vulcan began to wonder how many lives she might need to end in order to facilitate her own survival.

Vaughn turned over the sheer *How-the-hell-did-I-end-up-here?* of his situation and tried to push those thoughts out of his mind. This wasn't how he had wanted to find himself in command of a mission: by dint of a murderous Klingon. Miller had seemed so effortlessly in control of his situation, even to the very end as he bled to death there on the deck, while Vaughn was still struggling to gather in the scope of where he was and what it meant. Miller's experience had given Elias the belief that they could make this mission succeed. Without him, all that was left to rely on was Kaj's desire for vengeance, the unreadable motivations Valeris kept hidden, and Vaughn's dogged determination not to fail.

And he had no idea if it would be enough. Vaughn pulled at his jacket, in the place where his rank insignia would have lain, if it were a Starfleet uniform. *This is where you are, Lieutenant,* he told himself. *You've got no choice but to make it work.*

He looked up and met Kaj's fiery eyes as he crossed the

gloomy circular space of the hub deck. The rest of the landing party teams were assembled in a loose knot around her, grumbling and surly with the cold.

Kaj threw a look at Urkoj and pointed in the direction of Valeris. The Orion reacted instantly by drawing a knife as long as Elias's forearm and pulling the Vulcan woman into a headlock. He pressed the tip of the weapon to her throat and she immediately ceased any attempt to struggle.

When Vaughn looked back at Kaj, all her men had drawn their pistols and taken aim at his chest. "So this is how it's going to be, then?"

"Have you enjoyed your sport, convict?" Kaj spat at Valeris. "Tell me, did something go wrong? Did you bring us here with intent to flee, or have us ambushed? Did your cohorts leave you twisting in the wind?"

"Where are you getting that from?" Vaughn demanded, determined to draw her attention. "Did you expect Valeris to deliver your sister's killers wrapped like a gift box?"

Mentioning Kaj's sibling made the tension in the chamber leap, and the major's simmering glare finally turned on him. She looked at the lieutenant as if she were picturing a point in the middle of his head and contemplating how to get there the hard way. "I should execute you both. There is nothing here," she said, her voice low and loaded with menace. "The Kriosians are gone! The convict has led us down a blind canyon!"

"Not so," Valeris managed, talking around Urkoj's unmoving grip. "We found traces—"

"From the isolytic weapons," Vaughn broke in. He quickly explained what they had discovered, the assembly room and the radiation readings.

Kaj folded her arms. He noticed that the strange gene alteration the major had undertaken was turning her skin a shade of violet that seemed to darken as she spoke. "Finding the spoor of your prey has no value if you cannot track it any farther. Tell me, Lieutenant Vaughn. How do you propose to use this data to lead us to the Thorn?" When he didn't answer at once, she gave a dismissive snarl. "Do you still trust this Vulcan? Do you think Miller would trust her now?"

Vaughn's jaw hardened. "Yes," he said firmly, "to both questions." *No time for doubts now,* he told himself.

"If . . ." Valeris said, half gasping, ". . . if I may offer a suggestion?"

Kaj gestured to the Orion. "Let the convict speak."

Urkoj relaxed his grip on her, but only a little. "Whoever assembled those weapons exposed themselves to a great deal of energetic particulate radiation. They would likely be in dire need of urgent medical attention."

"No doubt," Kaj allowed. "But I ask you for the last time, Vulcan. How do we find them?"

"We do not," said Valeris. "The solution to our dilemma is eminently logical. We will let the Thorn find *us.*"

Object JDEK-3246553-AKV
Ikalian Asteroid Belt
Ty'Gokor Sector, Klingon Empire

"It feels like it should be cold in here," said Tulo, ducking to avoid an outcropping of rock. "Why isn't it cold?"

Rein threw a sideways glance at the thin-faced man and jutted his chin in the direction of the ceiling. "The minerals in the rocks," he told him. "The actinides and the metallics. The very same ores that hide us from the scopes of the tyrants. They have thermal properties."

"Isn't that . . . dangerous?" Tulo blinked.

"No more dangerous than anything we have done." Rein looked away, to the slab-sided walls rising up around them, cut by phaser beams from the original network of natural caverns that threaded through the asteroid. The rocky chamber had been retrofitted with gear from an elderly Tellarite mining rig, and it was in many ways a crude mirror of the equipment they had left behind on Xand Depot.

Inside the shimmering envelopes of force walls and radiation baffles, figures in heavy environment suits moved with sluggish, careful motions. They crowded around the weapon, which sat on its cradle like an exploded technical diagram, pieces of its framework gathered in clumps, coming together with painstaking effort. Rein frowned and absently brushed at his pigmentation lines. They were quite a way behind schedule, and the move from the depot to the blind here had only added more days to the construction regimen. It didn't help that his most experienced men were unable to work, too sickened by radiation exposure.

As if on cue, Tulo spoke again. "We need to move quicker."

Rein made a bowing gesture. "You have my blessing to go in there and help. Of course, we're shy of suits, so it would have to be as you are now."

Tulo colored slightly. "That's not what I, uh, meant. Perhaps we could run the shifts longer? Keep the men working for more—"

"Tired men make mistakes!" Rein exploded, turning on him with a flash of sudden fury. "We've seen the result of that already! Our first two blows, hobbled!" He prodded Tulo hard in the chest. "That won't happen again. This time it will be done right!"

Tulo's mouth opened and closed, and finally he managed to find his voice again. "Is . . . is that the only reason, Rein?"

"Watch where you take this," he warned. "I'm not in the mood!"

"Colen . . ." Tulo said the name of Rein's brother and then halted, trying to find the right words. "His bravery is an example to all of us, but he knew . . . he knew what he was doing. And so do they." He pointed at the figures on the other side of the shields. "They volunteered for it."

Rein's lips thinned. His anger wasn't just spared for his frustration; Colen had lied to him, kept his illness hidden for as long as he could. Worse, his brother had encouraged the other men similarly afflicted to do the same, so as not to cause a distraction. There had been two deaths already on the journey back from Xand Depot, and Rein did not want to think about who might be the next to succumb.

Rein took the energy of the emotion churning inside him and channeled it. He turned and grabbed Tulo's shoulder. The other man was startled. "You trust me, don't you?"

Tulo nodded. "Of . . . of course I do, Rein. Have I done something to make you think otherwise?"

"No, no. Never." Rein gripped him tightly, his gaze intense. "But at times like this, I need to hear you say it. This is a difficult path we walk, my friend. One mistake and we are done for."

"I know. We all know that."

Rein nodded back at him. He remembered when Tulo had first joined the group; he had been directionless and afraid, and they had given him purpose. "Good. *Good.*"

Tulo licked dry lips. "It is just that . . . perhaps, if we had remained at the depot, then—"

"*No,*" Rein stopped him before he could go on, his tone hard and sharp. Tulo reacted, and Rein realized he had overstepped the mark. "No," he repeated, metering his voice. "If there had been any other option open to us, I would have taken it. I never wanted us to return to that derelict . . . We should have abandoned it years ago and never returned . . . But we needed a location that was distant from this one." Rein gestured at the rocky walls. "I only took us back to Xand Depot because we needed a place to meet with our new patrons. To keep this bolt-hole unknown to them, do you see?"

Tulo nodded.

Rein went on: "I hope I have succeeded in that. To keep this haven safe. We've risked so much . . ." He looked back at Tulo, eyes narrowing. "I know what the men have been saying. I hear them speaking. You want to strike while the iron is hot, yes? Take the killing blow to the heart of the tyrants . . ."

Tulo's head bobbed again. "If we wait too long . . . if they find us . . ."

"They can't stop us!" Rein snapped. "Do you know what we have done? Before, no matter what blows we struck, we were an insect to them, fleabites against a wolf's hide. And then we abased ourselves, drew into collusion with the very beings we wished dead!" He scowled. "The thorn in their sides . . . but nothing more than an irritant!"

"You changed that," Tulo told him.

"I did!" Rein replied. "And look at us now! Striking from the darkness, leaving destruction in our wake. We have the tyrants turned about, looking in all the wrong places. The mighty Klingon wolf, barking at shadows!" He gave Tulo's shoulder another squeeze. "And soon we will kill the beast. We'll cut out its heart and watch the body wither and die . . . and that's when the tyrants will know, when it is too late for them to stop us. They will learn that the men of one single world can cripple an empire of a hundred star systems, if their resolve is strong enough." He released his grip and stepped away. After a moment he spoke again. "We will do these things, and we will do them *right*. No more mistakes. No more imprudence. I won't waste lives needlessly. I lead, and the responsibility falls to me."

He gave Tulo a look that dared him to disagree, but the other man said nothing, instead struggling to find a way to respond. In truth, Rein was not only sensing the pressure from his own men to strike the final blow in their campaign, their patrons had also communicated a degree of "dismay" at the delays he had put in place. But the third attack would not be squandered on an objective of middling importance: it had to be a high-value target, something much more than just the place where the Klingons and their Federation allies played at cooperation. It had to be a symbol, the loss of which would wound the tyrants for eternity.

He could make it happen. He just needed time, and men— but neither were in great supply.

Finally, Tulo found his voice again. "Colen and the others . . . What will be done with them? If we had their skills . . ."

"We do not have the medicines required to treat their sickness," Rein told him. The raw energy that had driven his words before suddenly bled away in the face of the hard reality.

He thought of the lesions and the weeping sores that Colen had kept hidden beneath his tunic, and a stab of guilt buried itself in his heart. *I drove him to that. He did these things for me, for the cause. Because I asked it of him.* "We cannot even lessen the pain of those . . ." he trailed off. "Colen cannot help us," Rein concluded. He heard footsteps approaching, and turned to see Gattin enter through the far hatch.

She stepped through the doorway, a ring of metal cut from an old starship and retrofitted to the stone walls with thick gobs of polymer sealants. "I can hear you talking all the way down the corridor," she told him, her perpetually severe face barely sparing Tulo a look. "You pick the poorest of times to give speeches. Do it in front of everyone, not just him."

Rein folded his arms. "You make it sound like my words are some cheap theater. I mean everything I say, Gattin. You've been my second long enough to know that by now."

"Morale is low," she retorted. "I understand your reasons for delaying the next strike, but without that to focus on, the men can only listen to the wounded moaning in the infirmary and wonder how long it will be before they join them."

"Only those who were exposed—"

Gattin spoke over him. "*Everyone* is afraid they were exposed, whether they admit it or not. Then every cough or ache seems a harbinger of slow, painful death." She shook her head. "We signed up for this fight willing to die in battle, Rein, not to perish by degrees like your brother."

He stepped closer, matching her gaze. "And what do you propose? Put them out of their misery?" Rein glared at her. "We are not like the tyrants! We don't put a knife in the chests of our wounded and pretend it is some kind of mercy!"

A rare flicker of emotion crossed Gattin's face: *disgust.* "I would never suggest such a thing. You know me better than that." She frowned. "I have a more proactive solution, one that will be of benefit to everyone." The woman pulled a padd from a holster on her belt and offered it to Rein.

He took it and examined the information it displayed. "What is this?"

"A communication from one of our supporters," she explained. While the core of their group was a relatively small cell, there were others who never picked up a weapon but kept eyes and ears open for them in return for coin or a chance to lend a hand to the resistance. "An Axanarri medical ship has been observed passing along the colonial border. They might have what Colen needs. We could mount a fast raid, take the supplies."

Rein held out the padd. "Too risky. Too many unknowns."

"We've done this sort of thing a dozen times over!" Gattin shook her head. "The men feel useless, Rein! This will give them something to do. They need that right now."

He frowned and turned to Tulo. "Is she right?"

The other man nodded once. "She is right."

With a flick of his wrist, Rein tossed the padd and Gattin caught it easily. "Then we'll do it," he said. "Ready the ship."

Kaitaama's Daughter
Ka'Vala Sector, Colonial Border
Klingon Empire

A generous description for the vessel could have been "warship," but the reality was that the dart-shaped craft was hardly a threat to any of the Klingon cruisers that regularly patrolled the border zone. The *Daughter* wasn't designed for toe-to-toe fights against the heavily armored ships of the Imperial Defense Force; it had been built in an age when the Kriosian military engaged in hit-and-fade skirmishes with their age-old adversaries on Valt Minor. When the Empire had finally thrown off the pretense of treaty and collaboration, moving in to annex the Krios System with troop carriers and battle cruisers, they had not even graced the Royal Fleet by meeting them on the field of conflict. Instead, they held the inner worlds hostage and forced the naval commanders to bring their ships home under pennants of surrender. A proxy force was left intact, but the majority of the craft were dismantled in the interests of what the invaders called "regional stability." Rather than risk the wholesale bombardment of their worlds, the Kriosian monarchy capitulated—but not all of their starship captains did the same.

Some fled, and for a few months they held out and attempted to mount a guerrilla war against the tyrants. But ultimately, one by one, the last holdouts were hunted down and ruthlessly exterminated by the Klingon military.

The *Daughter* was one of those that escaped, but her crew had, like their rebellious countrymen, been whittled down by the actions of time, battle, and frailty. The ship herself—a warp-capable cutter built for system patrol duties—had already been elderly at the time of the invasion. Nearly three decades later, she was kept alive by Rein and his people, having fallen into their possession during the rise of their movement. The vessel resembled a cross between a throwing dart and a sharp-edged buckler, the hull made up of a central fuselage and two dagger-tipped wings.

She was at best a raider. When the group went through leaner times, the *Daughter* had prowled the freight lanes beyond the Ikalian Belt and preyed on unlucky transports, the freedom fighters taking what they needed when the donations of their supporters back on Krios Prime were not enough. The crew had run attacks like this one many times—they went about the work soberly—but Rein detected a sense of anticipation on the ship's narrow bridge. Gattin had been correct: the moment he announced that they were taking out the *Daughter* for a sortie, the men were eager to go.

It concerned him that he hadn't realized that himself. He should have been aware of what was going on among the rest of the group, not concentrating on Colen's deterioration and the assembly of the last device. But then Gattin, for all her dour nature and coldness, was better at observing the mood of others than Rein had ever been. It was one of the reasons he kept her at his side. Her aloof manner—callous, even, at times—masked deeper insights that few were aware of.

The Axanarri transport wasn't difficult to locate. The *Daughter* caught it on the long range sensors several light-days from the dust clouds of the Ubeac Range. The vessel moved at low warp, a stubby metallic rod made up of numerous cargo modules arranged end to end. The scanners could not get a solid read on the contents of the pods, but Rein knew from experience that such ships were typically well stocked, making circuits around colony worlds without centralized hospital facilities, supplying drugs and medical gear to those who needed it.

As they closed, matching course with the target, Tulo noted that the scans remained fuzzy and indistinct; but then, the *Daughter* was an old ship, and warp travel caused ghosting on her sensor grid. They reached the point of no return as the Axanarri ship spotted them and reacted: Rein committed the cutter to the attack. To turn back now would only make him seem weak and indecisive in front of the others, and he needed their confidence to follow their mission through to the bitter end. And it *would* become bitter, he had no doubt of that.

Gattin settled herself at the flight yoke dangling from the helm console, and Rein gave the order to take the target. The *Daughter* dropped in at high velocity and swung around in front of the Axanarri ship, presenting the medical transport with the slimmest head-on profile. The cutter made a fast, jousting pass that veered lethally close to the cargo vessel, the forward particle beam emitters spitting out lances of crackling energy that swept over the defense shields.

The attack pattern had the desired effect, forcing the Axanarri ship to plummet back into normal space, bleeding off its faster-than-light velocity.

Rein perched on the edge of the command saddle behind Gattin, and peered into the drop-down periscope monitor feeding ranging data and sensor readings from the targeting grid. The *Daughter* cut back to impulse velocity and came about in a hard turn, standing on one blade-like wing to bring itself dagger-forward. Tulo called out an order to one of the other men, and a blanket of subspace jamming, ending all hopes of sending a distress call.

The transport was wallowing, moving slowly, but it seemed to have sustained very little damage in the initial attack. Rein refreshed the sensor sweep and noted the same effect Tulo had reported. The returns from the Axanarii ship were distorted and ill defined. At warp, that might have been expected, but now both ships were in normal space, and Rein expected a crisp detection.

Gattin was thinking the same thing: she wondered aloud if the medical transport was using a dispersal field, a passive transmitter designed to defeat attempts to gain a lock-on for weapons or matter transporters. But that technology was military in nature, and beyond the purview of all but the richest of freighter captains.

Rein gave the order to fire again, and this time demanded a full spread on the target from the four cannons mounted in the *Daughter*'s wing-roots. New spears of coherent energy crossed the distance between the two craft, and the medical ship tried to bank away.

And then, on the scanner screen, Rein saw very distinctly the passage of a beam right *through* the bow of the Axanarri vessel; where the shot touched, there was a momentary flicker, like oil moving over water.

"Something's wrong . . ." he muttered, then repeated his words in a shout. "Something's wrong!"

Gattin didn't ask him to explain himself; she knew better than to question him. Instead, the woman put the *Daughter* into another hard turn and veered off, pulling the arrow-shaped bow away from the target.

A power surge exploded on the sensors like a solar flare, and radiant beams of color shot from the Axanarri ship, emerging from the hull in places where no weapon emitters could be seen. But Rein recognized the hue and shimmer of Klingon disruptor batteries.

The medical ship glittered as if it were made of spun glass, and then it vanished. In its place, a *B'rel*-class bird-of-prey sat like a malignant raptor, wings folding downward as it fell into attack posture.

"It's a trap!" Gattin snarled. "Some kind of cloaking device?"

"How did they know?" Tulo was saying.

Gattin's hands gripped the control yoke and dragged it backward. "It doesn't matter. We need to get away."

"Do it!" Rein barked. He went to his feet, frustration boiling over. "We can't let them interfere now . . . We're too close . . ." He glared at Gattin. "All power to the drives. Now!"

She obeyed, but even as the *Daughter*'s warp engines throttled up, a cry of warning sounded out from one of the other men. Rein looked up and saw the bird-of-prey thundering toward them, fire bracketing the cutter as it turned to flee.

The deck shook under the impacts of multiple hits, and Rein staggered to one side, gripping the command saddle to stay on his feet.

"Deflectors are down," Tulo gasped. "Hits on the intercoolers . . . We're venting plasma . . ."

"Get us to warp!" he demanded.

"We can't!" Gattin shot back. "The engines will overload the moment we break the light barrier."

The blood drained from Rein's face and he felt sick inside. They had come so far, done so much for the struggle, only for it all to end here in the middle of the void, under the guns of some opportunistic Klingon corsair. "No . . ." he muttered, grabbing at his command console. "Not here, not like this. I will not let them have a victory . . ."

"What are you doing?" Tulo's voice was full of fear.

Rein ignored him, and drew up a systems menu. The governance controls for the *Daughter*'s fusion reactor were at hand. A few command strings and he could deactivate them, send the power core running hot and out of control, toward a critical overload. "This is not their victory," he said. Rein felt oddly dislocated from the moment, as if he were watching himself going through the motions. The deck shuddered again. Outside, the glitter of a tractor beam hazed the display on the viewscreen.

Gattin's hand came out of nowhere and grabbed Rein's wrist. "The tyrant ship is signaling us."

"Why?" he spat. "To gloat?"

She shook her head, her eyes hard. "Just listen." Gattin held out a wireless headset to him, and he snatched it from her.

"Who is this?" he demanded.

"*Kallisti,*" came the reply.

They materialized in a narrow compartment with a low ceiling, the walls all cut from a dull yellow metal, studded with curved grey hull spars that ran vertically every few meters. The walls fenced them in, and Vaughn glanced forward and back to see that two knots of worn, somber humanoids blocked any other method of escape.

He instinctively drew into a defensive wheel and noted Kaj and Valeris doing the same. Only the big Orion took his time about it.

"What is this?" asked one of the crewmen. He was thin, and like all the rest of them he had lines of pigment spots that ran the length of his neck, up his face to his temples. At last Valeris had led them to the Kriosians.

The Vulcan stepped out of the group and rolled back the hood of the traveling robe she wore, searching the faces of the others. She settled on one man, a whipcord figure with eyes like a wolf. He looked strung-out and furious; come to think of it, both those descriptions could have been hung on any one of the Kriosians. They had an air about them of near-feral desperation, like animals backed into a corner.

At Vaughn's side, Kaj's violet-hued face was darkening, and he saw her hand drift toward the disruptor pistol on her belt. Mentally he began to tick off the seconds before the shooting started.

Then Valeris spoke. "Rein. Do you remember me?"

The thin man nodded once. "Your face is one I'll never forget, Vulcan."

"I never revealed my identity to you. I am Valeris." She indicated the rest of them. "These are my associates."

The Kriosian aimed a finger at her. "I can't help but wonder if this is some cosmic joke on me. Is it mythic Akadar reaching from the heavens to taunt me?" His voice was tight and the false humor he showed ran thin. "You're like a sign, Vulcan. A bad omen."

"We should kill them while we have the chance." A grim-faced woman at Rein's shoulder offered a brisk throat-cutting gesture.

"I'm considering it, Gattin."

"That would be a mistake," Kaj told him. "The moment one of our bodies hits the floor, the *Chon'm* will obliterate this scow and everything aboard it."

"You make threats like a Klingon," Rein replied. "What are you? Your species isn't familiar to me."

Kaj showed him a mouth full of fangs. "I'm not from anywhere you want to visit."

"Kaj is a mercenary," explained Valeris. "Engaged by me and my colleague." She indicated Vaughn. "Her origin is not important."

"There are Klingons on that ship," said another of the Kriosians. "We scanned them!"

"Of course," Kaj said. "It's a Klingon ship. I needed some to crew it for me. But don't fret over it . . . They sold any loyalty they might have had for the Empire a long time ago, in exchange for latinum and bloodwine."

Vaughn did his best to maintain a stoic demeanor, but he had to admit it was impressive the way that Kaj had slipped effortlessly into the role of an alien privateer. Given the heat of the conversation they'd had on the *Chon'm* before the ambush, when Valeris first outlined her plan, he had never believed the Imperial Intelligence agent would go along with it. But here she was, playing the part, even as she stood across the room from the people responsible for murdering her sister. It had to be taking every iota of her self-control not to draw her gun and disintegrate Rein and the other Kriosians where they stood.

Elias remembered what Miller had said about the major: he had called her a "professional," as if that was the highest accolade a spy could earn. Kaj was certainly proving it now.

At first the Klingons had argued about taking the Kriosians when they fell into the trap, turning them over to Urkoj and the tender mercies of the mind-sifter in the *Chon'm*'s interrogation bay. But breaking the members of the Thorn would take precious time and perhaps cause the rest of their number to accelerate their attack schedule. Valeris's approach carried more risk, but it would get them to the heart of the terrorist organization much faster . . . if Rein could be convinced.

He came closer. "I've thought about ending you a hundred times," the Kriosian said to the Vulcan, his eyes glittering. "Do you know what happened to us when your conspiracy to kill that fool Gorkon collapsed? When Chang died we were revealed! We were forced to flee our home space, leave everything we knew. Our families were executed, our homes put to the torch by the tyrants because of our involvement with you . . . You and your cowardly master, Cartwright."

Vaughn took the cue to speak. "Cartwright is dead. Murdered in prison. Starfleet silenced him because of what he knew."

Rein gave him a sideways glance. "Is that so?"

He gestured at Valeris. "Federation security arrested her, threw her into the deepest, darkest hole they had. The rest of us . . . we were hunted, just like you."

"Vaughn was like me, a member of Starfleet, but part of our . . . coalition," said Valeris. "He helped me escape."

"And you came to find us?" The woman, Gattin, wasn't buying any of it. "There are a thousand places you could have gone to ground. But instead you come looking for the Thorn, laying a trap for us, just as we are about to—"

Rein hissed at her and she fell silent. He turned back to Valeris. "She makes a good point, Vulcan. Why come to us? Why *now*?"

"Because I do not wish to spend my life in hiding. Because I know what you have done." Valeris cocked her head. "At Da'Kel."

Rein sniffed, but Vaughn saw the tell on his face. The

woman had drawn him out. "That name means nothing to me."

Valeris's gaze remained steady, "Do not insult my intelligence. I know you are behind the attacks in the Da'Kel system. Do not forget, I studied your group for some time before we first made contact. I recognized the . . . fingerprints of the Thorn."

There was some truth in what Valeris was saying, and she wove it into her cover story without pause. There was something else Commander Miller had been right about: Vulcans could be exceptional liars, under the right circumstances.

Gattin went for her weapon, and some of the other Kriosians did the same. "That's it: they have to die—now!"

"No." Rein held up his hand. "I decide when—and if—that happens."

Valeris went on, "You need not be concerned. No one else knows that the Thorn instigated the attacks. For now, your hand in this remains hidden."

The Kriosian chuckled. "If anything, then, you've given us another good reason to kill you. Can you convince me not to let Gattin do as she wishes?"

"We want to assist you," said Valeris. "And you need our help."

"You almost destroyed our ship!" snarled one of the crewmen.

"Your crew were not injured, and only noncritical systems were targeted. That damage can be repaired. But the damage to your men cannot." Rein's expression hardened as she continued. "We visited Xand Depot, searching for you. The radiation traces there were quite clear." She let the implication hang.

"The Axanarii ship . . ." Gattin muttered. "Perfect bait."

Valeris nodded to Kaj, and the major spoke a command into a comm bead on her collar. Five olive-drab containers materialized in front of Rein's group. "These are Imperial Defense Force–issue emergency packs. The medicines they contain are for Klingons, but they should be compatible with

Kriosian physiology. Consider them a gesture of goodwill."

Gattin opened one of the crates and rifled through it. "She's telling the truth."

"I . . ." Valeris paused, and began again. "*We* were cut adrift and punished, just as you were after Gorkon's assassination. The plans failed. But together we can finish what was set in motion seven years ago. The sham treaty between the Federation and the Klingons must not endure. The Klingon Empire must be *defanged*."

Rein was silent for a long time, conflict warring across his face; then he crossed the rest of the distance to stand directly in front of the Vulcan. He stood a good head taller than she did, and where Valeris was cool and controlled, the Kriosian was a bundle of tension and energy. "If you're lying to me," he said in a low voice, "I will teach you regret."

Valeris never blinked. "I have never lied to you," she replied.

Something drew Vaughn's gaze away, and for a brief moment he found himself looking into Major Kaj's dark eyes.

A shared, unspoken thought passed between them. *For better or worse, our lives are now in the hands of a convicted traitor.*

13

The return of the *Daughter* under tow by a Klingon ship created something akin to panic when it appeared on the base's sensors, but a swift communication from Rein stopped those they had left behind from unveiling the hidden phaser batteries on the surface of the massive asteroid blind, and opening fire.

Gattin wouldn't go as far to concede that Rein had allayed their fears. Indeed, when the two ships hove into the landing bay, there were a handful of men waiting there with proton launchers and armor, ready to repulse a boarding operation; for the moment no one was aiming a weapon at anyone else.

For safety's sake, Kaj's mercenaries remained on board the bird-of-prey. She, the pet Orion, and the two ex-Starfleeters were granted permission to enter the Thorn base. But even that was almost too much for Gattin to tolerate.

The moment the medical supplies had been beamed over to the *Daughter*, she knew how the rest of the conversation would go. Rein was the best leader the Thorn had ever had, but his brother's illness was cutting into him and he could not stand by and let him die slowly. Gattin had no wish to see Colen suffer, either, but if it meant making pacts with the very same people who had cut them loose seven years ago . . . That would never sit well with her.

Valeris said the right things. Perhaps she was being truthful. Perhaps she had been as much a victim of the catastrophic failure of General Chang's grand plan as the Kriosians. Or perhaps she was there to stop them from achieving the victory that had been denied them for decades.

A lifetime of hating the tyrants, years of alternately running from or striking at them, had made Gattin a pragmatic woman. Some people thought she was coldhearted, but those people were idiots. She had simply grown to understand that the universe was an unfeeling place that bore no regard for the life that dwelled in it. Once you understood that, things became a lot clearer. Things like *justice* and *fairness* were not natural forces in the universe, they were the artificial constructs of sentient beings—and they needed to be applied with ruthless intent, or else they meant nothing.

Trust was something else that didn't occur naturally in Gattin's universe. It was rarer than iridium, and she had little to share with the new arrivals. At the first opportunity she slipped away from Rein's sight and headed up through the tunnels to the small cavern where they kept the subspace communications gear. Gattin ordered the man on monitor duty to take an unscheduled rest break, and when she was alone, she activated the system.

There were a number of protocols that had to be adhered to, but she'd learned them by rote, and within a few minutes the hyperchannel line connected. There was no voice transmission, no visual component; the data needed to provide them could have been detected by tyrant monitors. Instead, the conversation proceeded through a text-voice interface. Gattin spoke aloud and the computer rendered her words as a data string, encrypting them and parceling them out in bursts of signal that lasted less than a picosecond. The replies were formatted the same way, and the computer read them out to her in a flat, bland monotone.

"Are you ready to proceed?"

"That's not why I'm signaling you," she told them. "Something else has come up."

There was an appreciable interval before the reply came, doubtless some artifact of the distance and level of encoding in action at either end of the conversation. *"Gattin you need to make Rein understand time is of the essence."* The words flowed into one another. *"The longer he delays the greater the chance of discovery we have been very patient certain promises were made."*

She glared at the lines of green Kriosi pictographs on the display monitor, and wondered about who was on the far side of them. Gattin had never met the aliens, the ones that Rein liked to call "the patrons," and she trusted them about as much as she did the Vulcan woman and her mercenaries. But the patrons had at least proved their worth, giving the Thorn weapons and the means to use them against the tyrants. They had also shown they had a long reach, and at this moment that was all she was interested in. "It is vital that you pay attention at this time," she said into the pickup. "The future of our endeavors may depend on it."

There was a longer-than-normal delay before the reply came. *"Go on."*

With quick, economical phrases, Gattin told them what had happened out in space, the confrontation with the mercenary ship and the reappearance of Valeris after nearly a decade of silence. The machine-voice asked for more names and Gattin gave up those she was aware of. "I don't like the timing of this," she admitted. "I've never believed in coincidences. If these people are to be new recruits to our shared cause, we need to be sure of them. Do you agree?"

The reply came a few moments later. *"Yes, Gattin, we concur your caution is warranted; we will look into this and inform you of anything we learn."*

"Good. I will—"

Before she could say any more, the synthetic voice spoke again. *"In the meantime it would best for us all if you impress upon Rein the need to move swiftly. End communication."*

The screen went dark and, to her surprise, Gattin saw the distorted image of a face reflected in the blank monitor. She spun in her chair and found Rein watching from the corridor outside. His expression was fatigued. "You didn't want to tell me you were going to do this?" He pointed at the subspace radio. "Did you think I would forbid you?"

Gattin stood up. "You have a lot of things that demand your attention."

He snorted. "Don't pretend you were trying to spare me some worry, Gattin. I can read you like a picture-fold, and you made precious little attempt to hide your distrust of Valeris and the others. How many times did you suggest murdering them?"

"Not enough, it would seem."

Rein sighed. "Please don't try to think for me. And don't ever allow yourself to think that my focus is not on the mission at hand. Of course I love my brother, and of course I want to try to heal him, and the others. But that isn't going to blind me to what we're doing here. The war with the tyrants is always at the forefront of my every action. Second-guessing me undermines that."

She folded her arms. Gattin had expected him to unleash a tirade of criticism on her, but he was reasoned and measured. "I did what I thought was best," she said.

He nodded. "You did what I was going to do myself, you just got here faster. But I want you to know why I allowed the Vulcan in. It's not just because of the medicines. If it were only that, I would have let you shoot her the moment she gave them to us."

"Then why?" Gattin demanded. "*Kallisti* . . . the assassination was seven years ago! They burned us . . . We have no reason to trust her now!"

"Valeris was right when she said we need their help. We do." He gestured to the comm gear once again. "*They* won't send us more men, or accept any responsibility for the ones we've lost. But Valeris and Vaughn were Starfleet, so they have skills we can use . . . And that bird-of-prey? You saw how it could hide in plain sight. Think of what we could do with a vessel like that."

"Kaj doesn't seem like the kind to give up her ship willingly."

He shrugged. "Kaj is a mercenary, isn't she? If I put things in terms of profit and loss, she'll see it our way." Rein shook his head. "No, our patrons, as much as they have done for us, for all the aid they have given the fight for Krios's independence . . . It is important we don't rely on them alone. Dealing with that motherless cur Chang taught us that. Valeris represents an alternative. She says that there are other remnants from Cartwright's organization still extant in the Federation. She'll be of use to us, I know it."

Gattin scowled, her expression saying more than words.

Rein gave a grunt of amusement. "You don't agree."

"What was the first indication?" she retorted. "If the Vulcan wants to be trusted, then she'll need to do something to earn it—something more than just handing out a few containers of medical supplies." Gattin jabbed her finger in the air. "I want proof of her new loyalties."

"Of course you do," said Rein. "So we'll make our new friends give it to us."

Rein's subordinate Tulo came with a pair of armed men and demanded that Valeris and Vaughn accompany them into the lower levels of the asteroid complex. Kaj made a good show of appearing unconcerned about their fates, making no attempt to intervene.

"Unless, of course, the Vulcan wants to negotiate a bonus fee," she said, once more playing the soldier of fortune to the hilt. "Then I'll happily kill every one of these pattern-faced fools."

"That won't be required," said Valeris, but the unspoken part of the sentence was: *For now, do nothing.*

Vaughn wondered if Kaj would follow the inference: the major was the proverbial loose cannon, and her quick temper could be concealed for only so long. As they left Kaj and the Orion behind, he hoped that the Klingon operative would be able to hold fire until they had a better grasp on the situation they were in.

For all his doubts about her, Valeris had finally made good

on the promise that had been forged in the prison on Jaros II. She had brought them into the lair of the Thorn, face-to-face with the architects of the attack on Da'Kel. Now all they needed was to find a way to neutralize the Kriosian terrorists without getting themselves killed into the bargain.

This would have been so much easier if General Igdar wasn't a colossal pain in the ass, he thought. Ever since they arrived in the Ikalian Belt, Vaughn had been wondering how to get a message out to the Klingon forces. *But would they even believe me?* He recalled Igdar's reaction to the suggestion that a world as insignificant as Krios Prime could possibly be a threat to the Empire. The general had considered it a joke; he was unable to concede that anything less than another Klingon could be a match for his fleet.

Igdar's recalcitrant, lumbering manner had forced them to make choices that pushed this mission far into the realms of illegality. Vaughn, Valeris, and all of the *Chon'm*'s crew were now as much fugitives as the members of the Thorn, and their only hope of clearing their names was to take down the Kriosians before the terrorists could strike again.

But it was hard to tell how big a force they faced. Rein was no fool: he'd made sure that all corridors were cleared wherever the new arrivals went, that all hatches remained shut. For all Vaughn knew, the dozen or so faces he'd seen might represent the full manpower of the Thorn; but the asteroid base was built big enough to house hundreds of miners, and any one of the branching corridors could lead to barracks and training areas. He turned his analyst's skills to observation and silently took note of everything he was seeing around him. When the time came to move against Rein's people, they would likely have little opportunity to debate it. He had to be ready.

It grew warmer the deeper they went into the asteroid, until finally the curving corridors deposited them in a chamber filled with workstations and assembly gear. The similarity between it and the radiation-soaked compartment on Xand Depot immediately struck the lieutenant. Rein and Gattin were waiting for them.

"You wished to see us?" said Valeris, showing no signs that she had made the same connection as Vaughn.

"I want to believe you are sincere," Rein began, without preamble. "I really do. But my second lacks my willingness to accept new faces."

"And yet, she seemed so warm and welcoming on the ship," Vaughn said under his breath.

Rein smiled. "I don't want you to think I am ungrateful for your gifts of the medical supplies, but I'm going to need something more."

"We have no more medicines to give," Valeris told him.

"Not that," Gattin said irritably.

Beyond the barriers of force walls, Vaughn could clearly see manipulators and assembly platforms. "You're constructing another isolytic weapon, like the ones you used at Da'Kel." As he said the words, from nowhere a spark of cold fury kindled in Elias's chest. He thought of the crew of the *Bode*, dying in a blaze of radiation, never knowing who had attacked them or the reason why. He shuttered it away, burying the emotion deep.

"Not like them," Rein said with a swagger. "Something greater. Da'Kel was just the opening shot, the echo of the shout. What comes next will be heard around the galaxy."

"I see," said Valeris, moving to one of the humming force fields. "And you want us to help you finish assembling the device."

"You were both serving officers in the Federation Starfleet. You have skills that will speed the process along, yes?"

"Yes," agreed the Vulcan. She turned to look at Vaughn, and he fought to control his expression, to hide his shock.

Gattin went to a locker and drew out two exposure suits from within. She threw them at Vaughn and he caught the heavy garments with a grunt. "Put those on, unless you want to boil in your own skin."

"We'll consider this your . . . initiation," said Rein. "After all, it's much easier to find trust for someone willing to share in your labors. Don't you agree?"

• • •

Once they had both donned the thick, terra-cotta-colored suits, Vaughn and Valeris passed through a one-way field membrane that allowed the passage of slow-moving objects of large density, but deflected the majority of energetic particles. They moved clumsily through a sterilizing bay and into the assembly room proper.

Vaughn saw the framework of a mechanism that resembled the warhead of a photon torpedo but stripped of targeting systems and support gear. In the middle of the cluster were two halves of an orb of silvery metal, festooned with glowing cables and circuits. He recognized what had to be energy-exchange vanes and knots of spatial antennae, components more commonly suited to warp engines than weaponry.

The exposure gear they wore was Klingon surplus, like a lot of the hardware the Thorn utilized, likely captured during raids on their oppressors. It lacked the form and function of the Starfleet environment suits Vaughn was used to, but he gradually found his pace with it. The radiation exposure meter in the corner of his suit's dirty visor peaked alarmingly the moment they entered the chamber. He wondered how a scale calibrated for a more hardy Klingon user would fit to a frailer human being like him. Valeris, hailing from a desert world like Vulcan, would also have a greater tolerance than a man born under the skies of Berengaria VII.

Vaughn made a few experimental moves, flexing his hands and fingers as he got used to the coverall. Inside, the suit smelled stale—rancid, even—and he decided to breathe through his mouth. From a place near his right ear, a steady muttering crackle smothered any attempt to use the suit's internal communicator. The radiation in the workspace was enough to garble any transmission.

Instead, Valeris came to him and offered Vaughn a cable. He found a connector on the exposure suit's belt and snapped them together.

"Can you hear me?" said the Vulcan. He saw her mouth moving behind her visor, and he nodded. "We can speak freely via the hard-line," she went on. "The particle levels in this room are enough to disrupt any attempts to monitor us."

"Great," he replied. "We may get radiation poisoning, but at least we can have a private conversation."

She indicated the core of the isolytic device. "I assume you are somewhat familiar with this style of zero-point fusion initiator?"

"I took engineering courses at the Academy, so yes, somewhat . . ."

Valeris looked away, reaching for a tool. "You can assist me."

Vaughn grabbed her arm. "Assist you with *what*, exactly? Assembling a weapon of mass destruction for use by a terrorist organization? I never signed up for that!" He nodded at the incomplete weapon. "Look at this thing. Even I can tell that this device is a lot more powerful than the ones used at Da'Kel. The yield from a clean detonation . . ." He paused. "We're talking about a subspace fracture of *catastrophic* proportions."

She shook him off and set to work. "The longer you stand there watching me, the more Rein and his people will become suspicious. Please bring me a laser probe."

He frowned and glanced to the side. From the corner of the visor he could see the Kriosians observing them both from the far side of the field barriers. Reluctantly, Vaughn fetched the tool Valeris asked for, and under her direction, held it in place. "All right," he said. "So, how do we sabotage this thing?"

"I have no intention of rendering this device useless, Lieutenant," she told him. "They will know if we make any attempt to do so. This is a test we need to pass."

"We do that and we're committing a crime that carries a death sentence in Klingon space, and life without parole pretty much everywhere else!"

"Did you forget you recruited me from a prison?"

"There's a reason isolytic subspace weapons are banned by every sane species in the galaxy! You'll be handing Rein a loaded gun!"

"I am aware of that. Illuminate the tertiary manifold, please. Set at twenty nanometers."

Vaughn complied, still scowling. "We can't do this . . ."

"We *must*," Valeris insisted. "At this point, we do not know how many devices the Thorn have built, or where they have been deployed. We must stall for time."

"There's another option," he said. "We let Kaj off the chain. Her crew are all special forces. They may be able to take the base."

"The risk factor is too great. The actinides in the walls of this asteroid prevent beaming, so any attack would have to move directly from the landing bay. One word from Rein, and the bay could be isolated and opened to vacuum."

He shook his head. "Okay, another way, then. I'm sure Kaj has an idea."

Valeris's head bobbed behind her visor. "As am I, but I doubt it will resolve itself as anything else but brute force. The logical approach is to continue to . . . play along."

"For how long?" he demanded. "Until Rein has his finger on the button? Until the Thorn blow up something else?"

She met his gaze. "You do not trust me. Despite my actions since leaving Jaros II . . . taking the helm of the *Excelsior*, leading you to the Kriosians . . . You still do not have any conviction in me. You lied to Major Kaj at the Depot. I believe you hold me in as little regard as she does."

Vaughn was silent for a moment. "Miller was right. Nothing about this mission . . . this job . . . follows the book." He sighed. "Let me tell you why I'm here, Valeris. I owe it to Darius Miller to bring this to a close. To him and every single man and woman who died on board the *Bode*. I wonder if someone like you can appreciate that. Do you understand the meaning of the honor of the service?"

There was a brief flicker of something he couldn't read

in Valeris's eyes, and then she looked away, returning to the delicate work. "You think I am a traitor. But you should know, Lieutenant Vaughn, that everything I did to earn my imprisonment, I did because I, too, believed in *the honor of the service*. I did what I thought was right for my world and the Federation."

He snorted. "You thought it was right to provoke a war?"

She raised an eyebrow. "What war? If the Khitomer Accords had never been signed, I estimate the Klingon Empire would have collapsed within five-point-six-eight years. The so-called noble houses, turning on each other, self-destructing. They would burn themselves out. Starfleet's most lethal adversary would have fallen to ruin."

"Sounds like you've given it a lot of thought."

Valeris didn't look up. "There was little else to do on Jaros II."

"But what if it went another way?" Vaughn insisted. "The Klingons aren't known for their restraint. They would have become more aggressive, lashing out like a wounded animal . . ."

"Retract to eight nanometers," she ordered, working a set of micro-calipers. "The point is moot," Valeris went on. "Continued speculation has no value. But my statement remains: I am not a traitor. I consider myself a patriot."

"All too often that word is used to cover a multitude of sins."

The Vulcan stopped and spared him a glance. "I did what was logical." Her voice had an edge to it now, something Vaughn hadn't heard before.

The lieutenant shook his head. "You talk about what you did and you say the word 'logic,' like that'll explain it away. But I don't buy that, not for one damn second. You tell yourself your choices are about reason, but they're not. They're about *you*, Valeris. But you'll never allow yourself to admit that, because that would mean admitting you're like me . . . like the Klingons. Someone experiencing an *emotional reaction*."

Valeris's gaze went icy, and then Vaughn heard a dull buzz sound in his ear. On the environment suit's visor, the radiation meter was blinking red and green.

"Your exposure level is about to exceed the safe margin," she said flatly, dismissing him. "You need to leave the chamber and decontaminate." Valeris reached out and tugged the communications cable from the socket on Vaughn's suit, ending any further conversation.

Marina Green Park
San Francisco, Earth
United Federation of Planets

Malla Tancreda walked quickly across the path running parallel with Marina Boulevard and threw a look over her shoulder in the direction of the Golden Gate Bridge. Gray clouds, heavy with unspent rain, had been gathering over Richardson Bay all afternoon and now they were rolling slowly southward, inching closer to the city. The doctor had left her umbrella behind at Starfleet Medical, fooled by the morning sunshine into thinking that the whole day would be warm and temperate. She had yet to get used to San Francisco's changeable weather patterns; the city was much different from the familiar subtropical coasts of her home on Betazed. The wind off the bay pulled at her skirt, and Malla picked up the pace, deciding that she would summon a dronecab at the Fillmore Street intersection.

She saw the Vulcan coming toward her from the opposite direction. He was narrow and gaunt, wearing a tunic and trousers that seemed deliberately designed to be nondescript. He made eye contact with her and gave a solemn nod. "Doctor Tancreda." It wasn't a greeting or a question, just a statement.

"Hello?" She slowed to a halt and he did the same, inclining his head. "I'm so sorry," she went on, "have we met? I'm terrible with names . . ." As the doctor spoke, she pushed out a little with her more ephemeral senses and took the measure of the man. He was guarded and finely controlled, his thought process all hard edges and opaque, seamless surfaces.

"We have not met before," he replied. "I would like to trouble you for a few moments of your time."

Tancreda felt the first small stirrings of alarm. "Well, perhaps if you'd like to make an appointment with my office—"

"What I have to discuss would be better addressed in a setting like this one," said the Vulcan. "It is about a delicate matter."

She allowed herself to settle into a neutral, ready aspect. "Oh?"

He nodded once. "Specifically, the repayment of a debt owed. By your employer."

"I work for Starfleet Command, Mister, uh . . ."

He made no attempt to provide his name. "Your *other* employer, Doctor Tancreda."

The alarm in her thoughts became a clarion. "I think you have made some sort of mistake," she said, her tone cooling. "Please excuse me."

"If you leave now, it will become necessary to find another method of communication," he said as she turned away. "One less . . . amenable." And there, just beneath the static layer of control, she sensed a spike of violence, ready for release.

If he knew her name, then he had to know what she was. He'd deliberately allowed her telepathic senses to see that knife of brutality, the implied threat, as clearly as if he had opened his tunic to reveal a weapon tucked in his waistband. Tancreda halted and turned back. "Who are you?"

The Vulcan ignored the question. "In work such as ours, it is important that those on opposite sides maintain a certain level of . . . interaction. Do you agree?"

"I suppose so."

He nodded. "Sometimes it becomes necessary to maintain those links through unorthodox means. I believe the Terrans have a phrase for such a thing. A 'back channel'?"

Tancreda had a communicator bracelet around her wrist, and by now she had carefully moved her hand to it so she might tap a hidden key on the device. She smiled slightly. "Pardon me for asking, but your accent . . . I don't recognize it. I'm wondering what province of Vulcan you're from?"

And then, as briefly as he had shown her the intent of careful lethality, the man gave a flash of a feral smile. It was gone so fast that at first Tancreda thought she might have imagined it. "I think we both travel quite widely."

The breeze off the bay was growing cooler, stronger. She sensed the dampness in the air. "Why speak to me?"

"That will become clear," he said. "Section 31." He offered the words: "A clandestine group that exists within the structure of the Federation, dedicated to the preservation of that coalition at any cost. It draws agents from a diverse pool of skill sets and backgrounds . . . and it frequently acts in direct contravention of Starfleet and Federation policy for what is determined by it to be the greater good."

Tancreda said nothing. They were past the point of pretending. She would simply give him no reaction, no confirmation. By now Control would have received her panic signal and there would be people on the way. All she needed to do was wait.

But he had to be aware of that. There was little doubt in her mind that the man who stood before her was no more a Vulcan than she was. He was Romulan, most likely an operative of the Tal Shiar, the Star Empire's secret police. What he was doing here, on Starfleet Command's doorstep, was something she hesitated to speculate about.

Tancreda studied him carefully, committing everything about him to memory. "I'm curious about this . . . debt you mentioned. Perhaps you could explain that to me?"

"Kodiak Delta," he replied, as if the name would be explanation enough. It had no meaning to Tancreda. "We are calling in that marker. Certain agreements were made with your people."

"I don't—" Her comm bracelet hummed before she could answer. With the "Vulcan" watching her intently, she raised it to her mouth. "Yes?"

"Tell him exactly what he wants to know." The voice of Control was firm. She didn't question how he knew what was going on. *"Answer four questions. Nothing more."* The communicator clicked back into silence.

Her hand dropped away and she faked a smile. "Perhaps I can help you."

"You were previously assigned to monitor a convicted offender, a Vulcan female named Valeris. She has been observed in the company of a human male who calls himself Vaughn. Tell me how Valeris escaped from the Starfleet stockade on Jaros II."

The doctor didn't want to dwell on how a Tal Shiar agent knew the scope of her earlier mission. "Valeris didn't escape. She was released into the custody of operatives from Starfleet Intelligence."

The man raised an eyebrow in a gesture that was very Vulcan of him. "On whose authority?"

"Ambassador Spock."

"For what purpose?"

"To assist in the investigation of the bombing incidents in the Da'Kel System." She folded her arms. "You have one more question."

He was silent for a moment, looking away at the gray storm clouds. "Where is Valeris now?"

Tancreda hesitated. The news of the *Excelsior's* expulsion from Klingon space after the second attack was only just breaking here on Earth, but her superiors had learned of those events soon after they happened. What they had not expected was for Valeris, Lieutenant Vaughn, and Commander Miller to be missing from the ship's complement when Sulu's vessel crossed back into Federation space. The *Excelsior* would be arriving at Starbase 24 for repairs within the next ten hours, and their agent among the crew would give a full debrief— but Tancreda wouldn't be privy to any of that.

She answered as best she could. "We don't know where Valeris is. She's now considered to be a . . . rogue element."

Tancreda felt the first drops of rain landing around her on the sidewalk.

"The treaty as it currently stands between the Federation and the Klingons is not one of mutual benefit," said the man, glancing at the sky again. "The Federation gives much and receives little. It is both tactically and economically unsound."

"That's one way of looking at it."

"The collapse of that treaty would be welcomed by certain groups, Section 31 foremost among them. A weakened Klingon Empire, isolated and alone . . . Do you agree, Doctor?"

"I'm afraid I don't follow you," she said. The conversation, and not the cold in the air, was chilling her.

"If Valeris and the threat of what she knows were to . . . *disappear* . . . there would be one less impediment to the fall of the Klingons. Others would gain in return." He nodded to her. "Tell that to your employer." The man turned to go.

"*Jolan tru,*" she called after him.

He glanced back and gave the brief smile again. "*Jolan tru,* Doctor Tancreda."

And now the rain came, the sky above darkening as the clouds passed over, the raindrops bouncing off the sidewalk and the boulevard. She watched the man merge into a knot of people at the street crossing and lost sight of him. The downpour grew in strength, soaking her hair, and she wandered to the curbside and reached for the summons key on a taxi call-stand.

A cab pulled to a halt before she could even touch the button, the gull wing door rising open. The vehicle had a human driver. "Get in," he told her. "You'll be debriefed on the way."

"But what about—" Tancreda gestured toward the street crossing.

"We've got an agreement," interrupted the driver. "You just paid them what we owed. Now, get in."

She did as she was told, and the taxi glided away, its grav-impellors flaring.

14

Thirteen Years Earlier

Starfleet Command
San Francisco, Earth
United Federation of Planets

The summons had not been delivered to her through the usual manner, via the data queue in her terminal in the cadet barracks. Instead, a dour Cygnian wearing the tabs of a warrant officer came to the door of the quarters Valeris shared with her Andorian roommate. He wordlessly offered her a piece of paper—not a padd, but an actual slip of replicated paper—and waited while she read it.

When she was done, the noncom took the note back and left. She never saw him again. Her lectures for the day had just ended; it had been Valeris's intention to spend the rest of the afternoon engaged in quiet study, reading up on materials about navigational hazards near high-gravity bodies. Instead, she crossed the Academy quad and took the shuttle tram to the main building of Starfleet Command, the massive monolith of gray lunar stone and glass rising high into the sunny Terran sky.

She was expected. They gave her a temporary pass and the data-card displayed a small map to show her the way to the offices of the admiralty on the upper levels. There were precious few civilians here, she noted. Almost everywhere she looked, officers in Fleet uniforms went back and forth, intent on their duties. No one but her wore the tan-toned jumpsuit of a cadet, and her clothing drew a few sideways glances as she made her way across the marble floor of the atrium to the elevator bank. She paused only once, at the foot of the memorial wall. Beneath a massive Starfleet roundel made from beaten bronze and copper, atop a pedestal a stone bowl presented an eternally burning flame to commemorate the lives of those who had died in service.

As Valeris rode the turbolift upward, she reflected that a human cadet in her position would have been experiencing a fear reaction by this point. Certainly, she was unable to deny that a vague sense of trepidation was upon her, but definitely not anything that could be classed as alarm. That was beneath her. Instead, the Vulcan woman considered her current state to be one of heightened curiosity.

Her circumstances were highly irregular: a cadet in her second year of the Starfleet Academy curriculum, one with excellent marks in all her studies, abruptly summoned to a meeting with an officer of admiral's rank, without explanation. Such things tended to happen only when a question of expulsion or matters of similar seriousness were at hand.

Valeris could see no reason why she would be subject to such a thing. She had transgressed no rules or regulations. Perhaps, she reflected, the opposite was true. It could be that she had been singled out for some special accolade. Valeris was aware that she was on track to becoming the highest-scoring Vulcan student in the history of the Academy. Perhaps they wanted to discuss that with her?

The turbolift deposited her on the fortieth floor and she followed the pass's directions along the corridor. The one element of this that seemed the most unusual was the note. Typically, if an officer wished to speak with a cadet, a comm message would be sent, but the act of actually writing down words on a physical piece of paper . . . *What did that mean?* It seemed needlessly archaic. But then again, the summons would leave no trace in Starfleet Academy's communications database.

At last she reached the office, and the yeoman at the desk gestured at the door. "Go right in, Cadet," said the young man, barely glancing at her. "He's ready for you."

Valeris looked up, and a piece of the puzzle clicked into

place as she saw the name on the door: ADMIRAL LANCE CARTWRIGHT.

Inside, Cartwright's office was spacious, as befitting an officer of his status; the footprint of the room would have swallowed Valeris's cadet quarters and half as much again. Panoramic windows looked out across the bay, sunlight muted as the automatic polarizers cut down the afternoon glare.

The admiral's choice of décor was sparse, but precise. A couple of plants added splashes of greenery, and in a cabinet behind him she saw a case containing a dozen medals. Alongside it stood a shelf of real paper books with volumes by Sun Tzu, Vegetius, and Lee Kuan. There were some framed holopics arranged at the corners of his desk, and on a low coffee table stood a museum-quality model of a *Constitution*-class starship. Valeris glimpsed the name and registration across the saucer—U.S.S. ARK ROYAL NCC-1791—and felt a twitch of old, buried memory.

She pulled her gaze away, dismissing the impulse before it could distract her. The Vulcan drew up to parade-ground attention. "Cadet Valeris, reporting as ordered, sir."

Cartwright put down the padd he held and nodded. "At ease, Cadet."

Valeris saw a careworn paper notebook and a fountain pen near the admiral's right hand, and immediately knew where the summons had come from. "How may I be of service, Admiral?" she asked.

He didn't answer the question. "It's been a good few years since I last saw you." He glanced at the model starship, then back. "You've done well for yourself."

"Yes sir." He looked much as she remembered him, and as Valeris studied his face, noting the lines where human aging had marked his dark complexion, there was a curious sensation in the pit of her chest that she could not identify. Valeris considered it; it was some sort of reaction by association, she determined. A tension in her connected to a moment of recollection.

"I've been following your progress ever since Captain Spock sponsored your application to the Academy," continued the admiral. "I agree with his evaluation of you. You have the potential to become a fine officer one day, Valeris."

"That is my intention." Inwardly, she began to wonder where the conversation was leading. A man of Cartwright's stature would not have brought her all the way from the campus just to compliment her.

He smiled briefly. "You've certainly got the confidence for it." Then the smile vanished and his manner hardened. "But I wonder if you have the insight." He opened a drawer and removed another padd, dropping it on the desk where Valeris could get a good look at it. "You wrote this?"

The padd was displaying the cover page of a dissertation Valeris had assembled for her class in Advanced Federation Culture and Law. The assignment had been to write a thesis based on the topic of Starfleet's role as a military force serving a democratic confederacy. As she considered it, she recalled that her grading for the assignment was overdue. "I did."

Cartwright picked up the padd again. "That's quite a title: *The Federation-Klingon Conflict: A Study in Failures.* A solid ten thousand words of searing indictment of current policy."

"I felt I more than adequately attacked the subject at hand, sir."

The admiral eyed her. " 'Attacked' is right," he said. "One of your tutors brought this piece of work to my attention. To say that the tone of your writing here is highly incendiary would be an understatement, Cadet. And apparently this isn't the first time you've expressed such a . . . strident viewpoint."

Valeris hesitated, framing her reply. "I am reminded of a human aphorism, Admiral: 'I call it as I see it.' "

"Is that so?" Cartwright's lips thinned and he leaned forward in his chair, his hands coming together before him. "What you've presented goes against the grain of current Starfleet policy and the peaceable ethos our officers are sworn to uphold." He paged through the digital document and highlighted a section of text. "Here you talk about Starfleet's errors in judgment at a number of key confrontations with the Klingon Empire. Each time you suggest that a forceful military response would have been preferable to the more measured, diplomatic approach that was taken."

"History provides many examples of situations where peaceful overtures toward the Klingons have ultimately proven fruitless, sir. I reference several of them."

"It's a commonly held truth that your species are not a violent people, Cadet," Cartwright said, his tone hard. "And yet, here you are advocating something close to open warfare with a major galactic power!"

"I believe we *are* at war with the Klingons, Admiral," she replied. "In my opinion, we have never been at peace with them." Valeris pointed at the padd. "In section four, you can find my correlation between the Federation-Klingon conflict and the 'cold war' that existed on your planet between the capitalist and Communist states of the twentieth century—"

He cut her off. "I know my Earth history, Valeris. But what you suggest in this paper is that we adopt a similar course toward mutually assured destruction!"

Valeris tensed. The confidence she had felt before the conversation was crumbling. "With respect, sir, that is a gross simplification of the point of my thesis."

Cartwright frowned. "You understand, Cadet, that in the current political climate, a work like this will be a black mark against you? Did it not occur to you at any time that you were essentially passing judgment on the very organization you hope to serve in?"

Valeris couldn't find the right reply.

The admiral didn't wait for her. "This dissertation smacks of arrogance. It is the work of an unseasoned mind, and it *will* damage your academic record. Do you have anything to say to that?"

She found her voice, at last. "Admiral, the Klingon Empire represents a clear and present danger to the safety of the United Federation of Planets, and we have not yet risen to the challenge of dealing with them in a strong and unflinching manner." Valeris took a breath. "I am a Vulcan, and I do wish to strive for peace. But I would do so by keeping in mind the words of one of your human luminaries." She pointed at one of the books on Cartwright's shelf. "In his work *Epitoma rei militaris*, the Roman Vegetius states: *Si vis pacem, para bellum.*"

" 'If you want peace, prepare for war,' " the admiral translated. He smiled thinly. "You really are a student of our history, aren't you?"

She didn't hear him. Her thoughts were veering toward the chaotic. The idea that Valeris could have jeopardized her future in Starfleet through something as simple as a student paper. . . .

Cartwright got up and took the padd with him, coming around the desk toward her. "There are people in this building— ones who consider themselves doves among hawks—who would see you drummed out of the Academy for writing something like this." His expression shifted, becoming almost fatherly. "Especially after that debacle on Nimbus III and all the political fallout that followed. No one in government or the fleet wants to be the one to say that maybe the olive branch isn't working." He offered the padd to Valeris and she took it. "I've made sure that none of them will know about your dissertation, or your rather forthright opinions."

Valeris frowned. "Why would you do that, sir?"

"Because I am in agreement with you, Cadet." He came closer, speaking to her now almost as an equal. "I share your feelings about our most dogged foes. And that's not all we have in common, Valeris. You and I . . . we have both seen their real faces." Cartwright indicated the padd. "So, with that in mind, I suggest you delete this and write something much less confrontational. Something that won't draw unwanted attention and ruin your career before it even begins."

"Admiral, you are suggesting that I keep my opinions to myself."

He nodded. "For now. At least until the political winds change, and they will, eventually. Even if we have to help things along the way . . ." Cartwright moved to the windows. "I've been looking for people who share my point of view, Valeris. Officers among the ranks who can be counted on to understand the realities of our situation. I see that in you." He turned back to look at her. Cartwright's dark eyes bored into Valeris. "Am I mistaken?"

She shook her head. "No sir, you are not."

"I didn't think so." He smiled again. "I'll see that your brief lapse of good judgment is kept off the Academy's records. In return, I hope I can count on your reliability in the future."

"Of course, Admiral," Valeris said, weighing the padd in her hand and wondering what this meeting had set in motion.

"The Klingons are the greatest threat to the Federation," Cartwright told her, "but only a few of us can really see that. We must work together if we are to defeat our enemy."

"Aye, sir," Valeris replied, as she tapped the padd's DELETE key.

15

Gattin found Tulo in the main corridor, a rough-hewn tunnel that ran the length of the asteroid, from pole to pole. As he moved into the nimbus of light cast by one of the work lamps strung along the passage, the expression on his face told her what she wanted to know before he spoke.

"A new hyperchannel message?" she asked.

Tulo's head bobbed, and he traced the lines of his sallow pigment-spots. "It's not time," he said. "I don't know why they broke radio silence."

"I do," she said. Gattin held out her hand. "The reply code?"

Tulo hesitated. "I should inform Rein first—"

"He's busy with the work," Gattin insisted, stepping to block Tulo's path. "At this moment he's in a work suit on the other side of the lock-out hatch."

"In the assembly chamber?" The way Tulo said it made it sound like the gateway to a thousand hells.

She nodded. "He's in there with the Vulcan. The weapon is almost ready. Rein wanted to oversee the final stages personally." Gattin held out her hand. "I'll deal with this. The . . . patrons don't like to be kept waiting."

Tulo reluctantly handed over the strip bearing the string of pictographs and Gattin studied it. "Stay close by," she told him. "We may have to move **swiftly**."

"What's going on?" he asked.

"We'll find out soon enough," Gattin replied.

The Klingon environment suit had left Vaughn with the stink of sweat and old polymers in his nostrils, but the Kriosians were reluctant to provide him with anything like a standard Starfleet fresher cubicle where he could clean up. After a cursory decontamination, he made his way through the corridors that were open to him, up to the cave-space that served as the base's mess. With every step he took, he was aware that one of Rein's men was following on behind, making no attempt to conceal himself. They had a long way to go before they could win over the members of the Thorn; Elias had his doubts that playing the long game would work. He had a grim feeling that, sooner or later, the weapons were going to come out.

Conversation from the knot of Kriosians in the corner of the mess stopped briefly when he entered, then resumed as he crossed the oval-shaped room. He found Kaj at one of the metal tables that was impact-bolted to the stone floor. Her violet skin tone gave her a shadowy quality; somehow it made the woman look even more predatory than she had in her true Klingon aspect. Vaughn got a flask of water and settled himself on a bench across from the major.

He glanced around. "Where's the big guy?"

Kaj looked up from the bowl of dull, leafy shoots in front of her and jerked her head. "I sent Urkoj back to the ship. I think the dot-skins find him intimidating." She growled at her food and pushed it away. "How do they eat this tasteless trash? It's like chewing on ropes."

Vaughn saw that his Kriosian shadow was busy getting himself a beverage, and he shifted closer, lowering his voice. "It's worse than we thought," he told her. "The third weapon is a lot more powerful." Vaughn gave her a quick recap of his conversation with Valeris.

Kaj's expression remained stony and unchanged as he

spoke, but he could sense the fury lurking just below it. "When the moment comes, all of these fools will pay a blood cost," she told him. "You would be advised not to stand in my way."

"And how exactly are you going to make that happen? If we're going to deal with the Thorn, it has to be a lightning-strike attack or else it won't work. We have to take them all out at once. We leave a straggler, they could trigger the isolytic device or whatever other surprises Rein might have."

"We should destroy this place before they can deploy another weapon. Burn out the nest."

Vaughn sipped at the brackish, recycled water and made a face. "How? It'd take a couple of ships to crack this asteroid from the outside. Getting access to the subspace radio might be possible . . . If you think we can contact General Igdar—"

She gave a derisive snort, loud enough to draw the attention of the Kriosians. Kaj turned away. "That *politician* would never believe a word from my lips, nor yours. And certainly not the convict's. No, he's chasing the ghost-prey, and even if he knows it, he won't end the hunt. He would die before losing face."

Elias shook his head in disbelief. "Igdar's got to suspect that the House of Q'unat is a smoke screen, at the very least. He's a sector commander . . . You don't earn that rank by being an idiot."

Kaj gave him an arch look. "You think so? In some places the Empire is such a web of clannish inbreeding and privileged dolts, it's a miracle we haven't killed ourselves yet." She frowned. "Without your assistance after Praxis, we probably would have . . ." After a moment, the major went on. "What you fail to understand is that Igdar *does not care* who was behind the attacks. He sees only the quick gains the tragedy can net him. His honor is cheap; he builds a throne for himself from the corpses of the Thorn's victims. Igdar will let this go on as long as it means he gathers more power to him. He is an opportunist. The High Council is enraged at what has happened, so Igdar is given more ships to punish the criminals. Then he asks for more, and more, and they give it to him."

"And all the time, he's strengthening his own position instead of doing his job."

Kaj tapped the table with her cup. "Now the human sees. I am only sorry I won't get to put the knife in his liver myself."

There was a ring of fatality about her words that Elias didn't like. "What do you mean?"

"You are correct about any external attack. Two ships at least. But there's another option. A full-yield photon torpedo, fired from the *Chon'm*."

"But the *Chon'm* is parked in the landing bay."

"Exactly."

Vaughn felt the blood drain from his face. "That would be suicide. And you don't even know if it would work!"

"I think the odds are good. And it would be a noble way to die."

He took another drink to stifle his shock. "You are actually serious. What is it with your kind? Do you all have some kind of death wish?"

"Why are you so afraid to die?" Kaj retorted.

"Why are you so *eager*?" Vaughn shot back.

A shadow passed over the woman's face and he saw genuine sorrow in her dark eyes. "Because there is nothing left for me, human, nothing but my revenge." She glared around the room, the sadness fading and a feral hate taking its place. "My sister and I were the only remaining scions of the House of Tus'tai. She was betrothed . . . Our family line would have carried on. But now my clan dies with me."

"Isn't that all the more reason for you to live?" Vaughn said quietly, so his voice would not carry. "You could . . . find someone . . ."

She met his gaze. "I am barren. A price my career exacted from me many years ago."

"I'm sorry," he said, feeling a sudden jolt of empathy for the woman.

"And so," Kaj went on, "why not make my death have meaning?"

"Or," Vaughn added, "why not forget the whole death thing entirely and try something else?"

The major opened her long-fingered hands. "I see now why Miller liked you. The two of you are similar in spirit. Tenacious. Unwilling to face defeat." She sighed. "Tell me your plan."

He leaned in again. "We can't use transporters because the actinide deposits in the rock interfere with the locks, right? But what if we could get around that?"

Kaj showed some teeth. "You're talking about transponder beacons."

"We just need to secrete them in all the places we want to capture."

The major nodded slowly. "That could work. The only obstacle is convincing the Thorn to give us access to the most sensitive areas of their base."

Vaughn shrugged. "I never said it would be simple."

Gattin left Tulo outside the communications room and took the seat before the subspace radio. With a few keystrokes she ordered the system to extend the base's antenna, and out on the surface of the asteroid a hair-thin monomolecular wire extruded from a concealed nozzle. The sensors—the only ones that worked with any kind of real accuracy in the Ikalian belt—showed no signs of any vessels in the area, so for the moment it was safe to transmit. The antenna unspooled until several kilometers of it were adrift out in the void, soaking up the low-level spatial frequencies threaded through the hiss and hum of cosmic background radiation.

She typed in the reply code and went through the familiar motions of the communications protocols, waiting for the hyperchannel to connect. Nervous energy was collecting at the tips of her fingers, the same sensation that came upon her every time the Thorn embarked on a new sortie against the tyrants. Gattin was suddenly conscious of the weight of her weapon in the holster on her belt. She liked the feel of it in her hand, with her finger on the trigger plate: all the pain and fear that had dogged her from childhood would melt away. The weapon made her feel strong, just like the tyrants had been when they demolished the village she grew up in. It made things *even*.

The comm gear sounded a tone and she snapped back to the moment. The glyph signaling a strong connection was illuminated, and she bent to speak into the console's vox pickup. "This is Gattin. Proceed."

The pause before the reply was long, and for a second she wondered if the link might have been lost; but then the flat mechanical voice issued out, the words marching down the screen in synchrony. *"Gattin we confirm we have information your instincts were correct."*

"I knew it . . ." She tensed. "I knew this could not be a coincidence! Tell me!"

"We have determined that the Vulcan female Valeris is operating under the guidance of the Federation's covert intelligence bureau two humans are accompanying her Vaughn and Miller."

Gattin considered this. "There's only one human here, the once called Vaughn. The other could be on the ship. What about the mercenary, Kaj?"

"Kaj is known to us she is an agent of Klingon Imperial Intelligence highly resourceful and violent she should be dealt with immediately."

"The tyrants and their Federation allies, working in unison . . ."

"You must isolate and terminate these spies they will do all they can to undermine our partnership. You cannot delay any more. The third attack must proceed now."

"Yes, of course," she replied. "Leave it to me. I'll deal with the situation."

"If Rein will not proceed you must take over. Gattin we cannot protect you anymore do you understand?"

Gattin's hand slipped to her weapon. "I understand."

The hyperchannel connection ceased abruptly, and she rose to her feet. At last she pulled the laser pistol and checked the energy charge. There was no real need to do it—she had loaded a fresh power clip in that morning—but it felt necessary, like a ritual.

Tulo was still waiting out in the corridor, shifting anxiously from foot to foot. He saw the look on her face and became still. "It's not good news, is it?"

"That all depends on who you are," she told him. "Get everyone who isn't sick or on the work team together. Draw weapons and armor from the equipment pool, anything suitable for a boarding operation. Then talk to Drell."

"The healer?" Tulo sniffed. "I don't like the man. You want him to gear up too?"

Gattin shook her head. The group's medic hardly ever left the base's infirmary, and given his caustic personality, that was largely considered a good thing. But he had his uses. "Drell will have something you can use. He'll know what it is." She took a breath. "Now, listen to me carefully. These are your orders—"

Tulo held up a hand. "Wait, we're not waiting for Rein?"

She shook her head again. "We're not waiting for Rein."

"We'll need Valeris's help to make this work," said Vaughn as he led Kaj down the tunnel.

The major eyed him. "I don't think so. I consider her usefulness to me at an end."

He stopped and met her gaze. "What's that, Klingon code for 'time to slit her throat'?" Vaughn drew a line across his neck. "I'm not letting you do that."

Kaj looked back at him. "You know so little about us. We're not all the barbarians you think we are, human. She did what she said she would: she delivered us to the Thorn. So I won't kill her unless she gives me cause to."

"Fair enough," he said. "But my point stands. We could use her skills." Vaughn glanced over his shoulder as he heard footsteps approaching. It was his erstwhile shadow.

"I have more faith in my own abilities," Kaj replied as the Kriosian came closer.

"What are you two doing here?" demanded the other man. He was thickset, with a heavy brow and no hair on his scalp. "This part of the base is off-limits to outsiders."

"Oh, right," offered Vaughn. Up ahead, he could see an open hatch leading into a makeshift hydroponics garden. The level directly above was the main life support node, a vital target they would need to capture to take the asteroid from the Kriosians. "We were just . . . looking around."

Then Kaj did something Elias would never have expected in a million years. She let out a throaty, sultry chuckle and snaked one arm around his back, pulling herself to him. "We were just looking for somewhere we could be . . . together."

"Yeah," Vaughn added. "Together."

Kaj gave a coy smile. "Maybe your friend would like to join us?" she asked Vaughn, her hand passing out of sight toward her belt.

The Kriosian's eyes widened, more with moral outrage than enticement. "I am a bonded man!" he snapped. "And this is no place for you to amuse yourselves!"

"Pity," Kaj replied, and her hand came back up like a striking snake. The same slender dagger Vaughn had seen her use on the *Chon'm*'s bridge flashed in the half-light and buried itself in the man's chest. Kaj put a hand over the Kriosian's mouth to muffle his death cry.

"Damn it!" Vaughn staggered back a step, shocked by the speed of the execution. "What the hell are you doing?"

"Committing us to the course," Kaj replied, dragging the corpse into the hydroponics compartment. She found a row of planters and dumped the body out of sight behind them.

"If he's missed—"

She shot Vaughn a look. "We'll give them something else to think about." Kaj pulled a rod-shaped device from her pocket and threw it to him. "Here. Plant this on the rock wall. When we're done, I'll signal D'iaq to beam a squad in here and

they'll blow their way into the life support compartment."
She pointed at the ceiling.

Vaughn caught the transponder device and grudgingly
did as the major had ordered. "What about the power core
and the armory? We need to isolate those as well."

"Neither of those things will be important if you're
suffocating."

He frowned and turned away. "Wasn't this my idea?" he
muttered.

Kaj heard him and laughed. "It's a good plan. Just stand
clear until I complete it. You're innovative, that much is
certain, but what's needed now is experience."

"I could not agree more," said a voice from the hatchway.

Vaughn spun, reaching for his phaser, but there were four
Kriosians, each with weapons drawn and aimed, standing on
the threshold. Gattin was among them, a heavy laser pistol
in her hand.

She waved the weapon at him. "Drop it, human, or I'll
burn you down." He sighed and let the weapon fall to the
floor.

"Is there something wrong?" Kaj was almost conversational. "Do you have some sort of law against disturbing the
plants on Krios?"

"Your subterfuge is as clumsy and loutish as your race,
you Klingon *petaQ*!" Gattin's eyes flashed. "That disguise of
yours is worthless. You take us for fools, as you always do . . .
But not this time!"

Vaughn raised his hands. "Look, there's got to be some
kind of mistake here . . ."

But before he could continue, one of the Kriosians moved
forward and pointed into the shadows behind the planters.
"Gattin! It's Shero. He's dead."

"Ah," said Vaughn. "Him, yeah . . ."

"You've failed," Gattin told them, her anger building. "No
matter how many you kill, you can't stop us." She advanced
a step into the room, her men following. "I know what you
are. Our patrons cut through all your lies." The woman

aimed her weapon first at Vaughn, then swung it to bear on Kaj. "Federation Starfleet. Imperial Intelligence. You came to murder us . . . You should have destroyed our ship in space when you had the chance!"

Kaj's expression shifted by degrees, almost like a mask falling away from her features. Some element of the hard-eyed Klingon warrior Vaughn had first seen aboard the *Excelsior* rose back to the surface. "You're all going to die for what you have done," she told them.

"Likely," Gattin replied, "but you won't be there to see it. And we will send many more of your kind to the grave before that happens. Beginning with your crew."

Kaj snarled and slapped at the comm bead hidden in her collar. "D'iaq! *GhuHmoH!*"

Gattin's face twisted in a sneer. "They won't hear you. Tulo is leading an attack force aboard that scow of yours as we speak."

"Then Tulo will die like the vassal he is," Kaj retorted. She gestured around. "How many of you are there in this pitiful little band? Twenty? Less? You've tried to fool us into thinking there are more, but it's all a blind, just like everything you have done. This chamber proves it. You are *bok-rat* vermin pretending to be *targs!*"

Vaughn gave a nod. "Hydroponics for food and air . . . If you had an army here, you'd need something ten times the size of this room."

"You think we need legions to win? You're wrong." Gattin spat the words. "We're taking your ship, Klingon. I made sure Tulo has a little something to even the odds. We call it the Fell Breath, after the legend of the weapon used by Great Akadar."

Kaj stiffened. "What is she talking about?" said Vaughn. The name meant nothing to him.

"It is a gas, a nerve agent," said the major, glaring at the Kriosian. "Lethal to Klingons. A coward's weapon. The Thorn have used it many times in their raids, killing soldiers and civilians alike."

"So we have. I wish you could hear it, spy," said Gattin.

"The sound of your mongrel kindred choking to death on their own blood."

The woman's goading finally had the desired effect: Kaj exploded into motion, launching herself across the chamber with a feral shout of fury. She leapt over a rack of plants and dove on the nearest two Kriosians. There were blades in both her hands, as if conjured out of thin air, and she struck out, drawing blood as they all went down in a tumble.

Vaughn ducked low, scrambling to recover his phaser from where he had dropped it; but suddenly there was a shadow over him and one of Gattin's men was dragging him back up. His fingers slipped from the fallen weapon. Elias took a hard hit across the face that brought back sickening echoes of the blow he took on the *Chon'm*, but this time he was ready: he turned with the strike and shook it off. Vaughn brought up his arm and slammed the heel of his hand into the Kriosian's chest. He heard the crunch of a rib breaking and his attacker choked in pain, gasping out his breath.

The man staggered back, but Vaughn gave no quarter, stepping inside his guard to hit again. The Kriosian was bulky, and had they been wrestling, Elias would have lost—but the Starfleet officer had speed and agility, and he made them count. Vaughn lashed out with a snap-kick to the knee, and for good measure he threw a punch that cracked the other man's nose.

"Get him!" Gattin shouted, and another of the Kriosians fired a pulse of disruptor energy in his direction. Vaughn dove as the searing heat of the beam washed over him and cut across a rack of green shoots; the plants burst into smoky flame.

He scrambled along the floor, catching glimpses of Kaj as she took on all comers, her hands a whirlwind of blades. The woman plunged both knives into the chest of one attacker, then threw him at Gattin, cursing her in Klingon. In the next second a nimbus of blue-white fire enveloped the major, and Kaj stiffened. She crashed to the deck, dragging pieces of broken planter down with her.

Vaughn didn't hesitate, and he went for his phaser again, reaching for it where it lay beneath a skeletal hydroponics rack. This time the lieutenant grabbed hold and worked the beam setting, dialing the dispersal to wide-angle heavy stun.

The rack shuddered and tipped over, forced from its mountings by a hard shove from the other side. Vaughn tried to leap away, but metal supports, tubs of liquid growth media, and cascades of emerald leaves bombarded him. He fired the phaser blindly, but even as he did, he knew the shot's angle was all wrong, the energy dispersing harmlessly into the rocky ceiling. Another blow landed on the back of his knee and he stumbled.

Then there was the searing hot muzzle of a weapon being pressed into his neck and Gattin was there, her voice like thunder. "I told you to drop it," she snarled. "You should have listened."

"Wait!" came a shout. "Don't kill the human!" Rein entered the lab and pointed. "I want him alive!"

Valeris came with him, observing the situation with blank detachment.

Gattin tore the phaser from Vaughn's hand and then pushed him toward one of her men. She stalked across the chamber. "We have been invaded by spies," she told Rein. "A conspiracy of our enemies come to kill us before we could succeed." Gattin nodded to where Kaj lay crumpled on the ground. "The purple-skin is a Klingon assassin. The human is a Starfleet covert operative, and so is the—"

"The Vulcan, yes," said Rein. "I know." His calm manner was the polar opposite to Gattin's simmering fury.

"What?" The word fell from Vaughn's lips. He looked to Valeris, but the woman didn't acknowledge him.

"There was a communiqué," Gattin insisted. "Their duplicity is clear, just as I suspected. You were a fool to bring them here, Rein!"

The sound of the blow echoed like a thunderclap as Rein slapped his second across the face. Gattin was shocked into silence, but Rein's expression remained unchanged. "Don't forget your place," he told her. The Kriosian glanced at Valeris and then looked around at his people. "Everything I do has a reason. Never doubt that. Yes, these people are assassins sent to destroy us. You were right to take their ship, Gattin. But you should never move without my authority."

"How . . . did you know?" Gattin bit out the words, seething.

"Valeris has confessed the full truth to me."

"She *what?*" Vaughn could scarcely believe what he was hearing. He started toward the Vulcan, but strong arms grabbed him and held him in place. "Valeris, what the hell did you do?"

Rein answered for her. "What she did, Lieutenant Junior Grade Elias Vaughn of Starfleet Intelligence, was explain to me in complete detail the exact dimensions of the mission you were on and the true identities of you and your cohorts." He smiled slightly. "I admit, I was suspicious of you all, but I had no idea how far Starfleet would go to pursue us. And, of course, Valeris also offered to assist us in co-opting the bird-of-prey's systems."

"*Why?*" Vaughn shouted, his anger towering. "Answer me, Valeris! Answer, damn you! Why did you do this?"

And at last she looked at him. In those cool, steady eyes he saw not even the slightest glimmer of regret. "I did it as a gesture of good faith to my allies." Valeris inclined her head toward Rein. "I share common goals with the Thorn."

"You've betrayed us," Vaughn spat. "You betrayed the Federation!"

She studied him. "I have remained true to my intentions. You and the Federation consider me a traitor to my oath as a Starfleet officer, for my part in the death of Gorkon. So tell me, how could I betray it *again?*"

"I gave you my trust. So did Miller—and Spock!" Mentioning the name of her mentor got Vaughn the very smallest of reactions. "You betrayed *that.*"

Valeris came closer. "You have no understanding of me. None of you do. I have listened for decades to those who thought they knew me and knew how I should behave, what I should be. Everyone has been wrong." She sniffed. "The error was yours, Vaughn, you and Commander Miller and . . . and Spock. You want me to be something I am not. You condescendingly offer me a chance to 'redeem' myself, but never once did you consider that I did not wish for your redemption." At last, Valeris turned away. "Seven years ago, I began something that would change the galaxy for the better. And now the Thorn will see it through to the end."

"No." Vaughn struggled against his captors. "No!"

Rein nodded toward his men. "Take Vaughn and the Klingon to confinement. We're not done with them yet."

Valeris watched impassively as the Kriosians dragged Elias away.

The cells were little more than extended hemispherical spaces burned out of the rock face and closed off with grids of diagonal bars. The Kriosians threw Vaughn into one and the unconscious Kaj into another. The prison bars were sealed shut with the heavy thud of magnetic bolts and the two of them were left behind, with only the unblinking eye of a monitor drone to keep watch.

Vaughn observed the drone for a few minutes to get an idea of its scan pattern, and when he knew it was tracking away from him, he began a quick survey of the cell, searching for vulnerabilities or weak points he might be able to exploit. The only furniture was a worn plas-foam cot and a stained waste disposal unit. The rock was dense and thick with lines of heavy metals: nothing short of a phaser drill would be able to cut into it. Given the direction the Kriosians had taken them, moving deeper into the asteroid's core, it was also likely that beyond the confinement chamber there was nothing but meters and meters of inert stone.

He turned his attention to the bars and the mag-lock. Vaughn was aware that he was probably wasting his time, but he needed to do something to keep himself occupied. Otherwise the churn of anger inside him would break through.

The bars appeared to be cast rodinium, and he went from one end to the other, pulling on each one, testing the joints experimentally, looking for the smallest iota of movement. He found nothing.

With a sigh, he picked a single bar at random and gripped it. Vaughn planted his feet and angled himself, and then with all the strength he could muster he pushed and pulled, sweat beading on his face. The anger came, despite his best intentions, and he attacked the inert metal with all his might, cursing and kicking at it.

Eventually, when his rage at Valeris's betrayal had expended itself, he let go and dropped back onto the bunk's feculent foam mattress. His muscles sang with the effort and he leaned forward, his elbows on his knees, cupping his chin.

"Egan was right: I am a fool," he told the air. "An arrogant, stupid, unready greenhorn. I should have stayed at my desk and written a bloody memo."

From the next cell Vaughn heard the sounds of movement. A low moan, then boots scraping on the dusty floor.

"Major?" he called. "Kaj, can you hear me? It's Vaughn." He went to the bars. "Hello?"

Kaj said something under her breath that he didn't catch, but it had the tone of a gutter curse. He heard the Klingon spit. "This is not Sto'Vo'Kor," she said. "And you are not the herald of the Black Fleet. Tell me why we are both still alive."

"You're not gonna like it."

There was a long silence. When Kaj spoke again, her voice was cold. "The convict?"

"She gave us up. I don't think she even hesitated."

A low animal growl came from the neighboring chamber, and Vaughn instinctively backed off a step. He couldn't see what was taking place in Kaj's cell, but he could imagine the Klingon in there, the same stripe of anger he had felt coming to the fore in her. Suddenly Kaj let rip with a scream of pure rage and the rock wall vibrated as she pounded on it. A cacophony of metallic crashing and tearing sounds followed as she let her fury loose on the cell, ripping and smashing at everything she could get her hands on.

Finally the storm abated and Kaj dropped to the floor before taking in one last lungful of air. She tipped her head back and howled, a long, thunderous note that echoed down the length of the caverns. Vaughn recognized the cry for what it was: the Klingon death-ritual where a comrade of the honored dead would shout to the heavens—a warning that a warrior was on its way to the afterlife. Kaj gave the cry for D'iaq and all those who had served with her aboard the *Chon'm*. Vaughn nodded in grim appreciation.

"Feel better?" he asked.

"Not yet," Kaj replied. "After I tear out the convict's throat with my teeth and put those Kriosian dogs to the sword, then perhaps so." The Klingon paused. "She used us to bring her to the Thorn, to someone who shared her aims. She never intended to let us stop them. Her hate for my people runs deep."

Vaughn shook his head. "I thought . . ." He blew out a breath. "Damn it. I thought I had misjudged her."

"As did I," Kaj admitted.

"I gave Valeris a chance to do the right thing . . . and she threw it back in my face."

The bars on Kaj's cell rattled. "We are alive because Rein believes we have some value to him."

"You think he's going to interrogate us?"

"Perhaps," she mused. "If they know how to operate a mind-sifter . . . We have to escape these cages."

Vaughn felt ice in the pit of his gut. It was one thing to suffer treachery and failure, but the thought of being torn open to spill out every secret he knew . . . That sickened him to the core. "You get no argument from me. But they disarmed both of us, and without a beam cutter, there's no way to slice through these bars."

Kaj dropped to the floor of her cell. "They'll come back. When they do, we kill them and take their weapons."

"Just like that?" said Vaughn.

"I've done it quite often," said the major. "Just follow my lead."

"You make it sound easy."

Kaj gave a soft grunt of amusement. "Half of any victory is finding the right moment to strike."

"What's the other half?" asked Vaughn.

"Surviving."

16

Valeris followed the terse directions the Kriosians had given her and took a spiraling tunnel into the inner spaces of the asteroid. Down here, the gravity control plates were working sporadically, and more than once she was forced to call upon her microgravity environment training to negotiate some of the lengths of the passageway. The rock was at its densest here, layers of dark strata protecting the artificial caverns cut into the structure.

She passed through a set of heavy airlock doors; beyond was the infirmary. It was a sensible location, well shielded from the outside and easily defensible in the event of an invasion.

Valeris caught a snatch of conversation echoing down the narrow tunnel.

". . . a mistake," said a nasal voice. "Klingons are a handful at the best of times. This is not just some braggart soldier we're talking about. She's a covert operative, a hundred times more lethal. A thug with a brain!"

The reply was Rein's. "I know what Kaj is, even if you didn't."

"That wasn't my fault!" came the sharp retort. "She did something to herself! Some kind of gene-modification therapy. The bio-scanner couldn't break through the disguise."

Valeris was approaching the door to the infirmary, and she

slowed her pace so she could listen. A monitor drone standing guard turned lazily to study her.

"You should let Gattin execute her—and the Terran!" the voice went on.

"Soon," Rein answered. He sounded weary, as if he had gone through this conversation a dozen times already.

As the drone beeped a warning, the Vulcan stepped around it and entered the chamber. The walls were lined with plates of welded metal, and racks of medical capsules filled one side of the space. Each had a monitor screen displaying the status of the occupant, and Valeris saw that the majority were on life support, their bodies barely able to sustain themselves.

"What do you want?" A short Kriosian man, his face lined and heavy with age, gave her an acid glare.

"Drell, be quiet," said Rein, getting up from a chair by one of the capsules. "She's here because I told her to come." He glanced at Valeris. "You have something for me?"

Valeris nodded. "I was able to assist Tulo in bypassing the lock-outs on the bridge of the *Chon'm*. He estimates the bird-of-prey will be ready to fly within the hour." Despite herself, the Vulcan's nostrils flared. Inside the infirmary, the smell of organic decay was strong, and she looked in the direction of the scent. In a shadowed corner of the chamber, long, black tripolymer bags were laid out in a row, each one containing a dead body.

Rein saw her looking. "The fallen," he noted. "In our culture we hold the bodies for six days and nights before burning them. There hasn't been time to say the rites for these yet." He sighed and shook the thought away. "The ship, yes. That's what the tyrants call it: *Chon'm*? What does it mean?"

"I believe it is the name of one of their warrior-poets."

Drell snorted. "In my experience, the height of their culture is little more than mindless violence and shouting at each other."

"Kaj's crew," Rein went on. "They've all been neutralized?"

"Gattin is conducting a final sweep of the ship as we

speak," Valeris told him. "She has a most singular focus. I imagine anyone who survived the gas attack will not remain hidden from her for long. B'rel-class scouts are quite small vessels."

Rein nodded. "Good." He seemed distracted. "You . . . are proving very valuable to us, Valeris. I want to believe that I can trust you."

"I accept that you may be reticent," she went on. "I came to the Thorn under false pretenses. But it was necessary in order to get close to you."

The Kriosian medic folded his arms over his chest and eyed her. "That's the problem with turncoats, though," he said. "You can never be sure who they really serve."

Rein said nothing, watching her. Valeris nodded. "You are correct. I will give you no assurance, Drell. I will only say this: I serve myself, my own needs. And at this time, the needs of your group are in synchrony with mine. I want the Klingon Empire brought low."

"Mutual goals make strong allies," Rein said at last. He turned away, looking back at the medical pod while Drell walked away to tend to another.

Valeris came closer, and she saw the head and shoulders of a younger man through the clear observation bubble at the top of the capsule. His flesh was red, as if it had been burned, and there were lesions all over him. His hair was falling out in clumps.

"My brother, Colen," Rein said softly, without turning. "The medicines you provided have done much to ease his pain."

Valeris recognized the symptoms of radiation exposure and, glancing around, noted that most of the other pods were occupied by similarly affected victims.

"They paid a high price for striking the first blows," Rein went on. "They have suffered so much, even more than the brave souls who carried the devices to our enemy. They have not even been given the mercy of a swift end."

The Vulcan watched, evaluating the moment. The

vagaries of humanoid emotional response to death had always been a difficult subject for Valeris to grasp. On Jaros II, Doctor Tancreda suggested that stemmed from her inward-looking, self-focused manner. Valeris did not agree; she simply felt that the death of others was something that happened at a distance.

"How do you wish to proceed?" she asked, folding her arms behind her.

Rein spared her a look. "The weapon is being calibrated," he said. "Now that you have completed the primary assembly for us, the final checks are being made. And then it will be ready."

"You have a target in mind for the third isolytic device." It was not a question.

He gave a nod. "From the very start, Valeris. I must admit, I have had my doubts that we could reach it . . . But now, and with that ship . . . the possibility is very real. If I believed in fate, I might think it was smiling on us . . ." Rein looked away. "I am in the process of modifying my plans," he added, tapping a finger on his temple.

The Vulcan's curiosity threatened to get the better of her, and she reined it in. Given the size of the third device, if triggered correctly, it had the potential to obliterate something the size of a continent—and there were many targets of opportunity well within range of the bird-of-prey. The Imperial base at Ty'Gokor, the barracks on the moons of B'Moth—even the Federation facilities at Starbase 36—could all be reached in a matter of hours. She estimated that the Thorn's weapon of mass destruction would be able to cause a scale five subspace event, enough to consume a dozen starships or scar a planet.

"For the moment, another matter takes priority," Rein continued. He sat gently on the chair next to his brother's capsule.

"Colen."

He nodded again. "I must keep watch."

"It won't be long now," said Drell quietly. "Despite the

medication, he was too far gone to recover. The boy will take the long sleep."

"I was not aware—" Valeris began.

"It does not matter," said Rein. "The fault is mine. I pushed him too hard. He did these things to impress me, to show his dedication to the cause. And now I must break my promise to my brother."

"What promise?" asked Valeris, watching the play of emotion on the Kriosian's face.

"I told Colen that one day we would both stand on Krios Prime and see the flag of the Klingon Empire torn down. I swore to him on the graves of our parents that our clan and our freedom would be restored, and that he would be there to witness it." Rein gave a shuddering sigh. "My own ambition has made me a liar."

Valeris was unsure what to say. She sensed that some words of comfort would be appropriate, but Rein was still an unknown quantity and she could not predict how he might react. It was important for her to keep him on her side. "I am certain your sibling would not blame you for this turn of events," she said after a moment, looking at the comatose young man. "I imagine he understands the situation."

"But do *you* understand?" Rein shot her a fierce look, and he was suddenly the firebrand she remembered meeting on Xand Depot seven years ago. "Can you truly know why we fight?"

"To strike back at the Klingons."

"Let me tell you . . ." he said.

The two prisoners sat in silence, and Vaughn stared at the bars of the cell, in his mind turning over the moments before their capture, examining them for nuance.

He was an analyst first, after all. Looking for patterns and finding data was one of his key skills. There was something that Gattin had said, a phrase she used that pushed to the front of his thoughts: " 'Our patrons cut through all your lies.' "

"What did you say?" Kaj's voice came from the adjoining chamber.

"Not me," he replied. "It was Gattin. Before you tried to rip her head off, do you remember? She said she knew what we were."

"The Vulcan traitor told her."

"No," said Vaughn. "Gattin didn't know about Valeris until Rein arrived, after they'd stunned you. She was talking about someone else. 'Our patrons,' she said. Someone backing the Thorn . . ."

"It is likely," agreed the major. "The isolytic weapons, this facility, and the hideout at Xand Depot, along with the ships they used . . . I doubt a group like the Thorn could ever assemble all that on their own. They must have had outside assistance."

"The question is, who?" Vaughn frowned. "There's a phrase from Terran legal process that comes to mind: *Cui bono?* 'To whose benefit?'"

"The Klingon Empire has many enemies. It is the measure of our strength."

"I guess that's one way of looking at it. So we have to wonder: Who hates your race enough to see the alliance with the Federation broken? Who doesn't care about hurting your people or mine? Who wants a Klingon Empire riddled with infighting and starvation?"

"And a Federation afraid that we will turn on them?" He heard Kaj spit. "There is only one enemy we have in common that would stoop to such treachery. Must I even say the name?"

"The Romulans."

There was agreement in her voice. "It can be none other. Those honorless *yIntagh* have never abided by any treaty. I have no doubt they still possess isolytic weapons technology."

Vaughn didn't bother to mention that the Klingons and the Federation had probably kept copies of the same weapon specs as well. "If it's the Thorn using the bombs, the Romulans can keep their hands clean," Vaughn added. "The Kriosians do all the dirty work for them."

"Our mutual adversaries were as much a part of the Gorkon conspiracy as the renegades among our own commanders . . . and the Romulans have always been masters of the patient game."

"Nanclus," said Vaughn, thinking back. "He was the Romulan ambassador to the Federation seven years ago. He was in it with Chang and Cartwright and all the rest . . . But the man was extradited back to Romulus."

"Where he was tried for his crimes by tribunal and found guilty," Kaj went on, sarcasm dripping from every word. "His punishment was death by disintegration. A most convenient way to ensure no body remained for authentication."

"You think Nanclus is still alive? That he's part of this?"

When Kaj spoke again, her voice was almost a whisper. "I could be executed for what I am about to reveal to you, human. But considering I have been declared a deserter, the fact is moot." She sighed. "Imperial Intelligence believes that Nanclus was and remains to this day a key member of the Tal Shiar. We have made many attempts to track and isolate him, but none have succeeded. Before the attacks on Da'Kel, we intercepted traffic indicating that he was involved in some sort of ongoing operation near our borders. We had no specifics, however."

"It fits the bill, doesn't it?"

"Yes." She got to her feet and toyed with the bars once again. "The Tal Shiar sharpened the blade, then placed it in the hands of the Thorn to cut both our throats. It is the only explanation that rings true."

Vaughn said nothing, letting the scope of what they had discussed sink in. If that was right—*it had to be*—then the scale of the mission had just grown into something far larger, and far more deadly.

"We've got to get out of here," he told her. "Right *now*."

• • •

The bio-monitors muttered quietly to themselves, the rebreather systems working with low, mechanical sighs. Rein placed one hand on the glassy surface of the medical capsule, over Colen's blood-streaked face, and turned to study the Vulcan. She stood stiffly, her stance at parade ground rest. Her unblinking gaze gave him little in return. There was something at once compelling and disquieting about the impassive female—but then again, he wondered if Valeris really was truly without emotion. He had heard the edge of anger in her voice when she spoke to Vaughn: there was rage there, buried deep but still present. And rage was something Rein knew very well.

"We have always been a culture at war," he told her, stepping up to walk around the edges of the room. Being on his feet always helped him to concentrate. "Krios was born out of conflict. Our old enemies on Valt have been trying to destroy us for centuries, and the Sovereign Dynasty and the High Clans led the opposition against them. The will to resist is threaded through the soul of every Kriosian son and daughter. The tyrants understood that. They used it against us."

"They invaded your world," she said matter-of-factly.

"It wasn't an invasion," spat Drell, glaring from across the room. "Not to begin with."

"My father was the same age I am now when the Klingons came to Krios Prime," said Rein, recalling the stories his parents had told him. "The Valtians were becoming a greater threat with each passing season, and the Sovereign Guard were struggling to hold the line against them. We knew of the great and fearful Klingon Empire, but they had always chosen to leave us to our own devices. Until that day. They came in warships, but not to attack us. No, they came with an offer of *alliance*."

"A pact against your enemies?"

He nodded. "They wanted minerals, and we wanted to beat our old foes all the way back to Valt Minor. The First Monarch accepted."

"What else could she have done?" Drell grated. "It was

negotiation at the point of a gun! They came in peace, yes, but ready for battle if we refused them!"

"But the Klingons did not keep their bargain," said Valeris. "They cannot be trusted."

"No," Rein agreed, his expression turning grim. "Within a decade, through intimidation and violence, they expanded their so-called mining operations to include military facilities, and when the High Clans tried to oppose them, the tyrants suspended the monarchy and imposed martial law."

Drell's face soured. "They said it was for our own good."

"Oh, they kept the Valtians away," Rein noted, "but in return they annexed our worlds and began a systematic process of stripping them for all their resources. Dozens of vital ores. For thirty years they have been taking it from us. And in doing so, they planted the seeds of our resistance."

"We took the name *SeDveq*," said Drell. "The thorn in the hide of the stumbling, vicious beast."

Valeris cocked her head, musing on Rein's words as if they were some academic lecture filled with dry facts and not the blood-laced legacy that drove him and his cohorts. Her detachment began to irritate him.

"There is indeed one thing that I do not understand," said the Vulcan. "I have seen your passion and your dedication to your cause firsthand. And yet, I find it difficult to rationalize it with one fact."

"And that's what?" Drell demanded.

"If your loathing for the Klingon Empire is so strong, then explain to me why you and your leader Seryl were willing to ally yourselves with General Chang. Would not a Klingon officer like the general be a sworn enemy of the Thorn?"

Drell's expression darkened. "Don't you ever dare accuse us of collaboration, you cold-eyed—"

"*Drell!*" Rein barked. "Shut your mouth! Valeris's question is valid, and it deserves an answer."

"Seryl made the decision," said Valeris. "Am I correct?"

He nodded. "I'll admit, it was a hard thing to accept. But I have learned that, to reach the final goal, one must sometimes take a path through the darkest of places." Rein brushed his hand over Colen's capsule as if he were stroking his brother's face.

Rein told her how it had come to pass. Some fifteen years earlier, before Chang had ascended to the role of chief military advisor to the Klingon High Council, he had served a tour of duty on the border zone and patrolled the Krios system. Chang had been the most persistent, most dangerous adversary the Thorn rebels had ever faced. Unlike his compatriots, in his own way the tyrant commander developed a grudging respect for the tenacity of the Kriosian freedom fighters. Whereas other Klingons saw them as upstart natives fit only for slavery, Chang treated them as warriors worthy of battle.

"Chang's attitude toward us displeased his superiors. He was dispatched back to the tyrant core worlds," Rein went on. "And then the Praxis moon was destroyed."

Valeris nodded. "An industrial accident inside one of their main energy production facilities." She frowned. "It was the catalyst for so much of what would occur."

"It was a death warrant for our homeworld, that's what it was . . ." muttered Drell. "Within mere *days* of Praxis exploding, a fleet of refinery ships and cargo barges arrived in orbit over Krios Prime!" He scowled at the Vulcan. "It was their emergency contingency. Without resources from Praxis, the tyrants needed something to fill the gap. Strip-mining quadrupled, more lands were forcibly annexed, and anyone who didn't clear out died when they sent in the digger-mechs!"

"We could only watch," Rein said solemnly. He thought about that day, recalling the sickening sensation as he saw his birthright ground into dust. "We tried to fight, but the tyrants put soldiers on every street corner. Not since the bloodiest battles with Valt had so many of our people perished."

"Then Chang came back," said Drell, a note of disbelief in his voice.

"Seryl thought it was a trick at first," Rein remembered the moment, his mentor furious at the Klingon's towering arrogance. "But the opportunity was too great to ignore.

Somehow Chang had arranged to have a dozen of our kinsmen, prisoners taken by tyrant arrests, to be released. They brought a message. He wanted to meet with us, in private, far from the eyes of his own people."

Valeris raised an eyebrow. "How did you know he was sincere?"

Rein shook his head. "I didn't. I carried a concealed cluster of photon grenades wired to a trigger, and I fully intended to destroy myself and take Chang with me . . . But his offer changed everything."

"He made a deal with Seryl." Drell picked up the thread of the conversation. "He pledged to make good on what the Klingons had promised from the very start. Chang would make sure the Empire gave Krios back its independence, and the weapons and ships we needed to invade Valt and conquer it. In return, the Thorn would serve his plans."

"His plans to assassinate Chancellor Gorkon," said Valeris. "Hence our meeting on the Xand station. The Thorn became his go-betweens."

"That was the intention." Rein frowned. "We knew what Chang wanted. With Gorkon dead, he would have little to stop him from rising to the chancellor's throne himself. If we helped him, he would help us." He sighed. "We never trusted him, you realize that? We were not fools. But we understood the reality of our circumstances. The tyrants would continue to ravage our planet, and we could only harry them, never defeat them. As much as we hated him, Chang's offer was a chance for true freedom."

"Or so Seryl told us," Drell said bitterly.

"You selected the logical alternative," Valeris noted.

Rein shot her a sharp look. "We had proof of Chang's meetings with us. If he had double-crossed us, we could have ruined him. And so we made the pact . . . and it almost destroyed us."

"How?" asked the Vulcan. "General Chang and his men were killed in orbit over Khitomer, when their ship was defeated by the *Enterprise* and the *Excelsior*. If he was dead—"

"He was a Klingon," Drell broke in. "A killer, a deceiver to the last, just like all the rest of them! He tried to take us down with him! After his death, the entire plan unraveled. Chang's agents, the ones on other worlds—they were hunted down by Gorkon's daughter and interrogated for all they knew."

"Chancellor Azetbur's first order of business was to spare no mercy for Chang's network of conspirators," said Rein. "And his men willingly gave us up to save their own necks—not that it did. In the end, Krios suffered *more* because of the alliance we made! Half our number were executed, and the rest of us went to ground here." He showed his teeth. "And now, all these years later, the Federation continues to play at the sham of peace with the Klingons, turning a blind eye to the plight of my people while the tyrants hold Krios in an iron grip!"

Valeris accepted this with a nod, his ire rebounding off her cool demeanor. "And as such, your will to strike back at them has grown stronger. I understand that desperation and anger can be the most powerful of motivators."

Drell came closer, until he was almost face-to-face with the Vulcan. "But here's you, a passionless creature from a passionless species. I look at those pointed ears and big eyes of yours and wonder what drives *you*." He sneered. "I mean, if you're not capable of hate and wrath, then what are you?" The healer waved a finger in her face. "Are you dead in there, alien?"

"Your attempts to goad me are fruitless," she told him calmly. "I will not respond to such a simplistic attempt to engage me. Suffice to say that you are not the only ones to resent the continued ascendance of the Klingons. I believe that the Klingon Empire is a threat and it must be hobbled. If not, their violence and aggression will spill out across the galaxy, and it will not just be Krios Prime that suffers under their brutality." Valeris turned away, and finally she came to the question that Rein had been waiting for her to utter. "Who gave you the isolytic weapons?"

He smiled thinly. "An ally. There are many who would see Klingon blood spilled and their empire in flames."

"And you were willing to trust these . . . allies?"

"Of course not," Rein replied, "just as I do not trust you, Valeris. But as you said yourself, we are not the only ones who share enmity toward the tyrants. And our patrons have been very, *very* generous." He paused. "I work with these outsiders because I understand them. And that is also why I am working with *you*."

The Vulcan gave him a quizzical look. "I am . . . curious to know how you came to such insight."

Rein met her gaze. "Because you are like me, Valeris. At the core of your being, there is a hate for the Klingons that cannot be extinguished."

"I do not—"

He halted her before she could voice the denial. "Don't pretend to me with all your claims of Vulcan dispassion. I see it in you. I saw it the very first time we met. Like knows like. You hate them so much that you cannot even encompass your awareness of it. You don't have the words to express it." Rein smiled coldly. "But not I. I know myself." He leaned in and felt his temper rising, felt the fire of it warming him. "It will not be enough to make the Klingons leave Krios. Not nearly victory enough. No, the blood cost is far higher than just the dead left by the isolytic bombs. This is only the beginning. If I could do so—if I could press a button and wipe every Klingon life from existence at once—there would be no hesitation in me."

"You would commit genocide?" Valeris said carefully. "Destroy an entire civilization?"

"I'd relish it," Rein replied, nodding. "And that night I would sleep untroubled, knowing I did the universe a kindness. You understand that, don't you? You see what we share?"

"I understand you," said Valeris, her words without weight. After a moment she tried another tack. "But if the Klingons have done so much to hurt you, and now you have the power to strike back at them, why do it from behind a mask?"

"Were you not paying attention, woman?" Drell demanded. "Did you miss the part about Azetbur's thugs running wild across Krios, killing our kinsmen?"

Rein watched her reactions, looking for any signs; she gave him nothing. "For now we strike from the shadows."

"You hide," Valeris corrected. "Disguised, using the name of discommended Klingons. Are you content to let the ghosts of the House of Q'unat take the credit for the Thorn's victories? Do you not wish the Empire to know who has wounded it?"

"Now *who* is trying to goad *who*?" Rein shot back. "To reveal ourselves now would be premature. The tyrants believe they wiped us out after the purge of Chang's network, so we let them stumble on in ignorance. We've silenced Kaj and her subordinates . . . It serves the Thorn to have our enemies chasing shadows." He leaned closer. "Because, Valeris, when we strike again, they will never see it coming. And only then, as the ashes choke the skies of their crumbling Empire, when it is too late for them to strike out at the civilians on our homeworld . . . *then* we will show our faces."

Drell smiled distantly. "Just in time to dance on their graves."

"I wanted to see that." The words were faint, the voice weak. Valeris saw Rein whirl and race back to the medical capsule where his brother lay. The support pods were of a comparatively crude design—Klingon military models, by the look of them. The units had been created for triage medicine, she noted; they had not been built for the kind of patients Drell was caring for.

"Colen?" Rein craned over the observation bubble at the far end of the pod, and she glimpsed movement inside, fingers scraping along the inside of the container. The Kriosian shot a look at his subordinate. "Open it," he ordered.

Drell hesitated. "That's not a sensible idea," he said. "The boy . . . I mean, he won't—"

"Do it now!" Rein shouted.

The healer frowned and nodded. "All right. Back away. Let me get in there." Drell worked a control pad on the surface of the pod, and with a whine of servos, the upper half of the capsule retracted backward. Immediately, the stink of sickly body fluids hit Valeris's senses. She smelled decay.

Colen's hand emerged. It was trembling, the shapes of the bones visible through papery, pale skin. Rein clasped it and sat next to his brother. "I'm here," he told him. "I'm sorry."

"Don't be." The words were a rasp. "My choice, Rein. For all of us. It has always been our choice."

Valeris watched. She knew little of how Kriosians approached mortality and she was curious. Drell stood at her shoulder. "Do you see?" he asked, his voice pitched so it would not carry. "Do you see this, alien?"

Colen coughed, a harsh, racking spasm that brought up thin bile. Rein held his brother until the agony subsided.

"His pain is considerable," she observed. "How long has he been in this condition?"

"Days now."

Valeris glanced at the healer. "If his death is assured, would you not consider euthanization to ease his suffering?"

Drell scowled at her. "It's not our way."

"But it is your way to let one of your own linger on in crippling agony?" There was no accusation in her words, only the stark truth.

He looked away. "For your own good, don't speak to me again." Drell crossed to the medical monitor.

Rein managed a smile for his sibling. "You have been so brave. You make me proud. Mother and father would say the same if they were here to see this. The Thorn grows strong from your effort, Colen. The tyrants will . . ." He cast a fleeting look back at Valeris. "They will know your name."

Colen tried to lift himself up and look up at her through milky cataracts. "Is that . . . the Vulcan?" he managed. *"Kallisti?"*

Rein nodded. "Her name is Valeris. She says she shares our fight."

The younger man gave a pained chuckle. "I hope she's ready . . . to follow the path as far . . . as far as it goes." He settled back into the pod.

Drell flinched as the sensor readings on the monitor twitched and shifted. The blinking indicator of the heartbeat tracker stuttered and went dark, panels of data showed null returns. "Rein—"

The Kriosian let his brother's limp hand drop from his grip, and with infinite care he reached out and closed Colen's eyes. "It's ended." Rein stood, his back to them, and dabbed at his face. When he had composed himself, the man turned around and Valeris saw the firm mask of determination he had set in place over his expression. "His death won't be in vain," Rein told her, controlling his tone. Valeris could sense the turmoil he was keeping in check, and it was clear he could barely manage to do so. Still, she said nothing, and let him find his way through the moment. "The Thorn will bring the tyrants to their knees, and we will write the names of the fallen . . . We will write them high." He snapped his fingers at Drell. "Give me your communicator."

The healer obeyed, handing over an oval clamshell unit. "What are—"

Rein silenced him with a wave of his hand. He was still looking directly at Valeris. "I pay this cost," he said to her. "I do it with no question. Will you do the same?" Rein tapped the TRANSMIT key without waiting for her to reply. "Gattin, answer me."

"I'm here," the Kriosian woman responded within seconds. "Colen?"

"Gone," Rein replied, almost dismissive of the question. "It's time," he went on. "Is the bird-of-prey secured?"

"That Orion brute was still alive. Found him in the cargo bay. Dead now, though."

"Good. Assemble the men. We're going ahead with the next strike."

"Now?" said Valeris. She hadn't expected the Thorn to move so quickly.

Rein ignored her. "Get the Klingon and the Starfleet spy from confinement, bring them up to the landing bay."

"What are we going to do with them?" asked Gattin.

"Pick the one you want to die first," the Kriosian said, meeting her steady gaze. "Valeris can execute them for us."

17

Nidrus Gamma
Nidrus System
Federation-Klingon Border

"**A**re you afraid, Valeris?" said her mother. "Speak honestly."

The young girl buried her hands inside the folds of her brown traveling robe and looked up at the woman. Her parent's dark hair still hung disordered and unkempt from where she had fallen against the inside of the groundcar during the ambush. A slight bruise, shading emerald, marred the otherwise smooth profile of her face. She was, by Vulcan aesthetic standards, considered quite agreeable in aspect.

"I am not afraid," Valeris said, holding her voice steady with effort and care. "Fear is an unproductive emotional state." She rubbed at her wrists where tripolymer tapes wound them against one another. Everyone in the room was similarly bound.

Her mother scanned her face. "You are not being entirely truthful." Before her daughter could respond, she dropped to the grubby, dusty floor of the storeroom and leaned closer, making their conversation confidential. "Remember your exercises," she said. "It is important we do not allow ourselves to become distracted." She paused. "And for future note, fear is *not* an unproductive state."

"Father says—"

"Fear," her mother continued, "is an intuitive reaction to outward danger stimuli. Study it as a warning, and address it, but do not allow it to overwhelm you." Pointedly, she looked across at the humans who had been in the vehicle with them. Valeris sensed their anxiety coming off them in waves. The driver, one of the simianoid natives of Nidrus, was weeping into his long-fingered hands.

"What is going to happen to us?" she asked.

"Do not concern yourself with that," said her mother. "Do as I told you. Consider this a lesson."

Those words were something that Valeris had often heard throughout her childhood, and despite her hopes that their repetition would lessen after her successful passage through the *kahs-wan* ritual, the reverse seemed to be true. She had hoped that being given permission at long last to accompany her parents on their duties for the Federation would mark the beginning of a new chapter in her life. It had been more of the same, just on alien worlds and in starship cabins rather than on the plains of Vulcan.

She did as she was told, running silently through the focal mantras, looking around the space, her eyes adjusting to the gloom. Walls of cracked thermoconcrete supported a heavy wooden roof, shafts of pale yellow sunlight from the Nidrusi star angling across the dusty interior through cracks in the planks. Judging from the bales of vacuum-sealed grasses stacked poorly on the far side of the room, Valeris guessed that they were most likely inside one of the freehold farming complexes that dotted the countryside of Nidrus Gamma.

It was a matter of concern for her that she had not applied herself toward a more accurate determination of where they were located. After the chaos of the attack on the bridge, the explosion of the fuel cells in the groundcar, and the gunfire . . . she was reluctant to admit that her fear reaction had, as her mother had warned, briefly overwhelmed her analytical thought processes. It was only after they had been traveling for some time in the vehicle driven by their abductors that it occurred to Valeris she should have been monitoring the speed and direction of travel from beneath the sackcloth hood over her head.

She looked down at the floor and felt a cold burn across

her cheeks. Her reactions continued to shame her, and she forced them away, burying the sensations deep.

Along with the rest of the group in the groundcar, Valeris and her mother had been brought here at the barrels of a dozen weapons, in the hands of hulking, muscular figures who did not show their faces and did not speak. However, she had been on Nidrus Gamma long enough to know that they did not smell like the natives. These people were off-worlders, just like the Federation diplomatic party.

Then the door to the storeroom opened and her questions were answered.

A thickset man in a dark uniform with metallic copper accents entered and stalked across the room toward them. The humans reacted with gasps of terror as they recognized the profile of a Klingon warrior. His accented cranial ridges were heavy and broad, layered with a web of scarring. His skin had an oily, swarthy tone to it, and a thin black beard accented his face. He had a pistol in his hand. The warrior radiated threat like heat from a fire.

The Nidrusi driver got to his feet as the Klingon approached, holding out his hands in a gesture of supplication. "Please!" he began. "I am not with them! I am only a servant!"

Without breaking his stride, the Klingon spun the disruptor around in his grip and cracked it hard across the driver's face. Blood sprayed from his shattered nasal bone and a few droplets settled on Valeris's cheek. The Nidrusi collapsed in a heap, clutching his ruined snout and moaning.

Valeris stiffened, as motionless as she would have been if a wild *le-matya* had entered instead. With great delicacy, her mother reached up with a small kerchief and dabbed away the driver's blood from Valeris's face.

"Speak only when you are spoken to!" shouted the Klingon, turning his fierce expression on the mother and daughter. His breath was hot and coarse with the scent of raw meats.

Valeris remained stoic inwardly; the shameful rush of powerful emotions struggled at their bonds. She was not yet thirteen Vulcan summers old, and the girl had no wish to die on some dusty agricultural world hundreds of light-years from home.

The Klingon pulled a data slate from his tunic and scrutinized it. Something like amusement crossed his feral face, and he called out in his own language. Two more of his kind entered the storehouse, one a statuesque female carrying a heavy equipment case, the other a male with an athlete's build. This male carried himself with a swagger, and Valeris recognized him at once. It was the commander, the one she had glimpsed from the observation gallery during her father's meetings, a series of bronze-colored insignia tabs glittering on his uniform. The thuggish warrior had given him a deferential nod.

The commander took the slate, glanced at it, then handed it to the female. "You are T'Kio, wife of and assistant to Sepel," he told her mother, "of the Federation Diplomatic Service." He sounded out the words as if they meant something that sickened him.

"You have forcibly abducted us and broken several Nidrusi laws," said Valeris's parent. "Your actions constitute an interstellar incident. Your government will be notified. A formal complaint will be made."

The Klingon went on as if she had never spoken. "Your husband," he said, lingering over the words. "Does he love you?" He glanced down at the girl. "You and little . . . Valeris, isn't it?"

Her mother fell silent. She became impassive, reflecting nothing.

The commander went on. "I have always wondered if that's possible. Or are they passionless things, the marriages between your kind? A deed done only for the sake of propagating the species?" He gave Valeris an indulgent, sneering smile, showing his teeth.

Valeris couldn't stop herself: she felt compelled to answer. "My father cares for us both."

It was exactly the reply the Klingon wanted. "For your sake, child," he said, "I hope so."

He nodded to the female, who unlimbered the case and set it up on legs that she extended from the bottom of the container. The thug went back to the door and closed it halfway. Valeris got a glimpse of what was outside: she saw more farm outbuildings and the cab of the hover-truck that had brought them here.

Her attention returned to the case as the Klingon woman opened it to reveal a suite of military communications gear. There was a complex sensor head and a monitor screen that unfolded like a book.

The woman worked an inset console, then looked up. "Sensor mask is in place. Ready to transmit."

The commander nodded. "Hail them."

"What do you hope to achieve?" said one of the humans, a clerk on her father's staff. "The Nidrusi have already made their decision. It's done. You can't change anything! The negotiations are over!"

The Klingon gave a curt nod. "Yes, they are."

Today was they day they were going to leave. The groundcar was taking Valeris, her mother, and the others back to the spaceport. Her father and two senior staffers from his party had remained in the capital to confirm the final details of the local government's agreement with the Federation; the intention was that they would join them after sunset. It had been a problematic few weeks on Nidrus. Valeris wanted to leave. Now she began to wonder if any of them ever would.

Her father had told her, in one of his usual lectures, that while the Nidrus system itself was relatively peaceful, it sat in a zone of space that was considerably more hazardous. The indigenous ape-like species were relative newcomers to the galactic stage, having developed faster-than-light travel only in the last few decades, and until recently the Nidrusi had remained unaware that their worlds existed on the borders of the Klingon Empire. They had made contact with the United Federation of Planets and expressed interest at overtures of alliance—and the moons of Nidrus Gamma had a wealth of dilithium that would serve them well for interstellar trade, enough to pique Federation interest.

Nidrus was a nonaligned world, and that meant the Klingon Empire, under current treaty stipulations, could also tender an offer to the planetary government.

Ambassador Sepel of Vulcan had been dispatched aboard a civilian courier to put the Federation's case to the Nidrusi. The Klingons had arrived with a battle cruiser to show their flag.

Valeris was encouraged by her parents to observe the ambassadorial mission. They had both made very clear their expectations for their daughter: that she was being groomed to follow them into the diplomatic service. How Valeris's own intentions for her future factored into this had never been addressed.

From the start, she knew how the discussion would go. The natives, a race of peaceable beings who respected hard work, fair play, and directness, did not respond well to the veiled threats and braggadocio of the Klingons. Valeris agreed with the Nidrusi.

The Klingons were the antithesis of everything Valeris had grown up with: they were all raw emotion and aggression, noisy and dangerous. If forced to put a description to it, she would have said they frightened her.

"They cannot be trusted," she had told her father at the end of one day's round of talks.

"What do you base that statement upon?" he asked.

Valeris should have told him that her assertion was drawn from readings of past conduct on the part of Klingon commanders, or on cultural observation of their behavior patterns. Instead, she was truthful. *"An instinct."*

Sepel told his daughter that instincts were for animals and not rational, intelligent beings, then dismissed her.

At first, the Klingons paid lip service to the Nidrusi demands for an evenhanded negotiation. But as it became clearer that the natives were veering toward accepting the Federation's offer, they became belligerent. Finally, the Klingons threw off the last pretense at diplomacy and warned the governors of Nidrus that rejecting the Empire's demands would not end well for them.

Valeris's father chose that moment to question the credentials of K'Darg, the Klingon representative. The alien commander had been vague on that point from the very start; apparently, it was not unknown for officers of the Klingon military to act more in their own interests and claim it was for the good of their species after the fact.

There were harsh words and more threats. Valeris watched the Klingon commander storm from the meeting hall. She learned later that the officer's reaction was doubtless based on concerns for his own position and status. The captains of many Klingon ships were treated almost as privateers by their seniors, and the hierarchy among their crews was said to be similarly lawless. Returning home without a victory could be a death sentence.

In retrospect, it placed what happened next in an understandable context.

"Encryption is complete," said the Klingon female. "They won't be able to track the signal source."

"Be certain," said the commander. "If you fail me, I'll have your head."

The woman nodded grimly and he glared into the sensor unit. "Sepel!" he snarled. "This is Commander K'Darg! I know you are listening. Show yourself, Vulcan."

Valeris felt an odd flutter in her chest as her father's neutral expression appeared on the monitor screen. *I am here. I have been informed that my party has gone missing. Can I assume that you are responsible?*

My party. He did not mention Valeris or her mother by name.

"The Klingon Empire does what it must to retain the sovereignty of its borders," replied the commander. "You've promised these native fools the stars, but your promises are hollow. You can't even protect your own family!" He grabbed the sensor and aimed it at Valeris and her mother. "Your kind are weak, Vulcan, and I will prove it. This world needs strong leadership, and it will have it!"

"*You mean* mastery," Sepel replied calmly. "*All the Klingon Empire will bring to Nidrus is slavery. They made their choice. You must respect it. End this now.*"

"No." K'Darg drew his *d'k tahg*. "I have five of your people here, including your wife and your child." He made a show of flicking open the blade. "I will execute them one by one unless you agree to my terms."

Valeris's mother spoke up: "I was of the understanding that Klingons had a code of honorable behavior. Tell me, is the murder of unarmed women and children something that you will be lauded for among your species?"

In a flash, the commander spun and slapped T'Kio across the face with such force that she staggered backward a step. Valeris was unable to prevent a small gasp from escaping her lips. Her mother looked at her and shook her head.

"Klingon honor is for Klingons," said the female, glowering at them. "You insult us by suggesting you deserve such a privilege."

"Listen to me, Vulcan," said the commander. "You will withdraw from these negotiations. You will withdraw your authority on behalf of the Federation to Nidrus. And you will agree to leave this planet for us to . . . supervise."

"*What you ask for is impossible. Even if I were to agree, the letter of the agreement still stands. Starfleet would return to Nidrus to enforce the treaty.*"

"They would be welcome to *try*," retorted K'Darg.

Valeris knew that the Klingons would have the advantage if that scenario came to pass. Nidrus was out on the periphery here; by the time Starfleet managed to get starships deployed to this system, the Empire would have been able to reinforce their position. The locals certainly lacked the strength to stop them. And then she wondered if Starfleet Command would really be willing to go to war over a planet that was not even a member of the United Federation of Planets.

Her father's gaze did not waver. "*If the Federation agrees to leave Nidrus, the Klingon Empire will launch an invasion to annex these worlds. I cannot allow that to happen."*

"Perhaps the ambassador doesn't believe you are serious, sir?" said the female.

"That is a possibility," offered K'Darg. He turned and stabbed his blade into the trembling driver. The Nidrusi was robbed of the chance to scream; his body tensed and then fell slack.

Valeris went cold, as if she had been doused in icy water. She had never seen death so close at hand before. The brutal, horrific suddenness of it, the callous abandon of the act . . . It sickened her to her core. She turned and found the Klingon commander watching her, almost as if he were daring her to say something.

Ignoring the panicked utterances of the other hostages, he glanced back into the sensor. "No deadlines," he said. "No time to think it over. No stalling." The Klingon aimed his *d'k tahg* lazily in the direction of Valeris and her mother. "Agree now, or your wife dies and your child will bear witness. I will let the girl live long enough to ask you why you allowed this to happen."

Sepel's reply was immediate. *"I will not agree."*

"Father!" The word slipped from Valeris, and her hands tensed into fists. She could not believe what she was hearing.

"I will not agree," he repeated in the hectoring tone he so often used when he took it upon himself to criticize. *"I do not doubt you will do as you say. But still, I refuse to accede to your demands. They are illogical."*

K'Darg's face twisted and he crossed to Valeris's mother, resting the edge of his knife against her throat. "Are you so bloodless, *petaQ*? You will watch me end them, one after another? Your family and these mewling fools? You can save their lives with a single act!"

"He . . . will not." Her mother met her daughter's gaze, and in it Valeris saw something she could not fully understand, deep within the stoic mask.

"I cannot sacrifice the people of Nidrus . . . A handful

of deaths cannot be measured against the thousands of lives that will be lost in an invasion. No matter what you do in an attempt to coerce me, in the Federation's name I will never capitulate."

The Klingon grimaced and dragged T'Kio into the middle of the storeroom. "We'll see if you still feel the same after this one dies in front of you. This time it won't be quick. She'll bleed out."

"Father, please!" Valeris shouted. "Do what he wants!"

"No, daughter," came the reply. *"I am disappointed that you do not understand."*

But she did. She understood that her father was willing to allow her and her mother to be executed in order to prove an abstract point. He would do nothing, in the name of alien beings who were too weak, too foolish, to defend themselves against vicious predators like the Klingons.

For a moment Valeris felt herself cracking open as if she were a vessel made of clay. Her outer shell was crumbling, the years of unflinching, steady control imposed on her almost from birth, all of it on the verge of collapsing into nothing. She experienced shivers of response that were so foreign to her, she could barely comprehend them. Was this anger? Sadness? She couldn't tell. A directionless hurricane of emotion was welling up inside her, and Valeris had nowhere to release it.

She swept around the room. She saw the humans, fretting and self-obsessed, petrified that they were going to die next; her father's unmoving aspect, passing judgment on them all, ignorant of the child who had so often tried to gain his approval; her mother, resigned to her fate, exhausted and ineffectual . . . and the Klingons, terrible and monstrous, hateful and brimming with violence, shattering everything she loved.

Valeris looked down at her bound hands. They were trembling, and she was at once disgusted and horrified at her own emotional reaction. "Wh-what have you done?" she stuttered, digging deep to find a wellspring of defiance. She glared at the Klingon, ignoring the weapon in his hand. "What gives you the right to come here . . . and do these things?"

K'Darg showed his teeth once again and turned his bloodstained blade from her mother to hold it before Valeris's face. "This does," he said, nodding at the weapon.

In the next second there was a sound like the crackle of distant lightning, and all at once a series of new shafts of light snapped into being, emerging from the walls of the storeroom. The rays were bright and actinic, and each found a mark in the chest of one of the Klingons, threading back and forth so fast, it was only Valeris's acute Vulcan retinas that registered them.

The commander and the female, the thug at the door, all of them fell to the ground with smoking pits cut in their torsos. K'Darg stumbled and collapsed on the communications gear, severing the connection to Valeris's father. She rushed to her mother's side. T'Kio stood rigid, her face frozen.

"What . . . what happened?" said one of the others.

"Phaser beams. Fired through the walls," Valeris replied numbly.

A ripple of weapons discharges sounded outside, and the door swung open. Sunlight flooded in, framing an Andorian in Starfleet security armor, a phaser rifle in his hand. He advanced into the room, panning around with his weapon. "Clear!" he called, checking the bodies of their abductors. "I have the hostages." He waved a tricorder at them. "Negating dispersal field now."

Valeris heard the tinny reply over his helmet communicator. *"Good work, Lieutenant. Stand back, we're locking on to them."*

"Copy that, *Ark Royal*." The blue-skinned officer gave them all a nod. "We'll secure the site down here, look for any stragglers."

Valeris blinked into the bright light streaming in from outside; then she felt a prickling sensation wash over her skin, and the storeroom vanished into the haze of a transporter beam.

U.S.S. Ark Royal NCC-1791
Nidrus System
Federation-Klingon Border Zone

A human nurse in a beige tunic examined each of them, and after ensuring that Valeris was well, she escorted her to a small waiting area. The woman left her with a nervous smile and the girl found herself alone.

They had separated her mother from the rest of the recovered hostages within moments of rematerialization on board the starship. The nurse told her not to be concerned, but the human's body language made it clear she was attempting to mollify her.

Valeris got up from her seat and moved to the edge of the alcove so she could observe the corridor beyond. This was the medical section of the vessel: she recognized the uniform insignia colors of the crew moving back and forth. She took in her surroundings, uncertain of what she should do next. Waiting patiently felt like the wrong thing. Valeris was unsettled; her life had been within seconds of ending, and even though the danger was past, the energy of the moment had not dissipated. The calming mantras did not alleviate the problem.

The ship was of an older Starfleet design, judging by the construction and the systems visible to her. A cruiser, she guessed, perhaps one of the bigger *Constitution*-class vessels. The deck gave off a subtle vibration, and Valeris had some vague sense that the ship was in motion.

A door hissed open, and two officers in mid-conversation exited a room across the way. ". . . The fact is, if we hadn't been here, I hate to think how this would have turned out." The speaker was a human male, and Valeris estimated his age was in the midforties. Dark-skinned, with a weather-beaten face, he wore a blue-grey tunic and sported captain's insignia around his wrists. He was talking to the Andorian who had discovered them on the farmstead.

The security officer nodded, his antennae twitching. "Not well, sir. But the fates were on our side."

"Never believed in that sort of thing, Lieutenant," said the captain. "Luck is a fallacy. You get things done right by showing up and putting your shoulder to the grindstone." He frowned. "Has the ambassador been informed of the situation?"

Valeris stiffened at the mention of her father. The Andorian was nodding again.

"Aye, sir. He's, ah, chosen to remain down on the planet for the time being."

The human's frown deepened. "His wife has a severe concussion. Was that made clear to him?"

"It was," said the lieutenant. "Ambassador Sepel said he was quite certain that Starfleet's medical staff would be able to address her injuries."

Once again Valeris found her hands tightening into fists. With effort, she relaxed her fingers and continued to listen. The three-tone bosun's whistle over the intraship broke the line of the conversation.

"Bridge to Captain Cartwright," said a disembodied voice.

"Cartwright here, go ahead."

"Sir, the Klingon ship has just gone to warp. They're hightailing out of here, on a speed course straight back to their side of the border. What are your orders?"

"We could catch them before they get out of range," noted the Andorian. "A frigate-class ship like that would be no match for us."

"It is tempting to go for a little payback," admitted Cartwright, "but we have other concerns for now. Bridge?"

"Sir?"

"Let them go. Collate all the data we have on the vessel's identity and inform Starfleet Command. In the meantime, take us back to Nidrus Gamma. I'll be up there in a few moments. Cartwright out." He turned away from the intercom. "Even if we took them alive, the Klingon Empire would declare that ship and all of K'Darg's crew as renegades and claim they were acting alone."

"The ones on the ground fought us to the death," said the Andorian. "They wouldn't have let themselves be captured. It's not their way."

"'Their way'?" Cartwright repeated irritably. "Seems to me the Klingon way is preying on unarmed civilians and victims who can't fight back." He snorted as he walked away. "More fools, them, for thinking we'd send a diplomatic mission out here without fleet backup. K'Darg never would have shown his face if he knew *Ark Royal* was on the way."

"It's only a pity Sepel didn't summon us sooner," added the lieutenant.

Valeris processed what she was hearing: her father had called in the Starfleet vessel, doubtless after it became clear that the Klingons did not intend to allow Nidrus to choose the Federation. But why had he waited so long? Why had he insisted they come to Nidrus in an unarmed vessel in the first place? If Cartwright's ship had been there all along, none of this would have happened . . . and the Klingons would have been kept at bay.

They are *like animals,* she thought. *The Klingons have to be penned in, prevented from harming outsiders.* Valeris retreated into the alcove and took a hesitant step back toward the chair.

She looked down at her hands, at the darkened striations around her thin child's wrists where the restraint tapes had held them tightly. They were trembling as if she were cold.

The unfinished, ill-formed sensation that had come to her when K'Darg held his blade before Valeris returned like the surge of a tidal wave. Nameless emotion, potent and strong, shuddered through the Vulcan girl's body. She glanced around, but there was no one within sight, nobody to witness the sudden failure of her self-control.

Anger rose in Valeris, a flood-head that threatened to engulf her. It was more powerful than she had imagined it might be, and with it came fragments of terror, of sorrow, of razor-edged hate and raw animal panic. These things were anathema to her; never in her life had she allowed herself to *feel* like this.

Valeris had never experienced something so traumatic that it could open her so readily and spill out all these deeply buried sensations. It became a torrent that threatened to drown her.

She collapsed into the chair and her hands knitted together. Then, taking a lungful of air, Valeris took command of herself once more, and step by step the young girl isolated and excised the emotions spinning through her thoughts. She killed them off one at a time through a single-minded application of concentration. Anger at her father for a cold disregard for their lives, terror and panic as the echo of near death faded from her thoughts, and the empathy of sorrow for the man who had perished.

Finally, there was only the hatred. She rolled it back and forth in her mind as if it were a seething ember thrown from a fire, too hot to grasp. The emotion made her think of the Klingons, of all they were and the danger they represented. It gave her focus.

I will keep this one, she thought. *To remind myself.* With a final exercise of her resolve, Valeris pushed the ember away, hiding it in the darkness.

"Are you all right, child?" The voice seemed to come out of nowhere, and her head snapped up. The Andorian lieutenant stood in the doorway; she had been so consumed by her own inner turmoil that she had not heard him approaching. His expression was one of kindness and concern.

Valeris kept her aspect and voice neutral. "I was not injured."

He watched her carefully. "Some wounds don't appear all at once."

She raised an eyebrow. "I do not follow the logic of your statement." The moment of disconnect Valeris had experienced seconds earlier was fading now, as if it had never occurred. She felt her equilibrium returning.

"I mean, there's no shame in being afraid."

"Shame and fear are unproductive emotional states," Valeris said with finality. "I do not experience them."

18

Kaj's escape plan survived less than ten seconds. The Kriosians were not fools: they had spent their adult lives crossing swords with the Klingons, and they were still alive because they knew how to deal with them. They left Vaughn in his cell, ignoring his shouts, and six of them went into the compartment next to his, every one of them carrying shock-prods. Elias had seen the devices before: his uncle had a ranch on Berengaria VII that bred a local stripe of bison-like cattle, and the farmhands used them to keep the animals in check.

He didn't see what happened—he only heard the grunts and shouts from Kaj as she took on her assailants. Bones cracked and men screamed, but in the end the sparking of the prods drowned it all out.

They dragged Kaj's semiconscious form out and dumped her on the floor. Then the gate to Vaughn's cell opened and a man with a bloody nose beckoned him out. In his other hand, a shock-prod hummed like a hornet trapped inside a bottle. The inference was clear: *the easy way or the hard way.*

Vaughn walked out, his hands at his sides, and went to Kaj, lifting her up from the floor. She could barely stand, and all the Klingon's weight went on him. She was a lot heavier than she looked, and he grunted with the effort.

One of the other Thorn men sniggered, and Vaughn shot him an acid look. "Don't feel you need to help," he said. "I don't want to keep you from all the other women you need to beat on."

"Shut up and walk, Starfleet," said the one with the broken nose.

He was grateful for the slightly lower-than-Earth-standard gravity in the corridors outside: it made handling Kaj a little easier. The major staggered, managing to plant one foot in front of the other, and by degrees she shook off the effects of the attack. Her head drooped so she could whisper in Elias's ear. "They're going to kill us," she said.

The denial came automatically to him. "You don't know that."

"If they wanted to torture us, they would have done it by now," she went on. "I tell you this so you may make peace with your gods, Lieutenant."

"I never really believed in that kind of thing," he admitted.

Kaj eyed him. "Pity. You have courage. We might have been able to find you a posting in the Black Fleet."

"I'm not ready for Valhalla just yet," said Vaughn. "Where there's life, there's hope."

"I told you to shut up!" shouted the Kriosian. His new injury made his voice thick and nasal.

The rest of the forced march went on in silence. They were directed up the main spinal corridor to the levels at the northern "pole" of the elliptical asteroid. As far as Vaughn could tell, the Thorn base was arranged like a terrestrial building with tiers stacked one atop another, some cut into the rock, others fashioned across the naturally occurring caverns and places where minerals had been mined out.

They followed a spiraling ramp and emerged at a wide airlock gate that opened back into the main landing bay. The compartment was the largest open space Vaughn had seen inside the asteroid; at the far end, a wide slot looked out into the void, illuminated by a ring of force field projectors. The semitransparent barrier flickered now and then with discharges of blue light, keeping the atmosphere of the base contained but still permeable to objects of larger mass. Similar technology was used in starship shuttlebays: anything smaller than a man would be repelled by the energy membrane, but ships could enter and depart freely. Out beyond the barrier, a different curtain of light glowed: a holographic screen generated to conceal the mouth of the landing bay from any ships that might pass within visual range.

Despite the size of the bay, the space seemed cramped. There were clusters of cargo pods and wheeled tender-tractors here and there, remnants from the asteroid's days as a mine works. Among them stood the *Chon'm*, resting low on its landing gear with wings raised and boarding ramp down. The scoutship looked very much a mythical giant hawk settled on its talons, waiting to take flight. Several of the Thorn swarmed around it, apparently off-loading anything from inside the ship that might be of value. Vaughn heard Kaj hiss through her teeth at the sight of her vessel being plundered by the Kriosians.

Nearby, tucked under the bird-of-prey's port-side wing, the dart-like Kriosian cutter was crowded in with repair gantries. Hull panels lay discarded on the deck, and Vaughn could see exposed sections of the in-line warp nacelles where they had been damaged during the earlier engagement. The elderly cutter had been forgotten in favor of the captured Klingon vessel, and there were men moving equipment from one ship to the other in preparation . . . *for what?*

Kaj nudged him and jutted her head. "Look there."

He turned and saw the woman Gattin and her cohort Tulo supervising the movement of a metallic drum the length of a photon torpedo casing. Vaughn's blood ran cold to see the device again. "It's the subspace weapon," he began. "But it wasn't complete. It wasn't ready . . ."

"It is now," she grated.

Tulo guided the grav-trolley bearing the device in a slow, languid turn to orient it toward the bird-of-prey's boarding ramp. Gattin said something and left him to complete the task of loading, then strode toward the prisoners.

"What are you going to do with my ship?" Kaj demanded, as the severe woman approached them.

"*Your* ship?" Gattin mocked. "Not anymore. And as for the rest . . . ask *him*." The Kriosian nodded toward one of the other corridors that issued out into the echoing bay.

Rein emerged, crossing the metal deck quickly and purposefully. Valeris was a few steps behind him; she showed no interest in Vaughn's or Kaj's condition. To illustrate her opinion of the situation, the major drew up a mouthful of purple, blood-laced spittle, and ejected it onto the ground.

The Thorn's leader glared at her, offended by the action. He gestured for the guards to step back and caught sight of the man with the broken nose. "Which one of them did that?"

"The woman," came the terse reply.

Rein laughed. "Never underestimate the desperation of a cornered animal." He gave the two of them a measuring look. The Kriosian addressed Vaughn: "I admit, you did well. I was taken in at first; had there been time, you might even have won me over. The ship, you see . . . the ship turned my head." Then he glared at Kaj. "But as so often happens with beings like you . . . you underestimate us. You think that because you are citizens of your great Federation and Empire, you are somehow cleverer than those of us who hail from a single world. But we're not the parochial naïfs you believe us to be. Krios Prime was an empire of its own, long before your Federation even existed, human."

"Such an imperium," Kaj snorted. "A handful of dull worlds ruled by a cadre of moneyed snobs."

Gattin made a fist. "You know nothing about us, tyrant!"

Vaughn's patience was eroding by the second; he was sick of all the posturing. "Why the hell are we here, Rein?" he demanded. "If you think we're going to give you anything, you're way off base."

"Give me something?" Rein laughed again. "You think I want to interrogate you? Ransom you? Why would I waste my effort?"

He flicked his hand toward one of the guards, and two of the men came in and cracked Vaughn and Kaj across the backs of their legs. Elias staggered forward and caught himself before he collapsed to the deck. Beside him, Kaj was on her knees, her bruised face lit with fury.

Rein came closer. "You've already given me more than I could have hoped for." He pointed at the *Chon'm*. Running lights snapped on along the tips of the scout's wings, and the hum of internal systems grew louder: the vessel was making ready to depart. "I'll tell you a truth. Before you came along, I estimated that the chances of the Thorn making a third, successful strike against a tyrant target were less than one in five. I believed that, like the others before it, this would be a suicide mission, and even then it might not be enough to reach the objective." He looked at Kaj. "But then you came, with your lies, your subterfuge and your disrespect for us . . . And you brought your pretty ship. It's only right that it belongs to us now, because of your arrogance. A Klingon weapon turned against its masters. There's poetry in that, I think."

Vaughn blew out a breath. "You're actually going to do it, aren't you? Stand there and gloat at us like some kind of storybook villain." His jaw was set in a hard grimace, defiance etched on his features. "If you're waiting for us to do the whole begging-to-be-spared thing, that's not going to happen. So do what you have to do and be on your way."

At his side, Kaj gave a curt nod of approval. "What the human said."

Rein made a mock-sad face. "Oh, such bravery. But there will be no one to scream you into your idiotic afterlife, Klingon. And no one to remember your name, human." He took two steps away and then stopped. "Wait. No. That's not true. There *is* someone." He turned and beckoned. "Valeris. Come here. It's time to say farewell to your erstwhile comrades."

Vaughn stiffened as the Vulcan did as she was told.

"What is it that your people say? 'Live long and prosper'?" Rein went on, playing to his men. "That's a rather sarcastic farewell, considering how little life these two have remaining to them. I have a better idea, a better way to say good-bye." He drew a disruptor from his belt, grabbed Valeris's wrist, and slapped the butt of the pistol into her open palm. "There. That's much more honest."

"Rein . . ." Valeris met his gaze. "Is this necessary?"

"Yes," Gattin answered before anyone else could speak. "Because as corpses these two will become useful. We'll drop them near the detonation site, and if anything of them should happen to survive the subspace rupture, the DNA traces will set the tyrants running in circles for months."

"A Klingon and a human involved in the worst terrorist atrocity ever to strike the Empire. What will people say?" Rein cocked his head. "Kill them, Valeris. It's not like you've never done it before. Just two more."

The Vulcan walked slowly toward them, checking the settings of the gun in her hand. Kaj spat again and turned her head, unwilling to meet the eyes of a traitor, but Vaughn watched her all the way, never breaking his gaze.

"I regret it came to this," Valeris told him. "But there is no other way." She raised the disruptor, aiming it at his chest.

Carefully, Vaughn set his muscles and tensed, waiting for the right moment. *Closer. Just a little closer.* "Was there anything you said or did that was not a lie?" he asked her. "Any single act of real loyalty?"

" 'Loyalty' and 'treason' are relative terms," she replied. "They can be defined only by the points from which they are observed." For a fraction of a second Valeris's gaze broke away, flicking down to the weapon in her hand.

It was the instant Vaughn needed. He exploded into motion, throwing himself at the Vulcan with all the force he could muster. They collided, and he grabbed for the barrel of the disruptor, forcing it up and away. Valeris tried to block him, her free hand coming up to snag his, and for a brief second they struggled against each other. The Vulcan was stronger than her elfin frame made her appear, and Elias felt his joints lock as they pulled and pushed.

Then he felt something being pressed into the palm of his hand. Something small, hard-edged, the size of a coin. He

looked up in surprise and confusion. Valeris mouthed two
words to him.

Trust me.

Her hand came up in a palm strike and connected with
Vaughn's jawbone. Bright, sharp pain echoed through his
head and he stumbled backward, crashing back to the deck on
his hands and knees.

"Enough of this," he heard Gattin say. "Kill the human
first."

The object in his hand—the object Valeris had forced on
him—was a piece of a mechanism. He recognized it at once:
an emitter module from an energy weapon.

Elias looked up just as Valeris pulled the trigger.

The emotion behind Vaughn's eyes—was it surprise?
Resentment? She couldn't tell. Would he understand? *Would
either of them understand?*

Valeris didn't hesitate, knowing full well that the
chance before her would not come again. She squeezed the
disruptor's trigger plate and the energy weapon buzzed in
her hand, turning hot with the discharge. A lightning bolt
of red-orange flashed from the barrel and slammed into the
lieutenant's right shoulder, the energy turning into a puff
of flame as it atomized the outer layers of his clothing. The
shock effect punched him back and spun Vaughn to the deck
of the landing bay.

The gun was burning her skin, the power coils overcharging
as the Vulcan pivoted and fired again at the disguised Klingon,
even as the woman tried to spring at her. The second bolt hit
Kaj in the chest, another chug of fire bursting briefly over her
torso. The major fell hard, her limbs splaying. Wisps of thin
white smoke curled from the beam weapon's accelerator coils.

"It's done?" asked Rein.

Gattin raced to the fallen Klingon, a broad push-dagger
instantly in her grip, drawn from a pocket in the Kriosian's
sleeve. She had a fierce grin on her lips, and it occurred to

Valeris that the woman wanted some kind of souvenir from the body of her enemy. One of Rein's other people, the male with the facial injury, moved toward Vaughn.

Valeris turned back to where the Thorn leader stood waiting for her. He held his hand out for her to return his weapon. "You see?" he said. "Two. Two hundred. Two thousand. After a while, it's nothing but numbers."

What happened next occurred with great rapidity.

The man with the broken nose let out a wordless cry of alarm that was cut short by a sudden, concussive grunt. Vaughn, very much alive, landed a powerful punch in the Kriosian's gut, then followed it with a knee-strike to the crotch. The lieutenant threw his assailant off him and snatched at the pistol on the other man's belt, wrestling it free.

At the same moment, Kaj sat up sharply with such force that her forehead butted Gattin in the face, pulling a muffled howl from the other woman. Even though the major's cranial ridges had been smoothed for her alien camouflage, the density of a Klingon skull was still much greater than that of a Kriosian one, and the blow knocked Gattin aside. Her dagger fell from her hand and she staggered away.

There was a flurry of motion as multiple weapons were torn from their holsters, muzzles rising to draw a bead. Valeris was ready, however, and she pressed the trigger tightly, heat flaring in the gun once more. The Vulcan drew the disruptor across herself in an arc, sending a fan of crackling energy in the direction of Rein and his guards.

They scattered, one of them screaming as he caught a burst across his face. Rein dove for cover, and Valeris tried to strike back at him, but succeeded only in throwing a last pulse of flame at his retreating back. Finally, the weapon crackled and spat out a cloud of acrid smoke, the mechanism fused. Missing the vital emitter module she had detached from the phasing chamber, the disruptor's output had been reduced to mere sound and fury, enough to cause surface burning but not enough to disintegrate matter.

The Kriosians knew she had betrayed them. Beam fire

erupted from all sides of the landing bay, scoring black gouges in the metal decking and stone floor. Valeris broke into a full-tilt run as she heard Vaughn shout out, his voice carrying over the melee. "Get to cover!"

She was aware of Kaj moving off to the side, the Klingon hesitating long enough to backhand Gattin before sprinting for one of the parked cargo haulers and the train of container pods behind it. Before her, Vaughn was moving with an old Mark II phaser in his hand, laying down spears of brilliant fire.

The air around Valeris was thick with particle beam discharges and the screech of superheated oxygen molecules. She reached the cargo pods and vaulted over them, landing hard behind the low cover as heat and light splashed over the steel containers.

Vaughn fell into place next to her, popping back up to fire a spread of shots in all directions before ducking down once more. "What the hell are you doing?"

"Saving your life, Lieutenant Vaughn," she replied.

With a feral snarl, Kaj came up around the line of the parked cargo tractor. She, too, had a pistol in one fist, and Gattin's push-dagger gripped in the other. "You shot me," she growled. An angry purple-red weal marked her throat and cheek.

"I sabotaged the weapon. The injury was minimal to you both. There was no other alternative."

"More games?" Vaughn barked. "How many double crosses have you got?"

"We will argue about this later," said Kaj as more disruptor bolts and phaser discharges hissed over their heads. "We're pinned down here. The confusion won't last long; we need to move."

Valeris was surprised by the Klingon's calmness under fire: she seemed almost *Vulcan* in her manner, composed and singular in her focus. The major was also quite correct in her evaluation. The cargo tender and the pods on the trailers lay in a V-shape to the side of the landing bay—a single point of cover between Rein and his guards near the corridors to the right, and Gattin and the *Chon'm* to the left.

Valeris dropped to the deck and peered beneath the skids of the trailer. She heard Gattin shouting, but the woman's words were lost to her. Rein was visible behind a stanchion, and she saw him lean out of cover, gesturing wildly to his second in command.

"Gattin, the ship!" he was shouting. "Get to the ship! Forget them, just go!"

Vaughn heard the terrorist leader's orders as well. "They're going for the bird-of-prey . . ."

"No," Kaj retorted. "Give me covering fire." She tossed her stolen pistol to Valeris.

"Major, wait—"

The Klingon ignored the lieutenant's words and leapt high, mantling the cargo pods, breaking into a run. Vaughn swore and started firing wildly in the direction of Rein and his guards, blasting shots into the air to keep their heads down.

Valeris did the same as Kaj sprinted out after Gattin. The Kriosian woman had a long lead on the Klingon, and she made it to the drop ramp beneath the *Chon'm* while the major was still precious meters away. With a savage yell, Kaj returned Gattin's dagger to her, throwing it hard.

The stubby blade struck Gattin in the thigh, and she shrieked in pain; but the ramp was already lifting clear of the floor as thrusters along the underside of the scoutship rattled and ignited.

The ramp slammed shut, and with a surge of engine noise the *Chon'm* rose unsteadily into the air, wavering as whoever was at the helm got the feel of the flight controls. The bird-of-prey revolved in place, the massive wings swinging out as the ship's bow turned toward the glowing maw of the landing bay. The Klingon screamed in frustration as her ship showed its stern.

Across the chamber, Rein broke from his concealment and ran toward the corridor, his men falling back with him, laying down blasts of energy. Vaughn ducked back behind the sizzling, half-melted shapes of the cargo pods, glaring at the diminishing charge on his weapon.

Valeris kept her attention on Rein. He paused at an alcove and ducked inside; she remembered from her observations of the asteroid base's systems that similar control points were located throughout the facility. From any one of them, a person with the correct authority codes could access the primary control matrix.

And suddenly she knew what was going to happen next. Valeris shot to her feet, turning toward the mouth of the landing bay. The *Chon'm* was gliding toward it, the impulse grid glowing yellow; nothing could stop it now. Ahead, the white glow of the containment field grid flickered and began to fade.

"He's going to seal off the bay and vent the atmosphere," she snapped, then shouted to Kaj, "Major! The barrier!"

If the Klingon understood what Valeris meant, she did not have time to respond. Rein and his soldiers vanished behind saw-toothed steel hatches rising from the deck, just as an icy hurricane picked up across the chamber. The force field winked out as the *Chon'm* passed through it and into open space.

Pitiless vacuum embraced the pocket of atmosphere inside the asteroid, clawing at everything that wasn't secured to the deck. Empty containers, debris, scraps of metal, and loose tools were picked up, caught, and thrown out into the darkness.

Valeris felt the air being sucked from her lungs, a frigid polar wind lashing at her bare skin. Vaughn stumbled across the floor and grabbed at something near his feet; she saw a shaft of light flicker into being through a hatch in the deck. "A maintenance pit!" he bellowed, his words almost lost in the roaring chaos of the decompression. "Quickly!"

She tried to run to him, but her boots were slipping as patches of frost formed from vapor in the fading air. Vaughn slipped through the hatch and vanished. Valeris forced herself back up, clinging to the gridded deck plates, just as one of the cargo pods came loose from its tethers and clattered past her, tumbling end over end. The edge of the metal container clipped her arm and she spun, losing her grip.

The inexorable draw of the blackness took hold and Valeris slipped away, as if she were sliding down a slope into the abyss. She allowed herself to feel the emotion of *regret*.

But then a strong arm was pulling her back, gathering her up. With a monumental effort Kaj gathered the other woman to her and dragged them both toward the hatch, hand over hand. Vaughn, his face pale, pulled them into the maintenance pit and, with a shuddering gasp of relief, slammed his fist against the switch to seal the hatch behind them.

For a while the three of them lay in the cramped, uncomfortable space amid a mess of spilled tools and support gear, the air in the compartment thin and cold. Their breath emerged in puffs of white and none of them could stop shivering. Outside, the clank and rattle of unsecured items tumbling out into space faded to nothing, until the only sound was the creak of the hatch settling against the shift in external pressure.

Finally, Vaughn found his voice. He pointed to an oval panel on the far side of the long, narrow section. "Th-that's an accessway, I think. We can use it to get back into the main part of the base, to someplace with air."

Kaj didn't respond to him. Instead, she turned to study the Vulcan. The Klingon's face was discolored: the cold and the burn from the disruptor hit had damaged the artificial pigments in her flesh, and the violet hue she had worn was fading away, turning back to her natural dusky shade. "I am rarely surprised," she said, her tone hoarse with the chill. "But you continue to defy my attempts to categorize you, convict."

Valeris held her arms about herself, conserving her body heat. "You saved my life."

"For a second time," the lieutenant added.

Kaj shrugged, moving to examine the panel Vaughn had indicated. "What of it?"

"Why?" said Valeris. "Before, on the bridge of the

Chon'm . . . you needed me alive. But not so now. You placed yourself at considerable risk."

"Perhaps I want to kill you myself."

Valeris went on. "It would have been far easier to leave me to perish, but you chose otherwise. Given your attitude toward me, I have no idea what would motivate you."

Kaj rounded on her, eyes flaring. "Yes. That much is certain. You think you know me, but you know *nothing*." She took a warning step toward Valeris. "You judge me and every other Klingon by the actions of a craven few, by the very worst of our kind." Kaj pointed, taking in Valeris and Vaughn with the gesture. "I judge you, your Starfleet, and your Federation by honorable men like Darius Miller, the best of your kind." She turned away. "I saved your life because it was the right thing to do."

Valeris paused, mulling over the major's words. "You . . . have my gratitude."

Kaj pulled off the access panel and handed it to Vaughn; then, with a single, swift motion, she struck out and punched Valeris hard across the face. The blow sent the Vulcan reeling, opening a cut on her cheek.

"Whoa, stop!" Vaughn scrambled for his pistol, but Kaj was already moving away, her moment of anger spent.

"I've made my point," said the Klingon.

"Stifle those damn sirens," Rein ordered, moving quickly down the turns of the tunnel. "Someone get up to the operations center and put the barrier field back up: there are no remote terminals down here . . ."

The man at his side nodded. "On the way. It'll take a few moments." He hesitated. "Did . . . did Gattin make it out? Are they away?"

Rein stopped and gave the others a hard look. "She knows what the mission is, don't worry. We won't hear from her again until it is done." The Kriosian felt conflicted. On one hand, he had wanted to be on board the *Chon'm* himself, to be there when the deed was done and see it with his own eyes; but the needs of the moment had taken priority. That Vulcan witch had been playing them for fools all along, waiting for the chance to inveigle herself into the Thorn, to attack them from within. He should have let Gattin execute the lot of them at the first opportunity.

Rein nodded to himself. He had done the right thing. Every second the bird-of-prey sat on the deck was a moment more that Valeris and her fellow spies could use to thwart the Thorn's most deadly attack. Sending the ship was the right choice, and he had used the opportunity to deal with two problems at once.

But still . . . he had to be sure. "Come," he said, moving off again. "The infirmary is this way."

"But no one is hurt."

The Thorn leader shook his head. "The internal sensors in this place have never worked correctly. We'll need tricorders to scan for life-signs." He reached the door to the medical bay and strode inside.

Drell was waiting for them with a plasma pistol in his hand. "Akadar's blood! What did you do, lad?"

"I told you not to call me that," said Rein. He ignored the question and went to a rack where a cluster of old Federation surplus tricorders were recharging. "Here," he told the men. "Take these. Spread out and scan for anything that doesn't read as Kriosian. If you find something, shoot first."

"Rein!" Drell was at his heels. "Let me guess? The Vulcan spun a lie to you?"

He rounded on the acerbic medic. "Be silent, old man. Don't pretend she didn't turn your head as well."

"You're holding on too tightly!" Drell insisted. "I know it's you who was taking stimulants from the medical supplies! When was the last time you slept? Your judgment is impaired, and now look at what has happened!"

"Shut up!" Rein exploded with sudden fury, his cheeks reddening. He glared at the other men. "I gave you a command; now go and execute it!"

Reluctantly, they left to do as they had been told, and Drell backed away, aware that he had crossed a line with his outburst. "Rein . . . I am just concerned about you. After Colen got sick, and the stress of—"

"I told you to shut up!" he roared. The horrible truth of it was, Drell was right: he *had* helped himself to medications, to carry on when his body craved rest. It was important. He had to do it, to keep the Thorn ready. Things were at a critical juncture. No one else could be trusted to keep everything moving forward. The task was his, and his alone.

Drell reached out a hand, for a moment the healer's usual caustic manner abating and genuine disquiet taking its place. "We need you, lad. There are so few of us now. We need our leader to be strong."

"I *am* strong," he retorted, shaking off the other man's hand.

Out in the corridor, the sound of something heavy colliding with stone echoed down toward them. Drell opened his mouth to speak, but Rein silenced him with a look. He strained to listen, and caught the noise of cautious footsteps on metal and the squeaking of deck plates; then there was the skirl of a phaser shot.

Drell scrambled to grab his plasma gun. "They followed you down here?"

"Who is out there?" Rein demanded, pressing himself into the edge of the doorframe. "Answer me!"

"Rein—" The voice was that of one of his men, but before it could form a reply, it became a howl of pain that ended abruptly.

"She can't have survived that!" he snarled. "No. No! It's not possible! I blew them into space!" Rein yanked his spare pistol from the holster on his hip. "Face me!" he shouted, bellowing into the stony corridor. "Come and end this, if you dare."

"As you wish," came the reply.

From somewhere down the tunnel came a low, mechanical whine that rose in pitch with every passing second; then an object clattered into the light, bouncing off the walls. The sound grew louder as the object landed just across the threshold to the medical bay. Rein chanced a look and saw a phaser pistol lying on the floor, indicator lights flashing wildly as it built toward a forced overload.

Shocked into action, he threw his shoulder against the sliding hatch and tried to force it closed, but he was too slow.

The weapon self-destructed and threw a stunning crash of energy down the tunnel. The blast ripped into the half-closed hatch and blew it off its hinges. Rein went with it and slammed back into the infirmary proper, colliding with one of the bio-beds.

Hot dust burned off the stone walls choked the air, and Rein struggled to get to his feet, his ears ringing. Drell recovered quicker, letting off pulses of fire from his plasma gun into the ragged gap where the entrance had been. Shapes moved in the haze, and the healer attacked the nearest enemy with a guttural growl. He saw *her* face.

Drell tried to bring his weapon to bear on the Vulcan, but Valeris knocked his gun arm away and jammed her fingers into the nerve bunch at the base of his neck. Drell stiffened, his eyes misting, and sank to the floor.

Rein got free and staggered across the infirmary toward the stasis module where his brother's corpse still lay. He turned to see Vaughn rushing at him, the Klingon woman Kaj at his back.

"*No!*" he yelled, grabbing a tray of medical instruments and throwing them at the human. Rein's hand clasped a rod-like device and he drew it up, thumbing the activation switch.

"It's over, Rein!" said Kaj, aiming a weapon at him. "Surrender!"

The protoplaser's tip glowed blue, ready to cut through flesh with even the slightest pressure. Rein backed into Colen's pod and raised the rod, holding it at his own neck. "Stay away!" he shouted as loudly as he could. "I will never submit to you, tyrant sow!"

Vaughn hesitated, raising his hands to show he was unarmed. "Kaj is right. You're done here." The young human's face was covered in tiny scratches and dirty with smoke, but his eyes were hard like tempered steel. "Drop the protoplaser. You can still come out of this alive."

Rein laughed, and he heard the edge of hysteria in his own voice. "After all that has happened, you think I will capitulate now? On the eve of our triumph? Billions of tyrant lives are about to be snuffed out! You think a threat to me will stop any of that? I will kill myself first!"

"What do you mean, 'billions of lives'?" Kaj demanded, but Vaughn raised his hand, holding her back.

Rein felt the heat from the tip of the beam-cutter against his throat. "Stay away!" he shouted. "I'll do it!"

"So do it, then." Vaughn took a step closer.

"Lieutenant!" Valeris called. "We do not know the location of the third target. If Rein dies—"

But Vaughn paid no heed to the Vulcan. "Do it!" he barked. "Cut your own throat. This is your big chance to be a martyr, Rein. To show us all how powerful the will of the Thorn really is. So go on."

"I . . . I will . . ." The searing heat from the beam was crisping his flesh, and the pain was intense.

"You won't." Vaughn shook his head. "Because you're a coward. You're content to send your kinsmen off to die, people you call friends and brothers . . ." The human nodded toward the medical pods and the body bags. "You tell them it will be great and glorious, but you're just blinding them with lies. You spend the lives of others to fuel your own hate."

At his side, Colen's ruined features stared up at Rein from inside the pod. He refused to accept the human's words. He strained, trying to move the device, trying to slash it across his neck, but his muscles were frozen, his fear overwhelming him. Colen's final moments spiraled through his thoughts, the sight of the pain on his brother's face as death claimed him stark and terrifying. "I was willing to die!" Rein screamed, tears streaming from his face.

"Once, maybe," said Vaughn, "but not anymore." The Starfleet officer shot forward and struck him, knocking the protoplaser from his trembling hand.

"Sit down." Vaughn shoved Rein into a chair and used lengths of sealant tape to secure him in place. As Valeris watched, Kaj gathered up the plasma gun dropped by the old medic and moved back to the doorway. Drell lay unconscious in an untidy heap.

"Whoever is left of Rein's men will be on their way," said the major. "Now that we have him, we need to break him."

"I . . . will give you nothing . . ." said the Kriosian, sobbing. "I will not break . . ."

When Kaj looked back, her expression was menacing. "Everyone says that," she told him. "But everyone does, eventually."

"What are you suggesting?" said Valeris. "Forcible interrogation?"

Kaj gave a noncommittal shrug. "This infirmary has equipment that can be repurposed for that task."

"We are *not* going to torture this man," insisted the lieutenant, his lip curling in disgust. "That's not how we work."

"*We?*" echoed Kaj, turning to face him. "Remember where you are, Lieutenant Vaughn. That man is a terrorist, wanted by the Klingon Empire for multiple crimes. And this is Klingon space, where Klingon law applies. He has no rights." Her eyes narrowed. "You heard what Rein said. They must be targeting a major population center, one of the core worlds or the main colony stations. Families, Vaughn, not soldiers. We have no time for your Federation's bleeding-heart morality." Kaj aimed her pistol. "The torture of one terrorist *petaQ* in exchange for the safety of countless Klingon innocents is not a question at all. Now, step aside."

But Vaughn did not move. "You said yourself we're on the clock here. How long is it going to take to break him, Major?

Hours? Days? Even then, can you be sure that he will be telling the truth?"

"And what would you propose?" she retorted hotly. "The same thing you offered to the convict? The promise of eradication of all past crimes, freedom, and a new identity? An honorless *bribe*?"

Valeris studied Rein's pallid features. "You must give us the location," she told him. "You have no choice."

The Kriosian looked up at her. "I do not remember," he replied, with all the defiance he could muster.

A lie? The words resonated in her thoughts. *A choice.* Valeris heard her own voice echoing back from the past, from a similar moment seven years earlier on the bridge of the *Enterprise*. The recollection brought a shock of understanding to her, a surge of feeling so powerful that for a moment she struggled to assimilate it.

On that day, her mentor Spock had faced what she did now. A crisis rushing headlong toward death and destruction. A decision that pulled at reason and logic.

A chance to set right a past mistake.

She looked down at her hands, scratched and blemished from the chaotic escape from the landing bay, and Valeris knew what was being laid out before her.

"There's always a choice," she said softly.

She leaned closer and raised her hands to Rein's face, her fingers finding the points where the neural nerve clusters were closest to the surface of his skin.

"Don't . . ." Rein gasped out the word.

Valeris stared into the Kriosian's eyes. "My mind," she whispered, "to your mind."

19

Rein tried to resist her, but his mind was undisciplined and fraught with turmoil. Valeris was shocked to find how easy it was to invade his thoughts. A gentle, steady telepathic pressure and she felt herself sinking into his mind as if she were reaching into an ocean of thin, clinging oil.

Rein fought, but he was only raw emotion and brute force. Valeris, a Vulcan educated among the finest and most controlled minds in the galaxy, navigated the course of his surface thoughts, falling deeper and deeper toward the Kriosian's secrets.

His psyche was a dark and tormented place. Behind the façade of a confident, decisive leader he projected for his men, Rein was a mass of contradictions and self-doubt. He had a crude kind of control over his baser emotions, but it was a leaking dam, always in need of shoring up, forever on the verge of crumbling. The death of his brother shone brightly amid the gloom, the power of the feeling behind that moment pushed aside but impossible to dismiss. Rein was afraid to let himself feel the despair and the true loss that Colen's passing concealed; he knew that to open himself to that would be to admit his failures and take the full brunt of the blame for his brother's painful end.

Barriers of denial walled off great swathes of Rein's psyche, leaving only the well-trodden canyons of his mind, where baser emotions like hate and anger ran in crimson rivers.

But even as she went deeper, Valeris sensed Rein flailing to catch on to some fragment of her persona as a way of striking back. The mind-meld was, after all, a technique of sharing, not one of pure incursion, and as much as she looked into him, he saw into her. But where Rein opened to Valeris like a book with scattered, jagged pages, to the Kriosian all the Vulcan showed were flashes, sporadic glimpses of herself.

It was enough, though. *Like knows like.* In the communion of the meld, both of them uttered the words, but the mind that formed them was unclear. Rein reached out for something familiar in Valeris, and he found it, despite her attempts to hide it.

Hate. His primitive psyche flocked to the familiar emotion, hidden in the cages of the Vulcan's iron self-control. *You hate them as much as I do. But you pretend you are so evolved, so in command. You deny the potency of your own anger. But you cannot make it go away.*

For a brief moment, they shared. Raw, fluid odium washed back and forth across the bridge between their minds, and the power of it was seductive. Valeris saw the trembling walls of refusal erected in her own thoughts and encountered a spike of panic. The horrible admission of the truth at the base of Rein's words threatened to draw her away.

You told me you never lied. But that's all you've ever done.

She marshaled her will and pushed away, forcing him back. His wild, flailing attack had worked, but only for a heartbeat. Now Valeris turned it against him and cut through. Dimly, she was aware of taking gasping, shuddering breaths, of heat and sweat thick on her flesh.

The Vulcan passed through veils of memory, and flashes of Rein's past flared brightly. She saw his life as a child, the brusque and boorish manner of a surly noble youth denied what he considered his entitlement. The first kindling of a hatred for the barbarian alien tyrants. Disgust at his kind who

refused to oppose the Klingons, the commoner cattle who
bent the knee no matter who ruled them. And then the raw
potency of the acts of terror themselves: the first taking of a
life, the planning and the execution of kill after kill, bombing
after bombing. Valeris relived Rein's callous delight at the
deaths he had caused; she saw knives plunged into Klingon
hearts and explosive devices detonating inside buildings.

Another long-hidden emotion surged in her: *disgust.*
Rein had been directly responsible for attacks that had taken
the lives of his own kind—*collaborators!* he insisted—and
Klingon civilians as well as their soldiery—*all guilty!* he
cried, *all deserving!*—without remorse or sorrow.

Rein tried once more to fight back, raking at her psyche
like a wild beast. He pulled on skeins of memory and
sensation that she had kept carefully ordered, dragging out
her recollection of the meld with Spock and the exchange of
emotion that moment had brought her. The disappointment.
The confusion and misunderstanding. They had both failed,
both been so wrong.

You will fail now, said the meld-voice.

The Kriosian's last desperate defense finally collapsed, and
she could sense her hands clasped about his face, pressing into
his flesh. Rein gasped and shuddered and then his lips split
in a grin.

You want to see? I want you to see.

Rein let the barriers fall and showed Valeris the truth.
She saw the dream of his victory unfolding in his mind's
eye. A world, thick with population, rife with cities filled
with Klingon souls—soldiers, civilians, countless millions
of them—and all around, reaching to the sky, monuments
to arrogance and warfare. Brutalist castles and temples to
conflict. Gales of pennants and incarnadine flags bearing the
black trefoil of the Empire. And high above, set in a darkened
sky choked with acid rains and storm clouds, the shattered
husk of a distant moon.

We lay the knife here, Rein's voice muttered, *in the
monster's heart.*

• • •

Vaughn watched the strange transformation that passed over the faces of the Vulcan and the Kriosian as their minds came together in a forced, painful joining. Their lips moved in unison, half-spoken utterances mumbled at the edge of his hearing—until one word sounded clear and distinct, spoken in a chorus that made his blood run cold.

"*Qo'noS*," said Rein and Valeris.

"The homeworld," breathed Kaj, staggered by the import of the word. "The Thorn intend to strike at the Empire's capital . . ." He heard the disbelief in her tone.

"That's not possible," Vaughn replied. "It's one of the most heavily defended planets in the whole quadrant; they can't just waltz in through the security perimeter!"

"They can," Kaj said grimly. "The *Chon'm* can. These terrorists have Fek'lhr's luck . . . It's possible the ship could approach to near orbit before the planetary sensor grid detected any anomaly." The major fell silent for a moment. "Billions of lives. It would be mass murder on a colossal scale!"

"Yes." Valeris's voice was weak with effort.

Vaughn turned back as the Vulcan disengaged herself from the telepathic connection. "Are you . . . all right?"

"The experience was discomforting," she managed. "But I am unharmed."

Kaj pointed her gun at Rein. "And him?" He drooped in the chair, his head hung forward, his breathing fast and ragged. He was muttering under his breath.

"He will recover. But he has been forced to see the reality of certain truths."

"That's not nearly justice enough," growled the Klingon. "He has a price to pay." She grabbed a surgical blade, and for a second Vaughn thought Kaj was going to do what Rein had threatened and slit the Kriosian's throat. But instead she cut through the bonds that held him and dragged the man to his feet. "He will forfeit what he owes before the eyes of the Klingon people," she concluded.

Vaughn cast around the room, thinking out loud. "You're certain of this? The target?" he asked Valeris.

She gave a jerky nod: clearly the mind-meld had affected her more than she wanted to admit. "He could not lie to me. In the end, he did not wish to. Rein wanted me to know what he was planning." She glanced at the Kriosian. "He is proud of what he has done. He was tired of hiding it."

Rein managed a weak snigger. He seemed semiconscious, almost as if he were feverish. Whatever had happened between them in the meld, Vaughn concluded, the Thorn's leader had come off the worst.

"Then we have a very big problem." The lieutenant folded his arms across his chest. "Gattin has the bird-of-prey and the means to reach Qo'noS in, what? Six hours at high warp?"

"Ten," corrected Kaj, thinking it through. "They would have to operate under the holographic veil, most likely using the identity of a nonmilitary vessel to move without drawing any attention. At anything other than cruise speeds, they would be noticed."

"Of course. A fast ship would raise an alarm." He nodded.

Kaj frowned. "The *Chon'm* was built to be a deep-penetration vessel, Vaughn. With it, the Thorn will be able to reach any one of a number of targets of opportunity on or around Qo'noS—orbital shipyards, military platforms, settlements on the surface, even the First City—and they would never know it until the moment the Thorn detonate their isolytic device." Her expression darkened. "And I gave them the means."

"We have to break our silence, then," said Vaughn. "Contact Starfleet Command, let them know the situation."

"Given his previous behavior, General Igdar will not allow a Starfleet vessel to cross back over the border, no matter what the circumstances," noted Valeris. "And I doubt he will be receptive to calls from the Federation on matters of imperial security."

"Then *you* contact him," Vaughn said to Kaj. "Tell him the truth. Tell him we have evidence of a credible threat to the Klingon homeworld. Even Igdar's not a big enough ass to ignore something like that."

"Perhaps," the major admitted, "but my word would not be enough. Do not forget, we engaged his ships in open combat, killed his men in battle. In the general's eyes, we are all fugitives, wanted criminals little better than this vermin . . ." She gave Rein a shove. "Even if he believed me, Igdar would want to see the truth for himself, to be certain. We would lose vital time convincing him . . . if he did not simply execute us all on sight." Kaj shook her head. "No. We are alone in this. You are cut off from your Starfleet, just as I have been isolated from Imperial Intelligence."

Vaughn gave a nod. "All right, then. Just so we're all completely clear about how totally screwed we are." He sighed. "We have to stop the *Chon'm* ourselves." When none of them responded, he glanced around. "I'm open to any suggestions either of you might have."

"We need a ship," Kaj replied.

"*Useful* suggestions," Vaughn corrected.

Valeris's gaze turned inward for a moment; then she crossed to Rein and pulled a thick bracelet from his wrist, ignoring his weakened, mumbling protests. She showed it to them: a communicator. "We have a ship," Valeris said. "The *Kaitaama's Daughter*."

"That cutter?" snorted Kaj. "The elderly, half-dismantled wreck in the landing bay? An escape pod would be more impressive."

"It's not like we have a lot of options," said Vaughn. "Or, come to think of it, *any* other options."

"The Thorn's original plan was to use the *Daughter* to carry the third isolytic weapon to its target. The ship is equipped with a sensor countermeasures system that broadcasts a false transponder code. Any Klingon ships scanning it would read the vessel as an ore carrier of Kriosian origin under Klingon patronage."

Kaj considered this. "It might have worked. Krios Prime is an annexed world, so their cargo ships have some freedom of movement within Imperial space." She glanced at Valeris. "What patronage?"

"A shell company linked to the House of Q'unat."

"More blinds and subterfuge," said the major. "But the point is moot. That cutter would never be able to race a *B'rel*-class scout to the homeworld, even if it could get past perimeter security!"

"I disagree," Valeris replied. "The *Daughter*'s warp engines are salvaged Klingon technology from a K-6 gunboat. There is a substantial risk, but I believe it may be possible to modify the engines to exceed their safety limits and reach higher warp velocities."

Kaj's jaw set. "And you could kill us all in the attempt."

"As Lieutenant Vaughn said, there are no other options."

The infirmary fell silent as the reality of their predicament settled in. Finally, Vaughn spoke up. "So I guess we fight our way to the landing bay, get the force field back up, repressurize the bay, and then take the cutter. That's going to be a walk in the park for just the three of us."

Valeris worked the miniature keypad on the surface of the comm-bracelet. "A less hazardous approach would be preferable."

"What are you doing with that?" Kaj asked.

In the next second the humming glow of a transporter beam enveloped them, and the walls of the infirmary melted away.

In the aftermath of the *Chon'm*'s departure and the firefight in the landing bay, the remnants of the Thorn left behind were scattered through the asteroid base. Rein did not answer his communicator, and with their leader silent and Gattin gone, the chain of command was broken. In the time it took the other men to gather themselves into some semblance of order, Valeris and the others were already making their escape.

The *Daughter* had been left in hibernation mode, the ship sealed and empty of all crew; and when the power coils and running lights activated, at first no one noticed. By the time one of the Thorn soldiers called out a warning, it was too late to do anything to stop the cutter. The force field barrier was down, the landing bay still open to space. Above the debris-strewn deck, the ship's impulse engines flashed yellow-orange as they activated, and with a shudder the Kriosian vessel strained against the repair gantries clustered around it. Ion jets spat from maneuvering thrusters, and metal groaned, the noise echoing through the hull plates.

The dart-like ship trembled, pulling at the scaffolds like a corralled animal girding itself to break free of confinement. The thruster exhaust brightened as more power went to the jets, burning through steel grates and support stanchions, but it was not enough.

The throbbing impulse grids grew sun-bright and pushed the *Daughter* forward, breaking through the gantries with sudden, violent force. Metal spars spiraled away across the landing bay, and sparking cables were torn from sockets along the curved flanks of the cutter's fuselage. Like the loosed arrow it resembled, the Kriosian ship shot away across the open chamber, blasting hard flares of exhaust at the deck. The maneuver was risky and the vessel did not escape unscathed, trailing streamers of discharged plasma and fragments of hull metal; but it left the landing bay in disarray and powered out into the Ikalian Belt, vectoring up and away as the craft climbed rapidly toward one-quarter light velocity.

As a parting gift, a pulse of coherent light left the *Daughter*'s single aft cannon and obliterated the subspace communications antenna on the surface of the asteroid, silencing Rein's people before they could raise any alarm.

Kaitaama's Daughter
Ty'Gokor Sector
Klingon Empire

The bridge of the cutter was a cramped, narrow affair, and by Elias Vaughn's lights it was more a cockpit than a command center, with a ring of operator couches set below a raised saddle that had to be the equivalent of a captain's chair. None of them had taken the seat, however. Without waiting for permission, Valeris went straight to the helm the moment they entered the compartment, and Vaughn found the panel that served as both an engineering and weapons control station. Kaj hadn't accompanied them up from the *Daughter*'s tiny transporter room: the major insisted on securing their prisoner over all else.

The Kriosian technology was comparatively easy to read, but where Starfleet hardware was largely made up of touch-panel multifunction displays, the cutter's controls were like articulated gloves cabled to the consoles, each responding to hand motions and gestural strings. Still, a phaser cannon was a phaser cannon, and Vaughn had managed to take the shot that blasted the base's comm array without missing the chance.

"We will be clear of the belt in ninety seconds," noted Valeris, her attention focused on a pull-down monitor screen hanging from a support above her head. "Sensors are operating at reduced function, but currently no other vessels are within detection range."

Vaughn felt the motion of the *Daughter* in the pit of his stomach, the sluggish gravity compensators too slow to anticipate the quick, darting movements the Vulcan applied to the control yoke. She navigated through the asteroids with consummate skill, the same proficiency she'd shown days ago on board the *Excelsior*.

"You took a big chance, blasting us out of the bay on impulse engines," he told her. He nodded at the dagger-tips at the cutter's prow. "You could have pinned this thing to the deck like a lawn dart."

"I have done it before," she said offhandedly. "What is the status of the warp core?"

"Checking." He worked the clicking gloves to bring up a semicircle of sensor indicators. Dots of brilliant emerald and indigo icons made an arc across his board. "Looks good," he reported, glancing over his shoulder as the bridge hatch opened to admit Major Kaj. "We got green lights on almost everything."

Kaj frowned and leaned close over his shoulder, crowding him. "In Kriosian society, green is traditionally an indicator for danger." She tapped an auxiliary keypad and the icons switched to a more familiar color scheme: suddenly Vaughn's panel was swamped with hazard red.

"Ah, hell." He grimaced. "Well, at least we have impulse engines. I half expected us to find this scow gutted from the inside out."

Kaj moved to one of the other operations consoles. "You are not too far from the truth, Vaughn," she said. "There are several sections now sealed off where parts of the hull frame are open to space. We're lucky the transporter was even connected to the power train."

"It seemed like the most expedient method of boarding," Valeris explained. "We are now clear of the Ikalian Belt and entering open space. Setting course for the Klingon homeworld—"

"Wait." Kaj crossed to the pilot's station. "Let me. A direct route will send us right into the teeth of the Defense Force's patrol fleets. We'll stand a better chance of approaching undetected if we follow the freight routes past the Gorath system." Valeris held up her hands and let the major input the data.

Elias studied the navigational plot as it snaked across a star map on one of the tertiary displays. "So," he went on, "are you going to tell us what you did with Rein?"

Kaj didn't look up from her task. "This ship has been used for missions of piracy, so there are secured compartments on the lower decks. I found something that resembled a cell and locked him in."

"How can you be certain that he won't be able to escape?" Vaughn asked. "If I had a brig on my ship, I'd make sure I knew where the skeleton key was."

"I considered that," allowed the Klingon, "which is why I took a proximity detonator from the supply locker and placed it on the hatch. I made it clear that if Rein opens the door from the inside, he'll be blown apart."

"Thorough as ever," Vaughn remarked. Once again he could see what it was about Kaj that had earned her Commander Miller's professional respect.

"It's what keeps me alive," she replied. "There. Course set. You may proceed."

Valeris set the controls and the *Daughter* banked to port, accelerating across the void. "I estimate that in order to reach Qo'noS within the probable ten-hour deployment window, we will need to sustain a warp velocity of factor six-point-three."

"The drives from a K-6 can manage that, can't they?" Vaughn asked.

Kaj and Valeris both shook their heads. "Not on this spaceframe," said the Klingon. "They're designed for a ship half the mass of this one. If we push the engines, the warp field will collapse."

"At the very *least*," added Valeris. "It is more likely that a critical matrix imbalance will occur and the ship will be dragged into a wormhole effect."

Vaughn stepped up from the console and studied them both. "So, then. Solutions? Because if we arrive late to this party, all we've gone through will have been for nothing."

The Klingon and the Vulcan exchanged glances. "I believe it is possible to modify the warp field matrix to negate the collapse effect," Valeris explained. "Essentially, to force it to hold through the injection of controlled verteron bursts."

Vaughn took this in. What she was suggesting was the equivalent of pouring inflammable fluid on a raging fire; it would be enough to create a temporary surge, but it could just as easily result in a fatal blowback.

She saw the train of his thoughts on his face. "It will not be without a degree of risk."

"A *large* degree," corrected Kaj.

"Are you sure you can do this?" To say Vaughn had his doubts would have been an understatement of galactic proportions.

"My Starfleet training encompassed warp field theory and engineering process." Valeris seemed unconcerned; there was that damnable Vulcan arrogance again.

"Your training is almost a decade out-of-date," Kaj retorted, "and I imagine your familiarity with Klingon systems is passing at best."

Valeris nodded. "Indeed. Which is why you will need to assist me, Major. Together, we will be able to manage the warp matrix in real time."

Vaughn considered her reply and realized that both women were looking to him for the final word. *Great. Now the time comes for one of us to make a decision that could blow up the ship, and suddenly I'm the guy with command authority.* He took a breath. "Valeris, have you calculated the odds of us actually succeeding in this?"

She gave a nod. "Yes. Would you like me to tell you the figure?"

"No." He folded his arms. The way she had replied was answer enough. "Just go get it done."

"Lieutenant," Kaj warned, "a single error—"

"Will kill us all," he finished. Vaughn drew himself up and settled onto the command saddle. "So don't screw it up. That's an order."

Valeris raised her eyebrow at his tone but said nothing. Kaj only nodded and glanced at the other woman as she crossed back toward the hatch. "Follow me, convict," she said. "Now you'll get your chance to prove you're as good as you think you are."

The hatch clanked shut and Vaughn was alone. He surveyed the empty bridge and sighed. "Not exactly what I had in mind for my first starship command," he muttered, and pulled down the periscope monitor to study the path ahead.

Don't screw it up, repeated the voice in his head. It sounded like Darius Miller.

The warp core of the *Daughter* ran horizontally down the keel of the Kriosian cutter, the length of the main engineering spaces a slender compartment that was little wider than the ship's corridors. Control panels and monitoring gear lined the walls, while the thrumming column of light that contained the critical matter/antimatter reaction was beneath their feet. Pulses of light juddered into the dilithium chamber, flaring through gaps in the gridded deck plates. Valeris saw immediately from the rhythm and resonance of the pattern that the intermix was out of sync.

She moved to an observation station and frowned as pages of Kriosi pictographs scrolled down the screen in a waterfall of data. Like the rest of the alien warship, the warp core was antiquated. The Vulcan made an attempt to adjust some gross calibration vectors on the fly, but it became clear that little short of a dry-dock overhaul would return the *Daughter* to its optimal functionality.

"If we do this," Kaj was saying, "we'll run this craft into the ground. The human might not want to say it, but I will. The warp drives will be little but burned-out cinders by the time we reach the homeworld. *If* we reach the homeworld."

"You seem doubtful of our chances." Valeris didn't look up. "I have observed that the Klingons are a fatalistic people. Is it not one of your most oft-stated axioms that says, 'Today is a good day to die'?"

Kaj's lip curled. "Today is *not* a good day to die. Tomorrow, perhaps."

"How can you tell?"

"A Klingon can tell."

Valeris threw her a look. "I believe you are mocking me."

"And to think they say that Vulcans are too literal-minded to understand sarcasm." She ran her hands through a series of command strings. "Warp engines are ready to engage."

"I concur," said Valeris. She leaned forward to speak into an intercom grille. "Lieutenant Vaughn? Warp power is now available at your discretion."

"*I copy,*" he replied a moment later. The humming note

of the core grew faster, the pulses of light flickering. *"Here we go. Approaching light speed. Onset critical momentum in four seconds. Three. Two—"*

The cutter made the leap from normal space to warp travel with a heavy, shuddering groan that echoed down the length of the starship. Valeris gripped the edge of the console in front of her to steady herself as the deck trembled beneath her boots. Kaj muttered something darkly under her breath as the *Daughter* surged beyond the speed of light and continued to accelerate.

A disc-shaped gauge on the main engine display slowly filled with orange as the cutter moved up the warp scale, the dial crawling toward the warp six threshold. The acceleration brought with it increased vibration from the walls and the decking, and green warning lights began to blink on across the panels.

Kaj had a monitor displaying the four salvaged engines, the colors showing the status of the intercoolers and the meshing warp fields. "Stress levels are high," she reported. "The incompatibilities between the hull struts and the drive nacelles are more pronounced than I thought."

"Do we need to reduce speed?" asked Vaughn, a note of worry in his voice.

"Negative," Valeris insisted. "We are at factor four and climbing. Once we reach the target speed, we can normalize the field matrix."

The juddering of the hull was louder now. "This ship will tear itself apart if we push it too far!" Kaj snapped.

Valeris ignored her. "Warp five. Approaching warp six. Stand by for verteron pulse." She worked the controls, lining up the particle surge that would—if she was not in error—smooth the flight of the ship. *If my calculations are incorrect,* she considered, *none of us will live long enough to make an issue of it.*

The engine chamber was vibrating like a struck bell, and across every console cascades of danger-green icons flashed in unison. The *Daughter* crossed the warp six line and its velocity stabilized, but the same could not be said of the vessel itself.

"Structural integrity is dropping!" Kaj called. "Do it now, convict, or we will be atoms!"

She triggered the verteron surge and watched the flood of high-energy particles bombard the warp matrix. The fragile bubble of inverted space-time writhed, but ultimately it held. Slowly, the tremors lessened until the destructive thunder sank to a background rumble.

"*Warp six point five. How about that.*" The relief in Vaughn's voice was obvious. "*Now all we have to do is keep this up for ten hours. I hope they got some* raktajino *on this tub.*"

Valeris's reply was calm and steady. "We will monitor the warp matrix from here. Engine room out." She tapped the intercom control and turned to find Kaj watching her. The Klingon held a remote console in her hand, the padd-like device connected to the engine core with a thick, looped cable.

The violet skin tone that had characterized the major's disguise was almost totally gone now, save for a few mottled patches of discoloration on her neck and hands. She resembled the splinter breed of her species similar to humans, swarthy and dark-haired, but without the heavy cranial ridging. Kaj was measuring her silently.

Valeris realized that this was the first time she had been alone with the Klingon agent. A jolt of alarm echoed in her thoughts. The Vulcan still had a weapon in her belt, as did Kaj. Valeris estimated that the odds were even—her superior reflexes versus the Klingon's training and skill.

She voiced her thoughts. "Are you considering if you will kill me?"

A slow smile crossed Kaj's face. "Do you think I would do that, convict? Kill you to sate a desire for revenge over the chance to save countless lives? Does that seem rational . . . *logical* to you?"

"I have never considered rationality and logic to be components of the Klingon psyche." The flat delivery of her response killed Kaj's smile immediately.

Once more, Kaj did what she had done so often when Valeris spoke to her: she sneered. "Your . . . *gratitude* is overwhelming. Such touching words." The major hesitated, then came closer. "You will answer a question for me," she ordered.

"If I can."

"Why did you choose to turn on Rein?" Kaj's eyes narrowed. "You could have left him to execute us there in the landing bay. All you needed to do was *nothing*. He would have carried out his attack, and you would have done your part in striking against a people you hate."

"I do not experience hatred." Valeris's reply was rote and automatic.

Kaj continued. "Afterward, you could have escaped. Found whatever freedom you wanted. Why not, convict? Why did you do that?"

"My name is not *Convict*," said Valeris, ice forming on the words. "And I do not expect you to understand."

"*Why?*" Kaj snapped back. "Because I am a Klingon? An unsophisticated thug from a barbarian culture, incapable of thinking at your level?" She snorted. "Your conceit is immense, Vulcan."

Valeris turned away. A faint resonance sounded deep inside her—the ghost of an emotion. "I do not have to justify myself to you."

Kaj grabbed her by the shoulder and spun her around. "No," she agreed, "but you will have to justify it one day. To yourself, if no other!" The Klingon prodded her in the chest. "I know why you hate us, Valeris. I know what happened to you!"

"You do not know me," she insisted, but there was a tremor in her words.

"I read the report on what happened at Nidrus Gamma." Kaj said the name and it made Valeris feel sick inside. "After

Captain Sulu revealed that you were on board the *Excelsior*, at the first opportunity I downloaded every piece of data I could find on you from the archives of Imperial Intelligence. It wasn't just about the death of Gorkon . . . I went deeper. There was a surprising amount of information on Commander K'Darg's ill-conceived attempt to influence the local government on Nidrus all those years ago. His first officer gave a full report to the admiralty in order to ensure he was not charged with the same crimes."

"Crimes?" Valeris blinked, concentrating on maintaining her outward expression of neutrality; but within, her thoughts were churning.

"Disregarding orders. K'Darg was an opportunistic fool, operating far beyond his remit. He presumed too much and paid the price for his greed. He had no authority to do what he did. The taking of prisoners for ransom is the act of a desperate coward." Valeris saw genuine loathing in Kaj's eyes. The Klingon's sneer faded. "I know revenge very well, Vulcan. My culture is built upon its bloody bedrock. You have good reason to hate my kind."

"I do not experience—" Valeris caught herself, her voice rising. "My enmity toward the Klingon species is based in logic and fact, not emotional response," she insisted. "You cannot be trusted! Your empire is a clear and present danger to the Federation. First the Empire was an enemy, interested only in deceit and conquest, and now it has become a parasite, taking support while biding time to turn against us once more!"

"But never an ally?" Kaj replied. She became cold. "You could never accept that, could you? That our peoples might find common ground at last?" She prodded her again. "The mere thought of that *terrified* you."

"I do not fear you." Valeris reached into herself and found a wellspring of defiance—but dark emotions spun and turned there, like ink through clear water.

"Vulcans cannot lie," Kaj said, walking away across the

deck. "How many times has that falsehood been uttered, by fools who mistake logic for truth?" She pointed back at Valeris. "But the fact is Vulcans *always* lie. They lie to themselves." The major shook her head. "You're not machines. You deny what you are; you deny your emotions. That's what you are afraid of."

Valeris tried to find a counterargument, but nothing seemed to fit. She could hear her blood thundering in her ears. The dark emotion inside her was brimming, colliding with flashes of memory from that day in the storehouse. *The knife in her face, K'Darg's leering eyes, the smell of blood and ozone . . .*

. . . and the fear . . .

"Your argument is flawed," Kaj told her. "If it were reason alone that drove you, then you would have let Vaughn and me perish. The success of Rein's plan would result in the logical outcome you've wanted for so long: the collapse of the Klingon Empire. But now you are going to help save the very thing you hate! Explain that!"

"I . . ." Valeris struggled to frame her reply—and failed. Her hands drew up into tight fists, her cheeks darkening with the rush of blood. Now the memories of Nidrus Gamma were swept away, overwritten by Rein's words and the fierce, brutal emotions that wreathed him like smoke.

If I could press a button and wipe every Klingon life from existence at once, there would be no hesitation in me. She remembered the perfect calm on his face as the Kriosian had said those words.

Once, there had been a time when Valeris might have done the same. There were acts she had committed without pause and only the faintest flashes of remorse. *The clandestine meetings. The corruptions of the* Enterprise *files, Kirk's stolen logs . . . the silencing of Burke and Samno.* They seemed like moments from some alien alternate of herself, distant and far removed.

It all flowed from the black diamond of hatred that had

buried itself in her three decades earlier. Valeris had learned to rationalize it, cloaked it in arrogance and bigotry and called it logic—but she had only built walls around her hate and denied it.

Spock's forced mind-meld had brought it screaming back to the surface, dragging it into the light where it was impossible to deny any longer. He showed her something in those brief, terrible moments, a truth about herself she did not wish to accept.

On Jaros II, in the wake of the assassination, Valeris had been searching for a way to leave that behind. A single day she could live without the knowledge that she had poisoned herself with emotion. A day without the hate.

And then there was Rein. He was a reflection of her, the same unbreakable will fueled by deep, old anger, the same lies cast against the same enemy. Rein believed what he was doing was for the good of Krios Prime, for freedom and victory. But his lies were her lies—it was only personal revenge dressed up like something noble. *Genocide, in return for past wounds.*

She saw it in his eyes as he watched his brother die moment by moment. Rein had allowed himself to be consumed by his emotions, driven by them until there was nothing left of the man he might have been. Valeris looked upon the leader of the Thorn and a greater fear came to her.

I could become like him.

She tried again. "I . . . It is difficult, once patterns of behavior have become entrenched, for one to accept a deviation. It does not come easily."

Kaj frowned. "Not every Klingon treats honor as a thing to be adhered to when it is convenient. Prejudice is born of this notion."

Valeris closed her eyes and, with a strength she had never believed she had, for the moment put out the old fires of her enmity. At length she nodded. "We will stop the Thorn," she said, a sense of purpose rising in her, "and perhaps together we may redress the balance."

20

The Kriosian cutter slowed steadily from warp speed to a careful impulse cruise, crossing the orbit of the outermost world of the Klinzhai system. As much as possible, the star system that was home to the Klingon species was a fortress in space: a boundary patrolled by a flotilla of guardian ships and protected by drones lay around it in a massive invisible sphere. These were the outer walls of the castle keep that was Qo'noS itself, and any ships making their approach along anything but the approved flight corridors were subject to attack without warning.

The *Daughter* followed the course that Major Kaj had programmed into its navigation console hours earlier, traveling along the primary entry vector that the Defense Force left open for civilian transports and freighters. But it was immediately clear that the entire sector was on alert status. The patrols were more numerous, and the craft that normally swarmed the heavily populated system were moving in slow chains, under the watchful eyes of battle cruisers.

Some observers said that the Klingon Empire was forever on a war footing, and the martial nature of the Klingon culture meant that there was some truth in that. However, the attacks on Da'Kel had sharpened the ever-present edge of tension in the skies of Qo'noS to a new degree. Suspicion was the watchword.

The cutter crossed into sensor range and immediately received a summons from the perimeter command authority.

A patrol cruiser was already being routed to intercept the alien vessel. If the craft performed any maneuvers that could be considered questionable, lethal force would be employed.

Lieutenant Vaughn listened to the automated warning message for a second time and rubbed his chin. There was a layer of unkempt stubble forming there; it was one more indicator of the time and distance this mission had put between him and the Starfleet career he thought he had. He caught a glimpse of himself in the reflective surface of the control console. The man looking back at him seemed to have aged years since that confrontation in Commander Egan's office; he didn't look like a green officer anymore. The Elias Vaughn he saw now was someone different, someone who had gone a long way off the grid.

But that's the job, right? he wondered. At that moment, more than anything he wished that Miller could be here. Elias felt the veteran spy's loss keenly. This had been his mission from the start, and Vaughn felt like a pretender trying to fill the man's shoes. *I'm in the deep end now,* he told himself. *Do this wrong and it'll mean disavowal by Starfleet and a lifetime of breaking rocks on Rura Penthe . . . If I'm lucky.*

The hatch behind him opened and he turned as Kaj and Valeris entered. He drew his hand from his face self-consciously and the major smiled. "A beard might suit you, Vaughn. Humans have such weak chins. It would give you character."

"Thanks for the tip." He glanced at the engineering console. "Good work down there. You two kept this scow from falling apart *and* didn't kill each other. I'm impressed."

The Vulcan and the Klingon exchanged a loaded look that Vaughn couldn't read. "We . . . found a means of complementing each other's skill sets," said Valeris.

Vaughn frowned. Something had changed between the two women, that much was certain. *What happened while I was up here?* He decided not to press the issue: other matters were more urgent. "Border control has already hailed us. A ship is coming in. If you have any suggestion how we can sneak past them, now's the time to speak up, Major."

Kaj didn't reply immediately. Instead, she took a seat at the sensor panel and ran a long-range scan. A tactical plot opened on one of the tertiary monitors, sketching in the nearby planets and the zone around Qo'noS. Vaughn saw the orbital course of Corvix, the planet's one remaining moon, and the debris ring that was all that remained of shattered Praxis. The display grew a cluster of indicators, each one representing a starship. They were spread throughout the system, holding station, covering all avenues of approach.

"The Thorn are already here," Kaj pronounced, grim-faced.

"How can you tell?" said Vaughn.

Kaj gestured at the monitor. "We all knew from the start that this speed-course to Qo'nos would be a close run. I prayed that those Kriosian fools would make some error and attract the patrols, but the transit patterns visible here show ships on standby alert. The distribution of vessels would be markedly different if they had detected a viable threat."

"Maybe we got here before them?" he offered hopefully. "If we warn the Defense Force command—"

Valeris shook her head. "Negative. With their head start, the *Chon'm* was always guaranteed to reach Qo'noS first . . ." she trailed off as something on the screen took her attention. "One of the vessels displayed here . . . I recognize the transponder code from Da'Kel . . ."

Kaj's eyes narrowed. "It is the *No'Tahr*."

"General Igdar's flagship?" Vaughn blinked. "What's he doing here?"

"Summoned home to account for his actions, I imagine," said the major. "He would never pass up the opportunity to stand before the High Council and hold forth on his own merits." Kaj shook off the thought and worked the panel in front of her. "Perhaps, if we can isolate commercial traffic, we might be able to narrow down the targets. The Thorn would not risk dropping the *Chon'm*'s holographic veil until the last possible moment."

"I am detecting twenty-four cargo vessels in the system," Valeris reported, "and those are only the ones registering on the *Daughter*'s sensors. I remind you this ship's systems are considerably antiquated."

A strident buzz sounded from Kaj's panel. "There's a *K'tinga*-class battle cruiser approaching off the starboard bow. They're hailing us."

Vaughn took a breath. *Here we go.* "Let's hear it."

A gruff male voice growled from the bridge's speakers. *"Attention, Kriosian cargo vessel. Bring your ship to a halt and lower your shields for boarding and inspection."*

"They're targeting us," said Valeris.

"Standard procedure," Kaj noted. "If we don't respond in a few moments, they'll give us a mandatory warning and then open fire." She paused. "Of course, as we speak they are cross-checking the false transponder code this ship is broadcasting. If they determine the deception, they will fire immediately."

Vaughn looked at his periscope screen. The lethal hammerhead shape of the Klingon D-7 loomed large, overshadowing the smaller cutter. A livid crimson glow grew about the maw of the warship's forward photon torpedo launcher, signifying its readiness to launch.

"We can't fight a cruiser," he said, "but I'm damned if we'll show the white flag now." Vaughn drew himself up and looked to Kaj. "Last chance to pull rank, Major. Because the next order I give might be the last you ever hear."

"Miller had faith in you," she replied. "And I owe him a debt. Don't make either of us regret those choices."

"I assume my opinion is not required?" said Valeris, arching an eyebrow.

"On the contrary," Vaughn went on. "I want your opinion on the *Daughter*'s warp engines. Do they have anything left to give?"

The Vulcan's expression stiffened. "The field coils have been stressed beyond all operational limits, the plasma manifolds are on the verge of catastrophic failure, and the nacelle frames are riddled with micro-fractures. Engaging warp drive again for anything more than a few seconds will destroy this ship."

"Well, that was succinct." Vaughn shifted on the command saddle. "Take your stations."

"Attention, Kriosian cargo vessel." The Klingon voice was harsh and grating. *"Failure to comply with commands will result in your destruction. Obey now!"*

"You did hear what the Vulcan said, yes?" asked Kaj.

"Every word." He nodded, and glanced at Valeris. "Helm? Your heading is Qo'noS orbit. Maximum warp." Vaughn took a shuddering breath. *"Execute."*

Azure lightning flashed along the sides of the warp nacelles fitted into the flanks of the Kriosian cutter, the radiant flux of released energy spilling out into space. Resonating as if it had been struck by a massive hammer, the dart-shaped vessel trembled and burst into motion, leaping away at tremendous velocity from the lumbering D-7 before a tractor beam could snare it. Disruptors flashed, cutting through the vacuum where the *Daughter* had been a fraction of a second before; and then the Klingon ship vaulted after the cutter, racing past light speed to catch its new quarry.

As the stars turned into threads around them, the cruiser spat a fireball at the smaller ship's retreating stern. Trailing streamers of accelerated radiation, the photon torpedo crossed the gap between the two vessels and the *Daughter* banked hard, losing fragments of hull metal as the turn overstressed the already damaged fuselage.

The torpedo, proximity-fused for highest lethality, detonated in a sphere of annihilation, missing a direct hit on the cutter, but close enough to slam it with the edges of the expanding blast wave. Sparkling flickers spilling from overload buffers lashed along the blade-shaped planes of the Kriosian ship, and its speed bled away. In the few seconds that had passed, the pursuit had already crossed half the system and was now dangerously close to the homeworld. The D-7's crew had been fully briefed on what took place at Da'Kel; any threat to Qo'noS would not be allowed to stand. The cruiser's captain ordered a salvo of torpedoes.

Ahead of them, the *Daughter* was shedding pieces of itself, then suddenly the cutter's warp field collapsed like a bursting bubble and the vessel plummeted back into normal space.

The cruiser's helmsman was ready and reacted immediately, matching the punishing deceleration, dropping the D-7 out of warp, still on the cutter's stern.

"Jettison now!" The lieutenant had to shout to make himself heard over the hooting clarion of the *Daughter*'s warning sirens and the storm-noise of the tortured hull.

Valeris, ignoring the very real possibility that her next act would kill them all, stabbed at the activation key, sending the command to the struts securing the salvaged K-6 engines to the flanks of the Kriosian cutter. In a millisecond, explosive bolts sheared off the bracing rods and pinched shut the energy feeds connected to the nacelles. The drive modules were cut free, and they tumbled away from the starship, spinning end over end into the path of the Klingon cruiser.

She leaned in and pushed the flight control yoke to the stops. Valeris dropped the bow of the *Daughter* relative to the plane of the ecliptic, putting distance between the vessels at full impulse.

On the screen she saw the D-7 shift as her Klingon counterpart tried to mirror the escape maneuver, but the cruiser's mass was over twice that of the Kriosian vessel and it was slower on the turn.

The ejected warp nacelles, still crackling with unspent energy, reached the point of structural collapse and exploded within seconds of one another. Blasts of raging plasma bloomed in the darkness, spilling clouds of tritanium shards and dilithium hydroxides across the cruiser's course like an oil slick over water. The debris clogged the ramscoop collectors on the Klingon ship's warp engines and strangled their reaction. A cascade shutdown swept through the cruiser and set it adrift.

"*Qapla'!*" Kaj gave a triumphant shout.

However, Vaughn's reaction was more muted; he sighed and sagged against the command panel. "Great," he managed. "One ship down. Now all we need are some more warp engines to throw at the rest of the Klingon fleet, and we're set."

Valeris glanced at the sensor display. The warp jump had taken them into the high orbital zone over the Klingon homeworld, and the Defense Force was already reacting. Sensor drones were scanning them from multiple vectors, and the subspace frequencies were alight with encrypted communications from ground installations, orbital stations, and nearby ships. "They believe we have come to attack them," she said aloud.

"The *No'Tahr* is signaling planetary command," said Kaj. "They'll be coming after us."

Vaughn rubbed the bridge of his nose with his hand; the human's fatigue was evident. He appeared to be operating on little more than adrenaline and dogged tenacity. "No time to waste, then. Valeris, push all available power to the sensor grid, boost the gain as much as you can." He used the controller gloves to input a command string as he spoke.

She saw what he was attempting. The lieutenant had preprogrammed a scan subroutine to look for the energy signature of the Thorn's isolytic device. The sensors began a sweep of the surface of Qo'noS, searching for the unique radiation pattern of the subspace weapon.

"We've got the advantage," he explained, noting her scrutiny. Vaughn pulled a tricorder from his belt and showed it to her. "I secretly took a read of Rein's bomb while we were in the assembly chamber."

"The Defense Force has passive sensors at every viable target in the Empire," said Kaj. "They know what to look for. If the Thorn's isolytic device were there, they would know it."

The sensor returns showed only null readings. "That's not right . . ." said the human. "Unless . . . Could they have shielded the bomb somehow?" The frustration he was keeping silent finally burst out. and he slammed his fist against the panel. "Damn it! We have to find these bastards!"

"Perhaps it is beyond our scanning range on the far side of the planet, the night side," Valeris offered.

Kaj dismissed the suggestion. "There are no targets of high value there, only oceans and wilderness. The First City, Kri'stak, Qam-Chee . . . they all lie below us, and the scan reveals nothing. If the device is not on the homeworld . . ." Kaj turned a sharp glare on Valeris. "You told us this was the target! Rein deceived you—!"

"No," she insisted. "His mind was undisciplined. He could not lie to me. I saw his intentions. I saw Qo'noS."

"More Vulcan superiority?" Kaj demanded. "What if you are wrong?"

"I am not wrong." Behind her a warning chime sounded. Vessels were closing in on intercept headings.

"It has to be close," said Vaughn. "Think it through. If not on the surface, then where? On one of the stations . . . Maybe one of the ships out there is hiding the *Chon'm* . . ."

In that instant a jolt of insight struck Valeris like a slow bullet. "No," she repeated, snatching at the flight yoke. She applied power to the impulse drive, pivoting the *Daughter*'s bow away from the cloud-wreathed planet below.

"What are you doing?" demanded the Klingon.

"Realigning the sensor grid," she replied. "I estimate a sixty-two-point-eight percent probability that the isolytic device will be deployed from a location other than the planetary surface."

"Where?" asked Vaughn.

Valeris nodded at the monitor screen as a wide band of rocky debris swung up into view. The remnants of the moon Praxis lay spread out before them.

The Vulcan didn't wait for him to give the order: she applied power to the impulse drives and the *Daughter* shuddered as it raced away toward the glittering ring of rubble circling the planet.

What had once been a rocky satellite of similar dimensions to the moons of Vaughn's home on Berengaria VII was now an arc of shattered ruins, rocks, and dust stretched into a halo by the inexorable forces of gravitation. Seven years after the obliteration of Praxis, and the Klingon homeworld was still in turmoil from the loss of one of its orbital partners. On the surface, earthquakes and tidal shocks were common occurrences; the already challenging ecosphere of Qo'noS had been made far more severe, and meteor storms were now a frequent threat, as pieces of Praxis fell to the surface with alarming regularity. The meteors brought environmental damage with them, scarring the planet's atmosphere with heavy elements and toxic minerals.

Much of what most now called the "Praxis Ring" was made up of particles little bigger than grains of sand, but caught like a dark sapphire set in the band was a thicker clump of the largest fragments, the pieces that had survived the devastating explosion. Now they wheeled and tumbled in a shaggy cloud, a blot on the sky that passed over the heads of the citizens of Qo'noS like the blade of a *bat'leth* poised to fall upon them.

"The Thorn are there," said Valeris. "It is the only hypothesis that makes sense." She bent over the cutter's controls, working to keep the damaged ship stable.

"Supposing you're right," Vaughn said with a frown, gripping a support column to hold himself steady. "They're too far out to do serious damage. Even with the larger isolytic device, at most the blast might disrupt the debris ring, maybe damage ships and stations in near orbit . . ."

Kaj glanced at him, and her expression was bleak. "No, Lieutenant. The Vulcan is correct. Remember what Rein said? He threatened to destroy billions of Klingon lives. Speeding up the fall of a few meteors isn't enough. He was talking about destroying Qo'noS itself."

"The composition of Praxis was a major factor in its demise," Valeris said, speaking quickly. "Overmining and energy management errors caused a cascade effect—"

"I remember," Vaughn broke in. "Get to the point!"

"The structure of the moon was rich in boronite, pergium, and kemocite, all volatiles, all vital minerals for any spacefaring species. Each one of those ores is highly receptive to subspace particles."

A chill ran through him. "So if the isolytic weapon is detonated in the ring, what will happen?"

"An amplification effect," said Kaj. She looked stricken. "The particle stream will become self-sustaining, long enough to cause a spatial tear. A subspace rift large enough to consume the entire planet."

Valeris gave a nod. "Rein said these words to me: 'We will cut out the heart of the beast.' This is what he meant."

Elias tried to imagine what devastation such an event might wreak, the fabric of space-time itself ripping open to swallow a world whole. Nothing would survive as the atmosphere was flayed away and the planet disintegrated. It was almost too much to comprehend.

Then alarm tones blared from the sensor console, bringing him crashing back to the moment. Vaughn looked up at the main display as a photon torpedo went wide of the *Daughter*'s spiked prow, angling off into space.

"A warning shot," said Kaj. "Igdar's gunners on the *No'Tahr* are eager for our blood."

"We're not here to play shooting gallery," said the lieutenant. "Valeris, sweep the debris zone with the sensors, find Gattin!"

The cutter rattled and groaned as it passed through the inner edge of the Praxis Ring, energized specks of dust and larger clumps of rock sparking off the navigational deflectors. They were moving too fast to avoid them, but with Igdar's flagship at her back, the *Daughter* could not proceed with care. They dove into the denser regions of the debris belt, dodging around the wallowing motion of fragments as big as city blocks.

"You think Igdar will follow us in?" he asked.

"The High Council is watching," replied the woman. "The general likes to have an audience."

"Scanning." Valeris glanced at Kaj. "Major? Do you read anything?"

The Klingon gave a slow nod. "Detecting a power reading

at mark two-nine. It's difficult to be sure. The dust is acting like a scattering field."

"That's why we couldn't read the isolytic device," said Vaughn. "We'd have to be right on top of it—" The words had barely left his lips before Kaj's console sounded a warning. He peered over her shoulder. "What is that, a ship? Looks like a mining tender . . ."

It was drifting low over the surface of the largest remnant of Praxis, a dense bolus of rock striated with veins of dark minerals. The vast splinter was the size of a mountain range, cut loose and thrown into the void.

The *Daughter*'s scanner array showed the fuzzy image of a rectangular support vessel, the kind of craft that mined comets and rogue planetoids in deep space. The design resembled Axanarri technology.

Kaj showed her teeth. "That is not a mining ship." She made an aggressive, stabbing motion with the blade of her hand, and the control glove interpreted it. The cutter's forward weapons spat fire and hit the other vessel before it could react to their arrival. The disruption of the sensors worked both ways, hiding the *Daughter*'s approach until the very last moment.

Vaughn's gut tightened with shock, and for a second he had the sickening fear that the major might have attacked a shipload of civilians; but then a heartbeat later the holographic guise of the tender dissipated and the *Chon'm* rose up to meet them, the bird-of-prey dropping its wings into attack mode.

"Something on the surface of the fragment," Valeris was saying. "Life-signs."

Her words were drowned out as Kaj fired another barrage, this time scoring solid hits across the stern of the *Chon'm* as it banked to draw a bead on them.

The Vulcan worked at the flight yoke, but the Klingon scoutship was more agile than the aging, battle-damaged cutter. Even with Gattin's inexperienced crew on board, the *Chon'm* still had the edge.

Flashes of orange chain-fire burst from the muzzles of the disruptor cannons on the scoutship's wingtips. The bolts of light tore through the failing shields and ripped into the *Daughter*'s portside fuselage. Impulse power died as a chug of fat blue-white sparks vomited from the thruster grid and the ship fell into an uncontrolled spin. The cutter began a lazy tumble as its internal systems shut down, lumps of debris clanging off the hull.

Vaughn picked himself up from the deck; he had no memory of how he had gotten there. One moment he was clinging to the command saddle, shouting a warning; the next he was lying on the floor, his skull ringing with the pain of the impact. A hand reached for his, the skin warm, and he looked up to find Valeris. The cut on the Vulcan's face had reopened, and emerald blood lined her cheek.

"Kaj?" he asked.

"Here . . ." said the Klingon, coming to them through a haze of smoke that seemed to have appeared from nowhere. The major's face was lit by flickers of illumination from malfunctioning display consoles, casting her fierce aspect like the visage of some ghostly revenant. "Perhaps I was wrong," she told Valeris. "Perhaps today *is* a good day to die."

"All the same, I'd prefer not," Vaughn retorted. He stumbled to the periscope screen; his movements felt light and off balance. "Gravity control must have been hit."

"Life support remains stable, for the moment," reported Valeris. "Weapons, navigation, impulse power . . . all negative."

Vaughn shot Kaj a hard look. "Didn't we agree I was in command here? You fired without thinking!"

"I thought about it," she replied. "Hesitation would have been fatal. And I don't recall any formal declaration as to your command status. Major outranks lieutenant junior grade by a substantial margin."

"Fatal?" he snapped back. "What, like the situation we're in now?" Vaughn hammered at the damaged console without success. "Once the *Chon'm* swings around, we're dead!"

"Negative." Valeris was peering into a scanner hood. "The bird-of-prey has disengaged. They're returning to the fragment."

"The life-signs on the surface . . ." Kaj said, thinking aloud. "It must be an EVA team preparing the isolytic device for detonation. They're going back to get them."

"We can still stop Gattin." Valeris stood up. "The *Daughter*'s transporter system is operational. We can beam to the fragment, find the Thorn before they trigger the device."

"And get our molecules scrambled on the way," Vaughn retorted. "All those mineral compounds in the debris belt will play havoc with a transporter signal."

Kaj looked up from a systems diagnostic panel in front of her, and a wolfish smile played on her lips. "There's another way," she said. "But we need weapons and environment suits, and we must move *now*."

"What about Rein?" said Vaughn. "We're just going to leave him in the brig belowdecks?"

"Oh, he's still alive, I made certain of that," said the major, moving toward the hatch. "When we've dealt with Gattin and the others, we will be back for him. If this wreck holds together until then." The Klingon halted at the threshold. "Are you coming?"

Vaughn closed his eyes and heard himself say the words. "Lead the way."

Praxis Ring
Qo'noS Orbit
Klingon Empire

The escape pod was little more than an armored drum equipped with a cluster of thruster nozzles and a rudimentary life support system, at best a last resort for fleeing the Kriosian cutter if destruction was imminent.

It was a poor substitute for a ship's launch or shuttle, and the capsule spun through the darkness before landing unceremoniously on the surface of the largest planetesimal fragment. It touched down in a puff of dust and skidded to a halt, rolling over. The pod began to drift back off the fragment, the scant gravity of the massive scrap of rock too low to hold it. Before it could float away, the oval hatch along the aft snapped open and three figures in Defense Force–issue space suits spilled out. It was an ungainly, disordered exit, but they made it clear, scrambling into the lee of a jagged spike of granite.

Vaughn watched the capsule glide serenely back out into space, losing it in the jumble of the debris belt. "Some ride," he noted. "Now I know what being shot out of a torpedo tube must feel like."

"*We're here and we're alive,*" Kaj said over the helmet link. "*That's all that matters.*"

Valeris stood up, with care. The angular visor of her environment suit slowly turned this way and that. "*I see no sign that our arrival was observed.*"

"*The Thorn's attention will be on their weapon,*" Kaj replied. "*We must make use of the advantage while we still possess it.*"

Vaughn nodded wearily. "All right. How do we activate the gravity boots on these outfits?"

Kaj nodded, her helmet exaggerating the motion. "*Orange icon, right side of the visor.*"

"Got it." The lieutenant felt the bulky overshoes suddenly grow heavier as the grav-plates in the soles came online. The plates in the boots were attached to the surface of the planetesimal. He took a few practice steps. The Klingon military suits were more like battle armor than the protective gear used on Starfleet ships, and the movement was sluggish; it also didn't help that the outfit he was using was a half size too big. Vaughn had to lean into every move he made, or else his body shifted but the suit did not.

He looked up through the thick, gold-lensed visor and saw Kaj beckoning him. Her suit differed from Vaughn's and Valeris's with the addition of a larger backpack module, the function of which he couldn't be certain. What he was sure of was the curve of dull steel attached to a mag-strip at her shoulder; Kaj had found the *bat'leth* blade in the

Daughter's equipment locker and immediately claimed it as her own. Vaughn and the Vulcan both had heavy disruptors.

The suits had built-in tricorders, and while they lacked the fine detail of their Federation counterparts, they functioned well enough for the current circumstances. "Life-signs," Vaughn said, reading the display. He pointed. "That way."

Kaj loped over the rocky terrain, heading toward a ragged ridgeline. Vaughn followed at a steady pace, breathing hard. It was an effort to be inside the Klingon suit: the environmental settings were all off human standard, too warm, too moist. He glanced around, trying to keep his mind off the petty annoyances. Vaughn looked up past the "horizon" of the massive fragment—up there, the green orb of Qo'noS was visible through a cloud of smaller asteroids, constantly moving as the Praxis shard they stood upon slowly turned end over end. It made him feel dizzy, so the lieutenant put his head down. The rock all around was grey and black—dense, forbidding ground made of sharp planes and angular folds. *I'm standing on a stone island in the middle of nothing,* said a voice in his head. Vaughn frowned and dismissed the thought.

He dropped into a crouch as he came to the ridge alongside Kaj. Valeris fell in with him, sparing him a quick glance. Her expression was unreadable behind the visor.

"*See,*" said the Klingon, and pointed.

The ridgeline looked down on a shallow arroyo between two serrated hillsides, a vast wound that had been gouged in the surface of the planetesimal when Praxis had ripped itself apart. Off to one side, on a broad, cracked plate of fused silica, the *Chon'm* rested amid a haze of thruster gasses and disturbed rock-dust. The wings were raised high, and the drop ramp was open, a wan yellow light spilling out onto the black surface. Vaughn could see figures moving in the glow; they wore the same kind of environment suits, and their motions suggested a state of alarm.

He gave an involuntary look over his shoulder. "They must know the *No'Tahr* is closing in."

"It's a much bigger ship," said Kaj. "Igdar will come in slowly. But if we don't stop these terrorist petaQ, they'll be running for warp speed before he gets here."

"They have dug some kind of pit," Valeris observed, her keen Vulcan eyesight picking out a hollow in the rock. "Several meters from the bird-of-prey."

Vaughn saw it too. The skeletal shape of a phaser drill, the swan-like emitter head bowed, lay abandoned to one side. Dots of light—illuminator lamps mounted on suit helmets—bobbed like fireflies. A glint of silver caught his eyes, and he felt his gut tighten. "The device is down there. They've buried it in the rock." He swallowed hard. "We have to get to it."

"I concur," said Kaj, standing up. She tugged the bat'leth free and spun it around to a guard stance. "I will engage the ones at the ship and give you the distraction that you need."

"There's a dozen of them down there," said Vaughn. "Not good odds."

Kaj gave a brisk nod. "Be sure to tell Gattin that if you meet her before I do." The major drew back a few steps and then broke into a swift run. At the last second she threw herself off the top of the ridge and flew silently out over the gap.

Vaughn started after Kaj, too late to stop her. "What the hell is she doing? She'll fly off into space."

But then the function of the larger backpack became clear. Kaj did something with her glove, and puffs of white gas spurted from slits in the suit's shoulders. The Klingon's gear contained a basic thruster mechanism, and with it she dropped silently toward the knot of Kriosians dithering at the Chon'm's bow. In the silence of the vacuum, none of them could detect her approach. She raised her blade, coming down like an angel of vengeance.

Vaughn didn't wait to watch Kaj let loose; instead he beckoned Valeris to the lip of the ridge and they both stepped over, hunching low to slide down the steep incline in clumps of ebony dust. They hit the floor of the shallow rift and he pushed himself into a lumbering run, panting as the heavy suit dragged on his every motion.

Valeris sprinted past him, kicking up clumps of powder where her feet fell. Ahead, Vaughn could see more clearly now the pit the Thorn had dug. A grav-litter was off to one side, surrounded by discarded cables, and the rear third of the isolytic device was visible, projecting from the maw cut in the ground.

A figure in a suit stepped around the inert shape of the phaser drill and the blank face of its helmet jerked in surprise: they had been seen. Without hesitation, Vaughn leaned into a turn and ran headfirst into the Kriosian, the two of them colliding with a heavy, ringing impact.

They went down, and Vaughn lost sight of Valeris as dust billowed up around the two combatants like smoke.

Kaj's first kill was the man on guard at the foot of the ramp. He must have seen a shift in the shadows cast as she fell, and he looked up just in time to meet the tip of the *bat'leth* as it went through his faceplate. He fell in exaggerated slow motion as she landed, spinning, slamming the back edge of the weapon into the legs of the Kriosian's companion.

Another of the Thorn tried to pin her with a spear of light from a phaser, but she was moving faster than he expected and the shot went wide, flashing off the glassy surface of the asteroid. The only sound was the panting of her breath and the grunts of effort as she moved in and attacked in a whirl of blades. It seemed surreal to the woman, the dead silence across the airless landscape as she took down her foes. Kaj was used to the noises of battle, the ripping of flesh and the cries of the fallen. Here, in this moment, it was almost as if she were fighting wraiths who perished without a sound.

Behind her visor, she gave a feral grin. Wraiths or not, she would make the Thorn pay in kind for every drop of Klingon blood they had spilled. If these stony wastes were where she was to meet her end, at least it would be beneath the gaze of Qo'noS and the naked stars.

Snarling, she swung the *bat'leth* about and attacked once again.

• • •

Valeris almost stumbled as she dropped into the phaser-cut pit, her gloved hands unable to find purchase on the walls of the trench. The powerful beam that had torn open the ground had burned off the stone until it was smooth, the surface pitted with tiny cavities. The isolytic weapon lay cradled in the darkened furrow, the metallic shape of the device invasive and out of place among the black rock and powdery grey sand. Access panels along the sides of the object were open to the vacuum, and Valeris saw trains of indicator lights blinking back and forth within.

She recognized elements of her own work in the construction, the components of the firing core visible, suspended in a frame of duranium rods. Bunches of glowing optical cables ran the length of the casing, connecting to a trigger mechanism and other sub-modules that she could not immediately identify.

Valeris found the activation pad, and a flutter of emotion stuttered behind her chest. *The device is still in standby mode.* She took a breath and reached for it. *We are not too late—*

A hissing crackle sounded from the communicator bead in her ear, and Valeris winced at the sharp noise.

"You're too late," said a severe voice breaking in over the comm channel. A shape moved at the far end of the device, half hidden in shadows, and Valeris turned toward it. Another figure in a spacesuit emerged, and the helmet faceplate depolarized. Gattin's twisted, snarling face glared back at her. "*Run, traitor. Run away while you still can. In a few minutes, this will all be destroyed.*"

"You will not die here," said Valeris. "You are not like the ones Rein duped into giving their lives for the cause. You want to live to see it succeed. Your hatred demands nothing less."

"*What do you know of it, you passionless witch?*" Gattin said, advancing. Her hand hovered near the weapon on her belt. "*Nothing you say has any meaning. You say it is all logic and reason, but you only twist meaning to be what you wish it to be!*" She shook her head. "*If there ever was a spark of anything real in you, it was the hate. And you let that fade away. Be proud, Vulcan. You're as pale and colorless a soul as any of your kind!"*

"You have lost," Valeris told her. "This will end here."

The words triggered exactly the response she knew they would: Gattin leapt at her, reaching for her throat. It would not be enough for the Kriosian to shoot Valeris where she stood; Gattin wanted to end her life with her own hands.

Vaughn recognized the face of the man called Tulo as the Kriosian struck him with an elbow to the chest, the impact resonating through the suit armor. His adversary was more nimble than he expected, and Elias struggled to keep his balance as he dragged himself back up to his feet.

There was a part of him that wanted to give the Thorn member one last chance to surrender—the part of Elias Vaughn that had been instilled in him by his family and his training as a Starfleet officer. All his life, he had thought—he had *hoped*—that he lived in a universe where reason could win out. But Tulo and the rest of the Thorn seemed disconnected from reason. They had lost so much and become so saturated with their hatred that an act as apocalyptic as destroying a world was not beyond them.

One look at the feral anger on Tulo's face was enough to make Vaughn certain of it. This was not a man forced to fight but one who did not want redemption, did not want peace. The Thorn were mirrors of their leader: only death and more death would sate them.

You can't win, he wanted to say. *Hate consumes everything it touches. Violence only breeds more violence.*

Tulo drew his weapon and fired a wide shot, answering him. Vaughn slammed into the other man, deflecting the beam up and away. Their helmets clanked against one another and for an instant they were staring into each other's faces.

The man's eyes were dead, hollow things.

The weapon wavered between them, pushed back and

forth in their shared grip. Vaughn locked his legs and applied steady pressure. Tulo began to weaken. He knew what was coming and shouted silently behind his visor.

Then the weapon discharged for a second time and the Kriosian went limp, falling backward toward the dust. Glistening jewels of blood scattered from the wound on his chest, flash-freezing into crimson beads.

Vaughn staggered backward and turned away, sickened at the waste of it all.

Gattin screamed and beat at Valeris with her armored gloves, smashing into the joints where the Klingon suit's protective plates were thinnest. The Vulcan felt the impacts and tried to turn to avoid them, but the woman's assault was savage and swift. By reflex, Valeris managed a punch to the torso but Gattin shrugged it off.

Adrenaline and fury powered her on, and the Kriosian slammed Valeris into the wall of the trench with such force that her head rattled against the inside of the faceplate. Valeris tasted the metallic tang of blood in her mouth and blinked away bright spirals of pain.

Gattin did not tire. She grabbed Valeris's helmet in both hands and slammed it into the melt-smoothed rock, over and over. A spiderweb of fracture lines blossomed on the visor, and harsh red icons flared into life, warning of dangerous suit leaks. Valeris flailed against her attacker, but she couldn't recover. She was dizzy and it was becoming hard to concentrate. *I am losing air.*

But then Gattin gave her one last shove and pushed her away, letting Valeris slump and collapse to the dusty floor of the furrow.

Over their shared comm channel, the Vulcan heard Gattin panting with effort. The Kriosian went to the open panel on the side of the isolytic device and adjusted a control. New threads of indicator lights blinked on, and in the visible core of the weapon, the power modules glowed brightly.

Valeris struggled to get up, but Gattin came back to her with a swift kick that put her down once again. *"Death is the only coin for traitors,*" she hissed. "*And you've earned this a hundred times over.*"

Gattin broke into a run and disappeared over the edge of the trench. Valeris felt the broken ribs across her chest move as she shifted. Slowly, she made her way toward the device, each breath she took like razors.

Vaughn saw the figure in the suit rise into the weak light and hesitated. He raised a hand. "Valeris?"

With everyone wearing almost identical Klingon military-surplus gear it was hard to tell who was who. The question was answered as the other figure drew a weapon from their holster and fired a fan of disruptor bolts at him.

The lieutenant scrambled into the cover of a low boulder, fumbling for his own weapon. The bulky gloves made it awkward to grip the pistol. He chanced a look up and let off a shot of his own, but his target had not stopped to engage him: the assailant was fleeing back toward the *Chon'm*.

Which could only mean one thing. Vaughn looked down at the tricorder module built into the spacesuit's gauntlet. The sensor unit was reading a steady buildup of high-energy particles, growing with every passing second toward a point of critical mass.

Vaughn broke into a dash across the stony arroyo, half-running, half-stumbling, fighting the suit and the microgravity until he lurched down the furrow and skidded to a halt on the floor of the trench.

He found Valeris bent over the isolytic weapon, clinging to it with one hand, the other buried in a fist of torn-out cables and disconnected components.

"*The weapon is committed,*" she reported, breathy and fatigued. "*The discharge chamber is moments away from activation.*"

He reached out. "We've got to—"

She looked at him. "*I cannot stop it.*"

21

Vaughn could hear the building energies inside the isolytic device as a humming drone crackled across the open circuit of his helmet communicator, the surging knot of raw power bleeding out to disrupt the functions of his environment suit.

His hands opened and closed, and a horrible sense of powerlessness washed over him. Vaughn had never really believed that he would end his life like this, on some drifting shard of dead rock, his existence erased from the universe in one single blinding flash of force. *This isn't how it is supposed to go*, he told himself. *I'm supposed to make a difference. Isn't that why I'm here? Isn't that the reason for all of this?*

The motion of light and shadows drew his attention away for a moment. He looked up to see the bird-of-prey lifting off from the planetesimal, its wings dropping to flight mode. It turned and vanished over the jagged hillside, impulse engines flaring.

Vaughn looked back at Valeris. She seemed pale and weak, and belatedly he noticed the damage to her suit. He pulled the emergency patches from the utility pouch on his chest plate, but the Vulcan waved him away.

"I will . . . not live long enough to suffocate."

His throat became arid as his gaze was inexorably drawn back to the weapon. "How much time?"

"I estimate less than seventy seconds." She held out her

hand. "*Give me your disruptor, Lieutenant. Mine became lost in a struggle with Gattin . . .*"

He drew the pistol, holding it by the barrel. Vaughn's blood ran cold as his mind filled in her reasons. "Are you . . . ? I mean, do you want me to . . . ?" He couldn't finish the thought.

Valeris arched her eyebrow and she briefly showed the same disdain he had seen in her on their first meeting. "*I have no intention of taking my own life.*" She took the gun from him and adjusted the beam settings. "*The isolytic weapon will discharge no matter what we do. That event cannot be prevented.*" She raised the disruptor and aimed it into the open frame of the device. "*Only the outcome can be modified.*"

Vaughn jerked forward as he caught on to what she was doing. "What the—?"

"*I have an idea,*" she said, with no hint of concern, "*and if my hypothesis is incorrect, the only result will be that we will perish a few seconds sooner.*" Before he could stop her, Valeris pressed the disruptor's firing stud and released a pulse of light into the guts of the device.

Vaughn swore and flinched, bringing up his hand to cover the visor of his helmet as a massive shower of red sparks gouted from the isolytic weapon, cascading over the sides of the trench in a bright fountain. Streamers of plasma spurted into the vacuum and he saw lightning crackles crawling along the metal framework of the device. The buzzing howl of static was growing louder and louder, and even inside his suit, Vaughn could feel his skin prickling, the hairs on his flesh standing up.

"*We should run now,*" Valeris called, tugging at his arm. "*We need to get as far from the unit as possible.*"

He loped after her, up from the trench and across the clearing, toward a cluster of rocks in the near distance. His dumbstruck amazement at the Vulcan's perilous scheme finally broke and he called after her. "What did you do back there?"

"This is hardly the time—"

"Tell me, damn it!" he panted, fighting the exertion.

He heard Valeris's frown in her voice. *"Isolytic weapons gather extreme particle effects into an energetic mass . . . in order to punch a hole through space-time to create a destructive effect. Once activated, that process cannot be stopped."* She stumbled, catching herself on a stone, and fell forward.

Vaughn caught her arm and arrested her tumble, dragging her back up. They were less than ten meters from the rocks now, and something made him look back toward the trench.

"I destroyed the emitter node," she said as he scrambled after her. *"Without a discharge method, the particle stream will remain trapped. It will enter an uncontrolled quantum flux state and cause . . ."* Valeris ran out of breath and gasped. *"It will cause—"*

A spatial interphase effect. Vaughn remembered the term from his warp physics class at the Academy, and he remembered the look of dread on the face of the instructor who had explained what it could do to the fabric of reality.

He saw it happen. There was a momentary pulse of light, so bright that it burned a purple afterimage into his retinas; a visible discharge of the exotic radiation as it overwhelmed the pre-fire chamber inside the isolytic device. A thundering roar of static deafened Vaughn, and he shoved Valeris behind him, reflexively blocking her body with his.

He expected that the last thing he would see would be the wave-effect of a subspace discharge lashing out toward them, but the event he witnessed was something far stranger. Like a shimmering ripple across the surface of a lake, an orb of null-space energy emerged from the trench, bending the light all around them, twisting gravity and radiation.

Everything within the radius became gossamer and insubstantial. The rocks and the dust, the phaser drill and the bodies of the Thorn left behind by their comrades, all were suddenly as ghosts. Vaughn saw through them, and he saw the field effect coming closer. He felt a stab of fear—he would not be able to outrun it. It would overtake him, absorb him, and leave no trace that Elias Vaughn had ever existed.

The quantum flux negated the isolytic blast, but instead everything it touched turned into an unstable version of itself. With nowhere else to go, the energy collapsed into the spaces between dimensions, becoming *nothingness*.

The growing sphere hesitated, stopped short—and then finally dissolved. Vaughn watched as the ground less than a meter's length from him vanished. Suddenly he and Valeris were lying at the edge of a perfect bowl cut into the surface of the Praxis planetesimal. Everything in the arroyo had simply been *taken away*.

It seemed like hours before he got back to his feet, ignoring the flashing cascade of warning icons across the bottom of his visor. Vaughn helped Valeris from where she had fallen. "Did you know that was going to happen?"

"*Of course,*" she replied without hesitation. "*But it appears my calculations were wrong.*"

"Wrong?" He tensed at her answer, expecting the worst.

"*Indeed.*" The Vulcan nodded, frowning. "*I had estimated that the interphase field effect would not dissipate until well after we had been drawn into it. Clearly, I was in error.*"

"Clearly," he repeated, a giddy sense of relief washing over him. Vaughn blew out a breath. "Come on. We need to find a way off this rock before we both run out of air. We need to find Kaj, if she survived."

Valeris pointed up into the sky. "*It would appear that may not be an issue for either of us.*"

He looked up and cursed. An armored shape was turning back through the debris ring, heading down toward them. *Gattin. She must know we sabotaged the device.* "Maybe it's another bird-of-prey?" he offered.

Disruptor bolts lashed down and smashed boulders into powder across the arroyo, the shots marching across the ruined landscape toward them.

"Unlikely," said Valeris, diving into cover behind the rocks.

Vaughn went after her, heat washing over his back as the nimbus of a near hit turned the stone and powder into blackened glass. He fell as a black shadow passed over them, briefly blotting out the starlight.

The *Chon'm* moved off and made a lazy circle over the planetesimal's saw-toothed hillside; a crimson glow lit the weapons maw on the bow as the ship readied itself to unleash a photon torpedo. Vaughn got to his feet, scowling. *If I'm going to check out here, then I'll damn well do it standing up.*

"*I am sorry, Lieutenant.*" He heard Valeris say the words, unbidden.

"Yeah," he admitted, watching the ship. "Maybe you are."

The bird-of-prey angled toward the arroyo, picking up speed. The Thorn's plan was ruined now, but Rein's people had made a calling out of nurturing retribution, and Gattin was no different. Anyone else would have fled the system as quickly as possible, but Vaughn knew she was up there on the bridge of the *Chon'm*, glaring down at them, screaming for their blood from Kaj's command throne.

But then a shadow, grey as tempered steel and broad as a stormhead, rose up behind the vessel. Emerging from the streamers of dust and rocky debris of the Praxis Belt, the massive D-10 battle cruiser resembled a war hammer swinging in to strike a killing blow.

The gunners on the *No'Tahr* did not miss this time: a blazing salvo of energy streaked across the darkness, spears of bright lightning piercing the downswept wings of the smaller vessel. A swell of detonations flared inside the hull of the *Chon'm* and consumed it in an orange-red fireball.

The blast effect sent an earthquake tremor through the fragment where Vaughn and Valeris stood, and they struggled to keep their footing. Pieces of the scoutship's fuselage descended in a slow rain down all around them, trailing flaming streamers of gas.

"*Major Kaj . . .*" Valeris began. "*Do you think she was on board the* Chon'm?"

Vaughn shook his head. "She never struck me as the kind

to go out the easy way . . ." He trailed off as the big cruiser drifted closer, looming overhead with stately menace. Caught beneath its shadow, Elias had a very sudden, very strong sense of his own scale against the threat he faced.

Across the scarred clearing, glimmers of crimson energy formed out of nothing. Scattered here and there, the columns of light gained solidity and became figures in armored space suits. These ones differed from the utility gear worn by Vaughn and Valeris: they were heavy-duty, power-assisted units, hulking things with built-in weapons modules and enhanced musculature capable of ripping an enemy limb from limb.

The soldiers spread out, some surveying the aftermath of the interphase effect. One group of four made straight for the two survivors, and as they came closer Vaughn saw that the leader's armor was dressed with sigils denoting a warrior of high and exalted rank. The lieutenant's heart sank as General Igdar's glowering face peered out at him through a broad visor plate.

"*You,*" said the Klingon, turning the word into a curse. "*A pair of Federation weaklings. It is no surprise I find you cowering in the ashes. I will make you wish you chose death along with the rest of your worthless compatriots!*"

"*I would think it likely that you do not have a full understanding of what has taken place here,*" said Valeris, apparently unconcerned by how much her words would inflame the Klingon's manner.

As one, Igdar's escorts raised their right arms, each suit sporting the barrel of a disruptor at the wrist.

"*I understand what I see with my own eyes, convict,*" spat the general. "*It is as it was with the plot to murder Gorkon, the same schemes again! Turncoats and renegades, working with cowards within our own clans.*"

"The House of Q'unat was never part of this," Vaughn snapped, his reticence breaking in the face of the Klingon's monumental arrogance. "They were a smoke screen. You have to know that."

Igdar's gaze grew colder. *"That remains to be seen. I am certain my agents will find evidence of their involvement."*

"Even if it doesn't exist?" Vaughn countered.

The general snorted with derision and folded his arms. *"By all means, say your piece, human. With each word you utter, you bury yourself and your Federation a little deeper."* He pointed an armored finger at him. *"Your presence in this place alone is cause to throw our so-called treaty into the fire! You have lied and misled the Klingon people on the orders of Starfleet Command! I always knew we could never trust the Federation. I warned the High Council that one day you would stab us in the back!"*

"That's not true," Vaughn replied. "We stopped your homeworld from being obliterated." He jerked a thumb at Valeris. "In fact, *she* saved it. The convict and the traitor."

Igdar glanced at the Vulcan and sniffed as if he smelled something foul. *"Speaking of traitors, where is the spy Kaj? In hiding?"*

"The major is gone," said Vaughn, the words coming to him without pause.

"Dead?" sneered the general. *"A pity. I hoped to personally exact a recompense from her myself. She cost me a number of good men."* He approached them. *"You will have to suffice. I cannot wait to see how your president will justify the presence of a convicted criminal and a Starfleet intelligence agent at the site of a terrorist attack."* The general showed his teeth as he smiled. *"Such luck that I was here with my ship and able to intervene."*

"That's how you'll play it?" asked Vaughn. "You've been dragging this whole incident out, working the angles for your own advantage—and now you'll come back as the hero who saved Qo'noS."

"There's no better alternative," Igdar replied. *"The Empire needs strength. An alliance with your kind saps it."* He prodded Vaughn in the chest. *"So we will take your charity, human. And when we have had our fill, we'll take everything else we want from you."*

"*You do not make Imperial policy,*" Valeris retorted. "*The Chancellor—*"

Igdar spat harsh laughter. "*Azetbur won't last! And when she's gone, I will still be there to make my voice heard. I will ride the victory you have handed to me into the halls of the High Council.*"

"*For that, you would require our deaths,*" Valeris went on.

Igdar slowly raised his arm, the gun port on his wrist snapping open. "*Quite so.*"

"We are unarmed!" said Vaughn. "You'd kill two defenseless people under the eyes of your own planet?" He pointed into the sky, to Qo'noS overhead.

"*I would slit the throat of Kahless himself if it was in the Empire's best interests,*" came the reply. "*And as for witnesses? There are none. Our words will not carry beyond the Praxis Belt.*"

"No." Valeris shook her head, looking to the warriors the general had brought with him. "*Are you going to stand by and let him execute us in cold blood, without . . . without honor?*"

"*Do not presume to speak to Klingon honor, Vulcan!*" Igdar shouted. "*My soldiers are pragmatists! They understand what is right for the Empire!*" He slammed a mailed fist against his chest. "*The council is full of dithering old women panicked by storm clouds and acid rain! They have made us look weak in the eyes of the galaxy!*" He gestured at the rubble all around them. "*Look at this! They have allowed a race of slaves to strike at the heart of our race! I will not let that stand!*"

"Oh, General . . ." Vaughn flinched as he heard a familiar voice over the helmet communicator. "*Your arrogance is monumental. As if it were only a scion of the House of Igdar who may guide the future of the Klingon people . . .*"

"Kaj . . ." muttered Valeris, glancing around.

Igdar's face became stormy. "*That gutless witch . . . I knew she was too poisonous to die in silence! Show yourself, woman!*" He cast around, glaring into every shadowed place and fallen rock, then snarled at his men, *"Find her!"*

"Don't trouble yourself," said the major, emerging from behind the ridgeline. She made her way down into the arroyo, and Vaughn noted the damage to her armored suit. Kaj's motion was careful, and he knew at once that she'd been injured. But still she carried herself defiantly. *"I have nothing to fear from you."*

The general laughed again. *"If we had gods, I would praise them, for it can only be some divine providence that has made my luck so rich this day. Two collaborators and a traitor. A full bounty indeed!"* He took aim. *"My only question now is: Which of you should I kill first?"*

Kaj walked to Vaughn and, for a brief moment, clasped his arm as she passed him by. He felt something pressed into his grip and looked down: it was a Klingon tricorder, the data transmission system in full active mode. He spared Valeris a quizzical look as Kaj walked on, approaching the general at a steady, careful pace.

"General Igdar," Kaj said formally, *"you will stand down and surrender to my custody. I charge you with conduct unbecoming an officer of the Klingon Defense Force, failure to carry out your obligations, and willful disregard of your duties."* He let out a braying snarl of derision, but she went on, fearless in the face of the weapons trained on her. *"If you had been able to see past your own egotism and opportunist nature, the Thorn threat would have been neutralized immediately. Instead, you chose to disregard viable evidence because it came from Federation sources, because of personal bias . . . because it did not suit your plans to aggrandize yourself."* She was furious now. *"Your idiocy almost cost the lives of every being on the homeworld."* Kaj gestured toward Vaughn and Valeris. *"In the end, it was left to our allies to prevent an atrocity."*

Igdar glowered at her. *"Are you finished?"*

"No," said Kaj, and pointed at him. *"You are a relic. A remnant from the old ways when the Klingon Empire was nothing but and war and death. That path leads only to ruin.*

If we do not change, we will die." The major took a breath. *"By my authority as an agent of Imperial Intelligence, I place you under arrest."*

"Kill her!" Igdar snapped.

Vaughn held up the device in his hand, realization coming to him in a rush. "You don't want to do that. In fact, you should probably have been a lot more careful about what you said just now." He showed the general the tricorder. "See, if I'm reading this right, the major here set up a quick-and-dirty relay, from the comm frequency of these suits to the ship we left adrift out by the edge of the Praxis Belt. All the time you've been talking, it's been boosting the signal out and down to Qo'noS."

"I imagine Chancellor Azetbur will be displeased with some of the general's more incendiary statements," said Valeris.

Igdar swore violently and swept up his gun arm, but Kaj reacted faster, her less-bulky suit giving her the edge she needed to strike him in the knee. The general fell howling to the dust in a messy heap.

Kaj turned to face the rest of the warriors. *"He said that you know what is best for the Empire. No doubt you also know that Imperial Intelligence has a long, long reach. Those who defy it . . . defy what is best for the Empire."*

The soldiers shared a silent look—and then, as one, they lowered their weapons.

Six Days Later

I.K.S. No'Tahr
En Route to the Neutral Zone
Klingon Empire

A fist rang twice against the russet-colored hatch, and Valeris looked up from the sparse Klingon pallet where she rested. It took a moment before she realized that the person standing outside was waiting for her permission to enter the room. "Come in," she called. It was still something of a novelty for her to have quarters that were not governed by locked doors and security grids. The habits of years of living in cells were hard to break.

The hatch slid open and Vaughn crossed the threshold, hesitating in the doorway. "Lieutenant," she said with a nod. Valeris had not seen much of the Starfleet officer since they left Qo'noS, leaving Kaj behind along with Igdar and the commanding officer of the No'Tahr to appear before an emergency session of the Klingon High Council.

Both Vaughn and Valeris had given closed-session depositions to faceless interrogators from Imperial Intelligence, but they had seen only the edges of what was going on in the Klingon hierarchy. It was clear that Chancellor Azetbur was moving swiftly to bring the "Thorn incident" to a close as quietly as possible, and Igdar's unprincipled exploitation of his role in the Da'Kel investigation was to be dealt with silently and severely. The fact that the general's personal flagship had been stripped from him and was now ferrying them back to Federation space was doubtless some form of object lesson for Igdar's men.

Vaughn returned Valeris's nod, frowning. The young human's aspect had changed a great deal in the brief time since she had first met him on Jaros II, and in a way that she found difficult to articulate. He seemed to have both lost and gained something, but she could not say what. Experience, she reflected, could be a cruel teacher.

The death of Commander Miller had shocked Vaughn and forced him into circumstances that might otherwise have never occurred, but what those events had done to the man was not immediately apparent. Valeris briefly considered the pivotal moments from her own past that had altered the course of her life, and wondered how Vaughn's future might unfold for him.

"I've just come from the bridge," he began. "There was a transmission from Captain Sulu. The Excelsior will be waiting to pick us up when we cross the border. We should be there in a couple of hours." Vaughn paused. "I thought you'd want to know, so you could . . ."

"Prepare?" she answered. Valeris got up, gathering the jacket she had left on the table at the end of her bunk. "As a matter of fact, there is something I wish to do before we leave this ship, but it is not connected to my own circumstances."

Vaughn sighed. "I made a full report to Starfleet Intelligence Command and to Admiral Sinclair-Alexander. The details of your participation in this mission are all in there. Just the facts. I didn't make any . . . value judgments."

"Do you believe they will hold to the terms of our agreement?"

Vaughn took his time answering. "You kept up your end of the bargain. One way or another."

"That is not what I asked you."

He met her gaze. "It's not up to me."

"And if it were?" This time Vaughn didn't reply at all. Valeris pulled on the jacket and faced him. "I want an honest answer from you," she said. "You owe me that, if nothing else."

He walked into the room and sat on the edge of the table. "The truth is, I'm not sure how to deal with you. Part of me wants to put you back in the cells and throw away the key. You're sharp and you're tricky, and I'm not sure anyone can ever really know what goes on inside your head."

"That is not so." She answered without thinking, the words muted.

"Then there's a part of me that knows what you did out there." He sighed. "The risks that you took. The Klingon homeworld is still spinning because you risked your life to sabotage the Thorn's isolytic bomb. A planet full of people you professed to hate, and yet you saved their lives. Then there's what happened with Rein."

"Yes." Valeris looked away. Not a day had passed without some echo of the Kriosian's memories impinging on her thoughts. Meditation helped, but she sensed it would be some while before the specter of what she had been forced to do was fully excised. Rein's thoughts had burned into hers like acid, and it would take time to heal the wounds.

"I know it was hard for you to force the mind-meld on him, especially after what happened to you with Spock on the *Enterprise*. A weaker person . . . someone more damaged by that could never have done what you did."

She tensed. "I have never considered myself to be 'damaged.'"

"I read Tancreda's files too," he told her. "She had a lot to say about you."

"I do not doubt it." Inwardly, Valeris felt the rise of irritation as she listened to her own tone of voice. She was in danger of exhibiting an actual emotional response.

"I lost my mother when I was young. My dad and I . . . It was hard for us." Vaughn seemed to lose himself in a moment of memory. "Sometimes I think part of me died with her. Family makes us what we are." He looked up at her. "Tancreda talked about your family, your parents. Your *father*."

"I fail to see the relevance." But she did.

"Spock, Kirk, and Cartwright . . . Is that what you were doing, Valeris? Looking for a father figure to replace the one who let you down? But they all let you down, one way or another, didn't they? And you ended up cut adrift."

When she answered, her words were icy. "Is that the doctor's evaluation of me, or yours?"

"I don't judge people on who someone else thinks they are, or what theory some shrink uses to categorize them," said Vaughn. "I judge people on what they do."

She sensed the unspoken words. "And so?"

When he looked at her again, Vaughn's eyes were flinty. "What I believe is this: No matter what you've done to redeem yourself, it will never erase what you did seven years ago. You murdered two people in cold blood. You disavowed your sworn oath as a Starfleet officer. You aided and abetted men who wanted to bring us to war." He shook his head. "I can't excuse that."

"I see." Valeris felt a distant twist of emotion: on some level she had wanted him to absolve her. The Vulcan's expression stiffened, denying the impulse, wondering when it had taken root. "I appreciate your candor." She walked toward the door. "Now, if you will excuse me—"

"Valeris," he called after her. "You earned your freedom. When Commodore Hallstrom asks me, that's what I'll tell him. But what you've done . . . your crimes against Starfleet and the Federation . . . those are things you're going to have to live with for the rest of your life. And for a Vulcan, that's a long time."

The hatch opened and she paused. "I agree." Valeris did not turn back to face him as she spoke. "Perhaps, Lieutenant, you will live long enough to one day forgive me."

The tyrant guard woke Rein from his fitful sleep with a savage carillon of noise, dragging a shock-prod back and forth across the force wall that shuttered off his tiny cell from the corridor beyond. The snarl and spit of crackling energy made him jerk backward, pressing himself into the far corner. The Kriosian wondered if he would be interrogated again; his thoughts were still fogged with the chemicals they had used on him before.

Did I talk? Was I able to resist? He wanted to believe he had, but Rein was cursed with knowledge of himself. He was not as strong as he wished others to believe, and the tyrants . . . They were always stronger, always more numerous. He had become ruthless in his fight with them, and still he had lost.

Through the energy barrier, he saw the guard stalk away and in the Klingon's place there was a slimmer, elfin figure. He saw the face, the upswept eyebrows and the arrow-tip ears, and Rein spat in disgust. "You. The thrice-cursed traitor come to see the condemned man." Rein got up and crossed to the edge of the cell. It was her, without doubt. Even through his injured, swollen eye, he could see Valeris's calm, placid aspect. The only difference was a newly healed scar that marred her otherwise elegant features.

He hated that face: ever since she had touched him, invaded his thoughts, he could see the ghost of her lurking every time he closed his eyes, the echo of her voice ringing in the distance. "What do you want now?" he spat. "Tell me, do Vulcans gloat as well as they lie?"

"The Klingon Empire is in the midst of a crisis." Her tone was conversational, as if he were a colleague and this were a discussion over a cup of tea. "There are recriminations passing back and forth among the members of the High Council. The leaders of the largest noble families and the military have demanded action against the Thorn and their support network."

The words made him feel sick inside. Rein pictured the cities of Krios Prime in flames and tyrant soldiers walking the streets, killing his people in retribution for what he had done. He had thought that death would claim him long before this time. The tyrant witch Kaj had chained him in the belly of the *Daughter* and left him there to die as the ship was bombarded and then abandoned. Rein waited to perish from starvation or suffocation, from decompression or radiation—but instead the Klingons came to gather him up, kicking and screaming. They dragged him into a hell that seemed endless, and now there was this new torture.

Valeris went on. "Chancellor Azetbur called for moderation, however. She personally argued that more extreme measures would only stimulate future resistance against the Empire."

"Krios will always resist," Rein managed. "The people know what we have done . . ." His felt his voice rise. "They'll know! The Thorn were martyrs from the very start, and we will be so now!"

But the Vulcan shook her head. "No. It has been decided that the Da'Kel attacks will be blamed on the renegade House of Q'unat, as you intended. Your subterfuge will be used against you. No word of Kriosian involvement will be released. All information surrounding your attack on the Klingon homeworld has been suppressed. It will never be made public."

"You lie!" he roared, his fist glancing off the barrier. He howled in pain and denial.

"No," she said with a cursory flick of the head. She dismissed his contradiction with such indifference that he knew Valeris had to be speaking the truth. "Everything you have done will go unremembered. Only a handful of people will know the truth."

He stepped back, nursing the burnt skin on his knuckles. "Why are you telling me this?" Rein glared at the tyrant guard. "You! Kill me now, then! That's what you're here for, isn't it?"

"No," Valeris repeated. "You have been tried and convicted in absentia by the High Council. Of all the Thorn, only you now remain alive. Those left on the asteroid base were killed when the facility was destroyed."

"We have other bases!" he cried. "Other supporters! It doesn't matter what truth they try to hide, the Klingon occupation of Krios is wrong, it has always been an invasion! *We* are the victims, not *them*! They are the aggressors! The Thorn strike back the only way they can . . ." He choked, cutting off the words. Rein glared at Valeris. "If they execute me, more will rise to take my place!"

"You will not be executed."

"What?" The statement robbed him of all impetus. "What did you say?"

"My actions were instrumental in stopping your attack on Qo'noS. As such, the Klingons considered that a debt was owed to me. They offered to put aside my crimes against them. I declined that proposal."

"I don't understand."

"I asked for something else instead. Your life."

Rein sank slowly to the deck, shaking his head. She was in his thoughts as much as she was there beyond the force wall, dragging on him like an anchor. The reality of Rein's circumstances settled in on him. At last, after so long, after so much, he had embraced the need to give his life for his cause once more. There, on the *Daughter* as he waited for the end to come, he had made himself ready for it. It was the only way to gain any peace.

It was all he wanted, and the Vulcan was denying him that ending. "No . . . You cannot do this . . ."

"They were reluctant to agree, but honor demanded they do as I asked."

He began to shake, a torrent of tears welling up inside him. "I hate you," he hissed. "I hate you for this."

"You shared my thoughts," said Valeris. "So you know I have a sympathy for the plight of the people of Krios. Lieutenant Vaughn will report back to Ambassador Spock of the Federation Diplomatic Corps. He will put forward the case to press the Empire to release their grip on the Krios System."

He barely heard her words, instead wringing his hands and quaking where he sat. The faces of the dead whirled through his thoughts, mocking him and taunting his failure.

"Perhaps, in time, a solution can be found that will not involve bloodshed." Valeris looked away, her gaze turning inward. "A road without deceit and death."

The Vulcan turned to leave, and Rein surged back to his feet, shouting at her back. "Wait! *Wait!*"

Valeris halted and looked back.

"Why did you do this, traitor? Have you not betrayed enough? Now you turn against me once more, and this time you rob me of a righteous death? Why did you make the tyrants spare me?"

She met his gaze. "You will be taken to the penal facility on the planet Rura Penthe, and you will spend the rest of your natural life in confinement there." Valeris reached up and absently traced a fingertip over the new scar on her face. "You ask me why I prevented your execution? It is because of your responsibility. Because both of us need to live with what we have done."

The woman walked away into the gloom.

EPILOGUE

Four Months Later

Devoras Prime
Maelek Sector
Romulan Star Empire

The perpetual twilight of the Devoran sky made it difficult to remain unseen. Three suns ensured that even the depths of night still retained a good level of ambient illumination. To go hidden here meant that an extra effort was required—and for a man whose career was built around remaining undiscovered, it was a chore.

But a necessary one, he reflected. And if he could not hide, then neither could his enemies and his rivals. A balanced field of play was such a rarity in the business of espionage. *Perhaps I should savor it,* he thought.

He pulled his hood tighter over his head, the dark brown cloth and red trim presenting a modest aspect to the colonists passing him on the avenue. Had any of them stopped to look, they would have seen just another Romulan, an older male of typically hawkish stock. Perhaps a merchant or a shipmaster down from the starport: his clothes suggested someone of moderate but not ostentatious wealth. An ordinary and ultimately unremarkable person.

All of which was a carefully engineered lie, of course. His face was not the one he had been born with; circumstances had forced that change upon him, and although he would never speak of it openly, each day that he looked in the mirror and saw the cosmetic alterations, he nursed the same ember of annoyance that had ignited in him seven years earlier.

He saw the hostel up ahead and crossed the bridge over the river that would lead him to it. He had passed this way a few minutes earlier, and now he returned after doubling back on himself. The Romulan had done this so many times that it was rote to him, like muscle memory. Years of training had taught him how to determine if he was being followed, and his tradecraft was ingrained. He didn't need to look over his shoulder to know that he was free of surveillance.

The hostel's upper floor was lit by the faint glow of a lantern, visible through smoked-glass windows. He saw a shadow moving in the room.

They would all be there now, waiting for him. He was the last to arrive, and that was fitting. He had earned the right to that small privilege, and no one could deny it. His service to Romulus and her people was a matter of record, with sealed files full of mission reports that would have earned him a chest full of medals if only they could have been spoken of openly.

He was not bitter about that; no, his rancor had a different source. He laid the blame on the outsiders, the aliens he had been forced to spy on for so many years. It sickened him a little to think of those times now. Under open cover, he had moved among beings who thought they were the equal of Romulan perfection, stood at their tables and eaten at their state dinners. He had laughed and smiled and chatted, all the time thinking of how much he despised them.

And then it had all fallen apart. On the eve of what would have been his greatest accomplishment, a conspiracy of fools had collapsed, thanks to the weakness of a mongrel cousin. His lip curled to think of her. *A Vulcan. So superior to us, so disdainful. But in the end, frail and self-absorbed.*

One day, he decided, he would seek out the Vulcan and have her killed. He entertained the fantasy of it as he crossed the bridge. He'd have it done quietly, make it look like an accident. But before she perished, the assassin would ensure she knew whose hand had wielded the blade. The name that had been struck from his identity would be said aloud once again, just to let her know.

As he approached the hostel, he metered his expression, pushing the thoughts of revenge away. Now was not the time to dwell on the past. This meeting was an important one, and the cell leaders waiting for him would have much to discuss. These informal gatherings on colony worlds like Devoras Prime served to keep their activities out of sight and mind of the senators on Romulus, all the better to ensure that the great work went on without the interference of politicians. He had played the role of one for a long time and he knew how shortsighted they could be.

Better that the agents of the Tal Shiar met like this, in quiet places where the fates of worlds and men could be discussed in secret. *Let our enemies and the common folk stare up at the stately towers in the capital and believe we meet there.*

Tonight they would speak of the fires started on worlds along the borders of their great enemies, of the weapons and support funneled to proxy soldiers, the plans for covert murders and the exacerbation of conflicts. *The Star Empire is a most patient predator,* he thought. *She bleeds her foes white before the killing bite comes.*

Of course, there were missteps along the way: the expenditure of time and effort on the Klingon border with the Kriosians had fallen to nothing, for example. Like the inbred nationalist rabble of the Q'unat clan, they had self-destructed before they could do any real damage—but he was convinced that Krios Prime could still be a poison dagger with which to pierce the hide of the Klingon beast. As he climbed the staircase, he considered how he would address that matter. *We will try again. We will be the patient predator—*

The door before him opened to a room filled with silence and the stink of murder. The six men he was there to meet, each a cell leader of a Tal Shiar operations unit, all lay dead. Some slumped in chairs, throats slit open, others on the wooden floor in spreading pools of emerald blood.

He spun back for the door, his hand vanishing into his tunic for the disruptor concealed there, and it was then he saw the shadow at the back of the room.

From it emerged a woman, her face hard like plates of welded metal. She seemed like a native, with the heavier brow of many such Devoran-born Romulans; but something about her rang a wrong note with him. As the light fell on her, he saw blood on her jacket, and in her hands there were twin knives with barbed cleft-blades. The weapons were of Klingon design.

"*Jolan tru*, Ambassador Nanclus," she said.

The name. It belonged to a different part of his life, a different mission. That man had died along with the falsehood of his existence and he had been reborn with new purpose.

He tried to block her, but she moved too fast. The blades entered his torso, severing arteries in a puff of green vitae. He gasped, unable to scream.

"This is for my sister," she said, lowering him to the floor, watching him die. "For Kol, of the House of Tus'tai, and all those who perished at Da'Kel."

The room grew dark, and the pain rose to engulf him. When the woman spoke again, the last thing he heard was a curse to follow him into the afterlife.

"*Maghwl' chuH ghobe' Qib*," said the Klingon.

Russian Hill
San Francisco, Earth
United Federation of Planets

Vallejo Street was busy with weekend foot traffic, so Elias wandered into the park to shake off the stiffness from his run and found a place where he could work through his cool-down regimen. As an attempt to break up the patterns of his day, he'd taken to starting his exercise at random locations throughout the city; so far, it was working. He liked the runs: they narrowed his focus to a simple, mechanical action. One foot in front of the other, eating up the kilometers across the sidewalk. Vaughn could lose himself there, and slip away.

It was hard to find that distance, that peace of mind, elsewhere. Back in his apartment, the boxes were still there, half packed. If anything, returning home from the Da'Kel mission had made him feel even less connected to the city. And then there had been the endless rounds of questions, the debriefs—both casual and hostile—from officers way above his pay grade.

It all blurred together. The only thing that really stood out was the funeral. That he recalled with full and complete clarity, a rainy day in upstate New York where they buried an empty coffin for Darius Miller and handed his aging mother a folded Federation flag. Hallstrom had been there, and they shared a few words; but he had not seen the commodore since, and slowly Vaughn began to wonder if he had somehow been forgotten. He was back in the same role he had occupied at the Office of Intelligence Evaluation, almost as if nothing had happened; aside from the beard he'd started to grow, the only difference was that Commander Egan had flatly refused to have him return to his unit. Egan had apparently filed formal charges of insubordination against Vaughn, but like everything else, that seemed to fade away. Elias was now on a different desk, in a different building. The last connection to his former life was seeing Tracey Dale across the quad. He had waved, but she had not responded. That bothered him more than anything else.

He frowned and took a drink from his water bottle. *Here I go again.* He hated this train of thought, because it only led to one place. Vaughn felt trapped, like a fly in amber, his future on hold. *Are they going to drum me out for what I did? Give me a medal? Shuttle me off to some makeweight posting at the ass-end of the galaxy?* It was the silence from command that made it worse.

Vaughn remembered Sulu shaking his hand in the *Excelsior*'s transporter room, Valeris standing up on the pads waiting for him. *"You did what you thought was right,"* the captain had said. *"That's what it means to be an officer. You were there. No one else. Don't ever let them second-guess you."*

When he materialized at Starfleet Command, Valeris

wasn't with him. *Taken to another site for debriefing,* they had said. He hadn't seen her since that day.

"Excuse me?" In mid-stretch, he turned at the sound of a female voice. An attractive young woman with dusky skin and dark hair was smiling back at him. She had the deep, expressive eyes of a Betazoid.

Elias was returning the smile even before he was aware of it. "Yes?"

"Lieutenant Vaughn, right?" She came closer. "I thought I recognized you. I'd know a Starfleet haircut anywhere."

"There's a lot of them in this city," he allowed, holding the smile. "I'm sorry, have we met?"

"Not exactly," she replied. "I'm Malla Tancreda. I was on Jaros II . . ." she trailed off. "Some months ago."

Elias's defenses went up. He had never felt entirely comfortable around telepaths, and there was something about the disarming, easy grin on the doctor's face that unsettled him.

Tancreda must have sensed it. Her smile faded away. "I hoped I might run into you," she went on.

"Yes," Vaughn said carefully, "what are the odds?" He took another sip of water and studied her. "Look, Doctor. As nice to meet you as it is, if you're looking to talk to someone about our . . . mutual friend, I'm not that person."

"Our mutual friend," she repeated, weighing the words. "She's led a charmed life."

Vaughn thought of Valeris's face, and the hurt he glimpsed buried beneath it. "Not really." He frowned. *Rookie mistake. You're letting her draw you out.* "I should go." He clipped the water bottle to his belt and stepped away.

"Do you know where Valeris is now?"

"Who?" he said, and kept walking.

Tancreda gave a soft chuckle. "Nice try. A non-telepath might have believed you." She trailed after him. "Elias, don't you want to know? Aren't you curious about what's going to happen next? To her? To *you*?"

Those last two words brought him up short. He turned back to give her his full attention. "Who do you work for?"

"Starfleet Medical. The telepsychotherapy department."

"A mind-reading shrink. You must be great at your job."

"I like to think so," she demurred. "And I hear you are good at yours. A lot of people believe you have great potential."

"Always nice to hear." He folded his arms and let his instincts read the moment. Tancreda was sounding him out for something—but what, and why? He knew Starfleet Intelligence and this wasn't the way they worked with junior lieutenants. People like Vaughn got hauled up into the offices of men with rows of braid on their sleeves and told what to do, no questions asked. They did not get approached on their day off by pretty telepaths with a line in oblique conversation. He began to wonder what this woman's connection to Valeris's prison term could mean. *Did Hallstrom or Spock know?* "What do you want from me, Doctor?"

"The direct approach," she said with a nod. "That's what I expected. Truth is, Elias, I came here to offer you something. A job."

He stiffened. "I already have a career, thanks. I've got a desk and everything."

Her smile became brittle. "I'm not the enemy. Far from it. The people I represent are patriots, like you. Men and women who believe in the United Federation of Planets. People who want to get things done."

Ice flooded his gut. *Section 31.* He'd heard the name— no one could work in Starfleet Intelligence and not have— but it was a ghost story for the new recruits, an urban myth inside the espionage community. *A secret contingent within Starfleet and without, working to their own agenda, beyond oversight.*

Or perhaps this was something else. A test, maybe, to see which way he would jump.

"We need resourceful people like you, Elias. You could accomplish great things."

He had to admit, there was an iota of him that was tempted—but that moment passed quickly and he shook his head. "Thanks but no, thanks, Doctor. I'm not interested."

She frowned slightly. "I'm leaving Earth in less than an hour. I've been authorized to make this offer." Tancreda inclined her head toward the park entrance. "I walk away, the opportunity walks with me."

Vaughn eyed her. "I'm good at my job, remember? I think I could find you again."

The Betazoid chuckled again. "You really won't." She sighed. "Last chance. Unless of course you like the idea of flying an analysis desk in the bowels of the jigsaw department for the next thirty years?"

"Why now?" he demanded.

"What do you mean?"

"Why come to recruit me now, months after the fact? If you wanted me on board, why not ask me the day I got back?" A smile came to his lips, and he saw her hesitation at the reaction. "Do you know what I think? I think you're asking me today because you won't be able to tomorrow. I think tomorrow Commodore Hallstrom is going to be calling me into his office . . . and, one way or another, I'll know where I'm headed." He nodded. "And I think you know that too."

For a moment a flutter of irritation crossed Tancreda's face—but then it was gone, and the smile was back. "You *are* a sharp one, Lieutenant J.G. Elias Vaughn. And I'll be honest with you, I do believe you've got a great career ahead of you, as long as you keep a rein on that reckless streak of yours." She reached for a thick bracelet around her wrist and touched a control; he heard a soft answering beep. "Just be sure that we'll be watching you." A glitter of light hazed the air around Tancreda and she vanished into a transporter beam.

Vaughn stared at the blank spot on the path where the woman had been standing and rubbed the stubble on his chin, turning over her words in his mind.

After a long moment, he turned his back on it and began

the long jog back toward the air tram halt for the Starfleet Command grounds.

Sekir Settlement
Sigma Draconis V
United Federation of Planets

The starport lay on the edge of the desert expanse, looking out over the great rust-red erg toward the massive mountain range to the west. Mirage-heat wavered across the burning sands, blurring sight of the outlying homesteads that trailed out from the settlement like seedlings thrown from a *cir-cen* plant.

Many of the colonists who came from the homeworld remarked that this sector of the fifth planet was the one that most resembled the landscapes of Vulcan, and so it was that the majority of new arrivals made their new homes here. Sigma Draconis V was as Vulcan had been long ago, untouched by sentient hands and without the trials of the great tribal wars that had scarred Vulcan prehistory. Other species from Federation member worlds had also come to call the colony home, but they were a minority. It took a hardy being to adapt to such an environment, and those who did not hail from the desert found it difficult to make a life here.

The storms were the greatest threat, churning columns of sand whipped into corrosive hurricanes that could strip flesh from an unprotected body or ablate stone into fragments. It made ground travel and the fabrication of highways virtually impossible, and transporters were regularly disrupted by atmospheric ionization effects. Inside the city, behind the massive pergolas and windbreaks, underground maglevs carried the people and their cargoes, but beyond the limits of the main settlement the only contact could be by flyer.

On Sigma Draconis V, pilots were as valued as educators, healers, and ecologists, and the arrival of a new settler with that skill set was always met with approval.

V'Shel had been an administrator at Sekir Settlement for fifty-two-point-six rotations, and he had developed the ability to evaluate and parse the skill sets of each new colonial intake with speed and accuracy. The next interview would be the last of the day shift, and he deemed it would be a cursory matter. The applicant was already preapproved by the Federation's Office of Colonial Affairs and the Vulcan Citizen's Authority, and her résumé listed numerous talents that would be of value both in Sekir and the frontier townships.

The woman entered the reception room. V'Shel offered her the traditional Vulcan salute, and she was slow to return it. He had seen similar behavior in colonists who had spent long periods out of contact with fellow Vulcans, but in the new arrival it seemed unusual. He made a note of it, and she raised an eyebrow as he did so.

"Welcome to Sigma Draconis V," he began. "I am Administrator V'Shel. I am here to complete your final assignment."

She gave a shallow nod. "I am . . . T'Leris." The woman seemed to hesitate over her name, as if she were uncomfortable saying it aloud. She reached up and brushed a loose thread of hair back over her head.

Unlike many Vulcanoids, her hair was a light blond tone, and it framed her face in a manner that some might have considered aesthetically pleasing; V'Shel found it difficult to frame such concerns, however, and disregarded the thought. Still, he was drawn to study the scar on her right cheek, bisecting the rise of her cheekbone. It seemed peculiar; such an obvious blemish could easily have been removed with the application of a medical protoplaser. He decided to question her on that very issue.

"The scar is the result of . . . an accident," she said, haltingly at first. "I elected to keep it as a personal reminder of that event."

"Are your memories not vivid enough?" said V'Shel.

"No," T'Leris replied, and her tone indicated that she did not intend to speak further on the matter.

V'Shel moved on, checking that the woman had understood and assimilated the information from the orientation package and her colonial assignment documents. Her residence had already been listed—a small single-bedroom apartment on the shaded side of the city—but he found it curious that nothing more than a single bag of clothing had been shipped with her. She had no furniture, no items of luggage beyond that which she carried on her shoulder.

He picked up her citizen's identity card and handed it to her, cocking his head. "Your pilot's license is encoded on this card," he explained. "You have been logged into the municipal tasking schedule to begin work tomorrow morning. A run out to the farmlands in the salt sinks, I believe."

T'Leris nodded. "I am glad to be of service." Her tone remained flat and distracted.

V'Shel decided that it was important to impress upon the new arrival how fortunate she was to be accepted as a settler on Sigma Draconis V at such short notice. Several other applicants had been pushed back down the assignment list in favor of her, although V'Shel could not see any mitigating factors in play that made T'Leris a more valuable addition to the colony.

This he explained at length, concluding after several minutes. T'Leris only nodded. "Thank you for your clarification," she said, rising to her feet. "May I go now? I would like to visit the flyer depot."

V'Shel raised an eyebrow. "You're not needed there until tomorrow. Did I not make that clear?"

"You did," she noted. "But it has been some time since I have had the . . . the clarity of a flight control in my hands, and open sky before me. I would like to experience that once again. Before I begin my new life."

The administrator found her attitude peculiar and added another note to his padd. "I would suggest that a far better use of your time would be to remain in the city." He leaned forward, showing something close to enthusiasm. "I have been informed that Ambassador Spock is passing through the sector and will be arriving on-world to conduct a lecture for the colony. Perhaps you would be interested in attending? I understand he is a highly inspirational speaker."

The woman looked at him with an expression that, for a moment, seemed almost *human*. The emotion was difficult to interpret: Was it sorrow? V'Shel could not be sure.

"I have other plans," she said, striding out into the heat and the light of the day.

Acknowledgments

Thanks to: Kim Cattrall, Nicholas Meyer, Denny Martin Flynn, Michael A. Martin, Andy Mangels, Margaret Wander Bonnano, Steven H. Wilson, Geoffrey Mandel, Debbie Mirek, Larry Nemecek, Rick Sternbach, Michael Okuda and Denise Okuda, for their works in fiction and in reference.

My stalwart and supportive editors Jaime Costas, Emilia Pisani, Ed Schlesinger, and Margaret Clark, and fellow authors Dayton Ward and David Mack.

And with much love to my own Princess of *Pon farr*, Mandy Mills.

About the Author

James Swallow, a *New York Times* bestselling author, is proud to be the only British writer to have worked on a *Star Trek* television series, creating the original story concepts for the *Star Trek Voyager* episodes "One" and "Memorial." His other *Star Trek* writing includes the Scribe award winner *Day of the Vipers*, *Synthesis*, the *Myriad Universes* novella *Seeds of Dissent*, the short stories "The Slow Knife," "The Black Flag," "Ordinary Days," and "Closure" for the anthologies *Seven Deadly Sins*, *Shards and Shadows*, *The Sky's the Limit*, and *Distant Shores*, scripting the videogame *Star Trek Invasion*, and over 400 articles in thirteen different *Star Trek* magazines around the world.

As well as a nonfiction book (*Dark Eye: The Films of David Fincher*), James also wrote the *Sundowners* series of original steampunk westerns, *Jade Dragon*, *The Butterfly Effect*, and novels in the worlds of *Doctor Who* (*Peacemaker*), *Warhammer 40,000* (*Nemesis*, *Black Tide*, *Red Fury*, *The Flight of the Eisenstein*, *Faith & Fire*, *Deus Encarmine*, and *Deus Sanguinius*), *Stargate* (*Halcyon*, *Relativity*, *Nightfall*, and *Air*), and *2000AD* (*Eclipse*, *Whiteout*, and *Blood Relative*). His other credits feature scripts for video games and audio dramas, including *Deus Ex: Human Revolution*, *Battlestar Galactica*, *Blake's 7*, and *Space 1889*.

James Swallow lives in London, and is currently at work on his next book.